GOTHIC SHORT STORIES

GOTHIC
SHORT STORIES

◆

*Selected with an Introduction
and Notes by*
DAVID BLAIR

WORDSWORTH CLASSICS

First published in 2002 by Wordsworth Editions Limited
Cumberland House, Crib Street, Ware, Hertfordshire SG12 9ET

Wordsworth would like to thank A. P. Watt Ltd
for granting permission on behalf of the executors of
the late K. S. P. McDowall to include
'The Room in the Tower' by E. F. Benson in this selection.

ISBN 1 84022 425 8

Typeset by Antony Gray
Printed and bound in Great Britain by
Mackays of Chatham plc, Chatham, Kent

CONTENTS

General Introduction   VII

Foreword   VII

Introduction   VIII

Select Bibliography   XXVII

ANNA LETITIA AIKIN
Sir Bertrand: A Fragment (1773)   3

NATHAN DRAKE & AN ANONYMOUS HAND
Captive of the Banditti (1801)   7

ANONYMOUS
Extracts from Gosschen's Diary: No. 1 (1818)   16

CHARLES ROBERT MATURIN
The Parricide's Tale (1820)   21

ANONYMOUS
The Spectre Bride (1822)   32

SIR WALTER SCOTT
The Tapestried Chamber (1829)   40

EDGAR ALLAN POE
Berenice (1835)   52

CHARLES DICKENS
A Madman's Manuscript (1836)   60

J. S. LE FANU
Strange Event in the Life of Schalken the Painter (1839) 68

NATHANIEL HAWTHORNE
Ethan Brand (1850)   90

ELIZABETH GASKELL
The Old Nurse's Story (1852)   105

ROBERT LOUIS STEVENSON
The Body-Snatcher (1885)   124

CHARLOTTE PERKINS GILMAN
The Yellow Wallpaper (1892)   141

AMBROSE BIERCE
The Death of Halpin Frayser (1893)   156

M. R. JAMES
Canon Alberic's Scrapbook (1894)   170

RALPH ADAMS CRAM
No. 252 Rue M. le Prince (1895)   181

S. CARLETON
The Lame Priest (1901)   194

MARY WILKINS FREEMAN
Luella Miller (1902)   207

RICHARD MIDDLETON
The Bird in the Garden (1912)   219

E. F. BENSON
The Room in the Tower (1912)   223

Notes on Authors and Stories   235

GENERAL INTRODUCTION

Wordsworth Classics are inexpensive editions designed to appeal to the general reader and students. We commissioned teachers and specialists to write wide ranging, jargon-free introductions and to provide notes that would assist the understanding of our readers rather than interpret the stories for them. In the same spirit, because the pleasures of reading are inseparable from the surprises, secrets and revelations that all narratives contain, we strongly advise you to enjoy this book before turning to the Introduction.

General Adviser
KEITH CARABINE
Rutherford College
University of Kent at Canterbury

FOREWORD

The Notes that appear at the end of this volume give brief background information on the individual stories and their authors, plus, where necessary, some explanatory glosses on specific difficulties or allusions in the texts. Discussions of the tales occur in the Introduction below, but since they will certainly 'give too much away' for those who want to experience some of the stories' power to surprise, shock and disconcert, readers are especially advised to follow the generic advice of Keith Carabine in his General Introduction above.

D. B.

INTRODUCTION

The invention of literary Gothic is generally credited to Horace Walpole and dated to 1764. It was then a means of repossessing imaginative and emotional territories which had been largely surrendered in the rational, enlightened culture of the eighteenth century. In his short novel *The Castle of Otranto*, Walpole took the setting back to the 'Gothic' period of the Middle Ages – the 'dark' ages, as those living in the age of 'enlightenment' thought of them – because it seemed more appropriate to him to incorporate supernatural incidents in a fiction set at a period when belief in the supernatural was widespread. Such belief was frequently associated with Roman Catholic 'superstition', and where it existed in mid-eighteenth-century Britain, it was often seen as the aberration of uneducated minds – of servants, peasants or women. Any literary engagement with it could seem almost a self-conscious exercise in cultural anthropology or, as with *Otranto*, in antiquarianism. Only in the second edition of *Otranto* did Walpole admit his authorship of the story; the first edition had kept its 'Gothicism' at safe distance by claiming that it was translated from an Italian medieval manuscript.

Gothic writing thus began as part of an attempt to liberate and validate kinds of narrative – folkloristic, mythic, supernatural – that 'progress' and 'modernity' in their eighteenth-century versions had tended to exclude or marginalise. The results could combine extravagant incident with rather conventional morality in ways that seem clumsy and naïve to modern eyes. On the first page of *The Castle of Otranto*, a helmet of gigantic proportions appears from nowhere in the courtyard of the castle and crushes to death Conrad, the son and heir of Manfred, Duke of Otranto. Later a hand, arm and leg of similar proportions appear; and one of Manfred's ancestors steps down from his portrait and glides spectrally out of the room in apparent protest at his descendant's attempts to coerce into marriage the woman who was about to be his daughter-in-law until Conrad's fatal accident. At the end of the novel the fully-integrated gigantic spectre of Alfonso the Good (whose descendants Manfred's line had usurped), long dead but only bigger and better as a result, manifests itself to terminate Manfred's fraudulently maintained proprietorship of the dukedom, and then ascends into heaven. Naïve as they may seem, however, many of these elements remain recognisable as Gothic writing develops from the limited beginnings that Walpole had provided.

When Anna Letitia Aikin wrote her fragment, 'Sir Bertrand',
which opens this selection, literary Gothic was less than ten years
old. This early Gothic fiction does not purport to be a self-contained
'story' but presents itself as if extracted from a longer romance.
Aikin's orchestration of Gothic effects may suggest something of the
broader 'romance' narrative from which it might come, but admits
no dialogue and thus no explanations: just as a mouth is opened to
speak, the narrative disappears in a puff of dashes. 'Sir Bertrand',
however, in its original context, was written to illustrate a thesis. It
was appended to two short essays, 'On Romances' and 'On the
Pleasure derived from Objects of Terror', which speculated on the
issues of literary taste and aesthetics that arose from Gothic's currency in the 1760s and 1770s. Aikin there acknowledges that, once
engaged in any narrative, curiosity will carry the reader through
pages of (in some cases) tedium or (in the case of Gothic narrative)
terror, because 'we rather chuse to suffer the smart pang of a violent
emotion than the uneasy craving of an unsatisfied desire'. This is
what her hero experiences as 'resistless desire to finish the adventure'. However, readers go into Gothic narratives, she reflects,
knowing exactly what they are letting themselves in for and go in
regardless. What makes Gothic potent, she concludes, is 'the pleasure constantly attached to the excitement of surprise from new and
wonderful objects':

> A strange and unexpected event awakens the mind, and keeps it
> on the stretch; and where the agency of invisible beings is
> introduced, . . . our imagination, darting forth, explores with
> rapture the new world which is laid open to its view, [and] rejoices
> in the expansion of its powers.

Applied as a formula for generating Gothic narrative, the tendency
of this theory of Gothic is to generate just one strange thing after
another, as 'Sir Bertrand' shows. The hero is conducted through a
sequence of effects, each of which needs in some way to be more
'strange and unexpected' than the last. This yields a brilliant snap-
shot of how 'Gothic' was thought of and to an extent practised in its
very earliest years, but Aikin's reading of Gothic vocabulary as
merely a type of the 'new and wonderful' or the 'strange and
unexpected' appears to modern eyes too literal and too limiting.
   The most influential of the writers who developed Gothic in the
first sixty years after *Otranto* was Ann Radcliffe (1764–1823), author
of *The Mysteries of Udolpho* (1794) and other novels. Radcliffe and her
many imitators evolved the vocabulary of what can now be thought

of as 'classic' Gothic writing. The setting of the action in the past remained important, although the past was not always as Gothically distant as it had been in Walpole's novel – *Udolpho* was set in the 1580s. The castle remained a valuable albeit not indispensable setting – preferably ruined or partly ruined, helpfully endowed with vaults and labyrinthine passages, ideally with one section mysteriously sealed off. Radcliffe provided another recurrent source of danger by populating her landscapes with sinister *banditti*, always a lurking and sometimes a more active threat to her heroines. Abbeys and monasteries were also richly evocative, not just in their architectural promise, but also in the way that monastic life, with its semi-anonymity, its sexual denial and its ferocious insistence on orthodoxy and discipline, enabled further dramas of secret identity, suppressed histories and persecution. The extract from Charles Maturin's novel *Melmoth the Wanderer* (1820), that appears here as 'The Parricide's Tale', colourfully exemplifies this. One step further were the chambers and the machinery of the Inquisition, another potent type of the terror that Gothic man could visit upon man. As Gothic writing developed in these early years, the supernatural was not an essential element: Radcliffe famously practised a form of Gothic in which mysterious occurrences were *supposed* to be attributable to supernatural causes but were proved not to be. This shifted the focus of the narrative of terror from the outward monstrosities and manifestations that might occasion it to the inner imaginative processes of the victim. These processes Radcliffe herself, when at her most disapproving in commenting on her heroine's wayward inner life, could call 'a momentary madness'.

The main medium in which shorter Gothic fiction was practised and consumed in this period was that of the 'blue books' as they are generally known after the colour of their covers. These were compilations of stories produced to feed a huge public demand for sensational Gothic narrative. If novelists were developing the Gothic repertoire, the blue-book writers exercised that expanding repertoire rapidly, vigorously and cheaply. It is tempting, although perhaps too facile, to see the Gothic blue books as being down-market, parasitic offshoots of the 'classic' Gothic novel. Not all blue-book writing was crude and derivative, and not all Gothic novels were products of the kind of serious literary and stylistic endeavour that characterised Radcliffe's work. In the case of the story 'Captive of the Banditti', however, from an 1801 blue book, the charge of parasitism, or downright piracy, is hard to dodge. Here the blue-book publisher, unhampered by modern copyright protocols, has lifted a Gothic 'sketch' called 'Montmorenci' from a 1798 miscellany by literary collector and critic Nathan Drake entitled *Literary Hours; or Sketches, Critical, Narrative, and Poetical*. An anonymous hack has then been asked to 'finish' Drake's sketch and the two halves have been clamped together under a new and sensational title as a 'completed' Gothic story for the delectation of blue-book devotees.

What is thus delivered, while not especially satisfying as a narrative, even by blue-book standards, has interesting and enjoyable features – besides representing this particular phase of Gothic writing. Drake's original sketch had been composed as part of the literary defence of Gothic in the same spirit as Anna Letitia Aikin's 'fragment' of twenty-five years earlier. Drake, however, was an avowed admirer of Ann Radcliffe, and what he had laid down as a Gothic exercise shows her influence especially clearly. This is perhaps most apparent in the importance of extended passages of sublime landscape description, something that had featured strongly in Radcliffe's work and which Drake, elsewhere in *Literary Hours*, had commented on admiringly. This use of 'Gothicised' landscape was one of Radcliffe's significant extensions of the vocabulary of literary Gothic. The 'banditti' themselves, of course, have a Radcliffean pedigree, and Drake and his unintended collaborator also, like Radcliffe, equivocate with the supernatural. Drake toys with Walpole's gigantism: the landscape itself is vertiginously scaled-up, and the banditti themselves, when first seen by Montmorency, are 'gigantic figures in ponderous iron armour', like extras from *The Castle of Otranto*, the leader bearing 'a massy shield of immense circumference'. In the end, however, Montmorency has just run into an everyday scenario of Gothic banditry carried out by desperadoes who seem to be, at worst, a bit sturdier than the average. When the anonymous hand takes up the narrative thread the scene is described as 'a place fitted only for the residence of perturbed spirits', and Montmorency sees the approaching female figure in her white dress as 'supernatural'; but again quasi-supernaturalism, like quasi-gigantism, is an intermediate effect of this kind of Gothic and is dissolved by the narrative's explanations and resolutions. If the story thus bears the stamp of Radcliffe's influence, what we notice on the other hand is that the narrative remains male-centred, unlike Radcliffe's highly evolved 'female Gothic'. In this respect it still shows early Gothic's close relationship with medieval chivalric romance, as did 'Sir Bertrand' and, before it, *Otranto*. It is noticeable, even so, that when the anonymous portion of the tale is obliged to tie the narrative together using the fair

Dorothée's testimony, what ensues is something much closer to the more 'modern' Gothic, centred on female distress and victimisation, of which Radcliffe was the pre-eminent practitioner.

What is apparent looking back on the versions of Gothic evolving at the end of the eighteenth century is that in them the excitement of terror is only in part to do with their machinery of supernatural or quasi-supernatural incidents, of medieval superstition, violence or torture – of 'new and wonderful objects'. Often underpinning this machinery there are other agendas of anxiety. In *The Castle of Otranto* these are anxieties about property, dynastic alliance, inheritance, patrilinearity, the very foundations on which British society and political life were sustained. Radcliffe in her work picks up and develops from Walpole another urgent set of anxieties about male power and property, the tyranny exercised in law by fathers over daughters, husbands over wives, guardians over wards – anxieties which were finding at the same time a non-Gothic expression in the writing of feminists such as Mary Wollstonecraft. Furthermore, madness, momentary or otherwise, is a pointed concern in an age in which 'the spontaneous overflow of powerful feeling' (in William Wordsworth's famous formulation from the 1800 Preface to *Lyrical Ballads*) could be promoted rather than locked up or dismissed as aberrant. Such overflow, besides, if transferred to the political sphere, could threaten insurgence, even revolution, as had occurred in France in 1789. In this collection, 'Extracts from Gosschen's Diary: No. 1' and 'The Madman's Manuscript' centre on the negotiation between the violent overflow of 'insanity' and those who think of themselves as standing for 'normality'.

Gothic also dabbles in male – not merely female – sexual anxieties. In a striking episode in Matthew Lewis's infamous novel *The Monk* (1796), Don Raymond de Cisternas tells how, while bedridden due to an injury, he was visited nightly in his tapestried room by the hideous spectre of the Bleeding Nun of Lindenburg, a woman who had pursued unbridled sexual licence in life and now as a living corpse comes to the immobilised Don Raymond's bedchamber to claim him with a basilisk stare and deathly kisses. In what was to be an influential narrative in the development of a certain kind of Gothic, Lewis substitutes a male victim of Gothicised female sexual aggression for the entrapped, tremulous heroines of Radcliffe's female-centred Gothic, subject to unwanted visitation by predatory males. Sir Walter Scott's 1828 story 'The Tapestried Chamber' lifts this idea out of Lewis's novel, and it surfaces again spectacularly in the 1895 story

'No. 252 Rue M. le Prince' by Ralph Adams Cram, which is discussed later in this Introduction.

Other early pieces in this collection illustrate how the Gothic story spins off from the full-scale novel in the decades up to 1840. They illustrate also how perplexed in some ways the relationship between 'incident', 'story', 'romance' and 'novel' remain well into this period. 'Sir Bertrand' presents itself as a 'fragment'. 'Captive of the Banditti' is another fragment which a second hand has tried to convert into a 'tale'. Two further examples – those by Maturin and Dickens – are extracted from much longer novels; and even in 1850 Hawthorne's 'Ethan Brand' appears as 'a chapter from an aborted romance'. Gothic novels often tend to fragment into sub-narratives, such as that of Don Raymond and the Bleeding Nun from *The Monk*, thus allowing Scott to rework the episode as the core of his later story. Conversely, authors writing short fictions often embed them in meta-narrative frames, like Scott's *Chronicles of the Canongate*, for a second series of which 'The Tapestried Chamber' was originally intended, or Le Fanu's *Purcell Papers*, within which 'Strange Incident in the Life of Schalken the Painter' first appeared. Another of the early stories in this collection – this time from the periodical magazines which also carried much short Gothic fiction – promises to be merely the first 'Extract from Gosschen's Diary', although as it happens no others were forthcoming.

'Short Gothic', unencumbered by the need to provide plot and character on a novelistic scale, can seem sometimes, like Aikin's and Drake's early examples and much blue-book writing, to concentrate almost solely on effects. This is again visible in 'The Spectre Bride', a hugely extravagant farrago of Gothic nonsense from the magazines that covers all the territory between the sublime and the ridiculous but somehow survives because of its enormous *brio*. It is detectable too, however, in Scott's much more muted 'The Tapestried Chamber', in the way in which there is no real story: Browne arrives by chance at Lord Woodville's medieval castle, passes his 'painful night' in the eponymous chamber, where he is assailed by the spectre, identifies her in the morning from her portrait and then leaves. It is an incident, not a story. A story, properly and Gothically plotted, would have disclosed some sense in which the unearthly visitation was addressed specifically to Browne, obliging him to discover something suppressed about his own or his family's past that linked it to the darker parts of the Woodvilles' history. As it is, Browne has just been a rather desultory device for reworking the Gothic *topos* of spectral female iniquity, and he is not much more, in truth, than a modern Sir Bertrand in a less manic, more polished fragment.

To compare 'The Spectre Bride' with Le Fanu's story of 'Schalken the Painter' from the late 1830s is to see how, in reworking strands from earlier Gothic, writers at the beginning of the Victorian period were prepared to handle effect more subtly. In Le Fanu's story the scenario is recognisable – an innocent young woman trapped into marriage with a demon-husband – but whereas 'The Spectre Bride' was indecently eager to take us all the way to hell with the unhappy couple, Le Fanu cloaks the fate of Rose Velderkaust in a silence that is broken only by her one, terrible reappearance at her uncle's house when she seems to be making a last, doomed attempt to escape. Beyond that only Schalken's final dream in the church of Rotterdam hints at the nature of the life-in-death marriage to the 'livid and demoniac' Vanderhausen. It is not, however, just in the greater tact with which Gothic effects are handled that Le Fanu's tale transcends the 'Spectre Bride' model. Whereas Clotilda is romantically seduced by a demon-lover with a modicum of sub-Byronic charisma, Rose is brutally sold into marriage by her mercenary uncle: she is merely a commodity. The macabrely comic scene in which the palpably dead Vanderhausen comes to supper to meet the unsuspecting bride-to-be further roots the Gothic in recognisable social ritual and the grimmer facets of patriarchy. 'Gothic' here is not just a language of literal horrors but a metaphorical language wherein are explored waking anxieties. The 'advantageous' matches that were often forced on women by their fathers, uncles or guardians may have seemed little better, at root, than that forced on Rose with the ghoul Vanderhausen, as Le Fanu hints; and Schalken's dream, in which Rose draws aside the black curtains of the marriage-bed, gestures further towards the sexual horrors elided from the official narratives of such alliances.

When American writers turned to Gothic they faced difficulties that did not trouble writers in the European tradition. It was the Catholic European past and the detritus of European history – castles, catacombs and monasteries – that had provided early Gothic writers with their vocabulary of settings and effects. These spaces had retained custody of the darker narratives of the past and could be made to yield them up again. An American writer in the 1830s, however, had only just over two hundred years of an American past to look back on, and although that past had had its phases of superstition and darkness – most notably in the seventeenth-century witch-hunts and the persecution of the native peoples – these had

not left an infrastructure of sublime architectural ruins and subterranean vaults, although they had left a resonant enough legacy of
ruined lives and troubled consciences. American writers who chose
to pursue an American Gothic followed from the start different
paths. Writing in the 1790s, Charles Brockden Brown (1771–1810)
in his novels such as *Wieland* and *Edgar Huntley* had firmly located
the macabre and the bizarre in the American landscape. There was
an inevitable trade-off involved in this: the Gothic subject had to
change with the Gothic setting, and a properly Americanised Gothic
was not going to be driven by spectral dukes, mad monks and
bleeding nuns enacting the horrors of the past. Darkness enough,
however, could be found in the American scene – madness, persecution, violence and spiritual desolation had not been left behind in the
Old World. *Wieland* (1798), despite one spectacular incidence of
spontaneous combustion and the disruptions occasioned by the
presence of a voice-thrower, finds terror principally in the mind's
potential for catastrophic dysfunction. In *Edgar Huntley* (1799),
Brown demonstrates how the American landscape with its natural
wonders could function as a home-grown 'Gothic' resource, providing its own repertoire of terrors: journeying through the bizarre
landscape of frontier up-state Pennsylvania, the hero wanders in
complex cavern-systems that recall the subterranean vaults of the
Gothic castle or abbey, or the haunts of Nathan Drake's banditti,
threatened by wild beasts and hostile natives in ways that both
mirror and supplement the horrors of the disrupted mind itself.

   In the work of Poe and Hawthorne, the two major figures writing
what one can call Gothic short stories in America in the 1830s and
1840s, one can see some of the characteristic difficulties and some of
the distinctive triumphs of early American Gothic. Poe, who acknowledged openly the compelling precedent that Brown had set, is
nevertheless much more likely to be drawn back to the traditional
European theatre of the macabre in his most Gothic stories. The
most frequently anthologised of these, 'The Fall of the House of
Usher', exploits the very 'Gothic' idea of the degenerate legacy of a
decaying European aristocracy and with it the crumbling infrastructure of its architectural possessions. Like *The Castle of Otranto*,
it ends with the utter collapse of a dynasty and with it of the house
that it has possessed or mispossessed, a trope that Poe uses more than
once in his stories. 'Berenice', selected for this collection, also
centres on an aristocratic family and, like the better-known 'Usher',
uses madness, obsession and hints of incest and vampirism as lurid
indices of its degeneration.

Close as they are in date, 'Berenice' and the 'Madman's Manuscript', read by Mr Pickwick in Dickens's early novel, remind us of
the continued currency of madness as a subject in British and
American Gothic, and of the powerful legacy of the 'Gosschen' type
of insane-testimony from magazine Gothic of earlier in the century.
Dickens, like the 'Gosschen' author, carefully frames the maniacal
deposition both by the Pickwickian narrative that contains it and by
the diagnostic, hand-wringing comments that are appended to the
manuscript itself. It is, in contrast, characteristic of Poe's development of this kind of material that the first-person maniacal narrative
monopolises the text and the reader's attention, creating its own self-
defined, self-disrupted world.

Hawthorne could be drawn to European settings too (as in his
1844 story, 'Rappaccini's Daughter'), but by far the greater number
of his stories use local settings and invent an American Gothic, where
they do, by probing the American past for its own horrors. In stories
such as 'Young Goodman Brown' and 'Alice Doane's Appeal' (both
1835) these horrors are specifically associated with the Salem witch
trials of the early 1690s, in which Hawthorne's own great-great
grandfather had been involved as a prosecutor. The story selected
here, 'Ethan Brand', however, recreates Gothic differently, relying
less on history and instead deploying a clever allusiveness that
enables the story to participate in the European Gothic legacy while
remaining rooted in Massachusetts. Here is the cursed, wandering,
Faustian figure who has made a terrible compact with the forces of
darkness, the figure who has in various guises stalked through
European literature – as Faust himself, as the Wandering Jew (who
had made a guest appearance in Lewis's *The Monk* and is the
'stranger' of 'The Spectre Bride'), as Byron's Manfred and as
Melmoth, the demonic wanderer of Maturin's novel, who at the close
of the book comes to the end of the time allotted to his ill-purchased
life-span. If the figure of Ethan himself thus cues in memories of
European Gothic, so does Hawthorne's handling of the setting
among the lime-burners' kilns. Ethan's kiln, at which Bartram and
his son now toil, is described as a Gothic castle in miniature, a 'tower-
like structure', and, like the Gothic castle, a gateway between
normality and nightmare, 'a private entrance to the infernal regions'.
Abandoned kilns nearby 'look already like relics of antiquity'. Thus
Gothicised, this patch of an industrial New England landscape
transcends its utilitarian purpose as the arena of Bartram's daily
labours and becomes the lurid setting for the last chapter of Ethan's
dark night of the soul. As always in Hawthorne's and almost always in

Poe's work, the Gothic setting is the place of self-haunting and self-destructiveness.

This collection avoids as far as possible 'classic' ghost stories. Because, however, the ghost story was in the nineteenth century a major extension of Gothic writing, and the Victorian era's most distinctive contribution to the genre, it would be perverse to ignore it altogether. In Elizabeth Gaskell's 'Old Nurse's Story' it is possible to see especially clearly how Gothic can be simultaneously brought home (to nineteenth-century England) and kept at the margins (in this case rural north-west England), tinged now with characteristic Victorian strands of anxiety and sentiment – anxiety about social class and foreigners (that womanising music tutor) and sentiment about children. The Manor House in the story works very much as the Gothic castle or abbey had done in earlier, classic Gothic. Gloomy and labyrinthine, it has an east wing closed off and associated with dark events in the past, like the south wing of Castle Mazzini in Ann Radcliffe's *A Sicilian Romance* (1790). A servant called Dorothy shows the narrator parts of the building hung with portraits of previous inhabitants, conveying a sense of secrets lodged there and stories not to be told, just as a servant called Dorothée did for Emily St Aubert at Château Le Blanc in *The Mysteries of Udolpho*. The terrible secrets of Château Le Blanc were rooted, Radcliffe's reader and heroine later learned, in female sexual jealousy and murder, as they turn out to be also in Gaskell's story. Add the raging snow-storm and the ghost-child crying for admittance from the opening of Emily Brontë's *Wuthering Heights* – in part another 'old nurse's [Nellie Dean's] story' – in which another house in the middle of northern moors substitutes for the exotic semi-ruin of old Gothic – and the Gothic vocabulary of Gaskell's story is complete. The brutality with which the crime of the past is spectrally re-enacted at the tale's climax is very striking, but again recognisably looks back all the way to *Otranto* itself as the different 'parts' of the tale's Gothicity, the persons and clothes in the portraits, the ghostly organ-playing father, the lone girl-child and her wound, come together in a grand and hideous affirmation that the sins of the past will not be forgotten and must be answered for. The east wing will not contain them: it never can.

  Scores of Victorian ghost stories witness this adaptation of Gothic to the sensibilities and the anxieties of Victorian Britain. Prominent among these anxieties is that the carefully cultivated and regulated surface of Victorian respectability may conceal much darker energies or a hideous past that has been edited out of the official histories of the pillars of society. The latter is a central interest in many Victorian novels – think of Lady Dedlock in Dickens's *Bleak House* (1853), of Bulstrode in George Eliot's *Middlemarch* (1872) or of Henchard in Hardy's *The Mayor of Casterbridge* (1886) – and one that does not require the vocabulary of Gothic writing in order to be retold. Gothic, however, from *Otranto* onwards, had been adept at probing this particular terror, and often Victorian Gothic, in the ghost story and elsewhere, is used to develop it. In his novella *The Strange Case of Dr Jekyll and Mr Hyde* (1886), Robert Louis Stevenson produced what is arguably the century's most enduring parable of the dark underside of Victorian respectability; and at the start of 'The Body-Snatcher', another respectable Victorian medical practitioner suddenly confronts at the foot of an inn stairway a figure – the drunken Scotsman, Fettes – who was a participant in, and is the custodian of, his dark, pre-Victorian past – a Hyde to his Jekyll. By tracing the fictional Macfarlane's history back to the notorious 'body-snatching' scandal of 1820s' Edinburgh, Stevenson reminds us of the dark underside of medical practice itself – that uneasy and unacknowledged connection between the great, rich London practitioners and the corpses for dissection going in at the back doors of the medical schools. However, into this grim framework of nocturnal traffic with the dead Stevenson inserts another action, the arrival of the odious stranger, Gray, who has a dark, mysterious hold over the young Macfarlane and is thus, in a sense, an earlier version of Fettes himself at the story's opening, a point that Fettes has reinforced in his pointed remark to Macfarlane that 'we are not so easily shut of our acquaintance'. The story subtly integrates these two actions, each in its way Gothic without being supernatural, towards an even more macabre climax in which the past insists – again after the tradition of Walpole's Alfonso the Good – on reintegrating its scattered body parts and reanimating itself despite all attempts to eradicate it.

Although written by, in the estimation of many, the greatest of all ghost-story writers, 'Canon Alberic's Scrapbook' by M. R. James is not a ghost story at all, if we take a 'ghost' to be the manifestation of a dead person. In James's work, even when there are ghosts in this sense, they manifest themselves with striking physicality. Far from being wraith-like, his revenants often arrive in their decayed physical bodies, the water or earth or cobwebs of their burial places still dropping from them. The story of the Cambridge academic Dennistoun, and his scholarly quest to the Pyrenean cathedral town of St Bernard de Comminges (which really exists), is intensely Gothic without being 'ghostly'. Here, as Walpole had done at the birth of the Gothic and others after him, James exploits the culture of southern-European Catholic superstition. His English, rational, central figure, who approaches the Gothic past with a notebook and camera merely as a repository of antiquarian relics, is like the enlightenment man of the eighteenth century, only now he is a creature of the Victorian 'enlightenment', austere, scholarly and methodical. At Comminges he is disdainfully aloof from the jittery fearfulness of the old sacristan and his daughter, eyes fixed on the crucifix, 'telling her beads feverishly'; but what later manifests itself to Dennistoun cannot be fixed by reason and the tools of nineteenth-century historical enquiry. In James's story the very invention of Gothic is in a sense being re-enacted as the seemingly quaint lumber of a superstitious, medieval past discloses terrifyingly the things of darkness with which that past was in real contact. James himself, lightly disguised as Dennistoun, adores this lumber, and his enumeration of it gives the story authentic Gothic texture and atmosphere.

The development of the Gothic story in later nineteenth-century America is in many respects more interesting than its development in Britain at this period. Although American writers practise the ghost story, often in ways strikingly similar to writers in Britain albeit transplanted to local scenes, there is also a more vigorous re-exploration of other strands in the Gothic tradition. Accordingly, this collection includes a number of stories which show the diversity of setting and subject that is detectable in turn-of-the-century American Gothic writing: 'The Death of Halpyn Frayser' by Ambrose Bierce, 'The Lame Priest' by S. Carleton, 'Luella Miller' by Mary Wilkins Freeman and 'The Yellow Wallpaper' by Charlotte Perkins Gilman. Unlike Poe in many of his Gothic stories and Henry James, too, in *The Turn of the Screw* (1896), but like Hawthorne, all of these writers stay at home to find Gothic in the American landscape, townscape or housescape.

None of the tales is a ghost story, although Bierce and Freeman both wrote good conventional ghost stories. Bierce's 'The Death of Halpin Frayser' engages daringly with a converging set of Gothic possibilities, this convergence underpinned by the story's intense locus at a single point in the Californian landscape, a point which is a place of burial, of sleep, of nightmare, of murder, even of automatic writing, Frayser leaving as his final text blood-red quatrains in the manner of his ancestor Myron Bayne. As Hawthorne did in 'Ethan Brand', Bierce reminds us that the American landscape carries its own kinds of Gothic signifiers, here not just the graveyard but the ruined schoolhouse – 'a typical Californian substitute for what are known to guide-bookers abroad as "monuments of the past" ', as Bierce pointedly remarks. Structurally too the story is daring, Bierce's narrative voice taking on a kind of studied, almost heartless urbanity as it punctuates the chronicle of dream and death with his comments on Frayser and his past history. Thus the macabre dream of the blood-drenched forest and the shrouded ghoul-mother is interrupted by the retrospective story of the incestuous, possessive closeness of mother and son nurtured amid the macho Southern politicking of *post-bellum* Tennessee. Returning to mid-dream we now see how the ghoul-mother is acting out the vampiric subtext of that desire for incestuous possession that first led Frayser to flee west. Furthermore, this dream, as we learn only at the end, is being experienced while Frayser sleeps unknowingly on his murdered mother's grave. She herself had travelled west to find him, and he has momentarily woken from sleep in the story's opening paragraph with her unfamiliar remarried name on his lips, a sleep in which he is subsequently himself seemingly murdered by her murderer. The sounds of demoniac laughter come through the fog at the end of the tale – but is it that of Branscom/Larue? Was his the 'heartless' laughter that penetrated Frayser's nightmare? There is, as the detective, Jaralson, remarks, 'some rascally mystery here'. For the reader the conundrum is insoluble and unsettling because the giddy convergence of Gothic tropes – madness, nightmare, spirit visitation, murder, incest, the power of the past over the present – will not yield a single perspective or cohere into a single Gothic narrative. The story is an almost mischievous *tour-de-force* from a writer often bent on mischief.

'The Lame Priest' too is planted in the American landscape, transformed by winter snows as in some of the most memorable of Robert Frost's poems. For all the absolute difference of setting, style and effect of the two stories, however, it is at root doing the same kind of thing with Gothic as 'Canon Alberic's Scrapbook'. For Dennistoun's English scholarly detachment read the narrator's American backwoods pragmatism. For the superstitious French Catholic custodians of the secrets of Comminges read now Andrew's role as Native American custodian of the secrets of the evil spirits that are abroad in the land. It is Dennistoun's uncomfortable destiny in James's story to confront the forces that are at the root of the superstitions that he thinks of as being alien, as being 'Gothic'. So in Carleton's story the narrator who despises Andrew's 'silly mysteries' finds himself drawn into a new realisation of the forces at large in the world and discovers that the older – 'other' – set of beliefs derives not from intellectual backwardness but from a darker, more intimate knowledge. The map that is taken from him can be thought of as a metaphor for his intellectual 'map' of the world as he has supposed it to be: without it he must renegotiate both the physical and the metaphysical landscape.

In recreating this scenario Carleton also brilliantly reinvents and Americanises the 'werewolf' strand of Gothic. Werewolf narratives had crept into the blue books possibly as early as 1820, and the story that is the best-known example in the English tradition had appeared as an interpolated story in Captain Frederick Marryat's novel *The Phantom Ship* in 1839. Carleton's naturalisation is not only a matter of setting, or of using the structure of Native American superstition rather than European peasant superstition, but is also to do with the American Gothic focus on self-haunting and inward self-destruction. The lame priest is not the pitiless, often faceless predator of most European werewolf stories – in Marryat's example she doubles as the cruel stepmother of classic fairy-tale. Rather he is Poe's Roderick Usher or Hawthorne's Ethan Brand in werewolf's clothing, a figure in unutterable torment still in part tied to what Hawthorne calls 'the magnetic chain of humanity' but unable to control his own forces of darkness. Part of him is drawn to the narrator's 'better meat', but part must return to the freshly killed hare. Carleton's story revolves around taut passages of dialogue in which the priest conveys ob-liquely to the narrator and the reader his mental/spiritual condition, passages as striking in their way as the evocative descriptions of the winter landscape that also punctuate the tale.

'Luella Miller' is an equally striking relocation of the Gothic whose subtlety of effect is in large part a product of its 'folksiness'. This is partly a matter of setting – the provincial New England small town – but also a matter of voicing. The use of the regional narrative voice had featured from quite early in the Gothic tradition, partly as one means of suggesting the narrative's 'authenticity', partly counter-acting a tendency to bombastic 'literary' narrative styles. Scott had used the Scottish vernacular in his frequently anthologised story 'Wandering Willie's Tale', told within his novel *Redgauntlet* (1824). Stevenson, under Scott's direct influence, had done the same in 'The Tale of Tod Laphraik', told within his novel *Catriona* (1893), and in his much-admired story 'Thrawn Janet', published in 1891. Le Fanu had also created a vernacular female narrator using the dialect of north-eastern England in his 'Madam Crowl's Ghost' in 1871. The narrating voice of Lydia Anderson in 'Luella Miller' does not merely

impart vernacular colouring but entangles what is 'Gothic' about the
story in the jealous, gossipy, sometimes poisoned dynamics of small-
town life, an American Gothic trope that is visible still in the work of
Stephen King and in films such as David Lynch's 1986 *Blue Velvet*.
Those dynamics had, of course, played a part in what had happened
in Salem in 1691, and in Freeman's story Lydia remembers how
'folks said the days of witchcraft had come again'. What is 'wrong'
about Luella Miller is in large part that she is blonde, slender,
elegant, 'a type of beauty rather unusual in New England', in a
culture where Aunt Abby is considered 'a real good-lookin' woman,
tall and large, with a big, square face and a high forehead'. She is also
an outsider, who 'came here to teach the district school'; she is
impractical, indolent, manipulative; she 'gets' the man who was
showing interest in Lydia, and she in him, although she tries to deny
it. If Luella's Gothic literary ancestors are predatory ex-nuns and
vampiric women such as those in Le Fanu's *Carmilla* (1872) and
Bram Stoker's *Dracula* (1897), her non-Gothic literary ancestors are
the beautiful, useless, hypochondriac, blonde child-brides of the
Victorian novel, such as Dora Spenlow in Dickens's *David
Copperfield*. Dropped into small-town New England this pampered
female type of 'doll-baby', as Lydia describes her at one point,
becomes socially demonised, and the story thus equivocates very
subtly between presenting Luella as exploitative or parasitic and
disclosing her as truly uncanny. Filtering the story through Lydia
Anderson's embedded hostility raises issues that Freeman declines to
resolve: Luella remains an enigma, victim as well as vampire, wasting
away undiagnosed and unattended, a morning glory among weeds in
the story's closing, elegiac emblem of her.

'The Yellow Wallpaper' has in recent years become much read,
taught and discussed. This rise in the story's prestige has occurred in
part because of the way in which recent critical thinking about
Gothic has helped to fix Gilman's work. From Radcliffe's novels
onwards a recurrent image in Gothic narrative has been the cham-
ber-as-prison. Heroines are assigned to their rooms by the powerful
male characters and, once there, are trapped, unable to control
access to their space but unable to escape from it. This trope of
female entrapment has been central to the claiming of Gothic by
feminist literary criticism. Such criticism sees in it a powerful
expression of female anxiety about male persecution, dramatising
the threat of tyranny over the body and the male project to
marginalise or destroy the female mind and will. This has allowed
Gilman's story to be identified by its subtle reworking of this strand

of Gothic convention and not simply by its autobiographical genesis
in the author's mental history.

The psychological intensity of 'The Yellow Wallpaper' places it on
what now appears to be a cusp between, on the one hand, eighteenth-
and nineteenth-century Gothic, with its tradition of trappings,
machinery and manifestations of one kind or another, and, on the
other, twentieth-century modernism's obsession with the internalisation of and resultant disruptions to representations of experience.
We know perfectly well what has 'happened' at the end of *The Castle
of Otranto* or 'Ethan Brand' or 'The Old Nurse's Story', all of which
have a clearly discernible Gothic logic that is in part also a moral
logic of transgression and redress. But we are much less certain of
what has happened at the end of Bierce's and Freeman's stories, and
in 'The Yellow Wallpaper' the narrating voice can no longer explain
to the reader who she is or what has occurred. Is there – was there
ever? – the manifestation of a previous occupant of the room? Has
that 'other' occupant escaped into the present to possess the narrator? Precedents for this may lie in part in some of Poe's writing, but
Gothic in this phase no longer feels obliged to unfold its enigmas:
instead of resolving them, the story remains itself trapped within the
disruption and fragmenting of experience that has always been
characteristic of the genre. The 'Madman's Manuscript' that Mr
Pickwick read was followed by a note, perhaps by the clergyman to
whom the manuscript had belonged, that sought to locate the
narrator's insanity in 'medical theory', in theories of 'dissipation and
debauchery', of heredity, of 'morbid insanity'. In the madwoman's
manuscript that is 'The Yellow Wallpaper' the presumptive 'wisdom'
that would seek to ply medical theory, to diagnose and prescribe for
the morbid insanity of the subject, is now the voice of the patronising
husband, the colluding doctor. Gilman has brilliantly taken the
whole thrust of the diagnostic comment appended to the manuscript
confession in Dickens's piece and relocated it. It is not now a third-
party negotiation between the mad subject and the archetypal uneasy
reader, whose candle is 'just expiring in its socket'. Instead it is part of
the trope of the oppression of the (female) subject by the (male)
tyrant, and the claims it has to 'authority' are explicitly contested.
Like everything else in the story, it is relayed to us through the
consciousness of the Gothic subject herself; and instead of helping to
'account for' the Gothic, it has become entangled in its dynamics. No
intermediary here offers to help the reader negotiate her or his
unease, or her or his transition back into 'normality'. As a result
Gilman's reader may sleep less soundly than Mr Pickwick.

The internalisation that marks Gilman's practice of Gothic shows
a degree of assimilation between this development of Gothic writing
and mainstream modernist narrative. In Richard Middleton's odd,
disturbing story, 'The Bird in the Garden', we are somewhere
between the still Gothic space of 'The Yellow Wallpaper' and the
non-Gothic spaces of Virginia Woolf's novel *Jacob's Room*, written
ten years or so later. Disclosed suddenly in an unfamiliar half-light at
the end of Middleton's story, the basement room in which it has all
taken place is seen to be the arena for drunkenness, brutality and
murder, linking it to traditional Gothic subjects of entrapment,
persecution and violence. But the story has consistently embroiled
the reader in the phantasmagoric readings of that space which are
generated in the bizarre, dreamlike perceptions of the central child
subject, Toby. We try as readers to decode and to sort through these
perceptions to find out 'what has happened', who are 'real' people,
who phantasms or dreams, but the tale's design is to baffle and
disconcert as well as to shock.

This sort of writing grasps part of the cache of Gothic possibilities
at the turn of the twentieth century and heads off towards the stream-
of-consciousness novel, where what was distinctively 'Gothic' about
it begins to dissolve, as it is on the point of doing in 'The Bird in the
Garden'. On the other hand, the story by Ralph Adams Cram, 'No.
252 Rue M. le Prince', acts as a lurid reassurance that at the same
period the Gothic language of 'real' horrors is still being developed.
Here is an American author eschewing the American landscape or
townscape and heading back to old Europe with its complex architectural legacy and all its potential for trappings and machinery on a
grand Gothic scale. Cram's story shows, in its own poisonous way,
how these trappings can be reanimated and given new vibrancy. It is
in one sense just a night-in-a-haunted-house story, but at its heart is
that strand of anxiety about female sexuality that goes back to *The
Monk*'s Don Raymond and the Bleeding Nun of Lindenburg. Now,
however, that fear of aggressive female sexuality has become a very
specific horror of female anatomy. The house itself is called *la Bouche
d'Enfer* – the mouth of hell, like the lime-burner's kiln in 'Ethan
Brand' – and into it Sar Torrevieja was repeatedly seen to enter but
never to re-emerge. The hell-mouth here is the point of access to the
regions of the female body, and in the circular, domed room/womb
that the young men pass through as they explore the house there is a
grotesque, terrifying image of that body, splayed, red and naked,
crouching over and around the watchers. From its navel dangles a
dilated, externalised ovum – a 'roc's egg from *The Arabian Nights*'. In

what transpires for the narrator during his solitary watch, the Gothic, fetishised images of female sexuality are even more striking as the hypnotic, romantic beauty of the spectral eyes gives way to the paralysing horror of the 'wet, icy mouth' and its attendant slime. The ensuing image of the 'dead cuttle fish' will not be lost on anyone who remembers the tentacled succubus (a word that Cram himself uses) in Ridley Scott's 1979 movie *Alien*, that shoots from its pod to clamp itself to the face of John Hurt's character in order to impregnate him. In Cram's story, as in H. R. Giger's art-designs for *Alien*, a Gothic of the female body seems to be pathologically embedded in a way that goes beyond traditional misogyny and the traditional repertoire of Gothic anxieties.

In the final story in the collection, 'The Room in the Tower' by E. F. Benson, the setting appears again reassuringly English and reassuringly upper-middle-class: tea on the lawn, motor-cars (this is 1912, remember), golf matches, old 'schoolfellows', dressing (of course!) for dinner, and dinner followed by the society of 'the smoking- or billiard-room'. If 'Luella Miller' had taken Gothic possibilities into the rough democracy of the New England small town, Benson's story is rooted back in that Edwardian twilight wherein the century-old protocols of class, prosperity and social ritual are still being acted out. But even as we read of the disturbing undercurrent of dreams that afflicts the narrator we can see also how, as in Cram's story, the culture of the tale is one of male bonding, in which the women's parts of serving tea, assigning rooms to the guests and going early to bed are felt to conceal an indefinite evil. When that evil begins to take visible shape, in the portrait of Julia Stone that hangs in the room, the language in which it is described irresistibly recalls that in which the evil female apparition was described in Scott's 'The Tapestried Chamber'. Indeed, at the core of Benson's story is the same model that Scott was using, but now more developed and plotted, rising to a crescendo of macabre effects. As in many of M. R. James's tales, the smells and properties of the grave are present, and the narrator, Clinton and the male servant are all mysteriously stained with the female blood that oozes inexplicably from the portrait and is found at the conclusion to fill the dead woman's coffin. In Scott's story, female evil was felt through mere proximity and vague menace; here it results in laundry bills as well as frayed nerves.

Standing at the end of this collection, Benson's and Middleton's stories – the one richly macabre and vampiric, the other elusively teasing and inconclusive – exemplify a set of possibilities which can be seen as feeding into a developing Gothic tradition which, in 1912, was about to extend into cinematic as well as literary story-telling. Each, however, represents equally clearly a reworking of ideas and scenarios which go back to the origins of Gothic. Although Middleton probably did not know Gothic blue-book literature, his central figure, Toby, appears in his way to have been a captive of banditti, forced in the story's final moments to witness, like his distant and unlikely predecessor Montmorency, brutal, sordid acts committed in a place whose real scale and character have been consistently distorted by the narrative's phantasmagoric effects. As has been consistently seen though these stories, however, Gothic had, in the one hundred and fifty years between its beginnings and the second decade of the twentieth century, found ways of sustaining its traditions and its concerns while liberating itself from its original need to seek out the 'Gothic' past and exotic settings. Its narratives had relocated themselves much closer to home and so had continued to renew their potency.

DAVID BLAIR
University of Kent at Canterbury

SELECT BIBLIOGRAPHY

Once thin, the bibliography of studies of Gothic literature is now vast and expanding annually. The items selected for mention below will allow readers to follow up aspects of the Gothic tradition discussed in the Introduction to this collection.

Edith Birkhead, *The Tale of Terror: A Study of the Gothic Romance*, Constable, 1921

Fred Botting, *Gothic*, Routledge, 1996

E. J. Clery, *The Rise of Supernatural Fiction, 1762–1800*, Cambridge University Press, 1995

E. J. Clery and Robert Miles (eds), *Gothic Documents: A Sourcebook 1700–1820*, Manchester University Press, 2000

W. P. Day, *In the Circles of Fear and Desire: A Study of Gothic Fantasy*, Chicago University Press, 1985

Markman Ellis, *The History of Gothic Fiction*, Edinburgh University Press, 2000

Louis S. Gross, *Redefining the American Gothic: From 'Weiland' to 'The Day of the Dead'*, University of Michigan Press, 1989

Maggie Kilgour, *The Rise of the Gothic Novel*, Routledge, 1997

Elizabeth MacAndrew, *The Gothic Tradition in Fiction*, Columbia University Press, 1979

Robert D. Mayo, 'Gothic Romance in the Magazines', *Publications of the Modern Language Association of America*, 65 (1950), pp. 762–89

Robert Mighall, *A Geography of Victorian Gothic Fiction*, Oxford University Press, 1999

Robert Miles, *Gothic Writing 1750–1820: A Genealogy*, Manchester University Press, 2002

David Punter, *The Literature of Terror: A History of Gothic Fictions from 1765 to the Present Day*, revised edition, Longman, 1996

David Punter (ed.), *A Companion to the Gothic*, Blackwell, 2000

Donald A. Ringe, *American Gothic: Imagination and Reason in Nineteenth-Century Fiction*, University of Kentucky Press, 1982

Montague Summers, *A Gothic Bibliography*, Russell & Russell, 1964

Montague Summers, *The Gothic Quest: A History of the Gothic Novel*, Russell & Russell, 1964

Anne Williams, *Art of Darkness: A Poetics of Gothic*, University of Chicago Press, 1995

A number of websites concerned with the study of Gothic literature have sprung up. The best places to begin are probably the 'Literary Gothic' site (www.litgothic.com) and 'The Sickly Taper' site (www.toolcity.net/~frank/index.html). Both provide links to other Gothic and related sites.

GOTHIC SHORT STORIES

Sir Bertrand: A Fragment

ANNA LETITIA AIKIN

AFTER THIS ADVENTURE, Sir Bertrand turned his steed towards the
wolds, hoping to cross these dreary moors before the curfew. But ere
he had proceeded half his journey, he was bewildered by the different tracks, and not being able, as far as the eye could reach, to espy
any object but the brown heath surrounding him, he was at length
quite uncertain which way he should direct his course. Night over-
took him in this situation. It was one of those nights when the moon
gives a faint glimmering of light through the thick black clouds of a
lowering sky. Now and then she suddenly emerged in full splendour
from her veil; and then instantly retired behind it, having just served
to give the forlorn Sir Bertrand a wide extended prospect over the
desolate waste. Hope and native courage a while urged him to push
forwards, but at length the increasing darkness and fatigue of body
and mind overcame him; he dreaded moving from the ground he
stood on for fear of unknown pits and bogs, and alighting from his
horse in despair, he threw himself on the ground. He had not long
continued in that posture when the sullen toll of a distant bell struck
his ear – he started up, and turning towards the sound, discerned a
dim twinkling light. Instantly he seized his horse's bridle, and with
cautious steps advanced towards it. After a painful march he was
stopped by a moated ditch surrounding the place from whence the
light proceeded; and by a momentary glimpse of moonlight he had a
full view of a large antique mansion, with turrets at the corners, and
an ample porch in the centre. The injuries of time were strongly
marked on everything about it. The roof in various places was fallen
in, the battlements were half demolished and the windows broken
and dismantled. A drawbridge, with a ruinous gateway at each end,
led to the court before the building. He entered, and instantly the
light, which proceeded from a window in one of the turrets, glided
along and vanished; at the same moment the moon sank beneath a
black cloud, and the night was darker than ever. All was silent. Sir
Bertrand fastened his steed under a shed, and approaching the house,

traversed its whole front with light and slow footsteps. All was still as death. He looked in at the lower windows, but could not distinguish a single object through the impenetrable gloom. After a short parley with himself, he entered the porch and, seizing a massy iron knocker at the gate, lifted it up, and hesitating, at length struck a loud stroke. The noise resounded through the whole mansion with hollow echoes. All was still again. He repeated the strokes more boldly and louder – another interval of silence ensued. A third time he knocked, and a third time all was still. He then fell back to some distance that he might discern whether any light could be seen in the whole front. It again appeared in the same place and quickly glided away as before – at the same instant a deep sullen toll sounded from the turret. Sir Bertrand's heart made a fearful stop. He was awhile motionless; then terror impelled him to make some hasty steps toward his steed – but shame stopped his flight; and urged by honour, and a resistless desire of finishing the adventure, he returned to the porch; and working up his soul to a full readiness of resolution, he drew forth his sword with one hand and with the other lifted up the latch of the gate. The heavy door, creaking upon its hinges, reluctantly yielded to his hand – he applied his shoulder to it and forced it open – he quitted it and stepped forward – the door instantly shut with a thundering clap.

Sir Bertrand's blood was chilled – he turned back to find the door, and it was long ere his trembling hands could seize it – but his utmost strength could not open it again. After several ineffectual attempts, he looked behind him and beheld, across a hall, upon a large staircase, a pale bluish flame which cast a dismal gleam of light around. He again summoned forth his courage and advanced towards it. It retired. He came to the foot of the stairs, and after a moment's deliberation ascended. He went slowly up, the flame retiring before him, till he came to a wide gallery. The flame proceeded along it, and he followed in silent horror, treading lightly, for the echoes of his footsteps startled him. It led him to the foot of another staircase, and then vanished. At the same instant another toll sounded from the turret – Sir Bertrand felt it strike upon his heart. He was now in total darkness, and with his arms extended, began to ascend the second staircase. A dead cold hand met his left hand and firmly grasped it, drawing him forcibly forwards – he endeavoured to disengage himself, but could not – he made a furious blow with his sword, and instantly a loud shriek pierced his ears, and the dead hand was left powerless in his. He dropped it, and rushed forwards with a desperate valour. The stairs were narrow and winding, and interrupted by frequent breaches and loose fragments of stone. The staircase grew narrower and narrower and at length terminated in a low iron grate. Sir Bertrand pushed it open – it led to an intricate winding passage, just large enough to admit a person upon his hands and knees. A faint glimmering of light served to show the nature of the place. Sir Bertrand entered. A deep hollow groan resounded from a distance through the vault. He went forwards, and proceeding beyond the first turning, he discerned the same blue flame which had before conducted him. He followed it. The vault, at length, suddenly opened into a lofty gallery, in the midst of which a figure appeared, completely armed, thrusting forwards the bloody stump of an arm, with a terrible frown and menacing gesture, and brandishing a sword in his hand. Sir Bertrand undauntedly sprang forwards and aimed a fierce blow at the figure; it instantly vanished, letting fall a massy iron key. The flame now rested upon a pair of ample folding doors at the end of the gallery. Sir Bertrand went up to it, and applied the key to a brazen lock – with difficulty he turned the bolt – instantly the doors flew open and discovered a large apartment, at the end of which was a coffin rested upon a bier, with a taper burning on each side of it. Along the room on both sides were gigantic statues of black marble, attired in the Moorish habit, and holding enormous sabres in their right hands. Each of them reared his arm and advanced one leg forwards as the knight entered; at the same moment the lid of the coffin flew open, and the bell tolled. The flame still glided forwards, and Sir Bertrand resolutely followed, till he arrived within six paces of the coffin. Suddenly, a lady in a shroud and black veil rose up in it, and stretched out her arms towards him – at the same time the statues clashed their sabres and advanced. Sir Bertrand flew to the lady and clasped her in his arms – she threw up her veil and kissed his lips; and instantly the whole building shook as with an earthquake, and fell asunder with a horrible crash. Sir Bertrand was thrown into a sudden trance, and on recovering, found himself seated on a velvet sofa in the most magnificent room he had ever seen, lighted with innumerable tapers in lustres of pure crystal. A sumptuous banquet was set in the middle. The doors opening to soft music, a lady of incomparable beauty, attired with amazing splendour, entered, surrounded by a troop of gay nymphs more fair than the Graces. She advanced on the knight, and falling on her knees thanked him as her deliverer. The nymphs placed a garland of laurel on his head, and the lady led him by the hand to the banquet, and sat beside him. The nymphs placed themselves at the table and, a numerous train of servants entering, the feast was served, delicious music playing all the time. Sir Bertrand could not speak for astonishment – he could only return their honours by courteous looks and gestures. After the banquet was finished, all retired but the lady, who, leading back the knight to the sofa, addressed him in these words – – –

Captive of the Banditti

NATHAN DRAKE AND AN ANONYMOUS HAND

THE SULLEN TOLLING of the curfew was heard over the heath, and not a beam of light issued from the dreary villages, the murmuring cotter had extinguished his enlivening embers, and had shrunk in gloomy sadness to repose, when Henry de Montmorency and his two attendants rushed from the castle of A—y.

The night was wild and stormy, and the wind howled in a fearful manner. The moon flashed, as the clouds passed before her, on the silver armour of Montmorency, whose large and sable plume of feathers streamed threatening in the blast. They hurried rapidly on, and, arriving at the edge of a declivity, descended into a deep glen, the dreadful and savage appearance of which was sufficient to strike terror into the stoutest heart. It was narrow, and the rocks on each side, rising to a prodigious height, hung bellying over their heads; furiously along the bottom of the valley, turbulent and dashing against huge fragments of the rock, ran a dark and swollen torrent, and farther up the glen, down a precipice of near ninety feet, and roaring with tremendous strength, fell, at a single stroke, an awful and immense cascade. From the clefts and chasms of the crag, abrupt and stern, the venerable oak threw his broad breadth of shade, and bending his gigantic arms athwart the stream, shed, driven by the wind, a multitude of leaves, while from the summits of the rock was heard the clamour of the falling fragments that, bounding from its rugged side, leapt with resistless fury on the vale beneath.

Montmorency and his attendants, intrepid as they were, felt the inquietude of apprehension; they stood for some time in silent astonishment, but their ideas of present danger from the conflict of the elements being at length alarming, they determined to proceed; when all instantly became dark, whilst the rushing of the storm, the roaring of the cascade, the shivering of the branches of the trees, and the dashing of the rock, assailed at once their sense of hearing. The moon, however, again darting from a cloud, they rode forward, and, following the course of the torrent, had advanced a considerable way, when the piercing shrieks of a person in distress arrested their speed; they stopped and, listening attentively, heard shrill, melancholy cries repeated, at intervals, up the glen, which, gradually becoming more distant, grew faint and died away. Montmorency, ever ready to relieve the oppressed, couched his lance, and bidding his followers prepare, was hastening on; but again their progress was impeded by the harrowing and stupendous clash of falling armour, which, reverberating from the various cavities around, seemed here and there, and from every direction, to be echoed with double violence, as if a hundred men in armour had, in succession, fallen down in different parts of the valley. Montmorency, having recovered from the consternation into which this singular noise had thrown him, undauntedly pursued his course, and presently discerned, by the light of the moon, the gleaming of a coat of mail. He immediately made up to the spot, where he found, laid along at the root of an aged oak, whose branches hung darkling over the torrent, a knight wounded and bleeding: his armour was of burnished steel; by his side there lay a falchion, and a sable shield embossed with studs of gold; and, dipping his casque into the stream, he was endeavouring to allay his thirst, but, through weakness from loss of blood, with difficulty he got it to his mouth. Being questioned as to his misfortune, he shook his head and, unable to speak, pointed with his hand down the glen; at the same moment, the shrieks, which had formerly alarmed Montmorency and his attendants, were repeated, apparently at no great distance; and now every mark of horror was depicted on the pale and ghastly features of the dying knight; his black hair, dashed with gore, stood erect, and, stretching forth his hands towards the sound, he seemed struggling for speech, his agony became excessive, and groaning, he dropped dead upon the earth.

The suddenness of this shocking event, the total ignorance of its cause, the uncouth scenery around and the dismal wailings of distress, which still poured upon the ear with aggravated strength, left room for imagination to unfold its most hideous ideas; yet Montmorency, though astonished, lost not his fortitude and resolution, but determined, following the direction of the sound, to search for the place whence these terrible screams seemed to issue, and, recommending his men to unsheath their swords and maintain a strict guard, cautiously followed the windings of the glen until, abruptly turning the corner of an out-jutting crag, they perceived two corpses, mangled in a frightful manner, and a light glimmering through some trees that hung depending from a steep and dangerous part of the rock. Approaching a little nearer, the shrieks seemed evidently to proceed from that quarter, upon which, tying their horses to the branches of an oak, they ascended slowly and without any noise towards the light: but what was their amazement, when, by the pale glimpses of the moon, where the eye could penetrate through the intervening foliage, in a vast and yawning cavern, dimly lighted by a lamp suspended from its roof, they beheld half a dozen gigantic figures in ponderous iron armour; their visors were up, and the lamp, faintly gleaming on their features, displayed an unrelenting sternness capable of the most ruthless deeds. One, who had the aspect and the garb of their leader, and who, waving his scimitar, seemed menacing the rest, held on his arm a massy shield of immense circumference, which, being streaked with recent blood, presented to the eye an object truly terrific. At the back of the cave, and fixed to a brazen ring, stood a female figure, and, as far as the obscurity of the light gave opportunity to judge, of a beautiful and elegant form. From her the shrieks proceeded; she was dressed in white, and, struggling violently and in a convulsive manner, appeared to have been driven almost to madness from the conscious horror of her situation. Two of the banditti were high in dispute, fire flashed from their eyes and their scimitars were half unsheathed, and Montmorency, expecting that, in the fury of their passion, they would cut each other to pieces, waited the event; but when instead the authority of their captain soon checked the tumult, he rushed in with his followers, and hurling his lance, 'Villains,' he exclaimed, 'receive the reward of cruelty.' The lance bounded innocuous from the shield of the leader, who turning quickly upon Montmorency, a severe engagement ensued: they smote with prodigious strength, and the valley resounded to the clangour of their steel. Their falchions, unable to sustain the shock, shivered into a thousand pieces; whereupon Montmorency, instantly elevating with both hands his shield, dashed it with resistless force against the head of his antagonist; lifeless he dropped prone upon the ground and the crash of his armour bellowed through the hollow rock.

In the meantime, his attendants, although they had exerted themselves with great bravery, and had already dispatched one of the villains, were, by force of numbers, overpowered, and having bound them together, the remainder of the banditti rushed in upon Montmorency just as he had stretched their commander upon the earth and obliged him also, notwithstanding the most vigorous efforts of valour, to surrender. The lady who, during the encounter, had fainted away, waked again to fresh scenes of misery at the moment when these monsters of barbarity were conducting the unfortunate Montmorency and his companions to a dreadful grave. They were led by a long and intricate passage amid an immense assemblage of rocks, which, rising between seventy and eighty feet perpendicular, bounded on all sides a circular plain, into which no opening was apparent but that through which they came. The moon shone bright, and they beheld, in the middle of this plain, a hideous chasm; it seemed near a hundred feet in diameter, and on its brink grew several trees, whose branches, almost meeting in the centre, dropped on its infernal mouth a gloom of settled horror. 'Prepare to die,' said one of the banditti, 'for into that chasm shall ye be thrown; it is of unfathomable depth; and that ye may not be ignorant of the place ye are so soon to visit, we shall gratify your curiosity with a view of it.' So saying, two of them seized the wretched Montmorency, and dragging him to the margin of the abyss, tied him to the trunk of a tree, after which they treated his associates in the same manner. 'Look,' cried a banditto with a fiendlike smile, 'look and anticipate the pleasures of your journey.' Dismay and pale affright shook the cold limbs of Montmorency, and as he leant over the illimitable void, the dew sat in big drops upon his forehead. The moon's rays, streaming in between the branches, shed a dim light, sufficient to disclose a considerable part of the vast profundity whose depth lay hid; for a subterranean river, bursting with tremendous noise into its womb, occasioned such a mist from the rising spray as entirely to conceal the dreary gulf beneath. Shuddering on the edge of this accursed pit stood the miserable warrior; his eyes were starting from their sockets, and, as he looked into the dank abyss, his senses, blasted by the view, seemed ready to forsake him. Meantime the banditti, having unbound one of the attendants, prepared to throw him in; he resisted with astonishing strength, shrieking aloud for help, and just as he had reached the slippery margin, every fibre of his body racked with agonising terror, he flung himself with fury backwards on the ground; fierce and wild convulsions seized his frame, which being soon followed by a state of exhaustion, he was in this condition, unable any longer to resist, hurled into the dreadful chasm; his armour striking upon the rock, there burst a sudden effulgence, and the repetition of the stroke was heard for many minutes as he descended down its rugged side.

No words can describe the horrible emotions which, on the sight of this shocking spectacle, tortured the devoted wretches. The soul of Montmorency sank within him, and as they unbound his last fellow-sufferer, his eyes shot forth a gleam of vengeful light and he ground his teeth in silent and unutterable anguish. The inhuman monsters now laid hold of the unhappy man; he gave no opposition, and, though despair sat upon his features, not a shriek, not a groan escaped him: but no sooner had he reached the brink than, making a sudden effort, he liberated an arm, and grasping one of the villains round the waist, sprang headlong with him into the interminable gulf. All was silent – but at length a dreadful plunge was heard, and the sullen deep howled fearfully over its prey. The three remaining banditti stood aghast; they durst not unbind Montmorency, but resolved, as the tree to which he was tied grew near the mouth of the pit, to cut it down and, by that means, he would fall along with it into the chasm. Montmorency, who, after the example of his attendant, had conceived the hope of avenging himself, now saw all possibility of effecting that design taken away; and as the axe entered the trunk, his anguish became so excessive that he fainted. The villains, observing this, determined, from a malicious prudence, to forbear, as at present he was incapable of feeling the terrors of his situation. They therefore withdrew, and left him to recover at his leisure.

Not many minutes had passed away when, life and sensation returning, the hapless Montmorency awoke to the remembrance of his fate. 'Have mercy,' he exclaimed, the briny sweat trickling down his pallid features, 'O Christ, have mercy' – then looking around him, he started at the abyss beneath, and, shrinking from its ghastly brink, pressed close against the tree. In a little time, however, he recovered his perfect recollection, and, perceiving that the banditti had left him, became more composed. His hands, which were bound behind him, he endeavoured to disentangle, and, to his inexpressible joy, after many painful efforts, he succeeded so far as to loosen the cord and, by a little more perseverance, effected his liberty. He then sought around for a place to escape through, but without success; at length, as he was passing on the other side of the chasm, he observed a part of its craggy side, as he thought, illuminated, and, advancing a little nearer, he found that the moon's rays were shining through a large cleft of the rock, and at a very considerable depth below the surface. A gleam of hope now broke in upon his despair; and gathering up the ropes which had been used for himself and his associates, he tied them together, and fastening one end to the bole of a tree and the other to his waist, he determined to descend as far as the illuminated spot. Horrible as was the experiment, he hesitated not a moment in putting it into execution, for, when contrasted with his late fears, the mere hazard of an accident weighed as nothing, and the apprehension that the villains might return before his purpose was secure accelerated and gave vigour to his effort. Soon was he suspended in the gloomy abyss, and neither the roaring of the river, nor the dashing of the spray, intimidated his daring spirit, but, having reached the cleft, he crawled within it, then, loosing the cord from off his body, he proceeded onwards and, at last, with a rapture no description can paint, discerned the appearance of the glen beneath him. He knelt down, and was returning thanks to heaven for his escape, when suddenly –

*   *   *

CONCLUSION – *by Another Hand*

– his attention was attracted by a figure at the entrance of a forest which was on his left hand. Whole shades seemed to declare it a place fitted only for the residence of perturbed spirits, or that of the ferocious and remorseless banditti. The figure was dressed in white; and in the disordered eye of Montmorency appeared infinitely to surpass the human stature. For a few moments he paused, being transfixed with astonishment at an appearance which, in his present situation, he could not help looking on as supernatural.

At length he began to recover from the terror which this new adventure, together with the danger which had threatened him in his former one, had inspired in his breast; when perceiving the mysterious object still before him, he advanced towards it. Forgetting that he was standing on a craggy piece of the rock, he fell to the ground. Stunned with the blow, he lay for some time deprived of sense and motion. On coming to himself, to his no small surprise, he found he was supported by the same figure which had so forcibly engrossed his attention on his first emerging from the horrid chasm, where his unfortunate retinue had met with a fate the most dreadful that barbarity could possibly inflict. The stranger no sooner saw him open his eyes, than she, in the tenderest manner, enquired if he had received any hurt from his fall; to which he answered in the negative; and in his turn demanded who she was, and for what reason she had been induced to wander in that solitary place, and at that mysterious hour (for it was then very near midnight).

The fair fugitive readily complied with his request, and informed him that she was the only daughter of the renowned baron of Dunholm, and heiress to his vast domains. In consequence of which she had been surrounded by innumerable admirers, and those of the first rank, who all fought for her hand with the greatest avidity. Among these Count Edelbert, a knight of the most profligate manners, found means to ingratiate himself with the baron; who, lured by the ancestry of his family and the vast domains he pretended to be possessed of, readily accepted his proposals, and commanded Dorothée (for that was the name of the stranger) to look on him as her future husband. This, although her heart was entirely disengaged and the person of the count was by no means despicable, she could not comply with. A secret horror thrilled through her whole frame whenever her eyes met his. Impressed with these sensations, she ventured to declare her repugnance to the baron. Her father was inflexible, and the day was fixed for her union with the count. A few days previous to that appointed for the approaching nuptials, the count left Dunholm Castle with the utmost precipitation, apologising for his abrupt departure by saying that a relation of the family, from whom he had also great expectation, had sent for him as he found his dissolution fast approaching. The appointed moment at length arrived that was to unite the fair Dorothée to the abandoned count, but no Edelbert made his appearance; a circumstance which, at the same time as it created no small surprise in the bosom of the astonished baron, gave infinite pleasure to his afflicted daughter, as she now found her fate retarded a few days longer. In this state of mysterious suspense they remained about a week. Then, one evening, just as the sun had begun to retire behind the western mountains, a special messenger brought a packet for the baron from the Count Edelbert, informing her father that soon after her lover had arrived at the castle of his ancestors, the Danes having made an incursion, and penetrated as far as the castle, had not only spoiled and laid waste that and the whole of his domains, but were also very near taking him prisoner. Prejudiced in his favour, the baron readily gave credence to the contents of this epistle; and was on the point of sending him a consolatory answer, when he received another packet from a friend, who lived in the neighbourhood of the count, informing him that the whole of Edelbert's estates had been seized on to defray the debts which a life of debauchery and excess had drawn upon him. Enraged at his dissimulation, the baron instantly dispatched one of his vassals with a letter, forbidding him the castle and informing him that he was thoroughly acquainted with his perfidy. The count appeared much embarrassed on the receipt of this message; but endeavouring to conceal his emotion, he sent the servant back with an answer to the effect that being convinced of the integrity of his own actions, he should leave it to time to clear him from the vile aspersion he laboured under. 'From that time,' continued Dorothée, 'we heard no more of him; and concluded that in order to mend his battered fortunes, he had fled to some distant country; when yesterevening, as my father and myself were returning from Dunholm convent – where, as was our usual custom on an evening, we had been to hear mass – the uncommon fineness of the evening induced us to turn out of the road which led to the castle; when giving the rein to our horses, we were led insensibly to the narrow pass between the mountains; where we had not proceeded many steps before we were attacked by a numerous party of banditti. The baron defended himself with the greatest valour imaginable for a considerable time; when receiving a desperate wound in his side, near his heart, he fell. At that moment the chief of the banditti, in whose ruthless visage I then recognised the features of the profligate count, caused me to quit the horse I rode; and then placing me before him on his own, bore me off to his cavern, in spite of the piercing cries which I uttered in hopes of bringing some valiant knight to my assistance. Immediately on entering the cavern, I was confined in the manner you saw; in which situation I was doomed to pass my time until I should consent to become his mistress. From that horrid fate your timely interference preserved me, although you failed in effecting my liberty. I will not attempt to describe my feelings when I saw you overpowered by the banditti. I felt your misfortunes as acutely as my own; and when they led you and your domestics off, to inflict the horrid sentence they had passed on you, unable to bear the horrid ideas which at that moment oppressed me, I fainted a second time. On my recovery, I found the count, who had been only stunned by the blow, his helmet having broken the force thereof, and his vile associates flying up and down the cavern in the greatest confusion, vowing the most exemplary revenge on you; who I now perceived, to my inexpressible joy, had effected your escape in a most miraculous manner. Overwhelmed with fury and disappointment, the banditti at length left the cavern; when finding myself alone, I used every endeavour to obtain my liberty. For some time my exertions proved abortive; but the chain at length breaking, I quitted the cavern and fled on, without once looking behind me, to this very spot, where I have the happiness of meeting with you.'

Dorothée finished her narrative, and demanded of her deliverer to what singular circumstance she was indebted for his fortunate arrival. He then informed her that he had left the castle of A—y on the preceding evening during a tremendous storm, accompanied by two of his vassals, in order to relieve and assist such helpless fugitives as chance and misfortune might have exposed to the rude inclemencies of the weather; he then proceeded to inform her of what had passed previous to his attacking the banditti; which was scarcely finished when the ears of Montmorency were assailed by the sound of horses' feet. Raising his eyes, he saw the ferocious Edelbert advancing at the head of the surviving banditti. Driven to desperation, our hero was about to rush into the midst of them, and boldly meet his death, when he discovered another party coming full speed down the opposite side of the glen; they, on their near approach, proved, to his no small joy, to be a troop of his own domestics, collected together by one of his former retinue who had fled in the first engagement. They presented a sword to Montmorency and he, having mounted one of the horses, flew to the attack. The conflict was dreadful in the extreme, and for some time victory hung doubtful over the head of either. At length Edelbert falling by the hands of Montmorency, the day was declared in favour of the latter, who, having secured the banditti, conducted them, and the lady, to his castle. Thereafter, following the careful burial of the remains of Dorothée's father and a suitable period of mourning, she became the lawful mistress of A—y Castle by giving her hand to her valiant protector; and together they lived a life of uninterrupted happiness for many years, surrounded by the admiration of all people.

Extracts from Gosschen's Diary: No. 1

ANONYMOUS

The following striking narrative is translated from the manuscript memoirs of the late Revd Dr Gottlieb Michael Gosschen, a Catholic clergyman of great eminence in the city of Ratisbonne. It was the custom of this divine to preserve, in the shape of a diary, a regular account of all the interesting particulars which fell in his way during the exercise of his sacred profession. Two thick small quartos, filled with these strange materials, have been put into our hands by the kindness of Count Frederick von Lindénbäumenberg, to whom the worthy father bequeathed them. Many a dark story, well fitted to be the groundwork of a romance, many a tale of guilty love and repentance, many a fearful monument of remorse and horror, might we extract from this record of dungeons and confessionals. We shall from time to time do so, but sparingly, and what is still more necessary, with selection. EDITOR

NEVER HAD A MURDER so agitated the inhabitants of this city as that of Maria von Richterstein. No heart could be pacified till the murderer was condemned. But no sooner was his doom sealed, and the day fixed for his execution, than a great change took place in the public feeling. The evidence, though conclusive, had been wholly circumstantial. And people who, before his condemnation, were as assured of the murderer's guilt as if they had seen him with red hands, began now to conjure up the most contradictory and absurd reasons for believing in the possibility of his innocence. His own dark and sullen silence seemed to some an indignant expression of that innocence which he was too proud to avow; some thought they saw in his imperturbable demeanour, a resolution to court death, because his life was miserable and his reputation blasted; and others, the most numerous, without reason or reflection, felt such sympathy with the criminal as almost amounted to a negation of his crime. The man under sentence of death was, in all the beauty of youth, distinguished above his fellows for graceful accomplishments, and the last of a noble family. He had lain a month in his dungeon, heavily laden with irons. The first week he had been visited by several religionists, but he then fiercely ordered the jailor to admit no more 'men of God' – and till the eve of his execution he had lain in dark solitude, abandoned to his own soul.

It was near midnight when a message was sent to me by a magistrate that the murderer was desirous of seeing me. I had been with many men in his unhappy situation, and in no case had I failed to calm the agonies of grief and the fears of the world to come. But I had known this youth – had sat with him at his father's table – and I knew that there was in him a strange and fearful mixture of good and evil. I was aware that there were circumstances in the history of his progenitors not generally known – nay, in his own life – that made him an object of awful commiseration – and I went to his cell with an agitating sense of the enormity of his guilt, but a still more agitating one of the depth of his misery and the wildness of his misfortunes.

I entered his cell, and the phantom struck me with terror. He stood erect in his irons, like a corpse that had risen from the grave. His face, once so beautiful, was pale as a shroud and drawn into ghastly wrinkles. His black matted hair hung over it with a terrible expression of wrathful and savage misery. And his large eyes, which once were black, glared with a light in which all colour was lost, and seemed to fill the whole dungeon with their flashings. I saw his guilt – I saw what was more terrible than his guilt – his insanity – not in emaciation only – not in that more than deathlike whiteness of his face – but in *all* that stood before me – the *figure*, round which were gathered the agonies of so many long days and nights of remorse, and frenzy, and of a despair that had no fears of this world or its terrors but that was plunged in the abyss of eternity.

For a while the figure said nothing. He then waved his arm, making his irons clank and motioning me to sit down on the iron framework of his bed; and when I did so, the murderer took his place by my side.

A lamp burned on a table before us – and on that table there had been drawn by the maniac – for I must indeed so call him – a decapitated human body – the neck as if streaming with gore – and the face writhed into horrible convulsions, but bearing a resemblance not to be mistaken to that of him who had traced the horrid picture. He saw that my eyes rested on this fearful mockery – and, with a recklessness fighting with despair, he burst out into a broken peal of laughter, and said, 'Tomorrow will you see that picture drawn in blood!'

He then grasped me violently by the arm, and told me to listen to his confession – and then to say what I thought of God and his eternal Providence.

'I have been assailed by idiots, fools, and drivellers, who could understand nothing of me nor of my crime – men who came not here that I might confess before God but that I might reveal myself to them – and I drove the tamperers with misery and guilt out of a cell sacred to insanity. But my hands have played in infancy, long before I was a murderer, with thy grey hairs, and now, even that I am a murderer, I can still touch them with love and with reverence. Therefore my lips, shut to all beside, shall be opened unto thee.

'I murdered her. Who else loved her so well as to shed her innocent blood? It was I that enjoyed her beauty – a beauty surpassing that of the daughters of men – it was I that filled her soul with bliss, and with trouble – it was I alone that was privileged to take her life. I brought her into sin – I kept her in sin – and when she would have left her sin, it was fitting that I, to whom her heart, her body and her soul belonged, should suffer no divorcement of them from my bosom, as long as there was blood in hers – and when I saw that the poor infatuated wretch was resolved – I slew her; – yes, with this blessed hand I stabbed her to the heart.

'Do you think there was no pleasure in murdering her? I grasped her by that radiant, that golden hair – I bared those snow-white breasts – I dragged her sweet body towards me, and, as God is my witness, I stabbed and stabbed her with this very dagger, ten, twenty, forty times, through and through her heart. She never so much as gave one shriek, for she was dead in a moment – but she would not have shrieked had she endured pang after pang, for she saw my face of wrath turned upon her – she knew that my wrath was just, and that I did right to murder her who would have forsaken her lover in his insanity.

'I laid her down upon a bank of flowers – that were soon stained with her blood. I saw the dim blue eyes beneath the half-closed lids – that face so changeful in its living beauty was now fixed as ice, and the balmy breath came from her sweet lips no more. My joy, my happiness, was perfect. I took her into my arms – madly as I did on that night when first I robbed her of what fools called her innocence – but her innocence has gone with her to heaven – and there I lay with her bleeding breasts pressed to my heart, and many were the thousand kisses that I gave those breasts, cold and bloody as they were, which I had many million times kissed in all the warmth of their loving loveliness, and which none were ever to kiss again but the husband who had murdered her.

'I looked up to the sky. There shone the moon and all her stars. Tranquillity, order, harmony and peace glittered throughout the whole universe of God. "Look up, Maria, your favourite star has risen." I gazed upon her, and death had begun to change her into something that was most terrible. Her features were hardened and sharp – her body stiff as a lump of frozen clay – her fingers rigid and clenched – and the blood that was once so beautiful in her thin blue veins was now hideously coagulated all over her corpse. I gazed on her one moment longer, and all at once, I recollected that we were a family of madmen. Did not my father perish by his own hand? Blood had before been shed in our house. Did not that warrior ancestor of ours die raving in chains? Were not those eyes of mine always unlike those of other men? Wilder – at times fiercer – and oh! father, saw you never there a melancholy, too woeful for mortal man, a look sent up from the darkness of a soul that God never visited in his mercy?

'I knelt down beside my dead wife. But I knelt not down to pray. No: I cried unto God, if God there be – "Thou madest me a madman! Thou madest me a murderer! Thou foredoomedst me to sin and to hell! Thou, thou, the gracious God whom we mortals worship. There is the sacrifice! I have done thy will – I have slain the most blissful of all thy creatures; – am I a holy and commissioned priest, or am I an accursed and infidel murderer?"

'Father, you start at such words! You are not familiar with a madman's thoughts. Did I make this blood to boil so? Did I form this brain? Did I put that poison into my veins which flowed a hundred years since in the heart of that lunatic, my heroic ancestor? Had I not my being imposed, forced upon me, with all its red-rolling sea of dreams; and will you, a right holy and pious man, curse me because my soul was carried away by them as a ship is driven through the raging darkness of a storm? A thousand times, even when she lay in resigned love in my bosom, something whispered to me, "Murder her!" It may have been the voice of Satan – it may have been the voice of God. For who can tell the voice of heaven from that of hell? Look on this blood-crusted dagger – look on the hand that drove it to her heart, and then dare to judge of me and of my crimes; or comprehend God and all his terrible decrees!

'Look not away from me. Was I not once confined in a madhouse? Are these the first chains I ever wore? No. Remember things of old, that others may think I have forgotten. Dreams will disappear for a long, long time, but they will return again. It may have been someone like me that I once saw sitting chained, in his black melancholy, in a madhouse. I may have been only a stranger passing through that wild world. I know not. The sound of chains brings with it a crowd of thoughts that come rushing upon me from a dark and far-off world. But if it indeed be true, that in my boyhood I was not as other happy boys, and that even then the cloud of God's wrath hung around me – that God may not suffer my soul everlastingly to perish.

'I started up. I covered the dead body with bloody leaves, and tufts of grass, and flowers. I washed my hands from blood – I went to sleep – I slept – yes, I slept – for there is no hell like the hell of sleep, and into that hell God delivered me. I did not give myself up to judgment. I wished to walk about with the secret curse of the murder in my soul. What could men do to me so cruel as to let me live? How could God curse me more in black and fiery hell than on this green and flowery earth? And what right had such men as those dull heavy-eyed burghers to sit in judgment upon me, in whose face they were afraid to look for a moment, lest one gleam of it should frighten them into idiocy? What right have they, who are not as I am, to load me with their chains, or to let their villain executioner spill my blood? If I deserve punishment, it must rise up in a blacker cloud under the hand of God in my soul.

'I will not kneel – a madman has no need of sacraments. I do not wish the forgiveness nor the mercy of God. All that I wish is the forgiveness of her I slew; and well I know that death cannot so change the heart that once had life, as to obliterate from THINE the merciful love of me! Spirits may in heaven have beautiful bosoms no more; but thou, who art a spirit, wilt save him from eternal perdition, whom thou now knowest God created subject to a terrible disease. If there be mercy in heaven, it must be with thee. Thy path thither lay through blood: so will mine. Father! thinkst thou that we shall meet in heaven. Lay us at least in one grave on earth.'

In a moment he was dead at my feet. The stroke of the dagger was like lightning, and –

The Parricide's Tale

CHARLES ROBERT MATURIN

IT WAS IN THE MIDST of one of his most licentious songs that my
companion suddenly paused. He gazed about him for some time; and
faint and dismal as the light was by which we beheld each other, I
thought I could observe an extraordinary expression overshadow his
countenance. I did not venture to notice it. 'Do you know where we
are?' he whispered. – 'Too well; – in the vault of a convent, beyond
the help or reach of man – without food, without light, and almost
without hope.' – 'Aye, so its last inhabitants might well say.' – 'Its last
inhabitants! – who were they?' – 'I can tell you, if you can bear it.' – '*I
cannot bear it*,' I cried, stopping my ears, 'I will not listen to it. I feel
by the narrator it must be something horrid.' – 'It was indeed a
horrid night,' said he, unconsciously adverting to some circumstance
in the narrative; and his voice sank into mutterings, and he forbore to
mention the subject further. I retired as far from him as the limits of
the vault admitted; and, burying my head between my knees, tried to
forbear to think. What a state of mind must that be in which we are
driven to wish we no longer had one! – when we would willingly
become 'as the beasts that perish', to forget that privilege of humanity, which only seems an undisputed title to superlative misery! To
sleep was impossible. Though sleep seems to be only a necessity of
nature, it always requires an act of the mind to concur in it. And if I
had been willing to rest, the gnawings of hunger, which now began
to be exchanged for the most deadly sickness, would have rendered it
impossible. Amid this complication of physical and mental suffering,
it is hardly credible, sir, but it is not the less true, that my principal
one arose from the inanity, the want of occupation, inevitably
attached to my dreary situation. To inflict a suspension of action on
a being conscious of possessing the powers of action, and burning for
their employment – to forbid all interchange of mutual ideas or
acquirement of new ones to an intellectual being – to do this, is to
invent a torture that might make Phalaris[1] blush for his impotence of
cruelty.

I had felt other sufferings almost intolerable, but I felt this impossible to sustain; and, will you believe it, sir, after wrestling with it during an hour (as I counted hours) of unimaginable misery, I rose, and supplicated my companion to relate the circumstance he had alluded to, as connected with our dreadful abode. His ferocious good nature took part with this request in a moment; and though I could see that his strong frame had suffered more than my comparatively feeble one from the struggles of the night and the privations of the day, he prepared himself with a kind of grim alacrity for the effort. He was now in his element. He was enabled to daunt a feeble mind by the narration of horrors and to amaze an ignorant one with a display of crimes – and he needed no more to make him commence. 'I remember,' said he, 'an extraordinary circumstance connected with this vault. I wondered how I felt so familiar with this door, this arch, at first. I did not recollect immediately – so many strange thoughts have crossed my mind every day that events which would make a life-lasting impression on others pass like shadows before me, while thoughts appear like substances. *Emotions are my events* – you know what brought me to this cursed convent – well, don't shiver or look *paler* – you were pale before. However it was, I found myself in the convent, and I was obliged to subscribe to its discipline. A part of it was that extraordinary criminals should undergo what they called extraordinary penance; that is, not only submit to every ignominy and rigour of conventual life (which, fortunately for its penitents, is never wanting in such amusing resources), but act the part of executioner whenever any distinguished punishment was to be inflicted or witnessed. They did me the honour to believe me particularly qualified for this species of recreation, and perhaps they did not flatter me. I had all the humility of a saint on trial; but still I had a kind of confidence in my talents of this description, provided they were put to a proper test; and the monks had the goodness to assure me that I never could long be without one in a convent. This was a very tempting picture of my situation, but I found these worthy people had not in the least exaggerated. An instance occurred a few days after I had the happiness to become a member of this amiable community, of whose merits you are doubtless sensible. I was desired to attach myself to a young monk of distinguished family, who had lately taken the vows, and who performed his duties with that heartless punctuality that intimated to the community that his heart was elsewhere. I was soon put in possession of the business; from their ordering me to *attach* myself to him, I instantly conceived I was bound to the most deadly hostility against him. The friendship of convents is always a treacherous league – we watch, suspect and torment each other, for the love of God. This young monk's only crime was that he was suspected of cherishing an earthly passion. He was, in fact, as I have stated, the son of a distinguished family, who (from the fear of his contracting what is called a degrading marriage, i.e. of marrying a woman of inferior rank whom he loved, and who would have made him happy, as fools – that is, half mankind – estimate happiness) forced him to take the vows. He appeared at times broken-hearted, but at times there was a light of hope in his eye that looked somewhat ominous in the eyes of the community. It is certain that hope, not being an indigenous plant in the parterre of a convent, must excite suspicion with regard both to its origin and its growth.

'Some time after, a young novice entered the convent. From the moment he did so, a change the most striking took place in the young monk. He and the novice became inseparable companions – there was something suspicious in that. My eyes were on the watch in a moment. Eyes are particularly sharpened in discovering misery when they can hope to aggravate it. The attachment between the young monk and the novice went on. They were forever in the garden together – they inhaled the odours of the flowers – they cultivated the same cluster of carnations – they entwined themselves as they walked together – when they were in the choir, their voices were like mixed incense. Friendship is often carried to excess in conventual life, but this friendship was too like love. For instance, the psalms sung in the choir sometimes breathe a certain language; at these words, the young monk and the novice would direct their voices to each other in sounds that could not be misunderstood. If the least correction was inflicted, one would entreat to undergo it for the other. If a day of relaxation was allowed, whatever presents were sent to the cell of one were sure to be found in the cell of the other. This was enough for me. I saw that secret of mysterious happiness which is the greatest misery to those who never can share it. My vigilance was redoubled, and it was rewarded by the discovery of a secret – a secret that I had to communicate and raise my consequence by. You cannot guess the importance attached to the discovery of a secret in a convent (particularly when the remission of our own offences depends on the discovery of those of others).

'One evening as the young monk and his darling novice were in the garden, the former plucked a peach, which he immediately offered to his favourite; the latter accepted it with a movement I thought rather awkward – it seemed like what I imagined would be the reverence of a female. The young monk divided the peach with a knife; in doing so, the knife grazed the finger of the novice, and the monk, in agitation inexpressible, tore his habit to bind up the wound. I saw it all – my mind was made up on the business – I went to the Superior that very night. The result may be conceived. They were watched, but cautiously at first. They were probably on their guard; for some time it defied even my vigilance to make the slightest discovery. It is a situation incomparably tantalising, when suspicion is satisfied of her own suggestions, as of the truth of the gospel, but still wants the *little fact* to make them credible to others. One night that I had, by direction of the Superior, taken my station in the gallery (where I was contented to remain hour after hour, and night after night, amid solitude, darkness and cold, for the chance of the power of retaliating on others the misery inflicted on myself) – one night, I thought I heard a step in the gallery – I have told you that I was in the dark – a light step passed me. I could hear the broken and palpitating respiration of the person. A few moments after, I heard a door open, and knew it to be the door of the young monk. I knew it; for by long watching in the dark, and accustoming myself to number the cells, by the groan from one, the prayer from another, the faint shriek of restless dreams from a third, my ear had become so finely graduated, that I could instantly distinguish the opening of *that door*, from which (to my sorrow) no sound had ever before issued. I was provided with a small chain, by which I fastened the handle of the door to a contiguous one, in such a manner, that it was impossible to open either of them from the inside. I then hastened to the Superior, with a pride of which none but the successful tracer of a guilty secret in a convent can have any conception. I believe the Superior was himself agitated by the luxury of the same feeling, for he was awake and up in his apartment, attended by *four monks*, whom you may remember.' I shuddered at the remembrance. 'I communicated my intelligence with a voluble eagerness, not only unsuited to the respect I owed these persons but which must have rendered me almost unintelligible, yet they were good enough not only to overlook this violation of decorum, which would in any other case have been severely punished, but even to supply certain pauses in my narrative with a condescension and facility truly miraculous. I felt what it was to acquire importance in the eyes of a Superior, and gloried in all the dignified depravity of an informer. We set out without losing a moment – we arrived at the door of the cell, and I pointed out with triumph the chain unremoved, though a slight vibration, perceptible at our approach, showed the wretches within were already apprised of their danger. I unfastened the door – how they must have shuddered! The Superior and his satellites burst into the cell, and *I* held the light. You tremble – why? I was guilty, and I wished to witness guilt that palliated mine, at least in the opinion of the convent. I had only violated the laws of nature, but they had outraged the decorum of a convent, and, of course, in the creed of a convent, there was no proportion between our offences. Besides, I was anxious to witness misery that might perhaps equal or exceed my own, and this is a curiosity not easily satisfied. It is actually possible to become *amateurs*[2] *in suffering*. I have heard of men who have travelled into countries where horrible executions were to be daily witnessed, for the sake of that excitement which the sight of suffering never fails to give, from the spectacle of a tragedy, or an *auto-da-fé*,[3] down to the writhings of the meanest reptile on whom you can inflict torture and feel that torture is the result of your own power. It is a species of feeling of which we never can divest ourselves – a triumph over those whose sufferings have placed them below us, and no wonder – suffering is always an indication of weakness – we glory in our impenetrability. *I* did, as we burst into the cell. The wretched husband and wife were locked in each other's arms. You may imagine the scene that followed. Here I must do the Superior reluctant justice. He was a man (of course from his conventual feelings) who had no more idea of the intercourse between the sexes than between two beings of a different species. The scene that he beheld could not have revolted him more if he had seen the horrible loves of the baboons and the Hottentot women at the Cape of Good Hope; or those still more loathsome unions between the serpents of South America and their human victims, when they can catch them, and twine round them in folds of unnatural and ineffable union. He really stood as much astonished and appalled to see two human beings of different sexes, who dared to love each other in spite of monastic ties, as if he had witnessed the horrible conjunctions I have alluded to. Had he seen vipers engendering in that frightful knot which seems the pledge of mortal hostility, instead of love, he could not have testified more horror – and I do him the justice to believe he felt all he testified. Whatever affectation he might employ on points of conventual austerity, there was none here. Love was a thing he always believed connected with sin, even though consecrated by the name of a sacrament, and called marriage, as it is in our church. But, love in a convent! – Oh, there is no conceiving his rage; still less is it possible to conceive the majestic and overwhelming extent of that rage when strengthened by principle and sanctified by religion. I enjoyed the scene beyond all power of description. I saw those wretches, who had triumphed over me, reduced to my level in a moment – their passions all displayed, and the display placing me a hero triumphant above all. I had crawled to the shelter of their walls, a wretched degraded outcast, and what was my crime? Well – you shudder, I have done with that. I can only say want drove me to it. And here were beings whom, a few months before, I would have knelt to as to the images round the shrine – to whom, in the moments of my desperate penitence, I would have clung as to the "horns of the altar", all brought as low, and lower, than myself. "Sons of the morning," as I deemed them in the agonies of my humiliation, "how were they fallen!" I feasted on the degradation of the apostate monk and novice – I enjoyed, to the core of my ulcerated heart, the passion of the Superior – I felt that they were all men like myself. Angels, as I had thought them, they had all proved themselves mortal; and, by watching their motions, and flattering their passions, and promoting their interest, or setting up my own in opposition to them all while I made them believe it was only theirs I was intent on, I might make shift to contrive as much misery to others, and to carve out as much occupation to myself, as if I were actually living in the world. Cutting my father's throat was a noble feat certainly (I ask your pardon, I did not mean to extort that groan from you), but here were hearts to be cut – and to the core, every day, and all day long, so I never could want employment.'

Here he wiped his hard brow, drew his breath for a moment, and then said, 'I do not quite like to go through the details by which this wretched pair were deluded into the hope of effecting their escape from the convent. It is enough that I was the principal agent – that the Superior connived at it – that I led them through the very passages you have traversed tonight, they trembling and blessing me at every step – that . . . ' – 'Stop,' I cried, 'wretch! You are tracing my course this night step by step.' – 'What?' he retorted, with a ferocious laugh, 'you think I am betraying you, then; and if it were true, what good would your suspicions do you – you are in my power? My voice might summon half the convent to seize you this moment – my arm might fasten you to that wall, till those dogs of death, that wait but my whistle, plunged their fangs into your very vitals. I fancy you would not find their bite less keen from their tusks being so long sharpened by an immersion in holy water.' Another laugh, that seemed to issue from the lungs of a demon, concluded this sentence. 'I know I am in your power,' I answered; 'and were I to trust to that, or to your heart, I had better dash out my brains at once against these walls of rock, which I believe are not harder than the latter. But I know your interests to be some way or other connected with my escape, and therefore I trust you – because I must. Though my blood, chilled as it is by famine and fatigue, seems frozen in every drop while I listen to you, yet listen I must, and trust my life and liberation to you. I speak to you with the horrid confidence our situation has taught me – I hate – I dread you. If we were to meet in life, I would shrink from you with loathings of unspeakable abhorrence, but here mutual misery has mixed the most repugnant substances in unnatural coalition. The force of that alchemy must cease at the moment of my escape from the convent and from you; yet, for these miserable hours, my life is as much dependent on your exertions and presence, as my power of supporting them is on the continuance of your horrible tale – go on, then. Let us struggle through this dreadful day. *Day!* a name unknown *here*, where noon and night shake hands that never unlock. Let us struggle through it, "hateful and hating one another", and when it has passed, let us curse and part.'

As I uttered these words, sir, I felt that terrible *confidence of hostility* which the worst beings are driven to in the worst of circumstances, and I question whether there is a more horrible situation than that in which we cling to each other's hate, instead of each other's love – in which, at every step of our progress, we hold a dagger to our companion's breast, and say, 'If you falter for a moment, this is in your heart. I hate – I fear, but I must bear with you.' It was singular to me, though it would not be so to those who investigate human nature, that, in proportion as my situation inspired me with a ferocity quite unsuited to our comparative situations, and which must have been the result of the madness of despair and famine, my companion's respect for me appeared to increase. After a long pause, he asked, might he continue his story? I could not speak, for, after the slightest exertion, the sickness of deadly hunger returned on me, and I could only signify, by a feeble motion of my hand, that he might go on.

'They were conducted here,' he continued; 'I had suggested the plan, and the Superior consented to it. He would not be present, but his dumb nod was enough. I was the conductor of their (intended) escape; they believed they were departing with the connivance of the Superior. I led them through those very passages that you and I have trod. I had a map of this subterranean region, but my blood ran cold as I traversed it; and it was not at all inclined to resume its usual

temperament as I felt what was to be the destination of my attendants. Once I turned the lamp, on pretence of trimming it, to catch a
glimpse of the devoted wretches. They were embracing each other –
the light of joy trembled in their eyes. They were whispering to each
other hopes of liberation and happiness, and blending my name in
the interval they could spare from their prayers for each other. That
sight extinguished the last remains of compunction with which my
horrible task had inspired me. They dared to be happy in the sight of
one who must be for ever miserable – could there be a greater insult?
I resolved to punish it on the spot. This very apartment was near – I
knew it, and the map of their wanderings no longer trembled in my
hand. I urged them to enter this recess (the door was then entire),
while I went to examine the passage. They entered it, thanking me
for my precaution – they knew not they were never to quit it alive.
But what were their lives for the agony their happiness cost me? The
moment they were enclosed, and clasping each other (a sight that
made me grind my teeth), I closed and locked the door. This
movement gave them no immediate uneasiness – they thought it a
friendly precaution. The moment they were secured, I hastened to
the Superior, who was on fire at the insult offered to the sanctity of
his convent, and still more to the purity of his penetration, on which
the worthy Superior piqued himself as much as if it had ever been
possible for him to acquire the smallest share of it. He descended
with me to the passage – the monks followed with eyes on fire. In the
agitation of their rage, it was with difficulty they could discover the
door after I had repeatedly pointed it out to them. The Superior,
with his own hands, drove several nails, which the monks eagerly
supplied, into the door, thus effectually joining it to the staple, *never
to be disjoined*; and every blow he gave, doubtless he felt as if it was a
reminiscence to the accusing angel to strike out a sin from the
catalogue of his accusations. The work was soon done – the work
never to be undone. At the first sound of steps in the passage, and
blows on the door, the victims uttered a shriek of terror. They
imagined they were detected, and that an incensed party of monks
were breaking open the door. These terrors were soon exchanged for
others – and worse – as they heard the door nailed up, and listened to
our departing steps. They uttered another shriek, but oh, how
different was the accent of its despair! – they knew their doom.

*   *   *

It was my penance (no – my delight) to watch at the door, under the
pretence of precluding the possibility of their escape (of which they

knew there was no possibility); but, in reality, not only to inflict on me the indignity of being the convent gaoler, but of teaching me that callosity of heart, and enduration of nerve, and stubbornness of eye, and apathy of ear that were best suited to my office. But they might have saved themselves the trouble – I had them all before ever I entered the convent. Had I been the Superior of the community, I should have undertaken the office of watching the door. You will call this cruelty, I call it curiosity – that curiosity that brings thousands to witness a tragedy, and makes the most delicate female feast on groans and agonies. I had an advantage over them – the groan and the agony I feasted on were real. I took my station at *the door* – that door which, like that of Dante's hell, might have borne the inscription, 'Here is no hope' – with a face of mock penitence, and genuine – cordial delectation. I could hear every word that transpired. For the first hours they tried to comfort each other – they suggested to each other hopes of liberation – and as my shadow, crossing the threshold, darkened or restored the light, they said, 'That is he.' Then, when this occurred repeatedly, without any effect, they said, 'No – no, it is not he,' and swallowed down the sick sob of despair, to hide it from each other. Towards night a monk came to take my place, and to offer me food. I would not have quitted my place for worlds; but I talked to the monk in his own language, and told him I would make a merit with God of my sacrifices, and was resolved to remain there all night, with the permission of the Superior. The monk was glad of having a substitute on such easy terms, and I was glad of the food he left me, for I was hungry now, but I reserved the appetite of my soul for richer luxuries. I heard them talking within. While I was eating, I actually lived on the famine that was devouring them, but of which they did not dare to say a word to each other. They debated, deliberated, and, as misery grows ingenious in its own defence, they at last assured each other that it was impossible the Superior had locked them in there to perish by hunger. At these words I could not help laughing. This laugh reached their ears, and they became silent in a moment. All that night, however, I heard their groans – those groans of physical suffering that laugh to scorn all the sentimental sighs that are exhaled from the hearts of the most intoxicated loves that ever breathed. I heard them all that night. I had read French romances, and all their unimaginable nonsense. Madame Sevigné[4] herself says she would have been tired of her daughter in a long tête-à-tête journey, but clap me two lovers into a dungeon, without food, light or hope, and I will be damned (that I am already, by the by) if they do not grow sick of each other within the first twelve hours. The second day, hunger and darkness had their usual influence. They shrieked for liberation, and knocked loud and long at their dungeon door. They exclaimed they were ready to submit to any punishment; and the approach of the monks, which they would have dreaded so much the preceding night, they now solicited on their knees. What a jest, after all, are the most awful vicissitudes of human life! – they supplicated now for what they would have sacrificed their souls to avert four-and-twenty hours before. Then, as the agony of hunger increased, they shrank from the door, and grovelled apart from each other. *Apart!* – now I watched that. They were rapidly becoming objects of hostility to each other – oh, what a feast to me! They could not disguise from each other the revolting circumstances of their mutual sufferings. It is one thing for lovers to sit down to a feast magnificently spread, and another for lovers to crouch in darkness and famine – to exchange that appetite which cannot be supported without dainties and flattery, for that which would barter a de-scended Venus for a morsel of food. The second night they raved and groaned (as occurred); and, amid their agonies (I must do justice to women, whom I hate as well as men), the man often accused the female as the cause of all his sufferings, but the woman never – never reproached him. Her groans might indeed have reproached him bitterly, but she never uttered a word that could have caused him pain. There was a change which I well could mark, however, in their physical feelings. The first day they clung together, and every movement I felt was like that of one person. The next the man alone struggled, and the woman moaned in helplessness. The third night – how shall I tell it? – but you have bid me go on. All the horrible and loathsome excruciations of famine had been undergone; the disunion of every tie of the heart, of passion, of nature, had commenced. In the agonies of their famished sickness they loathed each other – they could have cursed each other, if they had had breath to curse. It was on the fourth night that I heard the shriek of the wretched female – her lover, in the agony of hunger, had fastened his teeth in her shoulder; – that bosom on which he had so often luxuriated, became a meal to him now.'

*   *   *

'Monster! and you laugh?' – 'Yes, I laugh at all mankind, and the imposition they dare to practise when they talk of hearts. I laugh at human passions and human cares – vice and virtue, religion and impiety; they are all the result of petty localities and artificial situation. One physical want, one severe and abrupt lesson from the

tintless and shrivelled lip of necessity, is worth all the logic of the
empty wretches who have presumed to prate it, from Zeno down to
Burgersdicius.[5] Oh! it silences in a second all the feeble sophistry of
conventional life, and ascititious[6] passion. Here were a pair who would
not have believed all the world on their knees, even though angels
had descended to join in the attestation, that it was possible for them
to exist without each other. They had risked everything, trampled on
everything human and divine, to be in each other's sight and arms.
One hour of hunger undeceived them. A trivial and ordinary want,
whose claims at another time they would have regarded as a vulgar
interruption of their spiritualised intercourse, not only, by its natural
operation, sundered it for ever, but, before it ceased, converted that
intercourse into a source of torment and hostility inconceivable,
except among cannibals. The bitterest enemies on earth could not
have regarded each other with more abhorrence than *these lovers*.
Deluded wretches! you boasted of having hearts, I boast I have none,
and which of us gained most by the vaunt let life decide. My story is
nearly finished, and so I hope is the day. When I was last here I had
something to excite me; – talking of those things is poor employment
to one who has been a witness to them. On the *sixth* day all was still.
The door was unnailed, we entered – they were no more. They lay
far from each other, farther than on that voluptuous couch into
which their passion had converted the mat of a convent bed. She lay
contracted in a heap, a lock of her long hair in her mouth. There was
a slight scar on her shoulder – the rabid despair of famine had
produced no further outrage. He lay extended at his length – his
hand was between his lips; it seemed as if he had not strength to
execute the purpose for which he had brought it there. The bodies
were brought out for interment. As we removed them into the light,
the long hair of the female, falling over a face no longer disguised by
the novice's dress, recalled a likeness I thought I could remember. I
looked closer, she was my own sister – my only one – and I had heard
her voice grow fainter and fainter. I had heard – ' and his own voice
grew fainter – it ceased.

The Spectre Bride

ANONYMOUS

THE CASTLE OF HERNSWOLF, at the close of the year 1655, was the resort of fashion and gaiety. The baron of that name was the most powerful nobleman in Germany, and equally celebrated for the patriotic achievements of his sons and the beauty of his only daughter. The estate of Hernswolf, which was situated in the centre of the Black Forest, had been given to one of his ancestors by the gratitude of the nation and had descended with other hereditary possessions to the family of the present owner. It was a castellated, Gothic mansion, built, according to the fashion of the times, in the grandest style of architecture, and consisted principally of dark winding corridors and vaulted tapestry rooms, magnificent indeed in their size but ill suited to private comfort from the very circumstance of their dreary magnitude. A dark grove of pine and mountain ash encompassed the castle on every side, and threw an aspect of gloom around the scene, which was seldom enlivened by the cheering sunshine of heaven.

*   *   *

The castle bells rang out a merry peal at the approach of a winter twilight, and the warder was stationed with his retinue on the battlements to announce the arrival of the company who were invited to share the amusements that reigned within the walls. The Lady Clotilda, the baron's only daughter, had but just attained her seventeenth year, and a brilliant assembly was invited to celebrate the birthday. The large vaulted apartments were thrown open for the reception of the numerous guests. The gaieties of the evening had scarcely commenced when the clock from the dungeon tower was heard to strike with unusual solemnity, and on the instant a tall stranger, arrayed in a suit of deepest black, made his appearance in the ballroom. He bowed courteously on every side, but was received by all with the strictest reserve. No one knew who he was or whence he came, but it was evident from his appearance that he was a nobleman of the first rank, and though his introduction was accepted with distrust, he was treated by all with respect. He addressed himself particularly to the daughter of the baron, and was so intelligent in his remarks, so lively in his sallies, and so fascinating in his address, that he quickly interested the feelings of his young and sensitive auditor. In fine, after some hesitation on the part of the host, who, with the rest of the company, was unable to approach the stranger with indifference, he was requested to remain a few days at the castle, an invitation which was cheerfully accepted.

The dead of the night drew on, and when all had retired to rest, the dull heavy bell was heard swinging to and fro in the grey tower, though there was scarcely a breath to move the forest trees. Many of the guests, when they met the next morning at the breakfast table, averred that there had been sounds as of the most heavenly music, while all persisted in affirming that they had also heard awful noises proceeding, as it seemed, from the apartment which the stranger at that time occupied. He soon, however, made his appearance in the breakfast circle, and when the circumstances of the preceding night were alluded to, a dark smile of unutterable meaning played round his saturnine features, which then relapsed into an expression of the deepest melancholy. He addressed his conversation principally to Clotilda, and when he talked of the different climes he had visited, of the sunny regions of Italy, where the very air breathes the fragrance of flowers, and the summer breeze sighs over a land of sweets; when he spoke to her of those delicious countries where the smile of the day sinks into the softer beauty of the night, and the loveliness of heaven is never for an instant obscured, he drew tears of longing from the bosom of his fair auditor, and for the first time she regretted that she was yet at home.

Days rolled on, and every moment increased the fervour of the inexpressible sentiments with which the stranger had inspired her. He never discoursed of love, but he looked it in his language, in his manner, in the insinuating tones of his voice and in the slumbering softness of his smile, and when he found that he had succeeded in inspiring her with favourable sentiments, a sneer of the most diabolical meaning spoke for an instant and died again on his dark-featured countenance. When he met her in the company of her parents he was at once respectful and submissive, and it was only when he was alone with her, in their rambles through the dark recesses of the forest, that he assumed the guise of the more impassioned admirer.

As he was sitting one evening with the baron in the wainscoted apartment of the library, the conversation happened to turn upon supernatural agency. The stranger remained reserved and mysterious during the discussion, but when the baron in a jocular manner denied the existence of spirits, and satirically mocked their appearance, his eyes glowed with unearthly lustre and his form seemed to dilate to more than its natural dimensions. When the conversation had ceased, there was a fearful pause of a few seconds and then a chorus of celestial harmony was heard pealing through the dark forest glade. All were entranced with delight, but the stranger was disturbed and gloomy; he looked at his noble host with compassion and something like a tear swam in his dark eye. After the lapse of a few seconds, the music died gently in the distance, and all was hushed as before. The baron soon after quitted the apartment, and was followed almost immediately by the stranger. He had not long been absent when an awful noise, as of a person in the agonies of death, was heard, and the baron was discovered stretched dead along the corridor. His countenance was convulsed with pain, and the grip of a human hand was visible on his blackened throat. The alarm was instantly given, the castle searched in every direction, but the stranger was seen no more. The body of the baron, in the meantime, was quietly committed to the earth, and the remembrance of the dreadful transaction recalled but as a thing that once was.

*   *   *

After the departure of the stranger, who had indeed fascinated her very senses, the spirits of the gentle Clotilda evidently declined. She loved to walk early and late in the walks that he had once frequented; to recall his last words; to dwell on his sweet smile; and wander to the spot where she had once discoursed with him of love. She avoided all society, and never seemed to be happy but when left alone in the solitude of her chamber. It was then that she gave vent to her affliction in tears; and the love that the pride of maiden modesty concealed in public, burst forth in the hours of privacy. So beauteous, yet so resigned was the fair mourner, that she seemed already an angel freed from the trammels of the world and prepared to take her flight to heaven.

As she was one summer evening rambling to the sequestered spot that had been selected as her favourite retreat, a slow step advanced towards her. She turned round, and to her infinite surprise discovered the stranger. He stepped gaily to her side, and commenced an animated conversation. 'You left me,' exclaimed the delighted girl; 'and I thought all happiness was fled from me for ever; but you return, and shall we not again be happy?' – 'Happy!' replied the stranger, with a scornful burst of derision. 'Can I ever be happy again – can there . . . but excuse the agitation my love, and impute it to the pleasure I experience at our meeting. Oh! I have many things to tell you; aye! and many kind words to receive; is it not so, sweet one? Come, tell me truly, have you been happy in my absence? No! I see in that sunken eye, in that pallid cheek, that the poor wanderer has at least gained some slight interest in the heart of his beloved. I have roamed to other climes, I have seen other nations; I have met with other females, beautiful and accomplished, but I have met with but one angel, and she is here before me. Accept this simple offering of my affection, dearest,' continued the stranger, plucking a heath-rose from its stem; 'it is beautiful as the wild flowers that deck thy hair, and sweet as is the love I bear thee.' – 'It is sweet, indeed,' replied Clotilda, 'but its sweetness must wither ere night closes around. It is beautiful, but its beauty is short-lived, as the love evinced by man. Let not this, then, be the type of thy attachment; bring me the delicate evergreen, the sweet flower that blossoms throughout the year, and I will say, as I wreathe it in my hair, "The violets have bloomed and died – the roses have flourished and decayed; but the evergreen is still young, and so is the love of the heart!" – you will not – cannot desert me. I live but in you; you are my hopes, my thoughts, my existence itself: and if I lose you, I lose my all. I was but a solitary wild flower in the wilderness of nature until you transplanted me to a more genial soil; and can you now break the fond heart you first taught to glow with passion?' – 'Speak not thus,' returned the stranger, 'it rends my very soul to hear you; leave me – forget me – avoid me for ever – or your eternal ruin must ensue. I am a thing abandoned of God and man – and did you but see the scared heart that scarcely beats within this moving mass of deformity, you would flee me, as you would an adder in your path. Here is my heart, love, feel how cold it is; there is no pulse that betrays its emotion, for all is chilled and dead as the friends I once knew.' – 'You are unhappy, love, and your poor Clotilda shall stay to succour you. Think not I can abandon you in your misfortunes. No! I will wander with thee through the wide world, and be thy servant, thy slave, if thou wilt have it so. I will shield thee from the night winds, that they blow not too roughly on thy unprotected head. I will defend thee from the tempest that howls around; and though the cold world may devote thy name to scorn – though friends may fall off, and associates wither in the grave, there shall be one fond heart that shall love thee better in thy misfortune, and cherish thee, bless thee still.' She ceased, and her blue eyes swam with tears as she turned them, glistening with affection, towards the stranger. He averted his head from her gaze, and a scornful sneer of the darkest, the deadliest malice passed over his fine countenance. In an instant, the expression subsided; his fixed glassy eye resumed its unearthly chillness, and he turned once again to his companion. 'It is the hour of sunset,' he exclaimed; 'the soft, the beauteous hour, when the hearts of lovers are happy, and nature smiles in unison with their feelings; but to me it will smile no longer – ere the morrow dawns I shall be very far from the house of my beloved; from the scenes where my heart is enshrined, as in a sepulchre. But must I leave thee, dearest flower of the wilderness, to be the sport of the whirlwind, the prey of the mountain blast?' – 'No, we will not part,' replied the impassioned girl; *'where thou goest, will I go; thy home shall be my home; and thy God shall be my God.'* – 'Swear it, swear it,' resumed the stranger, wildly grasping her by the hand. 'Swear to the fearful oath I shall dictate.' He then desired her to kneel, and holding his right hand in a menacing attitude towards heaven, and throwing back his dark raven locks, he declaimed in a strain of bitter imprecation with the ghastly smile of an incarnate fiend, 'May the curses of an offended God haunt thee, cling to thee for ever in the tempest and in the calm, in the day and in the night, in sickness and in sorrow, in life and in death, shouldst thou swerve from the promise thou hast here made to be mine. May the dark spirits of the damned howl in thine ears the accursed chorus of fiends – may the air rack thy bosom with the quenchless flames of hell! May thy soul be as the lazar-house of corruption, where the ghost of departed pleasure sits enshrined, as in a grave; where the hundred-headed worm never dies; where the fire is never extinguished. May a spirit of evil lord it over thy brow, and proclaim, as thou passest by, "THIS IS THE ABANDONED OF GOD AND MAN;" may fearful spectres haunt thee in the night season; may thy dearest friends drop day by day into the grave, and curse thee with their dying breath; may all that is most horrible in human nature, more solemn than language can frame, or lips can utter, may this, and more than this, be thy eternal portion, shouldst thou violate the oath that thou hast taken.' He ceased – and hardly knowing what she did, the terrified girl acceded to the awful adjuration, and promised eternal fidelity to him who was henceforth to be her lord. 'Spirits of the damned, I thank thee for thine assistance,' shouted the stranger; 'I have wooed my fair bride bravely. She is mine – mine for ever. – Aye, body and soul both mine; mine in life, and mine in death. What? in tears my sweet one, ere yet the honeymoon is past? Why! indeed thou hast cause for weeping . . . When next we meet we shall meet to sign the nuptial bond.' He then imprinted a cold salute on the cheek of his young bride, and softening down the unutterable horrors of his countenance, requested her to meet him at eight o'clock on the ensuing evening at the chapel adjoining the castle of Hernswolf. She turned round to him with a burning sigh, as if to implore protection, but the stranger was gone.

On entering the castle, she was observed to be impressed with deepest melancholy. Her relations vainly endeavoured to ascertain the cause of her uneasiness; but the tremendous oath she had sworn completely paralysed her faculties, and she was fearful of betraying herself by even the slightest intonation of her voice or the least variable expression of her countenance. When the evening was concluded, the family retired to rest; but Clotilda, who was unable to take repose, from the restlessness of her disposition, requested to remain alone in the library that adjoined her apartment.

All was now deep midnight; every domestic had long since retired to rest, and the only sound that could be distinguished was the sullen howl of the bandog as he bayed at the waning moon. Clotilda remained in the library in an attitude of deep meditation. The lamp that burnt on the table at which she sat was dying away, and the lower end of the apartment was already more than half obscured. The clock from the northern angle of the castle tolled out the hour of twelve, and the sound echoed dismally in the solemn stillness of the night. Suddenly the oaken door at the farther end of the room was gently lifted on its latch, and a bloodless figure, apparelled in the habiliments of the grave, advanced slowly up the apartment. No sound heralded its approach as it moved with noiseless steps to the table where the lady was stationed. She did not at first perceive it but presently she felt a death-cold hand fast grasp her own and heard a solemn voice whisper in her ear, 'Clotilda.' She looked up: a dark figure was standing beside her; she endeavoured to scream, but her voice was unequal to the exertion; her eye was fixed, as if by magic, on the form, which slowly removed the garb that concealed its countenance and disclosed the livid eyes and skeleton shape of her father. It seemed to gaze on her with pity and regret, and mournfully exclaimed – 'Clotilda, the dresses and the servants are ready, the church bell has tolled, and the priest is at the altar, but where is the affianced bride? There is room for her in the grave, and tomorrow shall she be with me' –

'Tomorrow?' faltered out the distracted girl; 'the spirits of hell shall have registered it, and tomorrow must the bond be cancelled.'[1]

The figure ceased – slowly retired, and was soon lost in the obscurity of distance.

The morning and at length the evening of the fateful morrow arrived; and already, as the hall clock struck eight, Clotilda was on her road to the chapel. It was a dark, gloomy night, thick masses of dun clouds sailed across the firmament and the roar of the winter wind echoed awfully through the forest trees. She reached the appointed place; a figure was in waiting for her – it advanced – and discovered the features of the stranger. 'Why! this is well, my bride,' he exclaimed, with a sneer; 'and well will I repay thy fondness. Follow me.' They proceeded together in silence through the winding avenues beyond the chapel, until they reached the adjoining cemetery. Here they paused for an instant; and the stranger, in a softened tone, said, 'But one hour more, and the struggle will be over. And yet this heart of incarnate malice can feel, when it devotes so young, so pure a spirit to the grave. But it must – it must be,' he proceeded, as the memory of her past love rushed on his mind, 'for the fiend whom I obey has so witted it. Poor girl, I am leading thee indeed to our nuptials; but the priest will be death; thy parents, two of the mouldering skeletons that rot in heaps around; and the witnesses to our union, the lazy worms that revel on the carious bones of the dead. Come, my young bride, the priest is impatient for his victim.' As they proceeded, a dim blue light moved swiftly before them and displayed at the extremity of the churchyard the portals of a vault. It was open, and they entered it in silence. The hollow wind came rushing through the gloomy abode of the dead; and on every side were piled the mouldering remnants of coffins, which dropped piece by piece upon the damp marl. Every step they took was on a dead body; and the bleached bones rattled horribly beneath their feet. In the centre of the vault rose a heap of unburied skeletons whereon was seated a figure too awful even for the darkest imagination to conceive. As they approached it, the hollow vault rang with a hellish peal of laughter; and every mouldering corpse seemed endued with unholy life. The stranger paused, and as he seized his victim in his grasp, one sigh burst from his heart – one tear glistened in his eye. It was but for an instant; the figure frowned awfully at his vacillation and waved his gaunt hand.

The stranger advanced; he made certain mystic circles in the air, uttered unearthly words, and paused in excess of terror. On a sudden he raised his voice and wildly exclaimed – 'Spouse of the spirit of darkness, a few moments are yet thine; that thou may'st know to whom thou hast consigned thyself. I am the undying spirit of the wretch who curst his Saviour on the cross. He looked at me in the closing hour of his existence, and that look hath not yet passed away, for I am curst above all on earth. I am eternally condemned to hell and I must cater for my master's taste till the world is parched as is a scroll, and the heavens and the earth have passed away. I am he of whom thou may'st have read, and of whose feats thou may'st have heard. A million souls has my master condemned me to ensnare, and then my penance is accomplished, and I may know the repose of the grave. Thou art the thousandth soul that I have damned. I saw thee in thine hour of purity, and I marked thee at once for my home. Thy father did I murder for his temerity. I permitted him to warn thee of thy fate; and myself have I beguiled for thy simplicity. Ha! the spell works bravely, and thou shall soon see, my sweet one, to whom thou hast linked thine undying fortunes, for as long as the seasons shall move on their course of nature – as long as the lightning shall flash, and the thunders roll, thy penance shall be eternal. Look below and see to what thou art destined.' She looked and saw the vault split in a thousand different directions; the earth yawned asunder; and the roar of mighty waters was heard. A living ocean of molten fire glowed in the abyss beneath her, and, blending with the shrieks of the damned, the triumphant shouts of the fiends rendered horror more horrible than imagination. Ten millions of souls were writhing in the fiery flames, and as the boiling billows dashed them against the blackened rocks of adamant, they cursed with the blasphemies of despair; and each curse echoed in thunder cross the wave. The stranger rushed towards his victim. For an instant as he held her over the burning vista he looked fondly in her face and wept as he were a child. This was but the impulse of a moment; an instant longer he grasped her in his arms, then dashed her from him with fury; and as her last parting glance was cast in kindness on his face, he shouted aloud, 'Not mine is the crime, but the religion that thou professest; for is it not said that there is a fire of eternity prepared for the souls of the wicked; and hast not thou incurred its torments?' She, poor girl, heard not, heeded not the shouts of the blasphemer. Her delicate form bounded from rock to rock, over billow, and over foam; as she fell, the ocean lashed itself as it were in triumph to receive her soul, and as she sank deep in the burning pit, ten thousand voices reverberated from the bottomless abyss, 'Spirit of evil! here indeed is an eternity of torments prepared for thee; for here the worm never dies, and the fire is never quenched.'

The Tapestried Chamber

SIR WALTER SCOTT

ABOUT THE END of the American War, when the officers of Lord Cornwallis's army, which surrendered at Yorktown, and others, who had been made prisoners during the impolitic and ill-fated controversy, were returning to their own country to relate their adventures and repose themselves after their fatigues, there was amongst them a general officer of the name of Browne – an officer of merit, as well as a gentleman of high consideration for family and attainments.

Some business had carried General Browne upon a tour through the western counties, when, at the conclusion of a morning stage, he found himself in the vicinity of a small country town which presented a scene of uncommon beauty and of a character peculiarly English.

The little town, with its stately old church, whose tower bore testimony to the devotion of ages long past, lay amidst pastures and cornfields of small extent but bounded and divided with hedgerow timber of great age and size. There were few marks of modern improvement. The environs of the place intimated neither the solitude of decay nor the bustle of novelty; the houses were old, but in good repair; and the beautiful little river murmured freely on its way to the left of the town, neither restrained by a dam nor bordered by a towing-path.

Upon a gentle eminence, nearly a mile to the southward of the town, were seen, amongst many venerable oaks and tangled thickets, the turrets of a castle as old as the wars of York and Lancaster, but which seemed to have received important alterations during the age of Elizabeth and her successor. It had not been a place of great size; but whatever accommodation it formerly afforded was, it must be supposed, still to be obtained within its walls; at least, such was the inference which General Browne drew from observing the smoke arise merrily from several of the ancient wreathed and carved chimney-stalks. The wall of the park ran alongside the highway for two or three hundred yards; and through the different points by which the eye found glimpses into the woodland scenery it was seen to be well stocked. Other points of view opened in succession – now a full one of the front of the old castle, and now a side glimpse at its particular towers, the former rich in all the bizarrerie of the Elizabethan school, while the simple and solid strength of other parts of the building seemed to show that they had been raised more for defence than ostentation.

Delighted with the partial glimpses which he obtained of the castle through the woods and glades by which this ancient feudal fortress was surrounded, our military traveller was determined to enquire whether it might not deserve a nearer view and whether it contained family pictures or other objects of curiosity worthy of a stranger's visit. Leaving the vicinity of the park, he rolled through a clean and well-paved street and stopped at the door of a well-frequented inn.

Before ordering horses to proceed on his journey, General Browne made enquiries concerning the proprietor of the château which had so attracted his admiration and was equally surprised and pleased at hearing him to be a nobleman whom we shall call Lord Woodville. How fortunate! Much of Browne's early recollections, both at school and at college, had been connected with young Woodville, who, by a few questions, he now ascertained to be the same with the owner of this fair domain. He had been raised to the peerage by the decease of his father a few months before and, as the General learned from the landlord, the term of mourning being ended, he was now taking possession of his paternal estate, in the jovial season of merry autumn, accompanied by a select party of friends, to enjoy the sports of a country famous for game.

This was delightful news to our traveller. Frank Woodville had been Browne's fag at Eton,[1] and his chosen intimate at Christ Church;[2] their pleasures and their tasks had been the same; and the honest soldier's heart warmed to find his early friend in possession of so delightful a residence, and of an estate, as the landlord assured him with a nod and a wink, fully adequate to maintain and add to his dignity. Nothing was more natural than that the traveller should suspend a journey which there was nothing to render hurried to pay a visit to an old friend under such agreeable circumstances.

The fresh horses, therefore, had only the brief task of conveying the general's travelling-carriage to Woodville Castle. A porter admitted them at a modern Gothic lodge, built in that style to correspond with the castle itself, and at the same time rang a bell to give warning of the approach of visitors. Apparently the sound of the bell had suspended the separation of the company, bent on the

various amusements of the morning, for, on entering the court of
the château, General Browne found several young men lounging
about in their sporting-dresses, looking at and criticising the dogs
which the keepers held in readiness to attend their pastime. As he
alighted, the young lord came to the gate of the hall, and for an
instant gazed as at a stranger upon the countenance of his friend, on
which war, with its fatigues and its wounds, had made a great
alteration. But the uncertainty lasted no longer than till the visitor
had spoken, and the hearty greeting which followed was such as can
only be exchanged betwixt those who have passed together the
merry days of careless boyhood or early youth.

'If I could have formed a wish, my dear Browne,' said Lord
Woodville, 'it would have been to have you here, of all men, upon
this occasion, which my friends are good enough to hold as a sort of
holiday. Do not think you have been unwatched during the years you
have been absent from us. I have traced you through your dangers,
your triumphs, your misfortunes, and was delighted to see that,
whether in victory or defeat, the name of my old friend was always
distinguished with applause.'

The general made a suitable reply, and congratulated his friend on
his new dignities, and the possession of a place and domain so
beautiful.

'Nay, you have seen nothing of it as yet,' said Lord Woodville,
'and I trust you do not mean to leave us till you are better acquainted
with it. It is true, I confess, that my present party is pretty large, and
the old house, like other places of the kind, does not possess so much
accommodation as the extent of the outward walls appears to
promise. But we can give you a comfortable old-fashioned room,
and I venture to suppose that your campaigns have taught you to be
glad of worse quarters.'

The general shrugged his shoulders and laughed. 'I presume,' he
said, 'the worst apartment in your château is considerably superior to
the old tobacco-cask in which I was fain to take up my night's
lodging when I was in the bush, as the Virginians call it, with the
light corps. There I lay, like Diogenes himself, so delighted with my
covering from the elements that I made a vain attempt to have it
rolled into my next quarters; but my commander at the time would
give way to no such luxurious provision, and I took farewell of my
beloved cask with tears in my eyes.'

'Well, then, since you do not fear your quarters,' said Lord
Woodville, 'you will stay with me a week at least. Of guns, dogs,
fishing-rods, flies, and means of sport by sea and land, we have

enough and to spare; you cannot pitch on an amusement, but we will find the means of pursuing it. But if you prefer the gun and pointers, I will go with you myself, and see whether you have mended your shooting since you have been amongst the Indians of the back settlements.'

The general gladly accepted his friendly host's proposal in all its points. After a morning of manly exercise, the company met at dinner, where it was the delight of Lord Woodville to conduce to the display of the high properties of his recovered friend, so as to recommend him to his guests, most of whom were persons of distinction. He led General Browne to speak of the scenes he had witnessed; and as every word marked alike the brave officer and the sensible man, who retained possession of his cool judgement under the most imminent dangers, the company looked upon the soldier with general respect, as on one who had proved himself possessed of an uncommon portion of personal courage – that attribute, of all others, of which everybody desires to be thought possessed.

The day at Woodville Castle ended as usual in such mansions. The hospitality stopped within the limits of good order; music, in which the young lord was a proficient, succeeded the circulation of the bottle; cards and billiards, for those who preferred such amusements, were in readiness; but the exercise of the morning required early hours, and not long after eleven o'clock the guests began to retire to their several apartments.

The young lord himself conducted his friend, General Browne, to the chamber destined for him, which answered the description he had given of it, being comfortable, but old-fashioned. The bed was of the massive form used in the end of the seventeenth century, and its curtains were of faded silk, heavily trimmed with tarnished gold. But the sheets, pillows and blankets looked delightful to the campaigner, especially when he thought of his 'mansion, the cask'. There was an air of gloom in the tapestry hangings which, with their worn-out graces, curtained the walls of the little chamber and gently undulated as the autumnal breeze found its way through the ancient lattice-window, which pattered and whistled as the air gained entrance. The toilet-table, too, with its mirror, turbaned, after the manner of the beginning of the century, with a coiffure of murrey-coloured silk, and its hundred strange-shaped boxes, providing for arrangements which had been obsolete for more than fifty years, had an antique and consequently a melancholy aspect. But nothing could blaze more brightly and cheerfully than the two large wax candles; or if aught could rival them, it was the flaming, bickering faggots in the chimney, that sent at once their gleam and their warmth through the snug apartment, which, notwithstanding the general antiquity of its appearance, was not wanting in the least convenience that modern habits rendered either necessary or desirable.

'This is an old-fashioned sleeping-apartment, general,' said the young lord, 'but I hope you find nothing that makes you envy your old tobacco-cask.'

'I am not particular respecting my lodgings,' replied the general; 'yet were I to make any choice, I would prefer this chamber by many degrees to the gayer and more modern rooms of your family mansion. Believe me, when I unite its modern air of comfort with its venerable antiquity, and recollect that it is your lordship's property, I shall feel in better quarters here than if I were in the best hotel London could afford.'

'I trust – I have no doubt – that you will find yourself as comfortable as I wish you, my dear general,' said the young nobleman; and once more bidding his guest good-night, he shook him by the hand and withdrew.

The general once more looked round him, and internally congratulating himself on his return to peaceful life, the comforts of which were endeared by the recollection of the hardships and dangers he had lately sustained, undressed himself and prepared for a luxurious night's rest.

Here, contrary to the custom of this species of tale, we leave the general in possession of his apartment until the next morning.

The company assembled for breakfast at an early hour, but without the appearance of General Browne, who seemed the guest that Lord Woodville was desirous of honouring above all whom his hospitality had assembled around him. He more than once expressed surprise at the general's absence, and at length sent a servant to make enquiry after him. The man brought back information that General Browne had been walking abroad since an early hour of the morning, in defiance of the weather, which was misty and ungenial.

'The custom of a solder,' said the young nobleman to his friends; 'many of them acquire habitual vigilance, and cannot sleep after the early hour at which their duty usually commands them to be alert.'

Yet the explanation which Lord Woodville thus offered to the company seemed hardly satisfactory to his own mind, and it was in a fit of silence and abstraction that he awaited the return of the general. It took place near an hour after the breakfast bell had rung. He looked fatigued and feverish. His hair, the powdering and arrangement of which was at this time one of the most important occupations of a man's whole day, and marked his fashion as much as, at the present time, the tying of a cravat, or the want of one, was dishevelled, uncurled, void of powder and dank with dew. His clothes were huddled on with a careless negligence remarkable in a military man, whose real or supposed duties are usually held to include some attention to the toilet; and his looks were haggard and ghastly in a peculiar degree.

'So you have stolen a march upon us this morning, my dear general,' said Lord Woodville; 'or you have not found your bed so much to your mind as I had hoped and you seemed to expect. How did you rest last night?'

'Oh, excellently well – remarkably well – never better in my life!' said General Browne rapidly, and yet with an air of embarrassment which was obvious to his friend. He then hastily swallowed a cup of tea and, neglecting or refusing whatever else he was offered, seemed to fall into a fit of abstraction.

'You will take the gun today, general?' said his friend and host, but had to repeat the question twice ere he received the abrupt answer, 'No, my Lord; I am sorry I cannot have the honour of spending another day with your lordship; my post-horses are ordered and will be here directly.'

All who were present showed surprise, and Lord Woodville immediately replied, 'Post-horses, my good friend! What can you possibly want with them, when you promised to stay with me quietly for at least a week?'

'I believe,' said the general, obviously much embarrassed, 'that I might, in the pleasure of my first meeting with your lordship, have said something about stopping here a few days; but I have since found it altogether impossible.'

'That is very extraordinary,' answered the young nobleman. 'You seemed quite disengaged yesterday, and you cannot have had a summons today, for our post has not come up from town, and therefore you cannot have received any letters.'

General Browne, without giving any further explanation, muttered something of indispensable business, and insisted on the absolute necessity of his departure in a manner which silenced all opposition on the part of his host, who saw that his resolution was taken, and forbore all further importunity.

'At least, however,' he said, 'permit me, my dear Browne, since go you will or must, to show you the view from the terrace, which the mist, that is now rising, will soon display.'

He threw open a sash-window and stepped down upon the terrace as he spoke. The general followed him mechanically, but seemed little to attend to what his host was saying as, looking across an extended and rich prospect, he pointed out the different objects worthy of observation. Thus they moved on till Lord Woodville had attained his purpose of drawing his guest entirely apart from the rest of the company; then, turning round upon him with an air of great solemnity, he addressed him thus: 'Richard Browne, my old and very dear friend, we are now alone. Let me conjure you to answer me upon the word of a friend and the honour of a soldier. How did you in reality rest during the night?'

'Most wretchedly indeed, my lord,' answered the general, in the same tone of solemnity; 'so miserably, that I would not run the risk of such a second night, not only for all the lands belonging to this castle but for all the country which I see from this elevated point of view.'

'This is most extraordinary,' said the young lord, as if speaking to himself; 'then there must be something in the reports concerning that apartment.' Again turning to the general, he said, 'For God's sake, my dear friend, be candid with me and let me know the disagreeable particulars which have befallen you under a roof where, with consent of the owner, you should have met with nothing save comfort.'

The general seemed distressed by this appeal and paused a moment before he replied. 'My dear lord,' he at length said, 'what happened to me last night is of a nature so peculiar and so unpleasant that I could hardly bring myself to detail it, even to your lordship, were it not that, independent of my wish to gratify any request of yours, I think that sincerity on my part may lead to some explanation about a circumstance equally painful and mysterious. To others, the communication I am about to make might place me in the light of a weak-minded, superstitious fool, who suffered his own imagination to delude and bewilder him; but you have known me in childhood and youth and will not suspect me of having adopted in manhood the feelings and frailties from which my early years were free.'

Here he paused, and his friend replied: 'Do not doubt my perfect confidence in the truth of your communication, however strange it may be. I know your firmness of disposition too well to suspect you could be made the object of imposition, and am aware that your honour and your friendship will equally deter you from exaggerating whatever you may have witnessed.'

'Well, then,' said the general, 'I will proceed with my story as well as I can, relying upon your candour, and yet distinctly feeling that I would rather face a battery than recall to my mind the odious events of last night.'

He paused a second time, and then, perceiving that Lord Woodville remained silent and in an attitude of attention, he commenced, though not without obvious reluctance, the history of his nocturnal adventures in the Tapestried Chamber.

'I undressed and went to bed so soon as your lordship left me yesterday evening; but the wood in the chimney, which nearly fronted my bed, blazed brightly and cheerfully and, aided by a hundred recollections of my childhood and youth, which had been recalled by the unexpected pleasure of meeting your lordship, prevented me from falling immediately asleep. I ought, however, to say that these reflections were all of a pleasant and agreeable kind, grounded on a sense of having for a time exchanged the labour, fatigues and dangers of my profession for the enjoyments of a peaceful life and the reunion of those friendly and affectionate ties which I had torn asunder at the rude summons of war.

'While such pleasing reflections were stealing over my mind, and gradually lulling me to slumber, I was suddenly aroused by a sound like that of the rustling of a silken gown and the tapping of a pair of high-heeled shoes, as if a woman were walking in the apartment. Ere I could draw the curtain to see what the matter was, the figure of a little woman passed between the bed and the fire. The back of this form was turned to me, and I could observe, from the shoulders and neck, it was that of an old woman, whose dress was an old-fashioned gown, which, I think, ladies call a sacque – that is, a sort of robe, completely loose in the body, but gathered upon the neck and shoulders into broad plaits, which fall down to the ground and terminate in a species of train.

'I thought the intrusion singular enough, but never harboured for a moment the idea that what I saw was anything more than the mortal form of some old woman about the establishment, who had a fancy to dress like her grandmother, and who, having perhaps, as your lordship mentioned that you were rather straitened for room, been dislodged from her chamber for my accommodation, had forgotten the circumstances and returned by twelve to her old haunt. Under this persuasion I moved myself in bed and coughed a little, to make the intruder sensible of my being in possession of the premises. She turned slowly round, but, gracious heaven! my lord, what a countenance did she display to me! There was no longer any question what she was, or any thought of her being a living being. Upon a face which wore the fixed features of a corpse were imprinted the traces of the vilest and most hideous passions which had animated her while she lived. The body of some atrocious criminal seemed to have been given up from the grave, and the soul restored from the penal fire, in order to form, for a space, a union with the ancient accomplice of its guilt. I started up in bed, and sat upright, supporting myself on my palms, as I gazed on this horrible spectre. The hag made, as it seemed, a single and swift stride to the bed where I lay, and squatted herself down upon it, in precisely the same attitude which I had assumed in the extremity of horror, advancing her diabolical countenance within half a yard of mine, with a grin which seemed to intimate the malice and the derision of an incarnate fiend.'

Here General Browne stopped, and wiped from his brow the cold perspiration with which the recollection of his horrible vision had covered it.

'My lord,' he said, 'I am no coward. I have been in all the mortal dangers incidental to my profession, and I may truly boast that no man ever knew Richard Browne dishonour the sword he wears; but in these horrible circumstances, under the eyes, and, as it seemed, almost in the grasp, of an incarnation of an evil spirit, all firmness forsook me, all manhood melted from me like wax in the furnace, and I felt my hair individually bristle. The current of my lifeblood ceased to flow, and I sank back in a swoon, as very a victim to panic terror as ever was a village girl or a child of ten years old. How long I lay in this condition I cannot pretend to guess.

'But I was roused by the castle clock striking one, so loud that it seemed as if it were in the very room. It was some time before I dared open my eyes, lest they should again encounter the horrible spectacle. When, however, I summoned courage to look up, she was no longer visible. My first idea was to pull my bell, wake the servants, and remove to a garret or a hayloft, to be ensured against a second visitation. Nay, I will confess the truth, that my resolution was altered, not by the shame of exposing myself, but by the fear that, as the bell-cord hung by the chimney, I might, in making my way to it, be again crossed by the fiendish hag, who, I figured to myself, might be still lurking about some corner of the apartment.

'I will not pretend to describe what hot and cold fever-fits tormented me for the rest of the night, through broken sleep, weary vigils, and that dubious state which forms the neutral ground between them. A hundred terrible objects appeared to haunt me; but there was the great difference betwixt the vision which I have described and those which followed – that I knew the last to be deceptions of my own fancy and over-excited nerves.

'Day at last appeared, and I rose from my bed ill in health and humiliated in mind. I was ashamed of myself as a man and a soldier, and still more so at feeling my own extreme desire to escape from the haunted apartment, a desire which conquered all other considerations; so that, huddling on my clothes with the most careless haste, I made my escape from your lordship's mansion, to seek in the open air some relief to my nervous system, shaken as it was by this horrible encounter with a visitant, for such I must believe her, from the other world. Your lordship has now heard the cause of my discomposure, and of my sudden desire to leave your hospitable castle. In other places I trust we may often meet; but God protect me from ever spending a second night under that roof!'

Strange as the general's tale was, he spoke with such a deep air of conviction that it cut short all the usual commentaries which are made on such stories. Lord Woodville never once asked him if he was sure he did not dream the apparition, never once suggested any of the possibilities by which it is fashionable to explain away supernatural appearances as wild vagaries of the fancy or deceptions of the optic nerves. On the contrary, he seemed deeply impressed with the truth and reality of what he had heard; and, after a considerable pause, regretted, with much appearance of sincerity, that his early friend should in his house have suffered so severely.

'I am the more sorry for your pain, my dear Browne,' he continued, 'that it is the unhappy, though most unexpected, result of an experiment of my own. You must know that, for my father and grandfather's time, at least, the apartment which was assigned to you last night had been shut on account of reports that it was disturbed by supernatural sights and noises. When I came, a few weeks since, into possession of the estate, I thought the accommodation which the castle afforded for my friends was not extensive enough to permit the inhabitants of the invisible world to retain possession of a comfortable sleeping-apartment. I therefore caused the Tapestried Chamber, as we call it, to be opened and, without destroying its air of antiquity, I had such new articles of furniture placed in it as became the modern times. Yet, as the opinion that the room was haunted very strongly prevailed among the domestics and was also known in the neighbourhood and to many of my friends, I feared some prejudice might be entertained by the first occupant of the Tapestried Chamber, which might tend to revive the evil report which it had laboured under and so disappoint my purpose of rendering it a useful part of the house. I must confess, my dear Browne, that your arrival yesterday, agreeable to me for a thousand reasons besides, seemed the most favourable opportunity of removing the unpleasant rumours which attached to the room, since your courage was indubitable and your mind free of any preoccupation on the subject. I could not, therefore, have chosen a more fitting subject for my experiment.'

'Upon my life,' said General Browne, somewhat hastily, 'I am infinitely obliged to your lordship – very particularly indebted indeed. I am likely to remember for some time the consequences of the experiment, as your lordship is pleased to call it.'

'Nay, now you are unjust, my dear friend,' said Lord Woodville. 'You have only to reflect for a single moment in order to be convinced that I could not augur the possibility of the pain to which you have been so unhappily exposed. I was yesterday morning a complete sceptic on the subject of supernatural appearances. Nay, I am sure that, had I told you what was said about that room, those very reports would have induced you, by your own choice, to select it for your accommodation. It was my misfortune, perhaps my error, but really cannot be termed my fault, that you have been afflicted so strangely.'

'Strangely indeed!' said the general, resuming his good temper; 'and I acknowledge that I have no right to be offended with your lordship for treating me like what I used to think myself, a man of some firmness and courage. But I see my post-horses are arrived, and I must not detain your lordship from your amusement.'

'Nay, my old friend,' said Lord Woodville, 'since you cannot stay with us another day – which, indeed, I can no longer urge – give me at least half an hour more. You used to love pictures, and I have a gallery of portraits, some of them by Vandyke, representing ancestry to whom this property and castle formerly belonged. I think that several of them will strike you as possessing merit.'

General Browne accepted the invitation, though somewhat unwillingly. It was evident he was not to breathe freely or at ease till he left Woodville Castle far behind him. He could not refuse his friend's invitation, however; and the less so, that he was a little ashamed of the peevishness which he had displayed towards his well-meaning entertainer.

The general, therefore, followed Lord Woodville through several rooms into a long gallery hung with pictures, which the latter pointed out to his guest, telling the names and giving some account of the personages whose portraits presented themselves in progression. General Browne was but little interested in the details which these accounts conveyed to him. They were, indeed, of the kind which are usually found in an old family gallery. Here was a Cavalier who had ruined the estate in the royal cause; there was a fine lady who had reinstated it by contracting a match with a wealthy Roundhead. There hung a gallant who had been in danger for corresponding with the exiled court at St Germain's; here one who had taken arms for William at the Revolution; and there a third who had thrown his weight alternately into the scale of Whig and Tory.

While Lord Woodville was cramming these words into his guest's ear, 'against the stomach of his sense', they gained the middle of the gallery, whereupon he beheld General Browne suddenly start, and assume an attitude of the utmost surprise, not unmixed with fear, as his eyes were caught and suddenly riveted by a portrait of an old lady in a sacque, the fashionable dress of the end of the seventeenth century.

'There she is!' he exclaimed – 'there she is, in form and features, though inferior in demoniac expression to the accursed hag who visited me last night.'

'If that be the case,' said the young nobleman, 'there can remain no longer any doubt of the horrible reality of your apparition. That is the picture of a wretched ancestress of mine, of whose crimes a black and fearful catalogue is recorded in a family history in my charter-chest. The recital of them would be too horrible; it is enough to say that in yon fatal apartment incest and unnatural murder were committed. I will restore it to the solitude to which the better judgement of those who preceded me had consigned it; and never shall anyone, so long as I can prevent it, be exposed to a repetition of the supernatural horrors which could shake such courage as yours.'

Thus, the friends who had met with such glee parted in a very different mood – Lord Woodville to command the Tapestried Chamber to be unmantled and the door built up; and General Browne to seek in some less beautiful county, and with some less dignified friend, forgetfulness of the painful night which he had passed in Woodville Castle.

Berenice

EDGAR ALLAN POE

Dicebant mihi sodales si sepulchrum amicae visitarem curas meas aliquantulum fore levatas.
                                                            EBN ZAIAT

MISERY IS MANIFOLD. The wretchedness of earth is multiform. Overreaching the wide horizon as the rainbow, its hues are as various as the hues of that arch – as distinct too, yet as intimately blended. Overreaching the wide horizon as the rainbow. How is it that from beauty I have derived a type of unloveliness? – from the covenant of peace a simile of sorrow? But as, in ethics, evil is a consequence of good, so, in fact, out of joy is sorrow born. Either the memory of past bliss is the anguish of today, or the agonies which *are* have their origin in the ecstasies which *might have been*.

My baptismal name is Egaeus; that of my family I will not mention. Yet there are no towers in the land more time-honoured than my gloomy, grey, hereditary halls. Our line has been called a race of visionaries; and in many striking particulars – in the character of the family mansion – in the frescoes of the chief saloon – in the tapestries of the dormitories – in the chiselling of some buttresses in the armoury – but more especially in the gallery of antique paintings – in the fashion of the library chamber – and, lastly, in the very peculiar nature of the library's contents, there is more than sufficient evidence to warrant the belief.

The recollections of my earliest years are connected with that chamber, and with its volumes – of which latter I will say no more. Here died my mother. Herein was I born. But it is mere idleness to say that I had not lived before – that the soul has no previous existence. You deny it? – let us not argue the matter. Convinced myself, I seek not to convince. There is, however, a remembrance of aerial forms – of spiritual and meaning eyes – of sounds, musical yet sad – a remembrance which will not be excluded; a memory like a shadow, vague, variable, indefinite, unsteady; and like a shadow, too, in the impossibility of my getting rid of it while the sunlight of my reason shall exist.

In that chamber was I born. Thus awaking from the long night of what seemed, but was not, nonentity, at once into the very regions of fairyland – into a palace of imagination – into the wild dominions of monastic thought and erudition – it is not singular that I gazed around me with a startled and ardent eye – that I loitered away my boyhood in books and dissipated my youth in reverie; but it *is* singular that as years rolled away, and the noon of manhood found me still in the mansion of my fathers – it is wonderful what stagnation there fell upon the springs of my life – wonderful how total an inversion took place in the character of my commonest thought. The realities of the world affected me as visions, and as visions only, while the wild ideas of the land of dreams became, in turn – not the material of my everyday existence – but in very deed that existence utterly and solely in itself.

*　　*　　*

Berenice and I were cousins, and we grew up together in my paternal halls. Yet differently we grew – I ill of health and buried in gloom – she agile, graceful and overflowing with energy; hers the ramble on the hillside – mine the studies of the cloister – I living within my own heart, and addicted body and soul to the most intense and painful meditation – she roaming carelessly through life with no thought of the shadows in her path, or the silent flight of the raven-winged hours. Berenice! – I call upon her name – Berenice! – and from the grey ruins of memory a thousand tumultuous recollections are startled at the sound! Ah! vividly is her image before me now, as in the early days of her light-heartedness and joy! Oh! gorgeous yet fantastic beauty! Oh! sylph amid the shrubberies of Arnheim! Oh! Naiad among its fountains! – and then – then all is mystery and terror, and a tale which should not be told. Disease – a fatal disease – fell like the simoom upon her frame, and, even while I gazed upon her, the spirit of change swept over her, pervading her mind, her habits and her character, and, in a manner the most subtle and terrible, disturbing even the identity of her person! Alas! the destroyer came and went, and the victim – where was she? I knew her not – or knew her no longer as Berenice.

Among the numerous train of maladies superinduced by that fatal and primary one which effected a revolution of so horrible a kind in the moral and physical being of my cousin, may be mentioned, as the most distressing and obstinate in its nature, a species of epilepsy not unfrequently terminating in *trance* itself – trance very nearly resembling positive dissolution – from which her manner of recovery was, in most instances, startlingly abrupt. In the meantime my own disease – for I have been told that I should call it by no other appellation – my own disease, then, grew rapidly upon me, and assumed finally a monomaniac character of a novel and extraordinary form – hourly and momently gaining vigour – and at length obtaining over me the most incomprehensible ascendancy. This monomania, if I must so term it, consisted in a morbid irritability of those properties of the mind in metaphysical science termed the *attentive*. It is more than probable that I am not understood; but I fear, indeed, that it is in no manner possible to convey to the mind of the merely general reader an adequate idea of that nervous *intensity of interest* with which, in my case, the powers of meditation (not to speak technically) busied and buried themselves in the contemplation of even the most ordinary objects of the universe.

To muse for long unwearied hours with my attention riveted to some frivolous device in the margin or in the typography of a book; to become absorbed for the better part of a summer's day in a quaint shadow falling aslant upon the tapestry or upon the door; to lose myself for an entire night in watching the steady flame of a lamp or the embers of a fire; to dream away whole days over the perfume of a flower; to repeat monotonously some common word, until the sound, by dint of frequent repetition, ceased to convey any idea whatever to the mind; to lose all sense of motion or physical existence by means of absolute bodily quiescence, long and obstinately persevered in; – such were a few of the most common and least pernicious vagaries induced by a condition of the mental faculties not, indeed, altogether unparalleled, but certainly bidding defiance to anything like analysis or explanation.

Yet let me not be misapprehended. – The undue, earnest and morbid attention thus excited by objects in their own nature frivolous must not be confounded in character with that ruminating propensity common to all mankind, and more especially indulged in by persons of ardent imagination. It was not even, as might at first be supposed, an extreme condition, or exaggeration, of such propensity, but primarily and essentially distinct and different. In the one instance, the dreamer or enthusiast, being interested by an object usually *not* frivolous, imperceptibly loses sight of this object in a wilderness of deductions and suggestions issuing therefrom, until, at the conclusion of a daydream *often replete with luxury*, he finds the *incitamentum* or first cause of his musings entirely vanished and forgotten. In my case the primary object was *invariably frivolous*, although assuming, through the medium of my distempered vision, a refracted and unreal importance. Few deductions, if any, were made; and those few pertinaciously returned in upon the original object as a centre. The meditations were *never* pleasurable; and, at the termination of the reverie, the first cause, so far from being out of sight, had attained that supernaturally exaggerated interest which was the prevailing feature of the disease. In a word, the powers of mind more particularly exercised were, with me, as I have said before, the *attentive*, and are, with the daydreamer, the *speculative*.

My books, at this epoch, if they did not actually serve to irritate the disorder, partook, it will be perceived, largely, in their imaginative and inconsequential nature, of the characteristic qualities of the disorder itself. I well remember, among others, the treatise of the noble Italian Coelius Secundus Curio, *De Amplitudine Beati Regni Dei*; St Austin's great work, *The City of God*; and Tertullian, *De Carne Christi*, in which the paradoxical sentence, *Mortuus est Dei filius; credibile est quia ineptum est: et sepultus resurrexit; certum est quia impossibile est*,[1] occupied my undivided time for many weeks of laborious and fruitless investigation.

Thus it will appear that, shaken from its balance only by trivial things, my reason bore resemblance to that ocean-crag spoken of by Ptolemy Hephestion, which, steadily resisting the attacks of human violence and the fiercer fury of the waters and the winds, trembled only to the touch of the flower called Asphodel. And although, to a careless thinker, it might appear a matter beyond doubt that the alteration produced by her unhappy malady in the *moral* condition of Berenice would afford me many objects for the exercise of that intense and abnormal meditation whose nature I have been at some trouble in explaining, yet such was not in any degree the case. In the lucid intervals of my infirmity, her calamity, indeed, gave me pain, and, taking deeply to heart that total wreck of her fair and gentle life, I did not fail to ponder frequently and bitterly upon the wonder-working means by which so strange a revolution had been so suddenly brought to pass. But these reflections partook not of the idiosyncrasy of my disease, and were such as would have occurred, under similar circumstances, to the ordinary mass of mankind. True to its own character, my disorder revelled in the less important but more startling changes wrought in the *physical* frame of Berenice – in the singular and most appalling distortion of her personal identity.

During the brightest days of her unparalleled beauty, most surely I had never loved her. In the strange anomaly of my existence, feelings

with me *had never been* of the heart, and my passions *always* were of
the mind. Through the grey of the early morning – among the
trellised shadows of the forest at noonday – and in the silence of my
library at night, she had flitted by my eyes, and I had seen her – not as
the living and breathing Berenice, but as the Berenice of a dream –
not as a being of the earth, earthy, but as the abstraction of such a
being – not as a thing to admire, but to analyse – not as an object of
love, but as the theme of the most abstruse although desultory
speculation. And *now* – now I shuddered in her presence, and grew
pale at her approach; yet bitterly lamenting her fallen and desolate
condition, I called to mind that she had loved me long, and, in an evil
moment, I spoke to her of marriage.

The period of our nuptials was at length approaching, when, upon
an afternoon in the winter of the year – one of those unseasonably
warm, calm and misty days which are the nurse of the beautiful
Halcyon* – I sat (and sat, as I thought, alone) in the inner apartment
of the library. But uplifting my eyes I saw that Berenice stood before
me.

Was it my own excited imagination – or the misty influence of
the atmosphere – or the uncertain twilight of the chamber – or the
grey draperies which fell around her figure – that caused in it so
vacillating and indistinct an outline? I could not tell. She spoke no
word, and I – not for worlds could I have uttered a syllable. An icy
chill ran through my frame; a sense of insufferable anxiety oppressed me; a consuming curiosity pervaded my soul; and sinking
back upon the chair, I remained for some time breathless and
motionless, with my eyes riveted upon her person. Alas! its emaciation was excessive, and not one vestige of the former being lurked
in any single line of the contour. My burning glances at length fell
upon the face.

The forehead was high, and very pale, and singularly placid; and
the once jetty hair fell partially over it, and overshadowed the hollow
temples with innumerable ringlets, now of a vivid yellow and jarring
discordantly, in their fantastic character, with the reigning melancholy of the countenance. The eyes were lifeless, and lustreless, and
seemingly pupil-less, and I shrank involuntarily from their glassy
stare to the contemplation of the thin and shrunken lips. They
parted; and in a smile of peculiar meaning, *the teeth* of the changed

* For as Jove, during the winter season, gives twice seven days of warmth, men
  have called this clement and temperate time the nurse of the beautiful
  Halcyon.   SIMONIDES

Berenice disclosed themselves slowly to my view. Would to God that I had never beheld them, or that, having done so, I had died!

*   *   *

The shutting of a door disturbed me, and, looking up, I found that my cousin had departed from the chamber. But from the disordered chamber of my brain, had not, alas! departed, and would not be driven away, the white and ghastly *spectrum* of the teeth. Not a speck on their surface – not a shade on their enamel – not an indenture in their edges – but what that period of her smile had sufficed to brand in upon my memory. I saw them *now* even more unequivocally than I beheld them *then*. The teeth! – the teeth! – they were here, and there, and everywhere, and visibly and palpably before me; long, narrow, and excessively white, with the pale lips writhing about them, as in the very moment of their first terrible development. Then came the full fury of my *monomania*, and I struggled in vain against its strange and irresistible influence. In the multiplied objects of the external world I had no thoughts but for the teeth. For these I longed with a frenzied desire. All other matters and all different interests became absorbed in their single contemplation. They – they alone were present to the mental eye, and they, in their sole individuality, became the essence of my mental life. I held them in every light. I turned them in every attitude. I surveyed their characteristics. I dwelt upon their peculiarities. I pondered upon their conformation. I mused upon the alteration in their nature. I shuddered as I assigned to them in imagination a sensitive and sentient power and, even when unassisted by the lips, a capability of moral expression. Of Mad'selle Sallé[2] it has been well said '*que tous ses pas étaient des sentiments*', and of Berenice I more seriously believed *que toutes ses dents étaient des idées. Des idées!* – ah here was the idiotic thought that destroyed me! *Des idées!* – ah, *therefore* it was that I coveted them so madly! I felt that their possession could alone ever restore me to peace, in giving me back to reason.

And the evening closed in upon me thus – and then the darkness came, and tarried, and went – and the day again dawned – and the mists of a second night were now gathering around – and still I sat motionless in that solitary room; and still I sat buried in meditation, and still the *phantasma* of the teeth maintained its terrible ascendancy as, with the most vivid and hideous distinctness, it floated about amid the changing lights and shadows of the chamber. At length there broke in upon my dreams a cry as of horror and dismay; and thereunto, after a pause, succeeded the sound of troubled voices, intermingled with many low moanings of sorrow, or of pain. I arose from my seat, and throwing open one of the doors of the library, saw standing out in the antechamber a servant maiden, all in tears, who told me that Berenice was – no more. She had been seized with epilepsy in the early morning, and now, at the closing in of the night, the grave was ready for its tenant, and all the preparations for the burial were completed.

* * *

I found myself sitting in the library, and again sitting there alone. It seemed that I had newly awakened from a confused and exciting dream. I knew that it was now midnight, and I was well aware that since the setting of the sun Berenice had been interred. But of that dreary period which intervened I had no positive – at least no definite comprehension. Yet its memory was replete with horror – horror more horrible from being vague, and terror more terrible from ambiguity. It was a fearful page in the record of my existence, written all over with dim, and hideous, and unintelligible recollections. I strived to decipher them, but in vain; while ever and anon, like the spirit of a departed sound, the shrill and piercing shriek of a female voice seemed to be ringing in my ears. I had done a deed – what was it? I asked myself the question aloud, and the whispering echoes of the chamber answered me, 'What was it?'

On the table beside me burned a lamp, and near it lay a little box. It was of no remarkable character, and I had seen it frequently before, for it was the property of the family physician; but how came it *there*, upon my table, and why did I shudder in regarding it? These things were in no manner to be accounted for, and my eyes at length dropped to the open pages of a book and to a sentence underscored therein. The words were the singular but simple ones of the poet Ebn Zaiat, *Dicebant mihi sodales si sepulchrum amicae visitarem curas meas aliquantulum fore levatas.* Why then, as I perused them, did the hairs of my head erect themselves on end, and the blood of my body become congealed within my veins?

There came a light tap at the library door, and pale as the tenant of a tomb, a menial entered upon tiptoe. His looks were wild with terror, and he spoke to me in a voice tremulous, husky and very low. What said he? – some broken sentences I heard. He told of a wild cry disturbing the silence of the night – of the gathering together of the household – of a search in the direction of the sound; and then his tones grew thrillingly distinct as he whispered to me of a violated grave – of a disfigured body enshrouded, yet still breathing, still palpitating, still *alive*!

He pointed to my garments – they were muddy and clotted with gore. I spoke not, and he took me gently by the hand – it was indented with the impress of human nails. He directed my attention to some object against the wall; I looked at it for some minutes; it was a spade. With a shriek I bounded to the table, and grasped the box that lay upon it. But I could not force it open; and in my tremor it slipped from my hands, and fell heavily, and burst into pieces; and from it, with a rattling sound, there rolled out some instruments of dental surgery, intermingled with thirty-two small, white and ivory-looking substances that were scattered to and fro about the floor.

A Madman's Manuscript

CHARLES DICKENS

HE HAD TAKEN A FEW TURNS from the door to the window, and from the window to the door, when the clergyman's manuscript for the first time entered his head. It was a good thought. If it failed to interest him, it might send him to sleep. He took it from his coat-pocket, and drawing a small table towards his bedside, trimmed the light, put on his spectacles, and composed himself to read. It was a strange handwriting, and the paper was much soiled and blotted. The title gave him a sudden start, too; and he could not avoid casting a wistful glance round the room. Reflecting on the absurdity of giving way to such feelings, however, he trimmed the light again, and read as follows:

A Madman's Manuscript

'Yes! – a madman's! How that word would have struck to my heart, many years ago! How it would have roused the terror that used to come upon me sometimes; sending the blood hissing and tingling through my veins, till the cold dew of fear stood in large drops upon my skin and my knees knocked together with fright! I like it now though. It's a fine name. Show me the monarch whose angry frown was ever feared like the glare of a madman's eye – whose cord and axe were ever half so sure as a madman's grip. Ho! ho! It's a grand thing to be mad! to be peeped at like a wild lion through the iron bars – to gnash one's teeth and howl, through the long still night, to the merry ring of a heavy chain – and to roll and twine among the straw, transported with such brave music. Hurrah for the madhouse! Oh, it's a rare place!

'I remember days when I was *afraid* of being mad; when I used to start from my sleep, and fall upon my knees, and pray to be spared from the curse of my race; when I rushed from the sight of merriment or happiness, to hide myself in some lonely place, and spend the weary hours in watching the progress of the fever that was to consume my brain. I knew that madness was mixed up with my very blood, and the marrow of my bones; that one generation had passed away without the pestilence appearing among them and that I was the first in whom it would revive. I knew it *must* be so: that so it always had been, and so it ever would be: and when I cowered in some obscure corner of a crowded room, and saw men whisper, and point, and turn their eyes towards me, I knew they were telling each other of the doomed madman; and I slunk away again to mope in solitude.

'I did this for years; long, long years they were. The nights here are long sometimes – very long; but they are nothing to the restless nights, and dreadful dreams I had at that time. It makes me cold to remember them. Large dusky forms with sly and jeering faces crouched in the corners of the room, and bent over my bed at night, tempting me to madness. They told me in low whispers that the floor of the old house in which my father's father died was stained with his own blood, shed by his own hand in raging madness. I drove my fingers into my ears, but they screamed into my head, till the room rang with it, that in one generation before him the madness slumbered but that his grandfather had lived for years with his hands fettered to the ground, to prevent his tearing himself to pieces. I knew they told the truth – I knew it well. I had found it out years before, though they had tried to keep it from me. Ha! ha! I was too cunning for them, madman as they thought me.

'At last it came upon me, and I wondered how I could ever have feared it. I could go into the world now, and laugh and shout with the best among them. I knew I was mad, but they did not even suspect it. How I used to hug myself with delight when I thought of the fine trick I was playing them, after their old pointing and leering, when I was not mad but only dreading that I might one day become so! And how I used to laugh for joy, when I was alone, to think how well I kept my secret, and how quickly my kind friends would have fallen from me if they had known the truth. I could have screamed with ecstasy when I dined alone with some fine roaring fellow to think how pale he would have turned, and how fast he would have run, if he had known that the dear friend who sat close to him, sharpening a bright glittering knife, was a madman with all the power, and half the will, to plunge it in his heart. Oh, it was a merry life!

'Riches became mine, wealth poured in upon me, and I rioted in pleasures enhanced a thousandfold to me by the consciousness of my well-kept secret. I inherited an estate. The law – the eagle-eyed law itself – had been deceived, and had handed over disputed thousands to a madman's hands. Where was the wit of the sharp-sighted men of sound mind? Where the dexterity of the lawyers, eager to discover a flaw? The madman's cunning had overreached them all.

'I had money. How I was courted! I spent it profusely. How I was praised! How those three proud overbearing brothers humbled themselves before me! The old white-headed father, too – such deference – such respect – such devoted friendship – he worshipped me! The old man had a daughter, and the young men a sister; and all the five were poor. I was rich; and when I married the girl, I saw a smile of triumph play upon the faces of her needy relatives, as they thought of their well-planned scheme and their fine prize. It was for me to smile. To smile! To laugh outright, and tear my hair, and roll upon the ground with shrieks of merriment. They little thought they had married her to a madman.

'Stay. If they had known it, would they have saved her? A sister's happiness against her husband's gold. The lightest feather I blow into the air, against the gay chain that ornaments my body!

'In one thing I was deceived with all my cunning. If I had not been mad – for though we madmen are sharp-witted enough, we get bewildered sometimes – I should have known that the girl would rather have been placed, stiff and cold, in a dull leaden coffin, than borne an envied bride to my rich, glittering house. I should have known that her heart was with the dark-eyed boy whose name I once heard her breathe in her troubled sleep; and that she had been sacrificed to me to relieve the poverty of the old white-headed man and the haughty brothers.

'I don't remember forms or faces, now, but I know the girl was beautiful. I *know* she was; for in the bright moonlight nights, when I start up from my sleep, and all is quiet about me, I see, standing still and motionless in one corner of this cell, a slight and wasted figure with long black hair which, streaming down her back, stirs with no earthly wind, and eyes that fix their gaze on me, and never wink or close. Hush! the blood chills at my heart as I write it down – that form is *hers*; the face is very pale, and the eyes are glassy bright; but I know them well. That figure never moves; it never frowns and mouths as others do that fill this place sometimes; but it is much more dreadful to me, even than the spirits that tempted me many years ago – it comes fresh from the grave; and is so very deathlike.

'For nearly a year I saw that face grow paler; for nearly a year I saw the tears steal down the mournful cheeks, and never knew the cause. I found it out at last though. They could not keep it from me long. She had never liked me; I had never thought she did: she despised my wealth, and hated the splendour in which she lived; – I had not expected that. She loved another. This I had never thought of. Strange feelings came over me, and thoughts, forced upon me by some secret power, whirled round and round my brain. I did not hate her, though I hated the boy she still wept for. I pitied – yes, I pitied – the wretched life to which her cold and selfish relations had doomed her. I knew that she could not live long, but the thought that before her death she might give birth to some ill-fated being, destined to hand down madness to its offspring, determined me. I resolved to kill her.

'For many weeks I thought of poison, and then of drowning, and then of fire. A fine sight the grand house in flames, and the mad-man's wife smouldering away to cinders. Think of the jest of a large reward, too, and of some sane man swinging in the wind for a deed he never did, and all through a madman's cunning! I thought often of this, but I gave it up at last. Oh! the pleasure of stropping the razor day after day, feeling the sharp edge, and thinking of the gash one stroke of its thin bright edge would make!

'At last the old spirits who had been with me so often before whispered in my ear that the time was come, and thrust the open razor into my hand. I grasped it firmly, rose softly from the bed, and leaned over my sleeping wife. Her face was buried in her hands. I withdrew them softly, and they fell listlessly on her bosom. She had been weeping, for the traces of the tears were still wet upon her cheek. Her face was calm and placid; and even as I looked upon it, a tranquil smile lighted up her pale features. I laid my hand softly on her shoulder. She started – it was only a passing dream. I leant forward again. She screamed, and woke.

'One motion of my hand, and she would never again have uttered cry or sound. But I was startled, and drew back. Her eyes were fixed on mine. I know not how it was, but they cowed and frightened me; and I quailed beneath them. She rose from the bed, still gazing fixedly and steadily on me. I trembled; the razor was in my hand, but I could not move. She made towards the door. As she neared it, she turned, and withdrew her eyes from my face. The spell was broken. I bounded forward, and clutched her by the arm. Uttering shriek upon shriek, she sank upon the ground.

'Now I could have killed her without a struggle; but the house was alarmed. I heard the tread of footsteps on the stairs. I replaced the razor in its usual drawer, unfastened the door, and called loudly for assistance.

'They came, and raised her, and placed her on the bed. She lay bereft of animation for hours; and when life, look and speech returned, her senses had deserted her, and she raved wildly and furiously.

'Doctors were called in – great men who rolled up to my door in easy carriages, with fine horses and gaudy servants. They were at her bedside for weeks. They had a great meeting, and consulted together in low and solemn voices in another room. One, the cleverest and most celebrated among them, took me aside, and bidding me prepare for the worst, told me – me, the madman! – that my wife was mad. He stood close beside me at an open window, his eyes looking in my face and his hand laid upon my arm. With one effort, I could have hurled him into the street beneath. It would have been rare sport to have done it; but my secret was at stake, and I let him go. A few days after, they told me I must place her under some restraint: I must provide a keeper for her. I! I went into the open fields where none could hear me, and laughed till the air resounded with my shouts!

'She died next day. The white-headed old man followed her to the grave, and the proud brothers dropped a tear over the insensible corpse of her whose sufferings they had regarded in her lifetime with muscles of iron. All this was food for my secret mirth, and I laughed behind the white handkerchief, which I held up to my face as we rode home, till the tears came into my eyes.

'But though I had carried out my object and killed her, I was restless and disturbed, and felt that before long my secret must be known. I could not hide the wild mirth and joy which boiled within me and made me, when I was alone at home, jump up and beat my hands together, and dance round and round, and roar aloud. When I went out, and saw the busy crowds hurrying about the streets; or to the theatre, and heard the sound of music and beheld the people dancing, I felt such glee that I could have rushed among them, and torn them to pieces limb from limb, and howled in transport. But I ground my teeth, and struck my feet upon the floor, and drove my sharp nails into my hands. I kept it down; and no one knew I was a madman yet.

'I remember – though it's one of the last things I *can* remember: for now I mix up realities with my dreams, and having so much to do and being always hurried here, have no time to separate the two from some strange confusion in which they get involved – I remember how I let it out at last. Ha! ha! I think I see their frightened looks now, and feel the ease with which I flung them from me, and dashed my clenched fist into their white faces, and then flew like the wind and left them screaming and shouting far behind. The strength of a giant comes upon me when I think of it. There – see how this iron bar bends beneath my furious wrench. I could snap it like a twig, only there are long galleries here with many doors – I don't think I could find my way along them; and even if I could, I know there are iron gates below which they keep locked and barred. They know what a clever madman I have been, and they are proud to have me here, to show.

'Let me see; – yes, I had been out. It was late at night when I reached home and found the proudest of the three proud brothers waiting to see me – urgent business he said: I recollect it well. I hated that man with all a madman's hate. Many and many a time had my fingers longed to tear him. They told me he was there. I ran swiftly upstairs. He had a word to say to me. I dismissed the servants. It was late, and we were alone together – *for the first time*.

'I kept my eyes carefully from him at first, for I knew what he little thought – and I gloried in the knowledge – that the light of madness gleamed from them like fire. We sat in silence for a few minutes. He spoke at last. My recent dissipation, and strange remarks, made so soon after his sister's death, were an insult to her memory. Coupling together many circumstances which had at first escaped his observation, he thought I had not treated her well. He wished to know whether he was right in inferring that I meant to cast a reproach upon her memory, and a disrespect upon her family. It was due to the uniform he wore, to demand this explanation.

'This man had a commission in the army – a commission, purchased with my money and his sister's misery! This was the man who had been foremost in the plot to ensnare me and grasp my wealth. This was the man who had been the main instrument in forcing his sister to wed me, well knowing that her heart was given to that puling boy. Due to *his* uniform! The livery of his degradation! I turned my eyes upon him – I could not help it – but I spoke not a word.

'I saw the sudden change that came upon him beneath my gaze. He was a bold man, but the colour faded from his face, and he drew back his chair. I dragged mine nearer to him; and as I laughed – I was very merry then – I saw him shudder. I felt the madness rising within me. He was afraid of me.

' "You were very fond of your sister when she was alive," I said. "Very."

'He looked uneasily round him, and I saw his hand grasp the back of his chair: but he said nothing.

' "You villain," said I, "I found you out; I discovered your hellish plots against me; I know her heart was fixed on someone else before you compelled her to marry me. I know it – I know it."

'He jumped suddenly from his chair, brandished it aloft, and bid me stand back – for I took care to be getting closer to him all the time I spoke.

'I screamed rather than talked, for I felt tumultuous passions eddying through my veins and the old spirits whispering and taunting me to tear his heart out.

' "Damn you," said I, starting up and rushing upon him; "I killed her. I am a madman. Down with you. Blood, blood! I will have it!"

'I turned aside with one blow the chair he hurled at me in his terror and closed with him; and with a heavy crash we rolled upon the floor together.

'It was a fine struggle that; for he was a tall strong man, fighting for his life; and I, a powerful madman, thirsting to destroy him. I knew no strength could equal mine, and I was right. Right again, though a madman! His struggles grew fainter. I knelt upon his chest, and clasped his brawny throat firmly with both hands. His face grew purple; his eyes were starting from his head, and with protruded tongue, he seemed to mock me. I squeezed the tighter.

'The door was suddenly burst open with a loud noise, and a crowd of people rushed forward, crying aloud to each other to secure the madman.

'My secret was out; and my only struggle now was for liberty and freedom. I gained my feet before a hand was on me, threw myself among my assailants and cleared my way with my strong arm, as if I bore a hatchet in my hand, and hewed them down before me. I gained the door, dropped over the banisters, and in an instant was in the street.

'Straight and swift I ran, and no one dared to stop me. I heard the noise of feet behind and redoubled my speed. It grew fainter and fainter in the distance and at length died away altogether: but on I bounded, through marsh and rivulet, over fence and wall, with a wild shout which was taken up by the strange beings that flocked around me on every side and swelled the sound till it pierced the air. I was borne upon the arms of demons who swept along upon the wind, and bore down bank and hedge before them, and spun me round and round with a rustle and a speed that made my head swim, until at last they threw me from them with a violent shock, and I fell heavily upon the earth. When I woke I found myself here – here in this grey cell where the sunlight seldom comes, and the moon steals in in rays which only serve to show the dark shadows about me and that silent figure in its old corner. When I lie awake, I can sometimes hear strange shrieks and cries from distant parts of this large place. What they are, I know not; but they neither come from that pale form, nor does it regard them. For from the first shades of dusk till the earliest light of morning, it still stands motionless in the same place, listening to the music of my iron chain and watching my gambols on my straw bed.'

At the end of the manuscript was written, in another hand, this note:

> The unhappy man whose ravings are recorded above, was a melancholy instance of the baneful results of energies mis-directed in early life and excesses prolonged until their consequences could never be repaired. The thoughtless riot, dissipation and debauchery of his younger days produced fever and delirium. The first effects of the latter was the strange delusion, founded upon a well-known medical theory strongly contended for by some, and as strongly contested by others, that an hereditary madness existed in his family. This produced a settled gloom, which in time developed a morbid insanity, and finally terminated in raving madness. There is every reason to believe that the events he detailed, though distorted in the description by his diseased imagination, really happened. It is only a matter of wonder to those who were acquainted with the vices of his early career that his passions, when no longer controlled by reason, did not lead him to the commission of still more frightful deeds.

Mr Pickwick's candle was just expiring in the socket as he concluded the perusal of the old clergyman's manuscript; and when the light went suddenly out, without any previous flicker by way of warning, it communicated a very considerable start to his excited frame. Hastily throwing off such articles of clothing as he had put on when he rose from his uneasy bed, and casting a fearful glance around, he once more scrambled hastily between the sheets, and soon fell fast asleep.

Strange Event in the Life of Schalken the Painter

J. S. LE FANU

You will no doubt be surprised, my dear friend, at the subject of the following narrative. What had I to do with Schalken, or Schalken with me? He had returned to his native land, and was probably dead and buried before I was born; I never visited Holland nor spoke with a native of that country. So much I believe you already know. I must, then, give you my authority, and state to you frankly the ground upon which rests the credibility of the strange story which I am about to lay before you.

I was acquainted, in my early days, with a Captain Vandael, whose father had served King William in the Low Countries, and also in my own unhappy land during the Irish campaigns. I know not how it happened that I liked this man's society, spite of his politics and religion: but so it was; and it was by means of the free intercourse to which our intimacy gave rise that I became possessed of the curious tale which you are about to hear.

I had often been struck, while visiting Vandael, by a remarkable picture, in which, though no connoisseur myself, I could not fail to discern some very strong peculiarities, particularly in the distribution of light and shade, as also a certain oddity in the design itself, which interested my curiosity. It represented the interior of what might be a chamber in some antique religious building, and the foreground was occupied by a female figure, arrayed in a species of white robe, part of which is arranged so as to form a veil.

The dress, however, is not strictly that of any religious order. In its hand the figure bears a lamp, by whose light alone the form and face are illuminated; the features are marked by an arch smile, such as pretty women wear when engaged in successfully practising some roguish trick; in the background, and, excepting where the dim red light of an expiring fire serves to define the form, totally in the shade, stands the figure of a man equipped in the old fashion, with doublet and so forth, in an attitude of alarm, his hand being placed upon the hilt of his sword, which he appears to be in the act of drawing.

'There are some pictures,' said I to my friend, 'which impress one, I know not how, with a conviction that they represent not the mere ideal shapes and combinations which have floated through the imagination of the artist, but scenes, faces and situations which have actually existed. When I look upon that picture, something assures me that I behold the representation of a reality.'

Vandael smiled, and, fixing his eyes upon the painting musingly, he said: 'Your fancy has not deceived you, my good friend, for that picture is the record, and I believe a faithful one, of a remarkable and mysterious occurrence. It was painted by Schalken, and contains, in the face of the female figure which occupies the most prominent place in the design, an accurate portrait of Rose Velderkaust, the niece of Gerard Douw, who was the first and, I believe, the only love of Godfrey Schalken. My father knew the painter well, and from Schalken himself he learned the story of the mysterious drama, one scene of which the picture has embodied. This painting, which is accounted a fine specimen of Schalken's style, was bequeathed to my father by the artist's will, and, as you have observed, is a very striking and interesting production.'

I had only to request Vandael to tell the story of the painting in order to be gratified; and thus it is that I am enabled to submit to you a faithful recital of what I heard myself, leaving you to reject or to allow the evidence upon which the truth of the tradition depends, with this one assurance, that Schalken was an honest, blunt Dutchman, and, I believe, wholly incapable of committing a flight of imagination; and further, that Vandael, from whom I heard the story, appeared firmly convinced of its truth.

There are few forms upon which the mantle of mystery and romance could seem to hang more ungracefully than upon that of the uncouth and clownish Schalken – the Dutch boor – the rude and dogged, but most cunning worker in oils, whose pieces delight the initiated of the present day almost as much as his manners disgusted the refined of his own; and yet this man, so rude, so dogged, so slovenly, I had almost said so savage, in mien and manner, during his after successes, had been selected by the capricious goddess, in his early life, to figure as the hero of a romance by no means devoid of interest or of mystery.

Who can tell how meet he may have been in his young days to play the part of the lover or of the hero – who can say that in early life he had been the same harsh, unlicked and rugged boor that, in his maturer age, he proved – or how far the neglected rudeness which afterwards marked his air, and garb, and manners, may not have been the growth of that reckless apathy not unfrequently produced by bitter misfortunes and disappointments in early life?

These questions can never now be answered.

We must content ourselves, then, with a plain statement of facts, or what have been received and transmitted as such, leaving matters of speculation to those who like them.

When Schalken studied under the immortal Gerard Douw, he was a young man; and in spite of the phlegmatic constitution and unexcitable manner which he shared, we believe, with his country-men, he was not incapable of deep and vivid impressions, for it is an established fact that the young painter looked with considerable interest upon the beautiful niece of his wealthy master.

Rose Velderkaust was very young, having, at the period of which we speak, not yet attained her seventeenth year, and, if tradition speaks truth, possessed all the soft dimpling charms of the fair, light-haired Flemish maidens. Schalken had not studied long in the school of Gerard Douw when he felt this interest deepening into something of a keener and intenser feeling than was quite consistent with the tranquillity of his honest Dutch heart; and at the same time he perceived, or thought he perceived, flattering symptoms of a reci-procity of liking, and this was quite sufficient to determine whatever indecision he might have heretofore experienced and to lead him to devote exclusively to her every hope and feeling of his heart. In short, he was as much in love as a Dutchman could be. He was not long in making his passion known to the pretty maiden herself, and his declaration was followed by a corresponding confession upon her part.

Schalken, however, was a poor man, and he possessed no counter-balancing advantages of birth or position to induce the old man to consent to a union which must involve his niece and ward in the strugglings and difficulties of a young and nearly friendless artist. He was, therefore, to wait until time had furnished him with opportu-nity, and accident with success; and then, if his labours were found sufficiently lucrative, it was to be hoped that his proposals might at least be listened to by her jealous guardian. Months passed away, and, cheered by the smiles of the little Rose, Schalken's labours were redoubled, and with such effect and improvement as reasonably to promise the realisation of his hopes, and no contemptible eminence in his art, before many years should have elapsed.

The even course of this cheering prosperity was, however, destined to experience a sudden and formidable interruption, and that, too, in a manner so strange and mysterious as to baffle all investigation, and throw upon the events themselves a shadow of almost supernatural horror.

Schalken had one evening remained in the master's studio considerably longer than his more volatile companions, who had gladly availed themselves of the excuse which the dusk of evening afforded to withdraw from their several tasks in order to finish a day of labour in the jollity and conviviality of the tavern.

But Schalken worked for improvement, or rather for love. Besides, he was now engaged merely in sketching a design, an operation which, unlike that of colouring, might be continued as long as there was light sufficient to distinguish between canvas and charcoal. He had not then, nor, indeed, until long after, discovered the peculiar powers of his pencil, and he was engaged in composing a group of extremely roguish-looking and grotesque imps and demons, who were inflicting various ingenious torments upon a perspiring and potbellied St Anthony, who reclined in the midst of them, apparently in the last stage of drunkenness.

The young artist, however, though incapable of executing, or even of appreciating, anything of true sublimity, had nevertheless discernment enough to prevent his being by any means satisfied with his work; and many were the patient erasures and corrections which the limbs and features of saint and devil underwent, yet all without producing in their new arrangement anything of improvement or increased effect.

The large old-fashioned room was silent, and, with the exception of himself, quite deserted by its usual inmates. An hour had passed – nearly two – without any improved result. Daylight had already declined and twilight was fast giving way to the darkness of night. The patience of the young man was exhausted, and he stood before his unfinished production, absorbed in no very pleasing ruminations, one hand buried in the folds of his long dark hair, and the other holding the piece of charcoal which had so ill executed its office, and which he now rubbed, without much regard to the sable streaks which it produced, with irritable pressure upon his ample Flemish inexpressibles.

'Pshaw!' said the young man aloud, 'would that picture, devils, saint and all were where they should be – in hell!'

A short, sudden laugh, uttered startlingly close to his ear, instantly responded to the ejaculation.

The artist turned sharply round, and now for the first time

became aware that his labours had been overlooked by a stranger.

Within about a yard and a half, and rather behind him, there stood what was, or appeared to be, the figure of an elderly man: he wore a short cloak and broad-brimmed hat with a conical crown, and in his hand, which was protected with a heavy, gauntlet-shaped glove, he carried a long ebony walking-stick, surmounted with what appeared, as it glittered dimly in the twilight, to be a massive head of gold, and upon his breast, through the folds of the cloak, there shone what appeared to be the links of a rich chain of the same metal.

The room was so obscure that nothing further of the appearance of the figure could be ascertained, and the face was altogether overshadowed by the heavy flap of the beaver which overhung it, so that not a feature could be discerned. A quantity of dark hair escaped from beneath this sombre hat, a circumstance which, connected with the firm, upright carriage of the intruder, proved that his years could not yet exceed threescore or thereabouts.

There was an air of gravity and importance about the garb of this person, and something indescribably odd – I might say awful – in the perfect, stonelike movelessness of the figure, that effectually checked the testy comment which had at once risen to the lips of the irritated artist. He therefore, as soon as he had sufficiently recovered the surprise, asked the stranger, civilly, to be seated, and desired to know if he had any message to leave for his master.

'Tell Gerard Douw,' said the unknown, without altering his attitude in the smallest degree, 'that Mynher Vanderhausen, of Rotterdam, desires to speak with him tomorrow evening at this hour, and, if he please, in this room, upon matters of weight – that is all. Good-night.'

The stranger, having finished this message, turned abruptly, and, with a quick but silent step, quitted the room before Schalken had time to say a word in reply.

The young man felt a curiosity to see in what direction the burgher of Rotterdam would turn on quitting the studio, and for that purpose he went directly to the window which commanded the door.

A lobby of considerable extent intervened between the inner door of the painter's room and the street entrance, so that Schalken occupied the post of observation before the old man could possibly have reached the street.

He watched in vain, however. There was no other mode of exit.

Had the old man vanished, or was he lurking about the recesses of the lobby for some bad purpose? This last suggestion filled the mind of Schalken with a vague horror, which was so unaccountably intense as to make him alike afraid to remain in the room alone and reluctant to pass through the lobby.

However, with an effort which appeared very disproportioned to the occasion, he summoned resolution to leave the room, and, having double-locked the door and thrust the key in his pocket, without looking to the right or left he traversed the passage which had so recently, perhaps still, contained the person of his mysterious visitant, scarcely venturing to breathe till he had arrived in the open street.

'Mynher Vanderhausen,' said Gerard Douw within himself, as the appointed hour approached; 'Mynher Vanderhausen of Rotterdam! I never heard of the man till yesterday. What can he want of me? A portrait, perhaps, to be painted; or a younger son or a poor relation to be apprenticed; or a collection to be valued; or – pshaw! there's no one in Rotterdam to leave me a legacy. Well, whatever the business may be, we shall soon know it all.'

It was now the close of day, and every easel, except that of Schalken, was deserted. Gerard Douw was pacing the apartment with the restless step of impatient expectation, every now and then humming a passage from a piece of music which he was himself composing (for, though no great proficient, he admired the art), sometimes pausing to glance over the work of one of his absent pupils, but more frequently placing himself at the window, from whence he might observe the passengers who threaded the obscure bystreet in which his studio was placed.

'Said you not, Godfrey,' exclaimed Douw, after a long and fruitless gaze from his post of observation, and turning to Schalken – 'said you not the hour of appointment was at about seven by the clock of the Stadhouse?'

'It had just told seven when I first saw him, sir,' answered the student.

'The hour is close at hand, then,' said the master, consulting a horologe as large and as round as a full-grown orange. 'Mynher Vanderhausen, from Rotterdam – is it not so?'

'Such was the name.'

'And an elderly man, richly clad?' continued Douw.

'As well as I might see,' replied his pupil; 'he could not be young, nor yet very old neither, and his dress was rich and grave, as might become a citizen of wealth and consideration.'

At this moment the sonorous boom of the Stadhouse clock told, stroke after stroke, the hour of seven; the eyes of both master and student were directed to the door; and it was not until the last peal of the old bell had ceased to vibrate that Douw exclaimed – 'So, so; we shall have his worship presently – that is, if he means to keep his hour; if not, thou mayst wait for him, Godfrey, if you court the acquaintance of a capricious burgomaster. As for me, I think our old Leyden contains a sufficiency of such commodities, without an importation from Rotterdam.'

Schalken laughed, as in duty bound; and after a pause of some minutes, Douw suddenly exclaimed – 'What if it should all prove a jest, a piece of mummery got up by Vankarp, or some such worthy! I wish you had run all risks, and cudgelled the old burgomaster, stadholder, or whatever else he may be, soundly. I would wager a dozen of Rhenish, his worship would have pleaded old acquaintance before the third application.'

'Here he comes, sir,' said Schalken, in a low admonitory tone; and instantly, upon turning towards the door, Gerard Douw observed the same figure which had, on the day before, so unexpectedly greeted the vision of his pupil Schalken.

There was something in the air and mien of the figure which at once satisfied the painter that there was no mummery in the case, and that he really stood in the presence of a man of worship; and so, without hesitation, he doffed his cap, and courteously saluting the stranger, requested him to be seated.

The visitor waved his hand slightly, as if in acknowledgment of the courtesy, but remained standing.

'I have the honour to see Mynher Vanderhausen, of Rotterdam?' said Gerard Douw.

'The same,' was the laconic reply of his visitant.

'I understand your worship desires to speak with me,' continued Douw, 'and I am here by appointment to wait your commands.'

'Is that a man of trust?' said Vanderhausen, turning towards Schalken, who stood at a little distance behind his master.

'Certainly,' replied Gerard.

'Then let him take this box and get the nearest jeweller or goldsmith to value its contents, and let him return hither with a certificate of the valuation.'

At the same time he placed a small case, about nine inches square, in the hands of Gerard Douw, who was as much amazed at its weight as at the strange abruptness with which it was handed to him.

In accordance with the wishes of the stranger, he delivered it into the hands of Schalken and, repeating his directions, dispatched him upon the mission.

Schalken disposed his precious charge securely beneath the folds of his cloak, and rapidly traversing two or three narrow streets, he stopped at a corner house, the lower part of which was then occupied by the shop of a Jewish goldsmith.

Schalken entered the shop, and calling the little Hebrew into the obscurity of its back recesses, he proceeded to lay before him Vanderhausen's packet.

On being examined by the light of a lamp, it appeared entirely cased with lead, the outer surface of which was much scraped and soiled, and nearly white with age. This was with difficulty partially removed, and disclosed beneath a box of some dark and singularly hard wood; this, too, was forced, and after the removal of two or three folds of linen, its contents proved to be a mass of golden ingots, close packed, and, as the Jew declared, of the most perfect quality.

Every ingot underwent the scrutiny of the little Jew, who seemed to feel an epicurean delight in touching and testing these morsels of the glorious metal; and each one of them was replaced in the box with the exclamation – 'Mein Gott, how very perfect! not one grain of alloy – beautiful, beautiful!'

The task was at length finished, and the Jew certified under his hand the value of the ingots submitted to his examination to amount to many thousand rix-dollars.

With the desired document in his bosom, and the rich box of gold carefully pressed under his arm, and concealed by his cloak, he retraced his way, and, entering the studio, found his master and the stranger in close conference.

Schalken had no sooner left the room, in order to execute the commission he had taken in charge, than Vanderhausen addressed Gerard Douw in the following terms: 'I may not tarry with you tonight more than a few minutes, and so I shall briefly tell you the matter upon which I come. You visited the town of Rotterdam some four months ago, and then I saw in the church of St Lawrence your niece, Rose Velderkaust. I desire to marry her, and if I satisfy you as to the fact that I am very wealthy – more wealthy than any husband you could dream of for her – I expect that you will forward my views to the utmost of your authority. If you approve my proposal, you must close with it at once, for I cannot command time enough to wait for calculations and delays.'

Gerard Douw was, perhaps, as much astonished as anyone could be by the very unexpected nature of Mynher Vanderhausen's communication; but he did not give vent to any unseemly expression of surprise, for besides the motives supplied by prudence and politeness, the painter experienced a kind of chill and oppressive sensation, something like that which is supposed to affect a man who is placed unconsciously in immediate contact with something to which he has a natural antipathy – an undefined horror and dread while standing in the presence of the eccentric stranger, which made him very unwilling to say anything which might reasonably prove offensive.

'I have no doubt,' said Gerard, after two or three prefatory hems, 'that the connection which you propose would prove alike advantageous and honourable to my niece; but you must be aware that she has a will of her own, and may not acquiesce in what WE may design for her advantage.'

'Do not seek to deceive me, Sir Painter,' said Vanderhausen; 'you are her guardian – she is your ward. She is mine if YOU like to make her so.'

The man of Rotterdam moved forward a little as he spoke, and Gerard Douw, he scarce knew why, inwardly prayed for the speedy return of Schalken.

'I desire,' said the mysterious gentleman, 'to place in your hands at once an evidence of my wealth, and a security for my liberal dealing with your niece. The lad will return in a minute or two with a sum in value five times the fortune which she has a right to expect from a husband. This shall lie in your hands, together with her dowry, and you may apply the united sum as suits her interest best; it shall be all exclusively hers while she lives. Is that liberal?'

Douw assented, and inwardly thought that fortune had been extraordinarily kind to his niece. The stranger, he thought, must be both wealthy and generous, and such an offer was not to be despised, though made by a humorist, and one of no very prepossessing presence.

Rose had no very high pretensions, for she was almost without dowry; indeed, altogether so, excepting so far as the deficiency had been supplied by the generosity of her uncle. Neither had she any right to raise any scruples against the match on the score of birth, for her own origin was by no means elevated; and as to other objections, Gerard resolved, and, indeed, by the usages of the time was warranted in resolving, not to listen to them for a moment.

'Sir,' said he, addressing the stranger, 'your offer is most liberal, and whatever hesitation I may feel in closing with it immediately arises solely from my not having the honour of knowing anything of your family or station. Upon these points you can, of course, satisfy me without difficulty?'

'As to my respectability,' said the stranger drily, 'you must take that for granted at present; pester me with no enquiries; you can discover nothing more about me than I choose to make known. You shall have sufficient security for my respectability – my word, if you are honourable; if you are sordid, my gold.'

'A testy old gentleman,' thought Douw; 'he must have his own way. But, all things considered, I am justified in giving my niece to him. Were she my own daughter, I would do the like by her. I will not pledge myself unnecessarily, however.'

'You will not pledge yourself unnecessarily,' said Vanderhausen, strangely uttering the very words which had just floated through the mind of his companion; 'but you will do so if it is necessary, I presume; and I will show you that I consider it indispensable. If the gold I mean to leave in your hands satisfy you, and if you desire that my proposal shall not be at once withdrawn, you must, before I leave this room, write your name to this engagement.'

Having thus spoken, he placed a paper in the hands of Gerard, the contents of which expressed an engagement, entered into by Gerard Douw, to give to Wilken Vanderhausen, of Rotterdam, in marriage, Rose Velderkaust, and so forth, within one week of the date hereof.

While the painter was employed in reading this covenant, Schalken, as we have stated, entered the studio, and having delivered the box and the valuation of the Jew into the hands of the stranger, he was about to retire, when Vanderhausen called to him to wait; and, presenting the case and the certificate to Gerard Douw, he waited in silence until the latter had satisfied himself by an inspection of both as to the value of the pledge left in his hands. At length he said: 'Are you content?'

The painter said he would fain have another day to consider.

'Not an hour,' said the suitor, coolly.

'Well, then,' said Douw, 'I am content; it is a bargain.'

'Then sign at once,' said Vanderhausen; 'I am weary.'

At the same time he produced a small case of writing materials, and Gerard signed the important document.

'Let this youth witness the covenant,' said the old man; and Godfrey Schalken unconsciously signed the instrument which bestowed upon another that hand which he had so long regarded as the object and reward of all his labours.

The compact being thus completed, the strange visitor folded up the paper, and stowed it safely in an inner pocket.

'I will visit you tomorrow night, at nine of the clock, at your house, Gerard Douw, and will see the subject of our contract. Farewell.'

And so saying, Wilken Vanderhausen moved stiffly but rapidly out of the room.

Schalken, eager to resolve his doubts, had placed himself by the window in order to watch the street entrance; but the experiment served only to support his suspicions, for the old man did not issue from the door. This was very strange, very odd, very fearful. He and his master returned together, and talked but little on the way, for each had his own subjects of reflection, of anxiety and of hope.

Schalken, however, did not know the ruin which threatened his cherished schemes.

Gerard Douw knew nothing of the attachment which had sprung up between his pupil and his niece; and even if he had, it is doubtful whether he would have regarded its existence as any serious obstruction to the wishes of Mynher Vanderhausen.

Marriages were then and there matters of traffic and calculation; and it would have appeared as absurd in the eyes of the guardian to make a mutual attachment an essential element in a contract of marriage as it would have been to draw up his bonds and receipts in the language of chivalrous romance.

The painter, however, did not communicate to his niece the important step which he had taken in her behalf, and his resolution arose not from any anticipation of opposition on her part but solely from a ludicrous consciousness that if his ward were, as she very naturally might do, to ask him to describe the appearance of the bridegroom whom he destined for her, he would be forced to confess that he had not seen his face, and, if called upon, would find it impossible to identify him.

Upon the next day, Gerard Douw having dined, called his niece to him, and having scanned her person with an air of satisfaction, he took her hand, and looking upon her pretty, innocent face with a smile of kindness, he said: 'Rose, my girl, that face of yours will make your fortune.' Rose blushed and smiled. 'Such faces and such tempers seldom go together, and, when they do, the compound is a love-potion which few heads or hearts can resist. Trust me, thou wilt soon be a bride, girl. But this is trifling, and I am pressed for time, so make ready the large room by eight o'clock tonight, and give directions for supper at nine. I expect a friend tonight; and observe me, child, do thou trick thyself out handsomely. I would not have him think us poor or sluttish.'

With these words he left the chamber, and took his way to the room to which we have already had occasion to introduce our readers – that in which his pupils worked.

When the evening closed in, Gerard called Schalken, who was about to take his departure to his obscure and comfortless lodgings, and asked him to come home and sup with Rose and Vanderhausen.

The invitation was of course accepted, and Gerard Douw and his pupil soon found themselves in the handsome and somewhat antique-looking room which had been prepared for the reception of the stranger.

A cheerful wood-fire blazed in the capacious hearth; a little at one side, an old-fashioned table with richly-carved legs was placed – destined, no doubt, to receive the supper, for which preparations were going forward; and ranged with exact regularity, stood the tall-backed chairs, whose ungracefulness was more than counterbalanced by their comfort.

The little party, consisting of Rose, her uncle and the artist, awaited the arrival of the expected visitor with considerable impatience.

Nine o'clock at length came, and with it a summons at the street-door, which, being speedily answered, was followed by a slow and emphatic tread upon the staircase; the steps moved heavily across the lobby, the door of the room in which the party which we have described were assembled slowly opened, and there entered a figure which startled, almost appalled, the phlegmatic Dutchmen, and nearly made Rose scream with affright: it was the form, and arrayed in the garb, of Mynher Vanderhausen; the air, the gait, the height was the same; but the features had never been seen by any of the party before.

The stranger stopped at the door of the room, and displayed his form and face completely. He wore a dark-coloured cloth cloak, which was short and full, not falling quite to the knees; his legs were cased in dark purple silk stockings, and his shoes were adorned with roses of the same colour. The opening of the cloak in front showed the under-suit to consist of some very dark, perhaps sable material, and his hands were enclosed in a pair of heavy leather gloves which ran up considerably above the wrist, in the manner of a gauntlet. In one hand he carried his walking-stick and his hat, which he had removed, and the other hung heavily by his side. A quantity of grizzled hair descended in long tresses from his head, and its folds rested upon the plaits of a stiff ruff, which effectually concealed his neck.

So far all was well; but the face! – all the flesh of the face was coloured with the bluish leaden hue which is sometimes produced by the operation of metallic medicines administered in excessive quantities; the eyes were enormous, and the white appeared both above and below the iris, which gave to them an expression of insanity, which was heightened by their glassy fixedness; the nose was well enough, but the mouth was writhed considerably to one side, where it opened in order to give egress to two long, discoloured fangs, which projected from the upper jaw far below the lower lip; the hue of the lips themselves bore the usual relation to that of the face, and was consequently nearly black. The character of the face was malignant, even satanic, to the last degree; and, indeed, such a combination of horror could hardly be accounted for, except by supposing the corpse of some atrocious malefactor, which had long hung blackening upon the gibbet, to have at length become the habitation of a demon – the frightful sport of satanic possession.

It was remarkable that the worshipful stranger suffered as little as possible of his flesh to appear, and that during his visit he did not once remove his gloves.

When he had stood for some moments at the door, Gerard Douw at length found breath and collectedness to bid him welcome, and, with a mute inclination of the head, the stranger stepped forward into the room.

There was something indescribably odd, even horrible, about all his motions, something undefinable that was unnatural, unhuman – it was as if the limbs were guided and directed by a spirit unused to the management of bodily machinery.

The stranger said hardly anything during his visit, which did not exceed half an hour; and the host himself could scarcely muster courage enough to utter the few necessary salutations and courtesies; and, indeed, such was the nervous terror which the presence of Vanderhausen inspired that very little would have made all his entertainers fly bellowing from the room.

They had not so far lost all self-possession, however, as to fail to observe two strange peculiarities of their visitor.

During his stay he did not once suffer his eyelids to close, nor even to move in the slightest degree; and further, there was a deathlike stillness in his whole person owing to the total absence of the heaving motion of the chest caused by the process of respiration.

These two peculiarities, though when told they may appear trifling, produced a very striking and unpleasant effect when seen and observed. Vanderhausen at length relieved the painter of Leyden of his inauspicious presence; and with no small gratification the little party heard the street-door close after him.

'Dear uncle,' said Rose, 'what a frightful man! I would not see him again for the wealth of the States!'

'Tush, foolish girl!' said Douw, whose sensations were anything but comfortable. 'A man may be as ugly as the devil, and yet if his heart and actions are good, he is worth all the pretty-faced, perfumed puppies that walk the Mall. Rose, my girl, it is very true he has not thy pretty face, but I know him to be wealthy and liberal; and were he ten times more ugly – '

'Which is inconceivable,' observed Rose.

'These two virtues would be sufficient,' continued her uncle, 'to counterbalance all his deformity; and if not of power sufficient actually to alter the shape of the features, at least of efficacy enough to prevent one thinking them amiss.'

'Do you know, uncle,' said Rose, 'when I saw him standing at the door, I could not get it out of my head that I saw the old painted wooden figure that used to frighten me so much in the church of St Lawrence of Rotterdam.'

Gerard laughed, though he could not help inwardly acknowledging the justness of the comparison. He was resolved, however, as far as he could, to check his niece's inclination to ridicule the ugliness of her intended bridegroom, although he was not a little pleased to observe that she appeared totally exempt from that mysterious dread of the stranger which, he could not disguise it from himself, considerably affected him, as also his pupil Godfrey Schalken.

Early on the next day there arrived, from various quarters of the town, rich presents of silks, velvets, jewellery, and so forth, for Rose; and also a packet directed to Gerard Douw, which, on being opened, was found to contain a contract of marriage, formally drawn up, between Wilken Vanderhausen of the Boom-quay, in Rotterdam, and Rose Velderkaust of Leyden, niece to Gerard Douw, master in the art of painting, also of the same city, with engagements on the part of Vanderhausen to make settlements upon his bride, far more splendid than he had before led her guardian to believe likely, which were to be secured to her use in the most unexceptionable manner possible – the money being placed in the hands of Gerard Douw himself.

I have no sentimental scenes to describe, no cruelty of guardians, or magnanimity of wards, or agonies of lovers. The record I have to make is one of sordidness, levity and interest. In less than a week after the first interview which we have just described, the contract of marriage was fulfilled, and Schalken saw the prize which he would have risked anything to secure, carried off triumphantly by his formidable rival.

For two or three days he absented himself from the school; he then returned and worked, if with less cheerfulness with far more dogged resolution than before; the dream of love had given place to that of ambition.

Months passed away and, contrary to his expectation, and, indeed, to the direct promise of the parties, Gerard Douw heard nothing of his niece, or her worshipful spouse. The interest of the money, which was to have been demanded in quarterly sums, lay unclaimed in his hands. He began to grow extremely uneasy.

Mynher Vanderhausen's direction in Rotterdam he was fully possessed of. After some irresolution he finally determined to journey thither – a trifling undertaking, and easily accomplished – and thus to satisfy himself of the safety and comfort of his ward, for whom he entertained an honest and strong affection.

His search was in vain, however. No one in Rotterdam had ever heard of Mynher Vanderhausen.

Gerard Douw left not a house in the Boom-quay untried; but all in vain. No one could give him any information whatever touching the object of his enquiry, and he was obliged to return to Leyden nothing wiser than when he had left it.

On his arrival he hastened to the establishment from which Vanderhausen had hired the lumbering, though, considering the times, most luxurious, vehicle which the bridal party had employed to convey them to Rotterdam. From the driver of this machine he learned that, having proceeded by slow stages, they had late in the evening approached Rotterdam; but that before they entered the city, and while yet nearly a mile from it, a small party of men, soberly clad, and after the old fashion, with peaked beards and moustaches, standing in the centre of the road, obstructed the further progress of the carriage. The driver reined in his horses, much fearing, from the obscurity of the hour and the loneliness of the road, that some mischief was intended.

His fears were, however, somewhat allayed by his observing that these strange men carried a large litter, of an antique shape, which they immediately set down upon the pavement; whereupon the bridegroom, having opened the coach-door from within, descended, and having assisted his bride to do likewise, led her, weeping bitterly and wringing her hands, to the litter, which they both entered. It was then raised by the men who surrounded it and speedily carried towards the city, and before it had proceeded many yards the darkness concealed it from the view of the Dutch charioteer.

In the inside of the vehicle he found a purse, whose contents more than thrice paid the hire of the carriage and man. He saw and could tell nothing more of Mynher Vanderhausen and his beautiful lady. This mystery was a source of deep anxiety and almost of grief to Gerard Douw.

There was evidently fraud in the dealing of Vanderhausen with him, though for what purpose committed he could not imagine. He greatly doubted how far it was possible for a man possessing in his countenance so strong an evidence of the presence of the most demoniac feelings to be in reality anything but a villain; and every day that passed without his hearing from or of his niece, instead of inducing him to forget his fears, on the contrary tended more and more to exasperate them.

The loss of his niece's cheerful society tended also to depress his spirits; and in order to dispel this despondency, which often crept upon his mind after his daily employment was over, he was wont frequently to prevail upon Schalken to accompany him home and by his presence to dispel, in some degree, the gloom of his otherwise solitary supper.

One evening, the painter and his pupil were sitting by the fire, having accomplished a comfortable supper, and had yielded to that silent pensiveness sometimes induced by the process of digestion, when their reflections were disturbed by a loud sound at the street-door, as if occasioned by some person rushing forcibly and repeatedly against it. A domestic had run without delay to ascertain the cause of the disturbance, and they heard him twice or thrice interrogate the applicant for admission, but without producing an answer or any cessation of the sounds.

They heard him then open the hall-door, and immediately there followed a light and rapid tread upon the staircase. Schalken laid his hand on his sword and advanced towards the door. It opened before he reached it, and Rose rushed into the room. She looked wild and haggard, and pale with exhaustion and terror; but her dress surprised them as much even as her unexpected appearance. It consisted of a kind of white woollen wrapper, made close about the neck, and descending to the very ground. It was much deranged and travel-soiled. The poor creature had hardly entered the chamber when she fell senseless on the floor. With some difficulty they succeeded in reviving her, and on recovering her senses she instantly exclaimed, in a tone of eager, terrified impatience – 'Wine, wine, quickly, or I'm lost!'

Much alarmed at the strange agitation in which the call was made, they at once administered to her wishes, and she drank some wine with a haste and eagerness which surprised them. She had hardly swallowed it, when she exclaimed, with the same urgency – 'Food, food, at once, or I perish!'

A considerable fragment of a roast joint was upon the table, and Schalken immediately proceeded to cut some, but he was anticipated; for no sooner had she become aware of its presence than she darted at it with the rapacity of a vulture, and seizing it in her hands, she tore off the flesh with her teeth and swallowed it.

When the paroxysm of hunger had been a little appeased, she appeared suddenly to become aware how strange her conduct had been, or it may have been that other more agitating thoughts recurred to her mind, for she began to weep bitterly and to wring her hands.

'Oh! send for a minister of God,' said she; 'I am not safe till he comes; send for him speedily.'

Gerard Douw despatched a messenger instantly, and prevailed on his niece to allow him to surrender his bedchamber to her use; he also persuaded her to retire to it at once and to rest; her consent was extorted upon the condition that they would not leave her for a moment.

'Oh that the holy man were here!' she said; 'he can deliver me. The dead and the living can never be one – God has forbidden it.'

With these mysterious words she surrendered herself to their guidance, and they proceeded to the chamber which Gerard Douw had assigned to her use.

'Do not – do not leave me for a moment,' said she. 'I am lost for ever if you do.'

Gerard Douw's chamber was approached through a spacious apartment, which they were now about to enter. Gerard Douw and Schalken each carried a wax candle, so that a sufficient degree of light was cast upon all surrounding objects. They were now entering the large chamber, which, as I have said, communicated with Douw's apartment, when Rose suddenly stopped, and, in a whisper which seemed to thrill with horror, she said – 'O God! he is here – he is here! See, see – there he goes!'

She pointed towards the door of the inner room, and Schalken thought he saw a shadowy and ill-defined form gliding into that apartment. He drew his sword, and raising the candle so as to throw its light with increased distinctness upon the objects in the room, he entered the chamber into which the shadow had glided. No figure was there – nothing but the furniture which belonged to the room, and yet he could not be deceived as to the fact that something had moved before them into the chamber.

A sickening dread came upon him, and the cold perspiration broke out in heavy drops upon his forehead; nor was he more composed when he heard the increased urgency, the agony of entreaty, with which Rose implored them not to leave her for a moment.

'I saw him,' said she. 'He's here! I cannot be deceived – I know him. He's by me – he's with me – he's in the room. Then, for God's sake, as you would save me, do not stir from beside me!'

They at length prevailed upon her to lie down upon the bed, where she continued to urge them to stay by her. She frequently uttered incoherent sentences, repeating again and again, 'The dead and the living cannot be one – God has forbidden it!' and then again, 'Rest to the wakeful – sleep to the sleepwalkers.'

These and such mysterious and broken sentences she continued to utter until the clergyman arrived.

Gerard Douw began to fear, naturally enough, that the poor girl, owing to terror or ill-treatment, had become deranged; and he half suspected, by the suddenness of her appearance and the unseason-ableness of the hour and, above all, from the wildness and terror of her manner, that she had made her escape from some place of confinement for lunatics and was in immediate fear of pursuit. He resolved to summon medical advice as soon as the mind of his niece had been in some measure set at rest by the offices of the clergyman whose attendance she had so earnestly desired; and until this object had been attained, he did not venture to put any questions to her which might possibly, by reviving painful or horrible recollections, increase her agitation.

The clergyman soon arrived – a man of ascetic countenance and venerable age – one whom Gerard Douw respected much, forasmuch as he was a veteran polemic – though one, perhaps, more dreaded as a combatant than beloved as a Christian – of pure morality, subtle brain and frozen heart. He entered the chamber which communi-cated with that in which Rose reclined, and immediately on his arrival she requested him to pray for her, as for one who lay in the hands of Satan, and who could hope for deliverance only from heaven.

That our readers may distinctly understand all the circumstances of the event which we are about imperfectly to describe, it is necessary to state the relative position of the parties who were engaged in it. The old clergyman and Schalken were in the anteroom of which we have already spoken; Rose lay in the inner chamber, the door of which was open; and by the side of the bed, at her urgent desire, stood her guardian; a candle burned in the bedchamber, and three were lighted in the outer apartment.

The old man now cleared his voice, as if about to commence; but before he had time to begin, a sudden gust of air blew out the candle which served to illuminate the room in which the poor girl lay, and she, with hurried alarm, exclaimed: 'Godfrey, bring in another candle; the darkness is unsafe.'

Gerard Douw, forgetting for the moment her repeated injunctions in the immediate impulse, stepped from the bedchamber into the other, in order to supply what she desired.

'O God! do not go, dear uncle!' shrieked the unhappy girl; and at the same time she sprang from the bed and darted after him, in order, by her grasp, to detain him.

But the warning came too late, for scarcely had he passed the threshold, and hardly had his niece had time to utter the startling exclamation, when the door which divided the two rooms closed violently after him, as if swung to by a strong blast of wind.

Schalken and he both rushed to the door, but their united and desperate efforts could not avail so much as to shake it.

Shriek after shriek burst from the inner chamber, with all the piercing loudness of despairing terror. Schalken and Douw applied every energy and strained every nerve to force open the door; but all in vain.

There was no sound of struggling from within, but the screams seemed to increase in loudness, and at the same time they heard the bolts of the latticed window withdrawn, and the window itself grated upon the sill as if thrown open.

One LAST shriek, so long and piercing and agonised as to be scarcely human, swelled from the room, and suddenly there followed a deathlike silence.

A light step was heard crossing the floor, as if from the bed to the window; and almost at the same instant the door gave way, and, yielding to the pressure of the external applicants, nearly precipitated them into the room. It was empty. The window was open, and Schalken sprang to a chair and gazed out upon the street and canal below. He saw no form, but he beheld, or thought he beheld, the waters of the broad canal beneath settling ring after ring in heavy circular ripples, as if a moment before disturbed by the immersion of some large and heavy mass.

No trace of Rose was ever after discovered, nor was anything certain respecting her mysterious wooer detected or even suspected; no clue whereby to trace the intricacies of the labyrinth and to arrive at a distinct conclusion was to be found. But an incident occurred which, though it will not be received by our rational readers as at all approaching to evidence upon the matter, nevertheless produced a strong and a lasting impression upon the mind of Schalken.

Many years after the events which we have detailed, Schalken, then remotely situated, received an intimation of his father's death, and of his intended burial upon a fixed day in the church of Rotterdam. It was necessary that a very considerable journey should be performed by the funeral procession, which, as it will readily be believed, was not very numerously attended. Schalken with difficulty arrived in Rotterdam late in the day upon which the funeral was appointed to take place. The procession had not then arrived. Evening closed in, and still it did not appear.

Schalken strolled down to the church; he found it open – notice of the arrival of the funeral had been given – and the vault in which the body was to be laid had been prepared. The official who corresponds to our sexton, on seeing a well-dressed gentleman, whose object was to attend the expected funeral, pacing the aisle of the church, hospitably invited him to share with him the comforts of a blazing wood fire, which, as was his custom in wintertime upon such occasions, he had kindled on the hearth of a chamber which communicated, by a flight of steps, with the vaults below.

In this chamber Schalken and his entertainer seated themselves, and the sexton, after some fruitless attempts to engage his guest in conversation, was obliged to apply himself to his tobacco-pipe and can to solace his solitude.

In spite of his grief and cares, the fatigues of a rapid journey of nearly forty hours gradually overcame the mind and body of Godfrey Schalken and he sank into a deep sleep, from which he was awakened by someone shaking him gently by the shoulder. He first thought that the old sexton had called him, but the latter was no longer in the room.

He roused himself, and as soon as he could clearly see what was around him, he perceived a female form, clothed in a kind of light robe of muslin, part of which was so disposed as to act as a veil, and carrying in her hand a lamp. She was moving rather away from him and towards the flight of steps which conducted towards the vaults.

Schalken felt a vague alarm at the sight of this figure, and at the same time an irresistible impulse to follow its guidance. He followed it towards the vaults, but when it reached the head of the stairs, he paused; the figure paused also, and, turning gently round, displayed, by the light of the lamp it carried, the face and features of his first love, Rose Velderkaust. There was nothing horrible, or even sad, in the countenance. On the contrary, it wore the same arch smile which used to enchant the artist long before, in his happy days.

A feeling of awe and of interest, too intense to be resisted, prompted him to follow the spectre, if spectre it were. She descended the stairs – he followed; and, turning to the left, through a narrow passage, she led him, to his infinite surprise, into what appeared to be an old-fashioned Dutch apartment, such as the pictures of Gerard Douw have served to immortalise.

Abundance of costly antique furniture was disposed about the room, and in one corner stood a four-post bed, with heavy black-cloth curtains around it; the figure frequently turned towards him with the same arch smile; and when she came to the side of the bed, she drew the curtains, and by the light of the lamp which she held towards its contents, she disclosed to the horror-stricken painter, sitting bolt upright in the bed, the livid and demoniac form of Vanderhausen. Schalken had hardly seen him when he fell senseless upon the floor, where he lay until discovered, on the next morning, by persons employed in closing the passages into the vaults. He was lying in a cell of considerable size, which had not been disturbed for a long time, and he had fallen beside a large coffin which was supported upon small stone pillars, a security against the attacks of vermin.

To his dying day Schalken was satisfied of the reality of the vision which he had witnessed, and he has left behind him a curious evidence of the impression which it wrought upon his fancy in a painting executed shortly after the event we have narrated, and which is valuable as exhibiting not only the peculiarities which have made Schalken's pictures sought after, but even more so as present-ing a portrait, as close and faithful as one taken from memory can be, of his early love, Rose Velderkaust, whose mysterious fate must ever remain a matter of speculation.

The picture represents a chamber of antique masonry, such as might be found in most old cathedrals, and is lighted faintly by a lamp carried in the hand of a female figure, such as we have above attempted to describe; and in the background, and to the left of him who examines the painting, there stands the form of a man appar-ently aroused from sleep, and by his attitude, his hand being laid upon his sword, exhibiting considerable alarm: this last figure is illuminated only by the expiring glare of a wood or charcoal fire.

The whole production exhibits a beautiful specimen of that artful and singular distribution of light and shade which has rendered the name of Schalken immortal among the artists of his country. This tale is traditionary, and the reader will easily perceive, by our studiously omitting to heighten many points of the narrative, when a little additional colouring might have added effect to the recital, that we have desired to lay before him, not a figment of the brain, but a curious tradition connected with, and belonging to, the biography of a famous artist.

Ethan Brand

A Chapter from an Abortive Romance

NATHANIEL HAWTHORNE

BARTRAM THE LIME-BURNER, a rough, heavy-looking man, begrimed with charcoal, sat watching his kiln at nightfall, while his little son played at building houses with the scattered fragments of marble, when, on the hillside below them, they heard a roar of laughter, not mirthful, but slow, and even solemn, like a wind shaking the boughs of the forest.

'Father, what is that?' asked the little boy, leaving his play and pressing betwixt his father's knees.

'Oh, some drunken man, I suppose,' answered the lime-burner; 'some merry fellow from the bar-room in the village, who dared not laugh loud enough within doors, lest he should blow the roof of the house off. So here he is, shaking his jolly sides at the foot of Graylock.'

'But, father,' said the child, more sensitive than the obtuse, middle-aged clown, 'he does not laugh like a man that is glad. So the noise frightens me!'

'Don't be a fool, child!' cried his father, gruffly. 'You will never make a man, I do believe; there is too much of your mother in you. I have known the rustling of a leaf startle you. Hark! Here comes the merry fellow, now. You shall see that there is no harm in him.'

Bartram and his little son, while they were talking thus, sat watching the same limekiln that had been the scene of Ethan Brand's solitary and meditative life before he began his search for the Unpardonable Sin. Many years, as we have seen, had now elapsed, since that portentous night when the IDEA was first developed. The kiln, however, on the mountainside, stood unimpaired, and was in nothing changed since he had thrown his dark thoughts into the intense glow of its furnace, and melted them, as it were, into the one thought that took possession of his life. It was a rude, round, tower-like structure, about twenty feet high, heavily built of rough stones, and with a hillock of earth heaped about the larger part of its circumference; so that the blocks and fragments of marble might be drawn by cart-loads and thrown in at the top. There was an opening at the bottom of the tower like an oven-mouth, but large enough to admit a man in a stooping posture, and provided with a massive iron door. With the smoke and jets of flame issuing from the chinks and crevices of this door, which seemed to give admittance into the hillside, it resembled nothing so much as the private entrance to the infernal regions, which the shepherds of the Delectable Mountains were accustomed to show to pilgrims.

There are many such lime-kilns, in that tract of country, for the purpose of burning the white marble which composes a large part of the substance of the hills. Some of them, built years ago and long deserted, with weeds growing in the vacant round of the interior, which is open to the sky, and grass and wild-flowers rooting themselves into the chinks of the stones, look already like relics of antiquity, and may yet be overspread with the lichens of centuries to come. Others, where the lime-burner still feeds his daily and night-long fire, afford points of interest to the wanderer among the hills, who seats himself on a log of wood or a fragment of marble to hold a chat with the solitary man. It is a lonesome, and, when the character is inclined to thought, may be an intensely thoughtful occupation; as it proved in the case of Ethan Brand, who had mused to such strange purpose in days gone by while the fire in this very kiln was burning.

The man who now watched the fire was of a different order, and troubled himself with no thoughts save the very few that were requisite to his business. At frequent intervals, he flung back the clashing weight of the iron door, and, turning his face from the insufferable glare, thrust in huge logs of oak or stirred the immense brands with a long pole. Within the furnace were seen the curling and riotous flames, and the burning marble, almost molten with the intensity of heat; while without, the reflection of the fire quivered on the dark intricacy of the surrounding forest, and showed in the foreground a bright and ruddy little picture of the hut, the spring beside its door, the athletic and coal-begrimed figure of the lime-burner, and the half-frightened child, shrinking into the protection of his father's shadow. And when again the iron door was closed, then reappeared the tender light of the half-full moon, which vainly strove to trace out the indistinct shapes of the neighbouring mountains; and, in the upper sky, there was a flitting congregation of clouds, still faintly tinged with the rosy sunset, though thus far down into the valley the sunshine had vanished long and long ago.

The little boy now crept still closer to his father, as footsteps were heard ascending the hillside, and a human form thrust aside the bushes that clustered beneath the trees.

'Halloo! who is it?' cried the lime-burner, vexed at his son's timidity, yet half infected by it. 'Come forward and show yourself, like a man, or I'll fling this chunk of marble at your head!'

'You offer me a rough welcome,' said a gloomy voice, as the unknown man drew nigh. 'Yet I neither claim nor desire a kinder one, even at my own fireside.'

To obtain a distincter view, Bartram threw open the iron door of the kiln, whence immediately issued a gush of fierce light that smote full upon the stranger's face and figure. To a careless eye there appeared nothing very remarkable in his aspect, which was that of a man in a coarse, brown, country-made suit of clothes, tall and thin, with the staff and heavy shoes of a wayfarer. As he advanced, he fixed his eyes – which were very bright – intently upon the brightness of the furnace, as if he beheld, or expected to behold, some object worthy of note within it.

'Good-evening, stranger,' said the lime-burner; 'whence come you, so late in the day?'

'I come from my search,' answered the wayfarer; 'for, at last, it is finished.'

'Drunk! – or crazy!' muttered Bartram to himself. 'I shall have trouble with the fellow. The sooner I drive him away the better.'

The little boy, all in a tremble, whispered to his father and begged him to shut the door of the kiln, so that there might not be so much light, for there was something in the man's face which he was afraid to look at, yet could not look away from. And, indeed, even the lime-burner's dull and torpid sense began to be impressed by an indescribable something in that thin, rugged, thoughtful visage, with the grizzled hair hanging wildly about it, and those deeply-sunken eyes, which gleamed like fires within the entrance of a mysterious cavern. But, as he closed the door, the stranger turned towards him and spoke in a quiet, familiar way that made Bartram feel as if he were a sane and sensible man, after all.

'Your task draws to an end, I see,' said he. 'This marble has already been burning three days. A few hours more will convert the stone to lime.'

'Why, who are you?' exclaimed the lime-burner. 'You seem as well acquainted with my business as I am myself.'

'And well I may be,' said the stranger; 'for I followed the same craft many a long year, and here, too, on this very spot. But you are a newcomer in these parts. Did you never hear of Ethan Brand?'

'The man that went in search of the Unpardonable Sin?' asked Bartram, with a laugh.

'The same,' answered the stranger. 'He has found what he sought, and therefore he comes back again.'

'What! then you are Ethan Brand himself?' cried the lime-burner, in amazement. 'I am a newcomer here, as you say, and they call it eighteen years since you left the foot of Graylock. But, I can tell you, the good folks still talk about Ethan Brand in the village yonder, and what a strange errand took him away from his limekiln. Well, and so you have found the Unpardonable Sin?'

'Even so!' said the stranger, calmly.

'If the question is a fair one,' proceeded Bartram, 'where might it be?'

Ethan Brand laid his finger on his own heart.

'Here!' replied he.

And then, without mirth in his countenance, but as if moved by an involuntary recognition of the infinite absurdity of seeking throughout the world for what was the closest of all things to himself, and looking into every heart, save his own, for what is hidden in no other breast, he broke into a laugh of scorn. It was the same slow, heavy laugh that had almost appalled the lime-burner when it heralded the wayfarer's approach.

The solitary mountainside was made dismal by it. Laughter, when out of place, mistimed, or bursting forth from a disordered state of feeling, may be the most terrible modulation of the human voice. The laughter of one asleep, even if it be a little child – the madman's laugh – the wild, screaming laugh of a born idiot – are sounds that we sometimes tremble to hear, and would always willingly forget. Poets have imagined no utterance of fiends or hobgoblins so fearfully appropriate as a laugh. And even the obtuse lime-burner felt his nerves shaken as this strange man looked inward at his own heart and burst into laughter that rolled away into the night and was indistinctly reverberated among the hills.

'Joe,' said he to his little son, 'scamper down to the tavern in the village, and tell the jolly fellows there that Ethan Brand has come back, and that he has found the Unpardonable Sin!'

The boy darted away on his errand, to which Ethan Brand made no objection – indeed, seemed hardly to notice. He sat on a log of wood looking steadfastly at the iron door of the kiln. When the child was out of sight, and his swift and light footsteps ceased to be heard treading first on the fallen leaves and then on the rocky mountain-path, the lime-burner began to regret his departure. He felt that the little fellow's presence had been a barrier between his guest and himself, and that he must now deal, heart to heart, with a man who, on his own confession, had committed the one crime for which Heaven could afford no mercy. That crime, in its indistinct blackness, seemed to overshadow him. The lime-burner's own sins rose up within him, and made his memory riotous with a throng of evil shapes that asserted their kindred with the Master Sin, whatever it might be, which it was within the scope of man's corrupted nature to conceive and cherish. They were all of one family; they went to and fro between his breast and Ethan Brand's, and carried dark greetings from one to the other.

Then Bartram remembered the stories which had grown traditionary in reference to this strange man, who had come upon him like a shadow of the night, and was making himself at home in his old place, after so long absence that the dead people, dead and buried for years, would have had more right to be at home, in any familiar spot, than he. Ethan Brand, it was said, had conversed with Satan himself in the lurid blaze of this very kiln. The legend had been matter of mirth heretofore, but looked grisly now. According to this tale, before Ethan Brand departed on his search, he had been accustomed to evoke a fiend from the hot furnace of the limekiln, night after night, in order to confer with him about the Unpardonable Sin; the man and the fiend each labouring to frame the image of some mode of guilt which could neither be atoned for nor forgiven. And, with the first gleam of light upon the mountain-top, the fiend crept in at the iron door, there to abide the intensest element of fire until again summoned forth to share in the dreadful task of extending man's possible guilt beyond the scope of Heaven's else infinite mercy.

While the lime-burner was struggling with the horror of these thoughts, Ethan Brand rose from the log and flung open the door of the kiln. The action was in such accordance with the idea in Bartram's mind that he almost expected to see the Evil One issue forth red-hot from the raging furnace.

'Hold! hold!' cried he, with a tremulous attempt to laugh; for he was ashamed of his fears, although they overmastered him. 'Don't, for mercy's sake, bring out your devil now!'

'Man!' sternly replied Ethan Brand, 'what need have I of the devil? I have left him behind me, on my track. It is with such halfway sinners as you that he busies himself. Fear not, because I open the door. I do but act by old custom, and am going to trim your fire, like a lime-burner, as I was once.'

He stirred the vast coals, thrust in more wood, and bent forward to gaze into the hollow prison-house of the fire, regardless of the fierce glow that reddened upon his face. The lime-burner sat watching him, and half suspected his strange guest of a purpose, if not to evoke a fiend, at least to plunge bodily into the flames, and thus vanish from the sight of man. Ethan Brand, however, drew quietly back, and closed the door of the kiln.

'I have looked,' said he, 'into many a human heart that was seven times hotter with sinful passions than yonder furnace is with fire. But I found not there what I sought. No, not the Unpardonable Sin!'

'What is the Unpardonable Sin?' asked the lime-burner; and then he shrank further from his companion, trembling lest his question should be answered.

'It is a sin that grew within my own breast,' replied Ethan Brand, standing erect, with a pride that distinguishes all enthusiasts of his stamp. 'A sin that grew nowhere else! The sin of an intellect that triumphed over the sense of brotherhood with man and reverence for God, and sacrificed everything to its own mighty claims! The only sin that deserves a recompense of immortal agony! Freely, were it to do again, would I incur the guilt. Unshrinkingly I accept the retribution!'

'The man's head is turned,' muttered the lime-burner to himself. 'He may be a sinner, like the rest of us – nothing more likely – but, I'll be sworn, he is a madman too.'

Nevertheless he felt uncomfortable at his situation, alone with Ethan Brand on the wild mountainside, and was right glad to hear the rough murmur of tongues and the footsteps of what seemed a pretty numerous party stumbling over the stones and rustling through the underbrush. Soon appeared the whole lazy regiment that was wont to infest the village tavern, comprehending three or four individuals who had drunk flip beside the bar-room fire through all the winters, and smoked their pipes beneath the stoop through all the summers, since Ethan Brand's departure. Laughing boisterously, and mingling all their voices together in unceremonious talk, they now burst into the moonshine and narrow streaks of firelight that illuminated the open space before the limekiln. Bartram set the door ajar again, flooding the spot with light that the whole company might get a fair view of Ethan Brand and he of them.

There, among other old acquaintances, was a once ubiquitous man, now almost extinct, but whom we were formerly sure to encounter at the hotel of every thriving village throughout the country. It was the stage-agent. The present specimen of the genus

was a wilted and smoke-dried man, wrinkled and red-nosed, in a
smartly cut, brown, bob-tailed coat, with brass buttons, who, for a
length of time unknown, had kept his desk and corner in the bar-
room, and was still puffing what seemed to be the same cigar that he
had lighted twenty years before. He had great fame as a dry joker,
though, perhaps, less on account of any intrinsic humour than from
a certain flavour of brandy-toddy and tobacco-smoke which im-
pregnated all his ideas and expressions as well as his person. Another
well-remembered though strangely-altered face was that of Lawyer
Giles, as people still called him in courtesy; an elderly ragamuffin, in
his soiled shirtsleeves and tow-cloth trousers. This poor fellow had
been an attorney, in what he called his better days – a sharp
practitioner, in great vogue among the village litigants; but flip, and
sling, and toddy, and cocktails, imbibed at all hours, morning, noon
and night, had caused him to slide from intellectual to various kinds
and degrees of bodily labour, till at last, to adopt his own phrase, he
slid into a soap-vat. In other words, Giles was now a soap-boiler, in
a small way. He had come to be but the fragment of a human being,
a part of one foot having been chopped off by an axe, and an entire
hand torn away by the devilish grip of a steam-engine. Yet though
the corporeal hand was gone, a spiritual member remained; for,
stretching forth the stump, Giles steadfastly averred that he felt an
invisible thumb and fingers with as vivid a sensation as before the
real ones were amputated. A maimed and miserable wretch he was;
but one, nevertheless, whom the world could not trample on, and
had no right to scorn, either in this or any previous stage of his
misfortunes, since he had still kept up the courage and spirit of a
man, asked nothing in charity, and with his one hand – and that the
left one – fought a stern battle against want and hostile circumstances.

    Among the throng, too, came another personage, who with certain
points of similarity to Lawyer Giles had many more of difference. It
was the village doctor; a man of some fifty years, whom, at an earlier
period of his life, we introduced as paying a professional visit to Ethan
Brand during the latter's supposed insanity. He was now a purple-
visaged, rude and brutal, yet half-gentlemanly figure, with something
wild, ruined and desperate in his talk, and in all the details of his
gesture and manners. Brandy possessed this man like an evil spirit and
made him as surly and savage as a wild beast and as miserable as a lost
soul; but there was supposed to be in him such wonderful skill, such
native gifts of healing, beyond any which medical science could
impart, that society caught hold of him, and would not let him sink

out of its reach. So, swaying to and fro upon his horse, and grumbling thick accents at the bedside, he visited all the sick chambers for miles about among the mountain towns, and sometimes raised a dying man, as it were, by a miracle, or quite as often, no doubt, sent his patient to a grave that was dug many a year too soon. The doctor had an everlasting pipe in his mouth, and as somebody said, in allusion to his habit of swearing, it was always alight with hellfire.

These three worthies pressed forward and greeted Ethan Brand each after his own fashion, earnestly inviting him to partake of the contents of a certain black bottle, in which, as they averred, he would find something far better worth seeking for than the Unpardonable Sin. No mind, which has wrought itself by intense and solitary meditation into a high state of enthusiasm, can endure the kind of contact with low and vulgar modes of thought and feeling to which Ethan Brand was now subjected. It made him doubt – and, strange to say, it was a painful doubt – whether he had indeed found the Unpardonable Sin, and found it within himself. The whole question on which he had exhausted life, and more than life, looked like a delusion.

'Leave me,' he said, bitterly, 'ye brute beasts, that have made yourselves so, shrivelling up your souls with fiery liquors! I have done with you. Years and years ago, I groped into your hearts and found nothing there for my purpose. Get ye gone!'

'Why, you uncivil scoundrel,' cried the fierce doctor, 'is that the way you respond to the kindness of your best friends? Then let me tell you the truth. You have no more found the Unpardonable Sin than yonder boy Joe has. You are but a crazy fellow – I told you so twenty years ago – neither better nor worse than a crazy fellow, and the fit companion of old Humphrey here!'

He pointed to an old man, shabbily dressed, with long white hair, thin visage and unsteady eyes. For some years past this aged person had been wandering about among the hills, enquiring of all travellers whom he met for his daughter. The girl, it seemed, had gone off with a company of circus-performers; and occasionally tidings of her came to the village, and fine stories were told of her glittering appearance as she rode on horseback in the ring or performed marvellous feats on the tightrope.

The white-haired father now approached Ethan Brand, and gazed unsteadily into his face.

'They tell me you have been all over the earth,' said he, wringing his hands with earnestness. 'You must have seen my daughter, for she makes a grand figure in the world, and everybody goes to see her.

Did she send any word to her old father, or say when she was coming back?'

Ethan Brand's eye quailed beneath the old man's. That daughter, from whom he so earnestly desired a word of greeting, was the Esther of our tale, the very girl whom, with such cold and remorseless purpose, Ethan Brand had made the subject of a psychological experiment, and wasted, absorbed and perhaps annihilated her soul in the process.

'Yes,' murmured he, turning away from the hoary wanderer; 'it is no delusion. There is an Unpardonable Sin!'

While these things were passing, a merry scene was going forward in the area of cheerful light, beside the spring and before the door of the hut. A number of the youth of the village, young men and girls, had hurried up the hillside, impelled by curiosity to see Ethan Brand, the hero of so many a legend familiar to their childhood. Finding nothing, however, very remarkable in his aspect – nothing but a sunburnt wayfarer, in plain garb and dusty shoes, who sat looking into the fire, as if he fancied pictures among the coals – these young people speedily grew tired of observing him. As it happened, there was other amusement at hand. An old German Jew, travelling with a diorama on his back, was passing down the mountain-road towards the village just as the party turned aside from it, and, in hopes of eking out the profits of the day, the showman had kept them company to the limekiln.

'Come, old Dutchman,' cried one of the young men, 'let us see your pictures, if you can swear they are worth looking at!'

'Oh, yes, captain,' answered the Jew – whether as a matter of courtesy or craft, he styled everybody captain – 'I shall show you, indeed, some very superb pictures!'

So, placing his box in a proper position, he invited the young men and girls to look through the glass orifices of the machine, and proceeded to exhibit a series of the most outrageous scratchings and daubings, as specimens of the fine arts, that ever an itinerant showman had the face to impose upon his circle of spectators. The pictures were worn out, moreover, tattered, full of cracks and wrinkles, dingy with tobacco-smoke and otherwise in a most pitiable condition. Some purported to be cities, public edifices and ruined castles in Europe; others represented Napoleon's battles and Nelson's sea-fights; and in the midst of these would be seen a gigantic, brown, hairy hand – which might have been mistaken for the Hand of Destiny, though, in truth, it was only the showman's – pointing its forefinger to various scenes of the conflict, while its owner gave historical illustrations. When, with much merriment at its abominable deficiency of merit, the exhibition was concluded, the German bade little Joe put his head into the box. Viewed through the magnifying-glasses, the boy's round, rosy visage assumed the strangest imaginable aspect of an immense Titanic child, the mouth grinning broadly and the eyes and every other feature overflowing with fun at the joke. Suddenly, however, that merry face turned pale, and its expression changed to horror, for this easily impressed and excitable child had become sensible that the eye of Ethan Brand was fixed upon him through the glass.

'You make the little man to be afraid, captain,' said the German Jew, turning up the dark and strong outline of his visage from his stooping posture. 'But look again, and, by chance, I shall cause you to see somewhat that is very fine, upon my word!'

Ethan Brand gazed into the box for an instant and the,n starting back, looked fixedly at the German. What had he seen? Nothing, apparently; for a curious youth, who had peeped in almost at the same moment, beheld only a vacant space of canvas.

'I remember you now,' muttered Ethan Brand to the showman.

'Ah, captain,' whispered the Jew of Nuremburg, with a dark smile, 'I find it to be a heavy matter in my show-box – this Unpardonable Sin! By my faith, captain, it has wearied my shoulders this long day, to carry it over the mountain.'

'Peace,' answered Ethan Brand, sternly, 'or get thee into the furnace yonder!'

The Jew's exhibition had scarcely concluded, when a great, elderly dog – who seemed to be his own master, as no person in the company laid claim to him – saw fit to render himself the object of public notice. Hitherto, he had shown himself a very quiet, well-disposed old dog, going round from one to another, and, by way of being sociable, offering his rough head to be patted by any kindly hand that would take so much trouble. But now, all of a sudden, this grave and venerable quadruped, of his own mere notion, and without the slightest suggestion from anybody else, began to run round after his tail, which, to heighten the absurdity of the proceeding, was a great deal shorter than it should have been. Never was seen such headlong eagerness in pursuit of an object that could not possibly be attained; never was heard such a tremendous outbreak of growling, snarling, barking and snapping – as if one end of the ridiculous brute's body were at deadly and most unforgivable enmity with the other. Faster and faster, round about went the cur; and faster and still faster fled the unapproachable brevity of his tail; and louder and fiercer grew his yells of rage and animosity; until, utterly exhausted, and as far from the goal as ever, the foolish old dog ceased his performance as suddenly as he had begun it. The next moment he was as mild, quiet, sensible and respectable in his deportment as when he first scraped acquaintance with the company.

As may be supposed, the exhibition was greeted with universal laughter, clapping of hands and shouts of encore, to which the canine performer responded by wagging all that there was to wag of his tail but appeared totally unable to repeat his very successful effort to amuse the spectators.

Meanwhile, Ethan Brand had resumed his seat upon the log, and moved, it might be, by a perception of some remote analogy between his own case and that of this self-pursuing cur, he broke into the awful laugh which, more than any other token, expressed the condition of his inward being. From that moment, the merriment of the party was at an end; they stood aghast, dreading lest the inauspicious sound should be reverberated around the horizon, and that mountain would thunder it to mountain, and so the horror be prolonged upon their ears. Then, whispering one to another that it was late – that the moon was almost down – that the August night was growing chill – they hurried homewards, leaving the lime-burner and little Joe to deal as they might with their unwelcome guest. Save for these three human beings, the open space on the hillside was a solitude, set in a vast gloom of forest. Beyond that darksome verge, the firelight glimmered on the stately trunks and almost black foliage of pines, intermixed with the lighter verdure of sapling oaks, maples and poplars, while here and there lay the gigantic corpses of dead trees, decaying on the leaf-strewn soil. And it seemed to little Joe – a timorous and imaginative child – that the silent forest was holding its breath, until some fearful thing should happen.

Ethan Brand thrust more wood into the fire, and closed the door of the kiln; then looking over his shoulder at the lime-burner and his son, he bade, rather than advised, them to rest.

'For myself, I cannot sleep,' said he. 'I have matters that it concerns me to meditate upon. I will watch the fire, as I used to do in the old time.'

'And call the devil out of the furnace to keep you company, I suppose,' muttered Bartram, who had been making intimate acquaintance with the black bottle above-mentioned. 'But watch, if you like, and call as many devils as you like! For my part, I shall be all the better for a snooze. Come, Joe!'

As the boy followed his father into the hut, he looked back at the wayfarer, and the tears came into his eyes, for his tender spirit had an intuition of the bleak and terrible loneliness in which this man had enveloped himself.

When they had gone, Ethan Brand sat listening to the crackling of the kindled wood, and looking at the little spirits of fire that issued through the chinks of the door. These trifles, however, once so familiar, had but the slightest hold of his attention, while deep within his mind he was reviewing the gradual but marvellous change that had been wrought upon him by the search to which he had devoted himself. He remembered how the night dew had fallen upon him – how the dark forest had whispered to him – how the stars had gleamed upon him – a simple and loving man, watching his fire in the years gone by, and ever musing as it burned. He remembered with what tenderness, with what love and sympathy for mankind, and what pity for human guilt and woe, he had first begun to contemplate those ideas which afterwards became the inspiration of his life; with what reverence he had then looked into the heart of man, viewing it as a temple originally divine, and, however desecrated, still to be held sacred by a brother; with what awful fear he had deprecated the success of his pursuit and prayed that the Unpardonable Sin might never be revealed to him. Then ensued that vast intellectual development, which, in its progress, disturbed the counterpoise between his mind and heart. The Idea that possessed his life had operated as a means of education; it had gone on cultivating his powers to the highest point of which they were susceptible; it had raised him from the level of an unlettered labourer to stand on a starlit eminence, whither the philosophers of the earth, laden with the lore of universities, might vainly strive to clamber after him. So much for the intellect! But where was the heart? That, indeed, had withered – had contracted – had hardened – had perished! It had ceased to partake of the universal throb. He had lost his hold of the magnetic chain of humanity. He was no longer a brother-man, opening the chambers or the dungeons of our common nature by the key of holy sympathy, which gave him a right to share in all its secrets; he was now a cold observer, looking on mankind as the subject of his experiment, and, at length, converting man and woman to be his puppets, and pulling the wires that moved them to such degrees of crime as were demanded for his study.

Thus Ethan Brand became a fiend. He began to be so from the moment that his moral nature had ceased to keep the pace of improvement with his intellect. And now, as his highest effort and inevitable development – as the bright and gorgeous flower, and rich, delicious fruit of his life's labour – he had produced the Unpardonable Sin!

'What more have I to seek? what more to achieve?' said Ethan Brand to himself. 'My task is done, and well done!'

Starting from the log with a certain alacrity in his gait, and ascending the hillock of earth that was raised against the stone circumference of the limekiln, he thus reached the top of the structure. It was a space of perhaps ten feet across, from edge to edge, presenting a view of the upper surface of the immense mass of broken marble with which the kiln was heaped. All these innumerable blocks and fragments of marble were red-hot and vividly on fire, sending up great spouts of blue flame, which quivered aloft and danced madly, as within a magic circle, and sank and rose again, with continual and multitudinous activity. As the lonely man bent forward over this terrible body of fire, the blasting heat smote up against his person with a breath that, it might be supposed, would have scorched and shrivelled him up in a moment.

Ethan Brand stood erect and raised his arms on high. The blue flames played upon his face and imparted the wild and ghastly light which alone could have suited its expression; it was that of a fiend on the verge of plunging into his gulf of intensest torment.

'O Mother Earth,' cried he, 'who art no more my mother, and into whose bosom this frame shall never be resolved! O mankind, whose brotherhood I have cast off, and trampled thy great heart beneath my feet! O stars of heaven, that shone on me of old, as if to light me onward and upward! – farewell, all, and for ever! Come, deadly element of fire – henceforth my familiar friend! Embrace me, as I do thee!'

That night the sound of a fearful peal of laughter rolled heavily through the sleep of the lime-burner and his little son; dim shapes of horror and anguish haunted their dreams, and seemed still present in the rude hovel when they opened their eyes to the daylight.

'Up, boy, up!' cried the lime-burner, staring about him. 'Thank heaven, the night is gone, at last; and rather than pass such another, I would watch my limekiln, wide awake, for a twelve-month. This Ethan Brand, with his humbug of an Unpardonable Sin, has done me no such mighty favour in taking my place!'

He issued from the hut, followed by little Joe, who kept fast hold of his father's hand. The early sunshine was already pouring its gold upon the mountain-tops; and though the valleys were still in shadow, they smiled cheerfully in the promise of the bright day that was hastening onward. The village, completely shut in by hills, which swelled away gently about it, looked as if it had rested peacefully in the hollow of the great hand of Providence. Every dwelling was distinctly visible; the little spires of the two churches pointed upwards, and caught a fore-glimmering of brightness from the sun-gilt skies upon their gilded weathercocks. The tavern was astir, and the figure of the old, smoke-dried stage-agent, cigar in mouth, was seen beneath the stoop. Old Graylock was glorified with a golden cloud upon his head. Scattered likewise over the breasts of the surrounding mountains there were heaps of hoary mist, in fantastic shapes, some of them far down into the valley, others high up towards the summits, and still others, of the same family of mist or cloud, hovering in the gold radiance of the upper atmosphere. Stepping from one to another of the clouds that rested on the hills, and thence to the loftier brotherhood that sailed in air, it seemed almost as if a mortal man might thus ascend into the heavenly regions. Earth was so mingled with sky that it was a daydream to look at it.

To supply that charm of the familiar and homely, which Nature so readily adopts into a scene like this, the stagecoach was rattling down the mountain-road, and the driver sounded his horn, while Echo caught up the notes and intertwined them into a rich and varied and elaborate harmony of which the original performer could lay claim to little share. The great hills played a concert among themselves, each contributing a strain of airy sweetness.

Little Joe's face brightened at once.

'Dear father,' cried he, skipping cheerily to and fro, 'that strange man is gone, and the sky and the mountains all seem glad of it!'

'Yes,' growled the lime-burner, with an oath, 'but he has let the fire go down, and no thanks to him if five hundred bushels of lime are not spoiled. If I catch the fellow hereabouts again, I shall feel like tossing him into the furnace!'

With his long pole in his hand, he ascended to the top of the kiln. After a moment's pause, he called to his son.

'Come up here, Joe!' said he.

So little Joe ran up the hillock, and stood by his father's side. The marble was all burnt into perfect snow-white lime. But on its surface, in the midst of the circle – snow-white too, and thoroughly converted into lime – lay a human skeleton, in the attitude of a person who, after long toil, lies down to long repose. Within the ribs – strange to say – was the shape of a human heart.

'Was the fellow's heart made of marble?' cried Bartram, in some perplexity at this phenomenon. 'At any rate, it is burnt into what looks like special good lime; and taking all the bones together, my kiln is half a bushel the richer for him.'

So saying, the rude lime-burner lifted his pole, and, letting it fall upon the skeleton, he caused the relics of Ethan Brand to be crumbled into fragments.

The Old Nurse's Story

ELIZABETH GASKELL

You know, my dears, that your mother was an orphan, and an only child; and I dare say you have heard that your grandfather was a clergyman up in Westmoreland, where I come from. I was just a girl in the village school, when, one day, your grandmother came in to ask the mistress if there was any scholar there who would do for a nursemaid; and mighty proud I was, I can tell ye, when the mistress called me up, and spoke to my being a good girl at my needle, and a steady, honest girl, and one whose parents were very respectable, though they might be poor. I thought I should like nothing better than to serve the pretty young lady, who was blushing as deep as I was as she spoke of the coming baby and what I should have to do with it. However, I see you don't care so much for this part of my story, as for what you think is to come, so I'll tell you at once. I was engaged and settled at the parsonage before Miss Rosamond (that was the baby, who is now your mother) was born. To be sure, I had little enough to do with her when she came, for she was never out of her mother's arms, and slept by her all night long; and proud enough was I sometimes when missis trusted her to me. There never was such a baby before or since, though you've all of you been fine enough in your turns; but for sweet, winning ways, you've none of you come up to your mother. She took after her mother, who was a real lady born; a Miss Furnivall, a granddaughter of Lord Furnivall's, in Northumberland. I believe she had neither brother nor sister, and had been brought up in my lord's family till she had married your grandfather, who was just a curate, son to a shopkeeper in Carlisle – but a clever, fine gentleman as ever was – and one who was a right-down hard worker in his parish, which was very wide, and scattered all abroad over the Westmoreland Fells. When your mother, little Miss Rosamond, was about four or five years old, both her parents died in a fortnight – one after the other. Ah! that was a sad time. My pretty young mistress and me was looking for another baby, when my master came home from one of his long rides, wet and tired, and took the fever he died of; and then she never held up her head again, but just lived to see her dead baby, and have it laid on her breast, before she sighed away her life. My mistress had asked me, on her deathbed, never to leave Miss Rosamond; but if she had never spoken a word, I would have gone with the little child to the end of the world.

The next thing, and before we had well stilled our sobs, the executors and guardians came to settle the affairs. They were my poor young mistress's own cousin, Lord Furnivall, and Mr Esthwaite, my master's brother, a shopkeeper in Manchester; not so well-to-do then as he was afterwards, and with a large family rising about him. Well! I don't know if it were their settling, or because of a letter my mistress wrote on her deathbed to her cousin, my lord; but somehow it was settled that Miss Rosamond and me were to go to Furnivall Manor House, in Northumberland; and my lord spoke as if it had been her mother's wish that she should live with his family, and as if he had no objections, for that one or two more or less could make no difference in so grand a household. So, though that was not the way in which I should have wished the coming of my bright and pretty pet to have been looked at – who was like a sunbeam in any family, be it never so grand – I was well pleased that all the folks in the Dale should stare and admire when they heard I was going to be young lady's maid at my Lord Furnivall's at Furnivall Manor.

But I made a mistake in thinking we were to go and live where my lord did. It turned out that the family had left Furnivall Manor House fifty years or more. I could not hear that my poor young mistress had ever been there, though she had been brought up in the family; and I was sorry for that, for I should have liked Miss Rosamond's youth to have passed where her mother's had been.

My lord's gentleman, from whom I asked as many questions as I durst, said that the Manor House was at the foot of the Cumberland Fells, and a very grand place; that an old Miss Furnivall, a great-aunt of my lord's, lived there, with only a few servants; but that it was a very healthy place, and my lord had thought that it would suit Miss Rosamond very well for a few years, and that her being there might perhaps amuse his old aunt.

I was bidden by my lord to have Miss Rosamond's things ready by a certain day. He was a stern, proud man, as they say all the Lords Furnivall were; and he never spoke a word more than was necessary. Folk did say he had loved my young mistress; but that, because she

knew that his father would object, she would never listen to him, and
married Mr Esthwaite; but I don't know. He never married, at any
rate. But he never took much notice of Miss Rosamond; which I
thought he might have done if he had cared for her dead mother. He
sent his gentleman with us to the Manor House, telling him to join
him at Newcastle that same evening; so there was no great length of
time for him to make us known to all the strangers before he, too,
shook us off; and we were left, two lonely young things (I was not
eighteen) in the great old Manor House. It seems like yesterday that
we drove there. We had left our own dear parsonage very early, and
we had both cried as if our hearts would break, though we were
travelling in my lord's carriage, which I thought so much of once.
And now it was long past noon on a September day, and we stopped
to change horses for the last time at a little smoky town, all full of
colliers and miners. Miss Rosamond had fallen asleep, but Mr Henry
told me to waken her, that she might see the park and the Manor
House as we drove up. I thought it rather a pity; but I did what he
bade me, for fear he should complain of me to my lord. We had left
all signs of a town, or even a village, and were then inside the gates of
a large, wild park – not like the parks here in the south, but with
rocks, and the noise of running water, and gnarled thorn-trees, and
old oaks, all white and peeled with age.

The road went up about two miles, and then we saw a great and
stately house, with many trees close around it, so close that in some
places their branches dragged against the walls when the wind blew,
and some hung broken down; for no one seemed to take much
charge of the place – to lop the wood or to keep the moss-covered
carriageway in order. Only in front of the house all was clear. The
great oval drive was without a weed; and neither tree nor creeper was
allowed to grow over the long, many-windowed front; at both sides
of which a wing projected, which were each the ends of other side
fronts; for the house, although it was so desolate, was even grander
than I expected. Behind it rose the Fells, which seemed unenclosed
and bare enough; and on the left hand of the house, as you stood
facing it, was a little, old-fashioned flower-garden, as I found out
afterwards. A door opened out upon it from the west front; it had
been scooped out of the thick, dark wood for some old Lady
Furnivall; but the branches of the great forest-trees had grown and
overshadowed it again, and there were very few flowers that would
live there at that time.

When we drove up to the great front entrance, and went into the
hall, I thought we should be lost – it was so large, and vast, and grand.

There was a chandelier all of bronze, hung down from the middle of the ceiling; and I had never seen one before, and looked at it all in amaze. Then, at one end of the hall, was a great fireplace, as large as the sides of the houses in my country, with massy andirons and dogs to hold the wood; and by it were heavy, old-fashioned sofas. At the opposite end of the hall, to the left as you went in – on the western side – was an organ built into the wall, and so large that it filled up the best part of that end. Beyond it, on the same side, was a door; and opposite, on each side of the fireplace, were also doors leading to the east front; but those I never went through as long as I stayed in the house, so I can't tell you what lay beyond.

The afternoon was closing in, and the hall, which had no fire lighted in it, looked dark and gloomy; but we did not stay there a moment. The old servant, who had opened the door for us, bowed to Mr Henry, and took us in through the door at the farther side of the great organ, and led us through several smaller halls and passages into the west drawing-room, where he said that Miss Furnivall was sitting. Poor little Miss Rosamond held very tight to me, as if she were scared and lost in that great place; and as for myself, I was not much better. The west drawing-room was very cheerful-looking, with a warm fire in it, and plenty of good, comfortable furniture about. Miss Furnivall was an old lady not far from eighty, I should think, but I do not know. She was thin and tall, and had a face as full of fine wrinkles as if they had been drawn all over it with a needle's point. Her eyes were very watchful, to make up, I suppose, for her being so deaf as to be obliged to use a trumpet. Sitting with her, working at the same great piece of tapestry, was Mrs Stark, her maid and companion, and almost as old as she was. She had lived with Miss Furnivall ever since they both were young, and now she seemed more like a friend than a servant; she looked so cold, and grey, and stony, as if she had never loved or cared for anyone; and I don't suppose she did care for anyone, except her mistress; and owing to the great deafness of the latter, Mrs Stark treated her very much as if she were a child. Mr Henry gave some message from my lord, and then he bowed goodbye to us all – taking no notice of my sweet little Miss Rosamond's outstretched hand – and left us standing there, being looked at by the two old ladies through their spectacles.

I was right glad when they rang for the old footman who had shown us in at first and told him to take us to our rooms. So we went out of that great drawing-room, and into another sitting-room, and out of that, and then up a great flight of stairs, and along a broad gallery – which was something like a library, having books all down

one side, and windows and writing-tables all down the other – till we
came to our rooms, which I was not sorry to hear were just over the
kitchens; for I began to think I should be lost in that wilderness of a
house. There was an old nursery, that had been used for all the little
lords and ladies long ago, with a pleasant fire burning in the grate,
and the kettle boiling on the hob, and tea-things spread out on the
table; and out of that room was the night-nursery, with a little crib
for Miss Rosamond close to my bed. And old James called up
Dorothy, his wife, to bid us welcome; and both he and she were so
hospitable and kind that by and by Miss Rosamond and me felt quite
at home; and by the time tea was over, she was sitting on Dorothy's
knee, and chattering away as fast as her little tongue could go. I soon
found out that Dorothy was from Westmoreland, and that bound
her and me together, as it were; and I would never wish to meet with
kinder people than were old James and his wife. James had lived
pretty nearly all his life in my lord's family, and thought there was no
one so grand as they. He even looked down a little on his wife;
because, till he had married her, she had never lived in any but a
farmer's household. But he was very fond of her, as well he might be.
They had one servant under them, to do all the rough work. Agnes
they called her; and she and me, and James and Dorothy, with Miss
Furnivall and Mrs Stark, made up the family; always remembering
my sweet little Miss Rosamond! I used to wonder what they had
done before she came, they thought so much of her now. Kitchen
and drawing-room, it was all the same. The hard, sad Miss Furnivall,
and the cold Mrs Stark, looked pleased when she came fluttering in
like a bird, playing and pranking hither and thither, with a continual
murmur and pretty prattle of gladness. I am sure, they were sorry
many a time when she flitted away into the kitchen, though they
were too proud to ask her to stay with them, and were a little
surprised at her taste; though to be sure, as Mrs Stark said, it was not
to be wondered at, remembering what stock her father had come of.
The great, old rambling house was a famous place for little Miss
Rosamond. She made expeditions all over it, with me at her heels; all,
except the east wing, which was never opened, and whither we never
thought of going. But in the western and northern parts was many a
pleasant room; full of things that were curiosities to us, though they
might not have been to people who had seen more. The windows
were darkened by the sweeping boughs of the trees and the ivy which
had overgrown them; but, in the green gloom, we could manage to
see old china jars and carved ivory boxes, and great heavy books, and,
above all, the old pictures!

Once, I remember, my darling would have Dorothy go with us to tell us who they all were; for they were all portraits of some of my lord's family, though Dorothy could not tell us the names of every one. We had gone through most of the rooms, when we came to the old state drawing-room over the hall, and there was a picture of Miss Furnivall; or, as she was called in those days, Miss Grace, for she was the younger sister. Such a beauty she must have been! but with such a set, proud look, and such scorn looking out of her handsome eyes, with her eyebrows just a little raised, as if she wondered how anyone could have the impertinence to look at her, and her lip curled at us, as we stood there gazing. She had a dress on, the like of which I had never seen before, but it was all the fashion when she was young: a hat of some soft white stuff like beaver, pulled a little over her brows, and a beautiful plume of feathers sweeping round it on one side; and her gown of blue satin was open in front to a quilted white stomacher.

'Well, to be sure!' said I, when I had gazed my fill. 'Flesh is grass,[1] they do say; but who would have thought that Miss Furnivall had been such an out-and-out beauty, to see her now?'

'Yes,' said Dorothy. 'Folks change sadly. But if what my master's father used to say was true, Miss Furnivall, the elder sister, was handsomer than Miss Grace. Her picture is here somewhere; but, if I show it you, you must never let on, even to James, that you have seen it. Can the little lady hold her tongue, think you?' asked she.

I was not so sure, for she was such a little sweet, bold, open-spoken child, so I set her to hide herself; and then I helped Dorothy to turn a great picture that leaned with its face towards the wall and was not hung up as the others were. To be sure, it beat Miss Grace for beauty; and, I think, for scornful pride, too, though in that matter it might be hard to choose. I could have looked at it an hour, but Dorothy seemed half frightened at having shown it to me, and hurried it back again, and bade me run and find Miss Rosamond, for that there were some ugly places about the house, where she should like ill for the child to go. I was a brave, high-spirited girl, and thought little of what the old woman said, for I liked hide-and-seek as well as any child in the parish; so off I ran to find my little one.

As winter drew on, and the days grew shorter, I was sometimes almost certain that I heard a noise as if someone was playing on the great organ in the hall. I did not hear it every evening; but, certainly, I did very often, usually when I was sitting with Miss Rosamond, after I had put her to bed and was keeping quite still and silent in the bedroom. Then I used to hear it booming and swelling away in the

distance. The first night, when I went down to my supper, I asked
Dorothy who had been playing music, and James said very shortly
that I was a gowk² to take the wind soughing among the trees for
music; but I saw Dorothy look at him very fearfully, and Bessy, the
kitchen-maid, said something beneath her breath, and went quite
white. I saw they did not like my question, so I held my peace till I
was with Dorothy alone, when I knew I could get a good deal out of
her. So, the next day I watched my time, and I coaxed and asked her
who it was that played the organ; for I knew that it was the organ and
not the wind well enough, for all I had kept silence before James. But
Dorothy had had her lesson, I'll warrant, and never a word could I
get from her. So then I tried Bessy, though I had always held my
head rather above her, as I was evened to James and Dorothy, and
she was little better than their servant. So she said I must never,
never tell; and if ever I told, I was never to say *she* had told me; but it
was a very strange noise, and she had heard it many a time, but most
of all on winter nights and before storms; and folks did say it was the
old lord playing on the great organ in the hall, just as he used to do
when he was alive; but who the old lord was, or why he played, and
why he played on stormy winter evenings in particular, she either
could not or would not tell me. Well! I told you I had a brave heart;
and I thought it was rather pleasant to have that grand music rolling
about the house, let who would be the player; for now it rose above
the great gusts of wind, and wailed and triumphed just like a living
creature, and then it fell to a softness most complete, only it was
always music, and tunes, so it was nonsense to call it the wind. I
thought at first that it might be Miss Furnivall who played, unknown
to Bessy; but one day, when I was in the hall by myself, I opened the
organ and peeped all about it and around it, as I had done to the
organ in Crosthwaite Church once before, and I saw it was all broken
and destroyed inside, though it looked so brave and fine; and then,
though it was noonday, my flesh began to creep a little, and I shut it
up and ran away pretty quickly to my own bright nursery; and I did
not like hearing the music for some time after that, any more than
James and Dorothy did. All this time Miss Rosamond was making
herself more and more beloved. The old ladies liked her to dine with
them at their early dinner. James stood behind Miss Furnivall's
chair, and I behind Miss Rosamond's, all in state; and after dinner
she would play about in a corner of the great drawing-room as still as
any mouse, while Miss Furnivall slept, and I had my dinner in the
kitchen. But she was glad enough to come to me in the nursery
afterwards; for, as she said, Miss Furnivall was so sad, and Mrs Stark

so dull; but she and I were merry enough; and, by and by, I got not to care for that weird rolling music, which did one no harm, if we did not know where it came from.

That winter was very cold. In the middle of October the frosts began, and lasted many, many weeks. I remember one day, at dinner, Miss Furnivall lifted up her sad, heavy eyes, and said to Mrs Stark, 'I am afraid we shall have a terrible winter,' in a strange kind of meaning way. But Mrs Stark pretended not to hear, and talked very loud of something else. My little lady and I did not care for the frost; not we! As long as it was dry, we climbed up the steep brows behind the house, and went up on the Fells, which were bleak and bare enough, and there we ran races in the fresh, sharp air; and once we came down by a new path, that took us past the two old gnarled holly trees, which grew about halfway down by the east side of the house. But the days grew shorter and shorter, and the old lord, if it was he, played away, more and more stormily and sadly, on the great organ. One Sunday afternoon – it must have been towards the end of November – I asked Dorothy to take charge of little missy when she came out of the drawing-room, after Miss Furnivall had had her nap; for it was too cold to take her with me to church, and yet I wanted to go. And Dorothy was glad enough to promise, and was so fond of the child, that all seemed well; and Bessy and I set off very briskly, though the sky hung heavy and black over the white earth, as if the night had never fully gone away, and the air, though still, was very biting and keen.

'We shall have a fall of snow,' said Bessy to me. And sure enough, even while we were in church, it came down thick, in great large flakes – so thick, it almost darkened the windows. It had stopped snowing before we came out, but it lay soft, thick and deep beneath our feet as we tramped home. Before we got to the hall, the moon rose, and I think it was lighter then – what with the moon, and what with the white dazzling snow – than it had been when we went to church, between two and three o'clock. I have not told you that Miss Furnivall and Mrs Stark never went to church; they used to read the prayers together, in their quiet, gloomy way; they seemed to feel the Sunday very long without their tapestry-work to be busy at. So when I went to Dorothy in the kitchen, to fetch Miss Rosamond and take her upstairs with me, I did not much wonder when the old woman told me that the ladies had kept the child with them, and that she had never come to the kitchen, as I had bidden her, when she was tired of behaving pretty in the drawing-room. So I took off my things and went to find her, and bring her to her supper in the nursery. But when I went into the best drawing-room, there sat the two old ladies, very still and quiet, dropping out a word now and then, but looking as if nothing so bright and merry as Miss Rosamond had ever been near them. Still I thought she might be hiding from me – it was one of her pretty ways – and that she had persuaded them to look as if they knew nothing about her; so I went softly peeping under this sofa, and behind that chair, making believe I was sadly frightened at not finding her.

'What's the matter, Hester?' said Mrs Stark sharply. I don't know if Miss Furnivall had seen me, for, as I told you, she was very deaf, and she sat quite still, idly staring into the fire, with her hopeless face. 'I'm only looking for my little Rosy Posy,' replied I, still thinking that the child was there, and near me, though I could not see her.

'Miss Rosamond is not here,' said Mrs Stark. 'She went away, more than an hour ago, to find Dorothy.' And she, too, turned and went on looking into the fire.

My heart sank at this, and I began to wish I had never left my darling. I went back to Dorothy and told her. James was gone out for the day, but she, and me, and Bessy took lights, and went up into the nursery first; and then we roamed over the great, large house, calling and entreating Miss Rosamond to come out of her hiding-place and not frighten us to death in that way. But there was no answer; no sound.

'Oh!' said I, at last, 'can she have got into the east wing and hidden there?'

But Dorothy said it was not possible, for that she herself had never been in there; that the doors were always locked, and my lord's steward had the keys, she believed; at any rate, neither she nor James had ever seen them: so I said I would go back, and see if, after all, she was not hidden in the drawing-room, unknown to the old ladies; and if I found her there, I said, I would whip her well for the fright she had given me; but I never meant to do it. Well, I went back to the west drawing-room, and I told Mrs Stark we could not find her anywhere, and asked for leave to look all about the furniture there, for I thought now that she might have fallen asleep in some warm, hidden corner; but no! we looked – Miss Furnivall got up and looked, trembling all over – and she was nowhere there; then we set off again, everyone in the house, and looked in all the places we had searched before, but we could not find her. Miss Furnivall shivered and shook so much that Mrs Stark took her back into the warm drawing-room; but not before they had made me promise to bring

her to them when she was found. Well-a-day! I began to think she
never would be found, when I bethought me to look into the great
front court, all covered with snow. I was upstairs when I looked out;
but it was such clear moonlight, I could see, quite plain, two little
footprints, which might be traced from the hall-door and round the
corner of the east wing. I don't know how I got down, but I tugged
open the great stiff hall-door, and, throwing the skirt of my gown
over my head for a cloak, I ran out. I turned the east corner, and
there a black shadow fell on the snow; but when I came again into the
moonlight, there were the little footmarks going up – up to the Fells.
It was bitter cold; so cold, that the air almost took the skin off my
face as I ran; but I ran on, crying to think how my poor little darling
must be perished and frightened. I was within sight of the holly-
trees, when I saw a shepherd coming down the hill, bearing
something in his arms wrapped in his maud.[3] He shouted to me, and
asked me if I had lost a bairn; and, when I could not speak for crying,
he bore towards me, and I saw my wee bairnie, lying still, and white,
and stiff in his arms, as if she had been dead. He told me he had been
up the Fells to gather in his sheep, before the deep cold of night
came on, and that under the holly trees (black marks on the hillside,
where no other bush was for miles around) he had found my little
lady – my lamb – my queen – my darling – stiff and cold in the
terrible sleep which is frost-begotten. Oh! the joy and the tears of
having her in my arms once again! for I would not let him carry her;
but took her, maud and all, into my own arms, and held her near my
own warm neck and heart, and felt the life stealing slowly back again
into her little gentle limbs. But she was still insensible when we
reached the hall, and I had no breath for speech. We went in by the
kitchen-door.

'Bring the warming-pan,' said I; and I carried her upstairs, and
began undressing her by the nursery fire, which Bessy had kept up. I
called my little lammie all the sweet and playful names I could think
of – even while my eyes were blinded by my tears; and at last, oh! at
length she opened her large blue eyes. Then I put her into her warm
bed, and sent Dorothy down to tell Miss Furnivall that all was well;
and I made up my mind to sit by my darling's bedside the livelong
night. She fell away into a soft sleep as soon as her pretty head had
touched the pillow, and I watched by her till morning light; when she
wakened up bright and clear – or so I thought at first – and, my dears,
so I think now.

She said that she had fancied that she should like to go to Dorothy,
for that both the old ladies were asleep, and it was very dull in the

drawing-room; and that, as she was going through the west lobby, she saw the snow through the high window falling – falling – soft and steady; but she wanted to see it lying pretty and white on the ground; so she made her way into the great hall: and then, going to the window, she saw it bright and soft upon the drive; but while she stood there, she saw a little girl, not so old as she was, 'but so pretty,' said my darling; 'and this little girl beckoned to me to come out; and oh, she was so pretty and so sweet, I could not choose but go.' And then this other little girl had taken her by the hand, and side by side the two had gone round the east corner.

'Now you are a naughty little girl, and telling stories,' said I. 'What would your good mamma, that is in heaven, and never told a story in her life, say to her little Rosamond if she heard her – and I dare say she does – telling stories!'

'Indeed, Hester,' sobbed out my child, 'I'm telling you true. Indeed I am.'

'Don't tell me!' said I, very stern. 'I tracked you by your footmarks through the snow; there were only yours to be seen: and if you had had a little girl to go hand in hand with you up the hill, don't you think her footprints would have gone along with yours?'

'I can't help it, dear, dear Hester,' said she, crying, 'if they did not; I never looked at her feet, but she held my hand fast and tight in her little one, and it was very, very cold. She took me up the Fell-path, up to the holly trees; and there I saw a lady weeping and crying; but when she saw me, she hushed her weeping, and smiled very proud and grand, and took me on her knee, and began to lull me to sleep; and that's all, Hester – but that is true; and my dear mamma knows it is,' said she, crying. So I thought the child was in a fever, and pretended to believe her, as she went over her story – over and over again, and always the same. At last Dorothy knocked at the door with Miss Rosamond's breakfast; and she told me the old ladies were down in the eating parlour, and that they wanted to speak to me. They had both been into the night-nursery the evening before, but it was after Miss Rosamond was asleep; so they had only looked at her – not asked me any questions.

'I shall catch it,' thought I to myself, as I went along the north gallery. 'And yet,' I thought, taking courage, 'it was in their charge I left her; and it's they that's to blame for letting her steal away unknown and unwatched.' So I went in boldly, and told my story. I told it all to Miss Furnivall, shouting it close to her ear; but when I came to the mention of the other little girl out in the snow, coaxing and tempting her out, and willing her up to the grand and beautiful lady by the holly tree, she threw her arms up – her old and withered arms – and cried aloud, 'Oh! Heaven forgive! Have mercy!'

Mrs Stark took hold of her; roughly enough, I thought; but she was past Mrs Stark's management, and spoke to me, in a kind of wild warning and authority.

'Hester! keep her from that child! It will lure her to her death! That evil child! Tell her it is a wicked, naughty child.' Then Mrs Stark hurried me out of the room; where, indeed, I was glad enough to go; but Miss Furnivall kept shrieking out, 'Oh, have mercy! Wilt Thou never forgive! It is many a long year ago – '

I was very uneasy in my mind after that. I durst never leave Miss Rosamond, night or day, for fear lest she might slip off again, after some fancy or other; and all the more, because I thought I could make out that Miss Furnivall was crazy, from the odd ways about her; and I was afraid lest something of the same kind (which might be in the family, you know) hung over my darling. And the great frost never ceased all this time; and whenever it was a more stormy night than usual, between the gusts and through the wind we heard the old lord playing on the great organ. But, old lord, or not, wherever Miss Rosamond went, there I followed; for my love for her, pretty, helpless orphan, was stronger than my fear for the grand and terrible sound. Besides, it rested with me to keep her cheerful and merry, as beseemed her age. So we played together, and wandered together, here and there and everywhere; for I never dared to lose sight of her again in that large and rambling house. And so it happened that one afternoon, not long before Christmas Day, we were playing together on the billiard-table in the great hall (not that we knew the right way of playing, but she liked to roll the smooth ivory balls with her pretty hands, and I liked to do whatever she did); and, by and by, without our noticing it, it grew dusk indoors, though it was still light in the open air, and I was thinking of taking her back into the nursery, when, all of a sudden, she cried out –

'Look, Hester! look! there is my poor little girl out in the snow!'

I turned towards the long narrow windows, and there, sure enough, I saw a little girl, less than my Miss Rosamond – dressed all unfit to be out of doors such a bitter night – crying, and beating against the window panes, as if she wanted to be let in. She seemed to sob and wail, till Miss Rosamond could bear it no longer, and was flying to the door to open it, when, all of a sudden, and close upon us, the great organ pealed out so loud and thundering it fairly made me tremble; and all the more, when I remembered me that, even in the stillness of that dead-cold weather, I had heard no sound of little battering hands upon the window-glass, although the phantom child had seemed to put forth all its force; and, although I had seen it wail and cry, no faintest touch of sound had fallen upon my ears. Whether I remembered all this at the very moment, I do not know; the great organ sound had so stunned me into terror; but this I know, I caught up Miss Rosamond before she got the hall-door opened, and clutched her, and carried her away, kicking and screaming, into the large, bright kitchen, where Dorothy and Agnes were busy with their mince-pies.

'What is the matter with my sweet one?' cried Dorothy, as I bore in Miss Rosamond, who was sobbing as if her heart would break.

'She won't let me open the door for my little girl to come in; and she'll die if she is out on the Fells all night. Cruel, naughty Hester,' she said, slapping me; but she might have struck harder, for I had seen a look of ghastly terror on Dorothy's face which made my very blood run cold.

'Shut the back-kitchen door fast, and bolt it well,' said she to Agnes. She said no more; she gave me raisins and almonds to quiet Miss Rosamond; but she sobbed about the little girl in the snow, and would not touch any of the good things. I was thankful when she cried herself to sleep in bed. Then I stole down to the kitchen, and told Dorothy I had made up my mind. I would carry my darling back to my father's house in Applethwaite; where, if we lived humbly, we lived at peace. I said I had been frightened enough with the old lord's organ-playing; but now that I had seen for myself this little moaning child, all decked out as no child in the neighbourhood could be, beating and battering to get in, yet always without any sound or noise – with the dark wound on its right shoulder; and that Miss Rosamond had known it again for the phantom that had nearly lured her to death (which Dorothy knew was true); I would stand it no longer.

I saw Dorothy change colour once or twice. When I had done, she told me she did not think I could take Miss Rosamond with me, for that she was my lord's ward and I had no right over her; and she asked me would I leave the child that I was so fond of just for sounds and sights that could do me no harm; and that they had all had to get used to in their turns? I was all in a hot, trembling passion; and I said it was very well for her to talk, that knew what these sights and noises betokened, and that had, perhaps, had something to do with the spectre child while it was alive. And I taunted her so that she told me all she knew at last; and then I wished I had never been told, for it only made me more afraid than ever.

She said she had heard the tale from old neighbours that were alive when she was first married; when folks used to come to the hall sometimes, before it had got such a bad name in the countryside; it might not be true, or it might, what she had been told.

The old lord was Miss Furnivall's father – Miss Grace, as Dorothy called her, for Miss Maude was the elder, and Miss Furnivall by rights. The old lord was eaten up with pride. Such a proud man was never seen or heard of; and his daughters were like him. No one was good enough to wed them, although they had choice enough; for they were the great beauties of their day, as I had seen by their portraits, where they hung in the state drawing-room. But, as the old saying is, 'Pride will have a fall;' and these two haughty beauties fell in love with the same man, and he no better than a foreign musician, whom their father had down from London to play music with him at the Manor House. For, above all things, next to his pride, the old lord loved music. He could play on nearly every instrument that ever was heard of; and it was a strange thing it did not soften him; but he was a fierce, dour old man, and had broken his poor wife's heart with his cruelty, they said. He was mad after music, and would pay any money for it. So he got this foreigner to come; who made such beautiful music that they said the very birds on the trees stopped their singing to listen. And, by degrees, this foreign gentleman got such a hold over the old lord that nothing would serve him but that he must come every year; and it was he that had the great organ brought from Holland, and built up in the hall, where it stood now. He taught the old lord to play on it; but many and many a time, when Lord Furnivall was thinking of nothing but his fine organ, and his finer music, the dark foreigner was walking abroad in the woods with one of the young ladies: now Miss Maude and then Miss Grace.

Miss Maude won the day and carried off the prize, such as it was; and he and she were married, all unknown to anyone; and, before he made his next yearly visit, she had been confined of a little girl at a farmhouse on the moors, while her father and Miss Grace thought she was away at Doncaster Races. But though she was a wife and a mother, she was not a bit softened, but as haughty and as passionate as ever; and perhaps more so, for she was jealous of Miss Grace, to whom her foreign husband paid a deal of court – by way of blinding her – as he told his wife. But Miss Grace triumphed over Miss Maude, and Miss Maude grew fiercer and fiercer, both with her husband and with her sister; and the former – who could easily shake off what was disagreeable and hide himself in foreign countries – went away a month before his usual time that summer, and half-threatened that he would never come back again. Meanwhile, the little girl was left at the farmhouse, and her mother used to have her horse saddled and gallop wildly over the hills to see her once every week, at the very least; for where she loved she loved, and where she hated she hated. And the old lord went on playing – playing on his organ; and the servants thought the sweet music he made had soothed down his awful temper, of which (Dorothy said) some terrible tales could be told. He grew infirm, too, and had to walk with a crutch; and his son – that was the present Lord Furnivall's father – was with the army in America, and the other son at sea; so Miss Maude had it pretty much her own way, and she and Miss Grace grew colder and bitterer to each other every day; till at last they hardly ever spoke, except when the old lord was by. The foreign musician came again the next summer, but it was for the last time; for they led him such a life with their jealousy and their passions, that he grew weary, and went away, and never was heard of again. And Miss Maude, who had always meant to have her marriage acknowledged when her father should be dead, was left now a deserted wife, whom nobody knew to have been married, with a child that she dared not own, although she loved it to distraction; living with a father whom she feared and a sister whom she hated. When the next summer passed over, and the dark foreigner never came, both Miss Maude and Miss Grace grew gloomy and sad; they had a haggard look about them, though they looked handsome as ever. But, by and by, Miss Maude brightened; for her father grew more and more infirm, and more than ever carried away by his music; and she and Miss Grace lived almost entirely apart, having separate rooms, the one on the west side, Miss Maude on the east – those very rooms which were now shut up. So she thought she might have her little girl with her, and no one need ever know except those who dared not speak about it, and were bound to believe that it was, as she said, a cottager's child she had taken a fancy to. All this, Dorothy said, was pretty well known; but what came afterwards no one knew, except Miss Grace and Mrs Stark, who was even then her maid, and much more of a friend to her than ever her sister had been. But the servants supposed, from words that were dropped, that Miss Maude had triumphed over Miss Grace, and told her that all the time the dark foreigner had been mocking her with pretended love – he was her own husband. The colour left Miss Grace's cheek and lips that very day for ever, and she was heard to say many a time that sooner or later she would have her revenge; and Mrs Stark was forever spying about the east rooms.

One fearful night, just after the New Year had come in, when the
snow was lying thick and deep and the flakes were still falling – fast
enough to blind anyone who might be out and abroad – there was a
great and violent noise heard, and the old lord's voice above all,
cursing and swearing awfully, and the cries of a little child, and the
proud defiance of a fierce woman, and the sound of a blow, and a
dead stillness, and moans and wailings, dying away on the hillside!
Then the old lord summoned all his servants and told them, with
terrible oaths, and words more terrible, that his daughter had
disgraced herself, and that he had turned her out of doors – her and
her child – and that if ever they gave her help, or food, or shelter, he
prayed that they might never enter heaven. And, all the while, Miss
Grace stood by him, white and still as any stone; and, when he had
ended, she heaved a great sigh, as much as to say her work was done
and her end was accomplished. But the old lord never touched his
organ again, and died within the year; and no wonder! for, on the
morrow of that wild and fearful night, the shepherds, coming down
the Fell side, found Miss Maude sitting, all crazy and smiling, under
the holly trees, nursing a dead child, with a terrible mark on its right
shoulder. 'But that was not what killed it,' said Dorothy: 'it was the
frost and the cold. Every wild creature was in its hole, and every beast
in its fold, while the child and its mother were turned out to wander
on the Fells! And now you know all! and I wonder if you are less
frightened now?'

I was more frightened than ever; but I said I was not. I wished Miss
Rosamond and myself well out of that dreadful house for ever; but I
would not leave her and I dared not take her away. But oh, how I
watched her and guarded her! We bolted the doors and shut the
window-shutters fast an hour or more before dark, rather than leave
them open five minutes too late. But my little lady still heard the
weird child crying and mourning; and not all we could do or say
could keep her from wanting to go to her and let her in from the
cruel wind and snow. All this time I kept away from Miss Furnivall
and Mrs Stark as much as ever I could; for I feared them – I knew no
good could be about them, with their grey, hard faces, and their
dreamy eyes, looking back into the ghastly years that were gone. But,
even in my fear, I had a kind of pity for Miss Furnivall, at least. Those
gone down to the pit can hardly have a more hopeless look than that
which was ever on her face. At last I even got so sorry for her – who
never said a word but what was quite forced from her – that I prayed
for her; and I taught Miss Rosamond to pray for one who had done a
deadly sin; but often, when she came to those words, she would

listen, and start up from her knees, and say, 'I hear my little girl plaining and crying, very sad – oh, let her in, or she will die!'

One night – just after New Year's Day had come at last, and the long winter had taken a turn, as I hoped – I heard the west drawing-room bell ring three times, which was the signal for me. I would not leave Miss Rosamond alone, for all she was asleep – for the old lord had been playing wilder than ever – and I feared lest my darling should waken to hear the spectre child; see her I knew she could not. I had fastened the windows too well for that. So I took her out of her bed, and wrapped her up in such outer clothes as were most handy, and carried her down to the drawing-room, where the old ladies sat at their tapestry-work as usual. They looked up when I came in, and Mrs Stark asked, quite astounded, 'Why did I bring Miss Rosamond there, out of her warm bed?' I had begun to whisper, 'Because I was afraid of her being tempted out while I was away by the wild child in the snow,' when she stopped me short (with a glance at Miss Furnivall), and said Miss Furnivall wanted me to undo some work she had done wrong, and which neither of them could see to unpick. So I laid my pretty dear on the sofa, and sat down on a stool by them, and hardened my heart against them, as I heard the wind rising and howling.

Miss Rosamond slept on sound, for all the wind blew so; and Miss Furnivall said never a word, nor looked round when the gusts shook the windows. All at once she started up to her full height, and put up one hand, as if to bid us listen.

'I hear voices!' said she. 'I hear terrible screams – I hear my father's voice!'

Just at that moment my darling wakened with a sudden start: 'My little girl is crying, oh, how she is crying!' and she tried to get up and go to her, but she got her feet entangled in the blanket, and I caught her up; for my flesh had begun to creep at these noises, which they heard while Mrs Stark and I could catch no sound. In a minute or two the noises came, and gathered fast, and filled our ears; we, too, heard voices and screams, and no longer heard the winter's wind that raged abroad. Mrs Stark looked at me, and I at her, but we dared not speak. Suddenly Miss Furnivall went towards the door, out into the ante-room, through the west lobby, and opened the door into the great hall. Mrs Stark followed, and I durst not be left, though my heart almost stopped beating for fear. I wrapped my darling tight in my arms, and went out with them. In the hall the screams were louder than ever; they seemed to come from the east wing – nearer and nearer – close on the other side of the locked-up doors – close behind them. Then I noticed that the great bronze chandelier seemed all alight, though the hall was dim, and that a fire was blazing in the vast hearth-place, though it gave no heat; and I shuddered up with terror and folded my darling closer to me. But as I did so the east door shook, and she, suddenly struggling to get free from me, cried, 'Hester! I must go. My little girl is there! I hear her; she is coming! Hester, I must go!'

I held her tight with all my strength; with a set will, I held her. If I had died, my hands would have grasped her still, I was so resolved in my mind. Miss Furnivall stood listening, and paid no regard to my darling, who had got down to the ground, and whom I, upon my knees now, was holding with both my arms clasped round her neck; she still striving and crying to get free.

All at once, the east door gave way with a thundering crash, as if torn open in a violent passion, and there came into that broad and mysterious light, the figure of a tall old man, with grey hair and gleaming eyes. He drove before him, with many a relentless gesture of abhorrence, a stern and beautiful woman, with a little child clinging to her dress.

'O Hester! Hester!' cried Miss Rosamond; 'it's the lady! the lady below the holly trees; and my little girl is with her. Hester! Hester! let me go to her; they are drawing me to them. I feel them – I feel them. I must go!'

Again she was almost convulsed by her efforts to get away; but I held her tighter and tighter, till I feared I should do her a hurt; but rather that than let her go towards those terrible phantoms. They passed along towards the great hall-door, where the winds howled and ravened for their prey; but before they reached it, the lady turned; and I could see that she defied the old man with a fierce and proud defiance; but then she quailed – and then she threw up her arms wildly and piteously to save her child – her little child – from a blow from his uplifted crutch.

And Miss Rosamond was torn as by a power stronger than mine, and writhed in my arms, and sobbed (for by this time the poor darling was growing faint).

'They want me to go with them on to the Fells – they are drawing me to them. Oh, my little girl! I would come, but cruel, wicked Hester holds me very tight.' But when she saw the uplifted crutch, she swooned away, and I thanked God for it. Just at this moment – when the tall old man, his hair streaming as in the blast of a furnace, was going to strike the little shrinking child – Miss Furnivall, the old woman by my side, cried out, 'O father! father! spare the little innocent child!' But just then I saw – we all saw – another phantom shape itself, and grow clear out of the blue and misty light that filled the hall; we had not seen her till now, for it was another lady who stood by the old man, with a look of relentless hate and triumphant scorn. That figure was very beautiful to look upon, with a soft, white hat drawn down over the proud brows, and a red and curling lip. It was dressed in an open robe of blue satin. I had seen that figure before. It was the likeness of Miss Furnivall in her youth; and the terrible phantoms moved on, regardless of old Miss Furnivall's wild entreaty – and the uplifted crutch fell on the right shoulder of the little child, and the younger sister looked on, stony and deadly serene. But at that moment, the dim lights and the fire that gave no heat went out of themselves, and Miss Furnivall lay at our feet stricken down by the palsy – death-stricken.

Yes! she was carried to her bed that night never to rise again. She lay with her face to the wall, muttering low, but muttering always: 'Alas! alas! what is done in youth can never be undone in age! What is done in youth can never be undone in age!'

The Body-Snatcher

ROBERT LOUIS STEVENSON

EVERY NIGHT IN THE YEAR, four of us sat in the small parlour of the George at Debenham – the undertaker, and the landlord, and Fettes, and myself. Sometimes there would be more; but blow high, blow low, come rain or snow or frost, we four would be each planted in his own particular armchair. Fettes was an old drunken Scotchman, a man of education obviously, and a man of some property, since he lived in idleness. He had come to Debenham years ago, while still young, and by a mere continuance of living had grown to be an adopted townsman. His blue camlet cloak was a local antiquity, like the church-spire. His place in the parlour at the George, his absence from church, his old, crapulous, disreputable vices, were all things of course in Debenham. He had some vague radical opinions and some fleeting infidelities, which he would now and again set forth and emphasise with tottering slaps upon the table. He drank rum – five glasses regularly every evening; and for the greater portion of his nightly visit to the George sat, with his glass in his right hand, in a state of melancholy alcoholic saturation. We called him the Doctor, for he was supposed to have some special knowledge of medicine, and had been known, upon a pinch, to set a fracture or reduce a dislocation; but beyond these slight particulars, we had no knowledge of his character and antecedents.

One dark winter night – it had struck nine some time before the landlord joined us – there was a sick man in the George, a great neighbouring proprietor suddenly struck down with apoplexy on his way to Parliament; and the great man's still greater London doctor had been telegraphed to his bedside. It was the first time that such a thing had happened in Debenham, for the railway was but newly open, and we were all proportionately moved by the occurrence.

'He's come,' said the landlord, after he had filled and lighted his pipe.

'He?' said I. 'Who? – not the doctor?'

'Himself,' replied our host.

'What is his name?'

'Dr Macfarlane,' said the landlord.

Fettes was far through his third tumbler, stupidly fuddled, now nodding over, now staring mazily around him; but at the last word he seemed to awaken, and repeated the name 'Macfarlane' twice, quietly enough the first time, but with sudden emotion at the second.

'Yes,' said the landlord, 'that's his name, Dr Wolfe Macfarlane.'

Fettes became instantly sober; his eyes awoke, his voice became clear, loud and steady, his language forcible and earnest. We were all startled by the transformation, as if a man had risen from the dead.

'I beg your pardon,' he said, 'I am afraid I have not been paying much attention to your talk. Who is this Wolfe Macfarlane?' And then, when he had heard the landlord out, 'It cannot be, it cannot be,' he added; 'and yet I would like well to see him face to face.'

'Do you know him, Doctor?' asked the undertaker, with a gasp.

'God forbid!' was the reply. 'And yet the name is a strange one; it were too much to fancy two. Tell me, landlord, is he old?'

'Well,' said the host, 'he's not a young man, to be sure, and his hair is white; but he looks younger than you.'

'He is older, though; years older. But,' with a slap upon the table, 'it's the rum you see in my face – rum and sin. This man, perhaps, may have an easy conscience and a good digestion. Conscience! Hear me speak. You would think I was some good, old, decent Christian, would you not? But no, not I; I never canted. Voltaire might have canted if he'd stood in my shoes; but the brains' – with a rattling fillip on his bald head – 'the brains were clear and active, and I saw and made no deductions.'

'If you know this doctor,' I ventured to remark, after a somewhat awful pause, 'I should gather that you do not share the landlord's good opinion.'

Fettes paid no regard to me.

'Yes,' he said, with sudden decision, 'I must see him face to face.'

There was another pause, and then a door was closed rather sharply on the first floor and a step was heard upon the stair.

'That's the doctor,' cried the landlord. 'Look sharp, and you can catch him.'

It was but two steps from the small parlour to the door of the old George Inn; the wide oak staircase landed almost in the street; there was room for a Turkey rug and nothing more between the threshold and the last round of the descent; but this little space was every evening brilliantly lit up, not only by the light upon the stair and the great signal lamp below the sign, but by the warm radiance of the bar-room window. The George thus brightly advertised itself to passers-by in the cold street. Fettes walked steadily to the spot, and we, who were hanging behind, beheld the two men meet, as one of them had phrased it, face to face. Dr Macfarlane was alert and vigorous. His white hair set off his pale and placid, although energetic, countenance. He was richly dressed in the finest of broadcloth and the whitest of linen, with a great gold watch-chain, and studs and spectacles of the same precious material. He wore a broad-folded tie, white and speckled with lilac, and he carried on his arm a comfortable driving-coat of fur. There was no doubt but he became his years, breathing, as he did, of wealth and consideration; and it was a surprising contrast to see our parlour sot – bald, dirty, pimpled and robed in his old camlet cloak – confront him at the bottom of the stairs.

'Macfarlane!' he said somewhat loudly, more like a herald than a friend.

The great doctor pulled up short on the fourth step, as though the familiarity of the address surprised and somewhat shocked his dignity.

'Toddy Macfarlane!' repeated Fettes.

The London man almost staggered. He stared for the swiftest of seconds at the man before him, glanced behind him with a sort of scare, and then in a startled whisper, 'Fettes!' he said, 'you!'

'Ay,' said the other, 'me! Did you think I was dead too? We are not so easy shut of our acquaintance.'

'Hush, hush!' exclaimed the doctor. 'Hush, hush! this meeting is so unexpected – I can see you are unmanned. I hardly knew you, I confess, at first; but I am overjoyed – overjoyed to have this opportunity. For the present it must be how-d'ye-do and goodbye in one, for my fly is waiting, and I must not fail the train; but you shall – let me see – yes – you shall give me your address, and you can count on early news of me. We must do something for you, Fettes. I fear you are out at elbows; but we must see to that for auld lang syne, as once we sang at suppers.'

'Money!' cried Fettes; 'money from you! The money that I had from you is lying where I cast it in the rain.'

Dr Macfarlane had talked himself into some measure of superiority and confidence, but the uncommon energy of this refusal cast him back into his first confusion.

A horrible, ugly look came and went across his almost venerable countenance. 'My dear fellow,' he said, 'be it as you please; my last thought is to offend you. I would intrude on none. I will leave you my address, however – '

'I do not wish it – I do not wish to know the roof that shelters you,' interrupted the other. 'I heard your name; I feared it might be you; I wished to know if, after all, there were a God; I know now that there is none. Begone!'

He still stood in the middle of the rug, between the stair and doorway; and the great London physician, in order to escape, would be forced to step to one side. It was plain that he hesitated before the thought of this humiliation. White as he was, there was a dangerous glitter in his spectacles; but while he still paused uncertain, he became aware that the driver of his fly was peering in from the street at this unusual scene and caught a glimpse at the same time of our little body in the parlour, huddled by the corner of the bar. The presence of so many witnesses decided him at once to flee. He crouched together, brushing on the wainscot, and made a dart like a serpent, striking for the door. But his tribulation was not entirely at an end, for even as he was passing, Fettes clutched him by the arm and these words came in a whisper, and yet painfully distinct, 'Have you seen it again?'

The great rich London doctor cried out aloud with a sharp, throttling cry; he dashed his questioner across the open space, and, with his hands over his head, fled out of the door like a detected thief. Before it had occurred to one of us to make a movement, the fly was already rattling towards the station. The scene was over like a dream, but the dream had left proofs and traces of its passage. Next day the servant found the fine gold spectacles broken on the threshold, and that very night we were all standing breathless by the bar-room window, and Fettes at our side, sober, pale and resolute in look.

'God protect us, Mr Fettes!' said the landlord, coming first into possession of his customary senses. 'What in the universe is all this? These are strange things you have been saying.'

Fettes turned towards us; he looked us each in succession in the face. 'See if you can hold your tongues,' said he. 'That man Macfarlane is not safe to cross; those that have done so already have repented it too late.'

And then, without so much as finishing his third glass, far less waiting for the other two, he bade us goodbye and went forth, under the lamp of the hotel, into the black night.

We three turned to our places in the parlour, with the big red fire and four clear candles; and as we recapitulated what had passed, the first chill of our surprise soon changed into a glow of curiosity. We sat late; it was the latest session I have known in the old George. Each man, before we parted, had his theory that he was bound to prove; and none of us had any nearer business in this world than to track out the past of our condemned companion, and surprise the secret that he shared with the great London doctor. It is no great boast, but I believe I was a better hand at worming out a story than either of my fellows at the George; and perhaps there is now no other man alive who could narrate to you the following foul and unnatural events.

In his young days Fettes studied medicine in the schools of Edinburgh. He had talent of a kind, the talent that picks up swiftly what it hears and readily retails it for its own. He worked little at home; but he was civil, attentive and intelligent in the presence of his masters. They soon picked him out as a lad who listened closely and remembered well; nay, strange as it seemed to me when I first heard it, he was in those days well favoured, and pleased by his exterior. There was, at that period, a certain extramural teacher of anatomy, whom I shall here designate by the letter K. His name was subsequently too well known. The man who bore it skulked through the streets of Edinburgh in disguise, while the mob that applauded at the execution of Burke called loudly for the blood of his employer. But Mr K— was then at the top of his vogue; he enjoyed a popularity due partly to his own talent and address, partly to the incapacity of his rival, the university professor. The students, at least, swore by his name, and Fettes believed himself, and was believed by others, to have laid the foundations of success when he acquired the favour of this meteorically famous man. Mr K— was a *bon vivant* as well as an accomplished teacher; he liked a sly illusion no less than a careful preparation. In both capacities Fettes enjoyed and deserved his notice, and by the second year of his attendance he held the half-regular position of second demonstrator, or sub-assistant, in his class.

In this capacity the charge of the theatre and lecture-room devolved in particular upon his shoulders. He had to answer for the cleanliness of the premises and the conduct of the other students, and it was a part of his duty to supply, receive and divide the various subjects. It was with a view to this last – at that time very delicate – affair that he was lodged by Mr K— in the same wynd, and at last in the same building, with the dissecting-rooms. Here, after a night of turbulent pleasures, his hand still tottering, his sight still misty and confused, he would be called out of bed in the black hours before the winter dawn by the unclean and desperate interlopers who supplied the table. He would open the door to these men, since infamous throughout the land. He would help them with their tragic burden, pay them their sordid price, and remain alone, when they were gone, with the unfriendly relics of humanity. From such a scene he would return to snatch another hour or two of slumber, to repair the abuses of the night and refresh himself for the labours of the day.

Few lads could have been more insensible to the impressions of a life thus passed among the ensigns of mortality. His mind was closed against all general considerations. He was incapable of interest in the fate and fortunes of another, the slave of his own desires and low ambitions. Cold, light and selfish in the last resort, he had that modicum of prudence, miscalled morality, which keeps a man from inconvenient drunkenness or punishable theft. He coveted, besides, a measure of consideration from his masters and his fellow-pupils, and he had no desire to fail conspicuously in the external parts of life. Thus he made it his pleasure to gain some distinction in his studies, and day after day rendered unimpeachable eye-service to his employer, Mr K—. For his day of work he indemnified himself by nights of roaring, blackguardly enjoyment; and when that balance had been struck, the organ that he called his conscience declared itself content.

The supply of subjects was a continual trouble to him as well as to his master. In that large and busy class, the raw material of the anatomist kept perpetually running out; and the business thus rendered necessary was not only unpleasant in itself, but threatened dangerous consequences to all who were concerned. It was the policy of Mr K— to ask no questions in his dealings with the trade. 'They bring the body, and we pay the price,' he used to say, dwelling on the alliteration – '*quid pro quo*.' And, again, and somewhat profanely, 'Ask no questions,' he would tell his assistants, 'for conscience' sake.' There was no understanding that the subjects were provided by the crime of murder. Had that idea been broached to him in words, he would have recoiled in horror; but the lightness of his speech upon so grave a matter was, in itself, an offence against good manners, and a temptation to the men with whom he dealt. Fettes, for instance, had often remarked to himself upon the singular freshness of the bodies. He had been struck again and again by the hangdog, abominable looks of the ruffians who came to him before the dawn; and putting things together clearly in his private thoughts, he perhaps attributed a meaning too immoral and too categorical to the unguarded counsels of his master. He understood his duty, in short, to have three branches: to take what was brought, to pay the price, and to avert the eye from any evidence of crime.

One November morning this policy of silence was put sharply to the test. He had been awake all night with a racking toothache – pacing his room like a caged beast or throwing himself in fury on his bed – and had fallen at last into that profound, uneasy slumber that so often follows on a night of pain, when he was awakened by the third or fourth angry repetition of the concerted signal. There was a thin, bright moonshine; it was bitter cold, windy and frosty; the town had not yet awakened, but an indefinable stir already preluded the noise and business of the day. The ghouls had come later than usual, and they seemed more than usually eager to be gone. Fettes, sick with sleep, lighted them upstairs. He heard their grumbling Irish voices through a dream; and as they stripped the sack from their sad merchandise he leaned dozing, with his shoulder propped against the wall; he had to shake himself to find the men their money. As he did so his eyes lighted on the dead face. He started; he took two steps nearer, with the candle raised.

'God almighty!' he cried. 'That is Jane Galbraith!'

The men answered nothing, but they shuffled nearer the door.

'I know her, I tell you,' he continued. 'She was alive and hearty yesterday. It's impossible she can be dead; it's impossible you should have got this body fairly.'

'Sure, sir, you're mistaken entirely,' said one of the men.

But the other looked Fettes darkly in the eyes, and demanded the money on the spot.

It was impossible to misconceive the threat or to exaggerate the danger. The lad's heart failed him. He stammered some excuses, counted out the sum, and saw his hateful visitors depart. No sooner were they gone than he hastened to confirm his doubts. By a dozen unquestionable marks he identified the girl he had jested with the day before. He saw, with horror, marks upon her body that might well betoken violence. A panic seized him, and he took refuge in his room. There he reflected at length over the discovery that he had made; considered soberly the bearing of Mr K—'s instructions and the danger to himself of interference in so serious a business; and at last, in sore perplexity, determined to wait for the advice of his immediate superior, the class assistant.

This was a young doctor, Wolfe Macfarlane, a high favourite among all the reckless students, clever, dissipated and unscrupulous to the last degree. He had travelled and studied abroad. His manners were agreeable and a little forward. He was an authority on the stage, skilful on the ice or the links with skate or golf-club; he dressed with nice audacity and, to put the finishing touch upon his glory, he kept a gig and a strong trotting-horse. With Fettes he was on terms of intimacy; indeed, their relative positions called for some community of life; and when subjects were scarce the pair would drive far into the country in Macfarlane's gig, visit and desecrate some lonely graveyard, and return before dawn with their booty to the door of the dissecting-room.

On that particular morning, Macfarlane arrived somewhat earlier than his wont. Fettes heard him, and met him on the stairs, told him his story, and showed him the cause of his alarm. Macfarlane examined the marks on her body.

'Yes,' he said, with a nod, 'it looks fishy.'

'Well, what should I do?' asked Fettes.

'Do?' repeated the other. 'Do you want to do anything? Least said soonest mended, I should say.'

'Someone else might recognise her,' objected Fettes. 'She was as well known as the Castle Rock.'

'We'll hope not,' said Macfarlane, 'and if anybody does – well, you didn't, don't you see, and there's an end. The fact is, this has been going on too long. Stir up the mud, and you'll get K— into the most unholy trouble; you'll be in a shocking box yourself. So will I, if you come to that. I should like to know how any one of us would look, or what the devil we should have to say for ourselves, in any Christian witness-box. For me, you know there's one thing certain – that, practically speaking, all our subjects have been murdered.'

'Macfarlane!' cried Fettes.

'Come now!' sneered the other. 'As if you hadn't suspected it yourself!'

'Suspecting is one thing –'

'And proof another. Yes, I know; and I'm as sorry as you are this should have come here,' tapping the body with his cane. 'The next best thing for me is not to recognise it; and,' he added coolly, 'I don't. You may, if you please. I don't dictate, but I think a man of the world would do as I do; and I may add, I fancy that is what K— would look for at our hands. The question is, Why did he choose us two for his assistants? And I answer, Because he didn't want old wives.'

This was the tone of all others to affect the mind of a lad like Fettes. He agreed to imitate Macfarlane. The body of the unfortunate girl was duly dissected, and no one remarked or appeared to recognise her.

One afternoon, when his day's work was over, Fettes dropped into a popular tavern and found Macfarlane sitting with a stranger. This was a small man, very pale and dark, with coal-black eyes. The cut of his features gave a promise of intellect and refinement which was but feebly realised in his manners, for he proved, upon a nearer acquaintance, coarse, vulgar and stupid. He exercised, however, a very remarkable control over Macfarlane; issued orders like the Great Bashaw; became inflamed at the least discussion or delay and commented rudely on the servility with which he was obeyed. This most offensive person took a fancy to Fettes on the spot, plied him with drinks and honoured him with unusual confidences on his past career. If a tenth part of what he confessed were true, he was a very loathsome rogue; and the lad's vanity was tickled by the attention of so experienced a man.

'I'm a pretty bad fellow myself,' the stranger remarked, 'but Macfarlane is the boy – Toddy Macfarlane I call him. Toddy, order your friend another glass.' Or it might be, 'Toddy, you jump up and shut the door.' 'Toddy hates me,' he said again. 'Oh, yes, Toddy, you do!'

'Don't you call me that confounded name,' growled Macfarlane.

'Hear him! Did you ever see the lads play knife? He would like to do that all over my body,' remarked the stranger.

'We medicals have a better way than that,' said Fettes. 'When we dislike a dead friend of ours, we dissect him.'

Macfarlane looked up sharply, as though this jest were scarcely to his mind.

The afternoon passed. Gray, for that was the stranger's name, invited Fettes to join them at dinner, ordered a feast so sumptuous that the tavern was thrown into commotion, and when all was done, commanded Macfarlane to settle the bill. It was late before they separated; the man Gray was incapably drunk. Macfarlane, sobered by his fury, chewed the cud of the money he had been forced to squander and the slights he had been obliged to swallow. Fettes, with various liquors singing in his head, returned home with devious footsteps and a mind entirely in abeyance. Next day Macfarlane was absent from the class, and Fettes smiled to himself as he imagined him still squiring the intolerable Gray from tavern to tavern. As soon as the hour of liberty had struck, he posted from place to place in quest of his last night's companions. He could find them, however, nowhere; so returned early to his rooms, went early to bed, and slept the sleep of the just.

At four in the morning he was awakened by the well-known signal. Descending to the door, he was filled with astonishment to find

Macfarlane with his gig, and in the gig one of those long and ghastly packages with which he was so well acquainted.

'What?' he cried. 'Have you been out alone? How did you manage?'

But Macfarlane silenced him roughly, bidding him turn to business. When they had got the body upstairs and laid it on the table, Macfarlane made at first as if he were going away. Then he paused and seemed to hesitate; and then, 'You had better look at the face,' said he, in tones of some constraint. 'You had better,' he repeated, as Fettes only stared at him in wonder.

'But where, and how, and when did you come by it?' cried the other.

'Look at the face,' was the only answer.

Fettes was staggered; strange doubts assailed him. He looked from the young doctor to the body, and then back again. At last, with a start, he did as he was bidden. He had almost expected the sight that met his eyes, and yet the shock was cruel. To see, fixed in the rigidity of death and naked on that coarse layer of sack-cloth, the man whom he had left well clad and full of meat and sin upon the threshold of a tavern, awoke, even in the thoughtless Fettes, some of the terrors of the conscience. It was a *cras tibi* which re-echoed in his soul, that two whom he had known should have come to lie upon these icy tables. Yet these were only secondary thoughts. His first concern regarded Wolfe. Unprepared for a challenge so momentous, he knew not how to look his comrade in the face. He durst not meet his eye, and he had neither words nor voice at his command.

It was Macfarlane himself who made the first advance. He came up quietly behind and laid his hand gently but firmly on the other's shoulder.

'Richardson,' said he, 'may have the head.'

Now Richardson was a student who had long been anxious for that portion of the human subject to dissect. There was no answer, and the murderer resumed: 'Talking of business, you must pay me; your accounts, you see, must tally.'

Fettes found a voice, the ghost of his own: 'Pay you!' he cried. 'Pay you for that?'

'Why, yes, of course you must. By all means and on every possible account, you must,' returned the other. 'I dare not give it for nothing, you dare not take it for nothing; it would compromise us both. This is another case like Jane Galbraith's. The more things are wrong the more we must act as if all were right. Where does old K— keep his money?'

'There,' answered Fettes hoarsely, pointing to a cupboard in the corner.

'Give me the key, then,' said the other calmly, holding out his hand.

There was an instant's hesitation, and the die was cast. Macfarlane could not suppress a nervous twitch, the infinitesimal mark of an immense relief, as he felt the key between his fingers. He opened the cupboard, brought out pen and ink and a paper-book that stood in one compartment, and separated from the funds in a drawer a sum suitable to the occasion.

'Now, look here,' he said, 'there is the payment made – first proof of your good faith: first step to your security. You have now to clinch it by a second. Enter the payment in your book, and then you for your part may defy the devil.'

The next few seconds were for Fettes an agony of thought; but in balancing his terrors it was the most immediate that triumphed. Any future difficulty seemed almost welcome if he could avoid a present quarrel with Macfarlane. He set down the candle which he had been carrying all this time, and with a steady hand entered the date, the nature and the amount of the transaction.

'And now,' said Macfarlane, 'it's only fair that you should pocket the lucre. I've had my share already. By the by, when a man of the world falls into a bit of luck, has a few shillings extra in his pocket – I'm ashamed to speak of it, but there's a rule of conduct in the case. No treating, no purchase of expensive class-books, no squaring of old debts; borrow, don't lend.'

'Macfarlane,' began Fettes, still somewhat hoarsely, 'I have put my neck in a halter to oblige you.'

'To oblige me?' cried Wolfe. 'Oh, come! You did, as near as I can see the matter, what you downright had to do in self-defence. Suppose I got into trouble, where would you be? This second little matter flows clearly from the first. Mr Gray is the continuation of Miss Galbraith. You can't begin and then stop. If you begin, you must keep on beginning; that's the truth. No rest for the wicked.'

A horrible sense of blackness and the treachery of fate seized hold upon the soul of the unhappy student.

'My God!' he cried, 'but what have I done? and when did I begin? To be made a class assistant – in the name of reason, where's the harm in that? Service wanted the position; Service might have got it. Would *he* have been where *I* am now!'

'My dear fellow,' said Macfarlane, 'what a boy you are! What harm *has* come to you? What harm *can* come to you if you hold your tongue? Why, man, do you know what this life is? There are two squads of us – the lions and the lambs. If you're a lamb, you'll come to lie upon these tables like Gray or Jane Galbraith; if you're a lion, you'll live and drive a horse like me, like K—, like all the world with any wit or courage. You're staggered at the first. But look at K—! My dear fellow, you're clever, you have pluck. I like you, and K— likes you. You were born to lead the hunt; and I tell you, on my honour and my experience of life, three days from now you'll laugh at all these scarecrows like a high-school boy at a farce.'

And with that Macfarlane took his departure and drove off up the wynd in his gig to get under cover before daylight. Fettes was thus left alone with his regrets. He saw the miserable peril in which he stood involved. He saw, with inexpressible dismay, that there was no limit to his weakness, and that, from concession to concession, he had fallen from the arbiter of Macfarlane's destiny to his paid and helpless accomplice. He would have given the world to have been a little braver at the time, but it did not occur to him that he might still be brave. The secret of Jane Galbraith and the cursed entry in the day-book closed his mouth.

Hours passed; the class began to arrive; the members of the unhappy Gray were dealt out to one and to another, and received without remark. Richardson was made happy with the head; and before the hour of freedom rang Fettes trembled with exultation to perceive how far they had already gone toward safety.

For two days he continued to watch, with increasing joy, the dreadful process of disguise.

On the third day Macfarlane made his appearance. He had been ill, he said; but he made up for lost time by the energy with which he directed the students. To Richardson in particular he extended the most valuable assistance and advice, and that student, encouraged by the praise of the demonstrator, burned high with ambitious hopes, and saw the medal already in his grasp.

Before the week was out Macfarlane's prophecy had been fulfilled. Fettes had outlived his terrors and had forgotten his baseness. He began to plume himself upon his courage, and had so arranged the story in his mind that he could look back on these events with an unhealthy pride. Of his accomplice he saw but little. They met, of course, in the business of the class; they received their orders together from Mr K—. At times they had a word or two in private, and Macfarlane was from first to last particularly kind and jovial. But it was plain that he avoided any reference to their common secret; and even when Fettes whispered to him that he had cast in his lot with the lions and forsworn the lambs, he only signed to him smilingly to hold his peace.

At length an occasion arose which threw the pair once more into a closer union. Mr K— was again short of subjects; pupils were eager, and it was a part of this teacher's pretensions to be always well supplied. At the same time there came the news of a burial in the rustic graveyard of Glencorse. Time has little changed the place in question. It stood then, as now, upon a cross road, out of call of human habitations and buried fathom deep in the foliage of six cedar trees. The cries of the sheep upon the neighbouring hills, the streamlets upon either hand, one loudly singing among pebbles, the other dripping furtively from pond to pond, the stir of the wind in mountainous old flowering chestnuts and, once in seven days, the voice of the bell and the old tunes of the precentor were the only sounds that disturbed the silence around the rural church. The Resurrection Man – to use a byname of the period – was not to be deterred by any of the sanctities of customary piety. It was part of his trade to despise and desecrate the scrolls and trumpets of old tombs, the paths worn by the feet of worshippers and mourners, and the offerings and the inscriptions of bereaved affection. To rustic neighbourhoods, where love is more than commonly tenacious and where some bonds of blood or fellowship unite the entire society of a parish, the body-snatcher, far from being repelled by natural respect, was attracted by the ease and safety of the task. To bodies that had been laid in earth, in joyful expectation of a far different awakening, there came that hasty, lamp-lit, terror-haunted resurrection of the spade and mattock. The coffin was forced, the cerements torn, and the melancholy relics, clad in sackcloth, after being rattled for hours on moonless byways, were at length exposed to uttermost indignities before a class of gaping boys.

Somewhat as two vultures may swoop upon a dying lamb, Fettes and Macfarlane were to be let loose upon a grave in that green and quiet resting-place. The wife of a farmer, a woman who had lived for sixty years and been known for nothing but good butter and a godly conversation, was to be rooted from her grave at midnight and carried, dead and naked, to that faraway city that she had always honoured with her Sunday's best; the place beside her family was to be empty till the crack of doom; her innocent and almost venerable members were to be exposed to that last curiosity of the anatomist.

Late one afternoon the pair set forth, well wrapped in cloaks and furnished with a formidable bottle. It rained without remission – a cold, dense, lashing rain. Now and again there blew a puff of wind, but these sheets of falling water kept it down. Bottle and all, it was a sad and silent drive as far as Penicuik, where they were to spend the evening. They stopped once, to hide their implements in a thick bush not far from the churchyard, and once again at the Fisher's Tryst, to have a toast before the kitchen fire and vary their nips of whisky with a glass of ale. When they reached their journey's end the gig was housed, the horse was fed and comforted, and the two young doctors in a private room sat down to the best dinner and the best wine the house afforded. The lights, the fire, the beating rain upon the window, the cold, incongruous work that lay before them, added zest to their enjoyment of the meal. With every glass their cordiality increased. Soon Macfarlane handed a little pile of gold to his companion.

'A compliment,' he said. 'Between friends these little d—d accommodations ought to fly like pipe-lights.'

Fettes pocketed the money, and applauded the sentiment to the echo. 'You are a philosopher,' he cried. 'I was an ass till I knew you. You and K— between you, by the Lord Harry! but you'll make a man of me.'

'Of course we shall,' applauded Macfarlane. 'A man? I tell you, it required a man to back me up the other morning. There are some big, brawling, forty-year-old cowards who would have turned sick at the look of the d—d thing; but not you – you kept your head. I watched you.'

'Well, and why not?' Fettes thus vaunted himself. 'It was no affair of mine. There was nothing to gain on the one side but disturbance, and on the other I could count on your gratitude, don't you see?' And he slapped his pocket till the gold pieces rang.

Macfarlane somehow felt a certain touch of alarm at these unpleasant words. He may have regretted that he had taught his young companion so successfully, but he had no time to interfere, for the other noisily continued in this boastful strain: 'The great thing is not to be afraid. Now, between you and me, I don't want to hang – that's practical; but for all cant, Macfarlane, I was born with a contempt. Hell, God, Devil, right, wrong, sin, crime, and all the old gallery of curiosities – they may frighten boys, but men of the world, like you and me, despise them. Here's to the memory of Gray!'

It was by this time growing somewhat late. The gig, according to order, was brought round to the door with both lamps brightly shining, and the young men had to pay their bill and take the road. They announced that they were bound for Peebles, and drove in that direction till they were clear of the last houses of the town;

then, extinguishing the lamps, they returned upon their course, and followed a byroad towards Glencorse. There was no sound but that of their own passage, and the incessant, strident pouring of the rain. It was pitch dark; here and there a white gate or a white stone in the wall guided them for a short space across the night; but for the most part it was at a foot pace, and almost groping, that they picked their way through that resonant blackness to their solemn and isolated destination. In the sunken woods that traverse the neighbourhood of the burying-ground the last glimmer failed them, and it became necessary to kindle a match and reillumine one of the lanterns of the gig. Thus, under the dripping trees and environed by huge and moving shadows, they reached the scene of their unhallowed labours.

They were both experienced in such affairs, and powerful with the spade, and they had scarce been twenty minutes at their task before they were rewarded by a dull rattle on the coffin lid. At the same moment, Macfarlane, having hurt his hand upon a stone, flung it carelessly above his head. The grave, in which they now stood almost to the shoulders, was close to the edge of the plateau of the graveyard, and the gig lamp had been propped, the better to illuminate their labours, against a tree and on the immediate verge of the steep bank descending to the stream. Chance had taken a sure aim with the stone. Then came a clang of broken glass; night fell upon them; sounds alternately dull and ringing announced the bounding of the lantern down the bank, and its occasional collision with the trees. A stone or two, which it had dislodged in its descent, rattled behind it into the profundities of the glen; and then silence, like night, resumed its sway; and they might bend their hearing to its utmost pitch, but naught was to be heard except the rain, now marching to the wind, now steadily falling over miles of open country.

They were so nearly at an end of their abhorred task that they judged it wisest to complete it in the dark. The coffin was exhumed and broken open; the body inserted in the dripping sack and carried between them to the gig; one mounted to keep it in its place, and the other, taking the horse by the mouth, groped along by wall and bush until they reached the wider road by the Fisher's Tryst. Here was a faint, diffused radiancy, which they hailed like daylight; by that they pushed the horse to a good pace and began to rattle along merrily in the direction of the town.

They had both been wetted to the skin during their operations, and now, as the gig jumped among the deep ruts, the thing that stood propped between them fell now upon one and now upon the other. At every repetition of the horrid contact each instinctively repelled it with the greater haste; and the process, natural although it was, began to tell upon the nerves of the companions. Macfarlane made some ill-favoured jest about the farmer's wife, but it came hollowly from his lips and was allowed to drop in silence. Still their unnatural burden bumped from side to side; and now the head would be laid, as if in confidence, upon their shoulders, and now the drenching sackcloth would flap icily about their faces. A creeping chill began to possess the soul of Fettes. He peered at the bundle, and it seemed somehow larger than at first. All over the countryside, and from every degree of distance, the farm dogs accompanied their passage with tragic ululations; and it grew and grew upon his mind that some unnatural miracle had been accomplished, that some nameless change had befallen the dead body and that it was in fear of their unholy burden that the dogs were howling.

'For God's sake,' said he, making a great effort to arrive at speech, 'for God's sake, let's have a light!'

Seemingly Macfarlane was affected in the same direction; for, though he made no reply, he stopped the horse, passed the reins to his companion, got down, and proceeded to kindle the remaining lamp. They had by that time got no farther than the cross-road down to Auchenclinny. The rain still poured as though the deluge were returning, and it was no easy matter to make a light in such a world of wet and darkness. When at last the flickering blue flame had been transferred to the wick and began to expand and clarify, and shed a wide circle of misty brightness round the gig, it became possible for the two young men to see each other and the thing they had along with them. The rain had moulded the rough sacking to the outlines of the body underneath; the head was distinct from the trunk, the shoulders plainly modelled; something at once spectral and human riveted their eyes upon the ghastly comrade of their drive.

For some time Macfarlane stood motionless, holding up the lamp. A nameless dread was swathed, like a wet sheet, about the body, and tightened the white skin upon the face of Fettes; a fear that was meaningless, a horror of what could not be, kept mounting to his brain. Another beat of the watch, and he had spoken. But his comrade forestalled him.

'That is not a woman,' said Macfarlane, in a hushed voice.

'It was a woman when we put her in,' whispered Fettes.

'Hold that lamp,' said the other. 'I must see her face.'

And as Fettes took the lamp his companion untied the fastenings of the sack and drew down the cover from the head. The light fell very clear upon the dark, well-moulded features and smooth-shaven cheeks of a too familiar countenance, often beheld in dreams of both of these young men. A wild yell rang up into the night; each leaped from his own side into the roadway: the lamp fell, broke, and was extinguished; and the horse, terrified by this unusual commotion, bounded and went off towards Edinburgh at a gallop, bearing along with it, sole occupant of the gig, the body of the dead and long-dissected Gray.

The Yellow Wallpaper

CHARLOTTE PERKINS STETSON

IT IS VERY SELDOM that mere ordinary people like John and myself secure ancestral halls for the summer.

A colonial mansion, a hereditary estate, I would say a haunted house and reach the height of romantic felicity – but that would be asking too much of fate!

Still I will proudly declare that there is something queer about it. Else, why should it be let so cheaply? And why have stood so long untenanted?

John laughs at me, of course, but one expects that in marriage.

John is practical in the extreme. He has no patience with faith, an intense horror of superstition, and he scoffs openly at any talk of things not to be felt and seen and put down in figures.

John is a physician, and *perhaps* (I would not say it to a living soul, of course, but this is dead paper and a great relief to my mind), *perhaps* that is one reason I do not get well faster.

You see he does not believe I am sick!

And what can one do?

If a physician of high standing, and one's own husband, assures friends and relatives that there is really nothing the matter with one but temporary nervous depression – a slight hysterical tendency – what is one to do?

My brother is also a physician, and also of high standing, and he says the same thing.

So I take phosphates or phosphites – whichever it is, and tonics, and journeys, and air, and exercise, and am absolutely forbidden to 'work' until I am well again.

Personally, I disagree with their ideas.

Personally, I believe that congenial work, with excitement and change, would do me good.

But what is one to do?

I did write for a while in spite of them; but it *does* exhaust me a good deal – having to be so sly about it, or else meet with heavy opposition.

I sometimes fancy that in my condition, if I had less opposition and more society and stimulus – but John says the very worst thing I can do is to think about my condition, and I confess it always makes me feel bad.

So I will let it alone and talk about the house.

The most beautiful place! It is quite alone, standing well back from the road, quite three miles from the village. It makes me think of English places that you read about, for there are hedges and walls and gates that lock, and lots of separate little houses for the gardeners and people.

There is a *delicious* garden! I never saw such a garden – large and shady, full of box-bordered paths, and lined with long grape-covered arbours with seats under them.

There were greenhouses, too, but they are all broken now.

There was some legal trouble, I believe, something about the heirs and coheirs; anyhow, the place has been empty for years.

That spoils my ghostliness, I am afraid, but I don't care – there is something strange about the house – I can feel it.

I even said so to John one moonlight evening, but he said what I felt was a *draught*, and shut the window.

I get unreasonably angry with John sometimes. I'm sure I never used to be so sensitive. I think it is due to this nervous condition.

But John says, if I feel so, I shall neglect proper self-control; so I take pains to control myself – before him, at least, and that makes me very tired.

I don't like our room a bit. I wanted one downstairs that opened on the piazza and had roses all over the window, and such pretty old-fashioned chintz hangings! but John would not hear of it.

He said there was only one window and not room for two beds, and no near room for him if he took another.

He is very careful and loving, and hardly lets me stir without special direction.

I have a schedule prescription for each hour in the day; he takes all care from me, and so I feel basely ungrateful not to value it more.

He said we came here solely on my account, that I was to have perfect rest and all the air I could get. 'Your exercise depends on your strength, my dear,' said he, 'and your food somewhat on your appetite; but air you can absorb all the time.' So we took the nursery at the top of the house.

It is a big, airy room, the whole floor nearly, with windows that look all ways, and air and sunshine galore. It was nursery first and then playroom and gymnasium, I should judge; for the windows are barred for little children, and there are rings and things in the walls.

The paint and paper look as if a boys' school had used it. It is stripped off – the paper – in great patches all around the head of my bed, about as far as I can reach, and in a great place on the other side of the room low down. I never saw a worse paper in my life.

One of those sprawling flamboyant patterns committing every artistic sin.

It is dull enough to confuse the eye in following, pronounced enough constantly to irritate and provoke study, and when you follow the lame uncertain curves for a little distance they suddenly commit suicide – plunge off at outrageous angles, destroy themselves in unheard of contradictions.

The colour is repellent, almost revolting; a smouldering unclean yellow, strangely faded by the slow-turning sunlight.

It is a dull yet lurid orange in some places, a sickly sulphur tint in others.

No wonder the children hated it! I should hate it myself if I had to live in this room long.

There comes John, and I must put this away – he hates to have me write a word.

We have been here two weeks, and I haven't felt like writing before, since that first day.

I am sitting by the window now, up in this atrocious nursery, and there is nothing to hinder my writing as much as I please, save lack of strength.

John is away all day, and even some nights when his cases are serious.

I am glad my case is not serious!

But these nervous troubles are dreadfully depressing.

John does not know how much I really suffer. He knows there is no *reason* to suffer, and that satisfies him.

Of course it is only nervousness. It does weigh on me so not to do my duty in any way!

I meant to be such a help to John, such a real rest and comfort, and here I am a comparative burden already!

Nobody would believe what an effort it is to do what little I am able – to dress, and entertain, and order things.

It is fortunate Mary is so good with the baby. Such a dear baby!

And yet I *cannot* be with him, it makes me so nervous.

I suppose John never was nervous in his life. He laughs at me so about this wallpaper!

At first he meant to repaper the room, but afterwards he said that I was letting it get the better of me, and that nothing was worse for a nervous patient than to give way to such fancies.

He said that after the wallpaper was changed it would be the heavy bedstead, and then the barred windows, and then that gate at the head of the stairs, and so on.

'You know the place is doing you good,' he said, 'and really, dear, I don't care to renovate the house just for a three months' rental.'

'Then do let us go downstairs,' I said, 'there are such pretty rooms there.'

Then he took me in his arms and called me a blessed little goose, and said he would go down to the cellar, if I wished, and have it whitewashed into the bargain.

But he is right enough about the beds and windows and things.

It is as airy and comfortable a room as anyone need wish, and, of course, I would not be so silly as to make him uncomfortable just for a whim.

I'm really getting quite fond of the big room, all but that horrid paper.

Out of one window I can see the garden, those mysterious deep-shaded arbours, the riotous old-fashioned flowers, and bushes and gnarly trees.

Out of another I get a lovely view of the bay and a little private wharf belonging to the estate. There is a beautiful shaded lane that runs down there from the house. I always fancy I see people walking in these numerous paths and arbours, but John has cautioned me not to give way to fancy in the least. He says that with my imaginative power and habit of story-making, a nervous weakness like mine is sure to lead to all manner of excited fancies, and that I ought to use my will and good sense to check the tendency. So I try.

I think sometimes that if I were only well enough to write a little it would relieve the press of ideas and rest me.

But I find I get pretty tired when I try.

It is so discouraging not to have any advice and companionship about my work. When I get really well, John says we will ask Cousin Henry and Julia down for a long visit; but he says he would as soon put fireworks in my pillowcase as to let me have those stimulating people about now.

I wish I could get well faster.

But I must not think about that. This paper looks to me as if it *knew* what a vicious influence it had!

There is a recurrent spot where the pattern lolls like a broken neck and two bulbous eyes stare at you upside down.

I get positively angry with the impertinence of it and the everlastingness. Up and down and sideways they crawl, and those absurd, unblinking eyes are everywhere. There is one place where two breadths didn't match, and the eyes go all up and down the line, one a little higher than the other.

I never saw so much expression in an inanimate thing before, and we all know how much expression they have! I used to lie awake as a child and get more entertainment and terror out of blank walls and plain furniture than most children could find in a toy-store.

I remember what a kindly wink the knobs of our big, old bureau used to have, and there was one chair that always seemed like a strong friend.

I used to feel that if any of the other things looked too fierce I could always hop into that chair and be safe.

The furniture in this room is no worse than inharmonious, however, for we had to bring it all from downstairs. I suppose when this was used as a playroom they had to take the nursery things out, and no wonder! I never saw such ravages as the children have made here.

The wallpaper, as I said before, is torn off in spots, and it sticketh closer than a brother – they must have had perseverance as well as hatred.

Then the floor is scratched and gouged and splintered, the plaster itself is dug out here and there, and this great heavy bed which is all we found in the room, looks as if it had been through the wars.

But I don't mind it a bit – only the paper.

There comes John's sister. Such a dear girl as she is, and so careful of me! I must not let her find me writing.

She is a perfect and enthusiastic housekeeper, and hopes for no better profession. I verily believe she thinks it is the writing which made me sick!

But I can write when she is out, and see her a long way off from these windows.

There is one that commands the road, a lovely shaded winding road, and one that just looks off over the country. A lovely country, too, full of great elms and velvet meadows.

This wallpaper has a kind of sub-pattern in a different shade, a particularly irritating one, for you can only see it in certain lights, and not clearly then.

But in the places where it isn't faded and where the sun is just so –

I can see a strange, provoking, formless sort of figure, that seems to skulk about behind that silly and conspicuous front design.

There's sister on the stairs!

*   *   *

Well, the Fourth of July is over! The people are all gone and I am tired out. John thought it might do me good to see a little company, so we just had mother and Nellie and the children down for a week.

Of course I didn't do a thing. Jennie sees to everything now.

But it tired me all the same.

John says if I don't pick up faster he shall send me to Weir Mitchell in the fall.

But I don't want to go there at all. I had a friend who was in his hands once, and she says he is just like John and my brother, only more so!

Besides, it is such an undertaking to go so far.

I don't feel as if it was worth while to turn my hand over for anything, and I'm getting dreadfully fretful and querulous.

I cry at nothing, and cry most of the time.

Of course I don't when John is here, or anybody else, but when I am alone.

And I am alone a good deal just now. John is kept in town very often by serious cases, and Jennie is good and lets me alone when I want her to.

So I walk a little in the garden or down that lovely lane, sit on the porch under the roses, and lie down up here a good deal.

I'm getting really fond of the room in spite of the wallpaper. Perhaps *because* of the wallpaper.

It dwells in my mind so!

I lie here on this great immovable bed – it is nailed down, I believe – and follow that pattern about by the hour. It is as good as gymnastics, I assure you. I start, we'll say, at the bottom, down in the corner over there where it has not been touched, and I determine for the thousandth time that I *will* follow that pointless pattern to some sort of a conclusion.

I know a little of the principle of design, and I know this thing was not arranged on any laws of radiation, or alternation, or repetition, or symmetry, or anything else that I ever heard of.

It is repeated, of course, by the breadths, but not otherwise.

Looked at in one way each breadth stands alone, the bloated curves and flourishes – a kind of 'debased Romanesque' with *delirium tremens* – go waddling up and down in isolated columns of fatuity.

But, on the other hand, they connect diagonally, and the sprawling outlines run off in great slanting waves of optic horror, like a lot of wallowing seaweeds in full chase.

The whole thing goes horizontally, too, at least it seems so, and I exhaust myself in trying to distinguish the order of its going in that direction.

They have used a horizontal breadth for a frieze, and that adds wonderfully to the confusion.

There is one end of the room where it is almost intact, and there, when the crosslights fade and the low sun shines directly upon it, I can almost fancy radiation after all – the interminable grotesques seem to form around a common centre and rush off in headlong plunges of equal distraction.

It makes me tired to follow it. I will take a nap, I guess.

I don't know why I should write this.

I don't want to.

I don't feel able.

And I know John would think it absurd. But I *must* say what I feel and think in some way – it is such a relief!

But the effort is getting to be greater than the relief.

Half the time now I am awfully lazy, and lie down ever so much.

John says I mustn't lose my strength, and has me take cod liver oil and lots of tonics and things, to say nothing of ale and wine and rare meat.

Dear John! He loves me very dearly, and hates to have me sick. I tried to have a real earnest reasonable talk with him the other day, and tell him how I wish he would let me go and make a visit to Cousin Henry and Julia.

But he said I wasn't able to go, nor able to stand it after I got there; and I did not make out a very good case for myself, for I was crying before I had finished.

It is getting to be a great effort for me to think straight. Just this nervous weakness I suppose.

And dear John gathered me up in his arms, and just carried me upstairs and laid me on the bed, and sat by me and read to me till it tired my head.

He said I was his darling and his comfort and all he had, and that I must take care of myself for his sake, and keep well.

He says no one but myself can help me out of it, that I must use my will and self-control and not let any silly fancies run away with me.

There's one comfort, the baby is well and happy, and does not have to occupy this nursery with the horrid wallpaper.

If we had not used it, that blessed child would have! What a fortunate escape! Why, I wouldn't have a child of mine, an impressionable little thing, live in such a room for worlds.

I never thought of it before, but it is lucky that John kept me here after all, I can stand it so much easier than a baby, you see.

Of course I never mention it to them any more – I am too wise – but I keep watch of it all the same.

There are things in that paper that nobody knows but me, or ever will.

Behind that outside pattern the dim shapes get clearer every day.

It is always the same shape, only very numerous.

And it is like a woman stooping down and creeping about behind that pattern. I don't like it a bit. I wonder – I begin to think – I wish John would take me away from here!

It is so hard to talk with John about my case, because he is so wise, and because he loves me so.

But I tried it last night.

It was moonlight. The moon shines in all around just as the sun does.

I hate to see it sometimes, it creeps so slowly, and always comes in by one window or another.

John was asleep and I hated to waken him, so I kept still and watched the moonlight on that undulating wallpaper till I felt creepy.

The faint figure behind seemed to shake the pattern, just as if she wanted to get out.

I got up softly and went to feel and see if the paper *did* move, and when I came back John was awake.

'What is it, little girl?' he said. 'Don't go walking about like that – you'll get cold.'

I thought it was a good time to talk, so I told him that I really was not gaining here, and that I wished he would take me away.

'Why darling!' said he, 'our lease will be up in three weeks, and I can't see how to leave before.'

'The repairs are not done at home, and I cannot possibly leave town just now. Of course if you were in any danger, I could and would, but you really are better, dear, whether you can see it or not. I am a doctor, dear, and I know. You are gaining flesh and colour, your appetite is better, I feel really much easier about you.'

'I don't weigh a bit more,' said I, 'nor as much; and my appetite may be better in the evening when you are here, but it is worse in the morning when you are away!'

'Bless her little heart!' said he with a big hug, 'she shall be as sick as she pleases! But now let's improve the shining hours by going to sleep, and talk about it in the morning!'

'And you won't go away?' I asked gloomily.

'Why, how can I, dear? It is only three weeks more and then we will take a nice little trip of a few days while Jennie is getting the house ready. Really dear you are better!'

'Better in body perhaps – ' I began, and stopped short, for he sat up straight and looked at me with such a stern, reproachful look that I could not say another word.

'My darling,' said he, 'I beg of you, for my sake and for our child's sake, as well as for your own, that you will never for one instant let that idea enter your mind! There is nothing so dangerous, so fascinating, to a temperament like yours. It is a false and foolish fancy. Can you not trust me as a physician when I tell you so?'

So of course I said no more on that score, and we went to sleep before long. He thought I was asleep first, but I wasn't, and lay there for hours trying to decide whether that front pattern and the back pattern really did move together or separately.

On a pattern like this, by daylight, there is a lack of sequence, a defiance of law, that is a constant irritant to a normal mind.

The colour is hideous enough, and unreliable enough, and infuriating enough, but the pattern is torturing.

You think you have mastered it, but just as you get well underway in following, it turns a back-somersault and there you are. It slaps you in the face, knocks you down, and tramples upon you. It is like a bad dream.

The outside pattern is a florid arabesque, reminding one of a fungus. If you can imagine a toadstool in joints, an interminable string of toadstools, budding and sprouting in endless convolutions – why, that is something like it.

That is, sometimes!

There is one marked peculiarity about this paper, a thing nobody seems to notice but myself, and that is that it changes as the light changes.

When the sun shoots in through the east window – I always watch for that first long, straight ray – it changes so quickly that I never can quite believe it.

That is why I watch it always.

By moonlight – the moon shines in all night when there is a moon – I wouldn't know it was the same paper.

At night in any kind of light, in twilight, candlelight, lamplight, and worst of all by moonlight, it becomes bars! The outside pattern I mean, and the woman behind it is as plain as can be.

I didn't realise for a long time what the thing was that showed behind, that dim sub-pattern, but now I am quite sure it is a woman.

By daylight she is subdued, quiet. I fancy it is the pattern that keeps her so still. It is so puzzling. It keeps me quiet by the hour.

I lie down ever so much now. John says it is good for me, and to sleep all I can.

Indeed he started the habit by making me lie down for an hour after each meal.

It is a very bad habit I am convinced, for you see I don't sleep.

And that cultivates deceit, for I don't tell them I'm awake – Oh, no!

The fact is I am getting a little afraid of John.

He seems very queer sometimes, and even Jennie has an inexplicable look.

It strikes me occasionally just as a scientific hypothesis – that perhaps it is the paper!

I have watched John, when he did not know I was looking, and seen him come into the room suddenly on the most innocent excuses, and I've caught him several times *looking at the paper*! And Jennie too. I caught Jennie with her hand on it once.

She didn't know I was in the room, and when I asked her in a quiet, a very quiet voice, with the most restrained manner possible, what she was doing with the paper – she turned around as if she had been caught stealing, and looked quite angry, and asked me why I should frighten her so!

Then she said that the paper stained everything it touched, that she had found yellow smooches on all my clothes and John's, and she wished we would be more careful!

Did not that sound innocent? But I know she was studying that pattern, and I am determined that nobody shall find it out but myself!

Life is very much more exciting now than it used to be. You see, I have something more to expect, to look forward to, to watch. I really do eat better, and am more quiet than I was.

John is so pleased to see me improve! He laughed a little the other day, and said I seemed to be flourishing in spite of my wallpaper.

I turned it off with a laugh. I had no intention of telling him it was *because* of the wallpaper – he would make fun of me. He might even want to take me away.

I don't want to leave now until I have found it out. There is a week more, and I think that will be enough.

I'm feeling ever so much better! I don't sleep much at night, for it is so interesting to watch developments; but I sleep a good deal in the daytime.

In the daytime it is tiresome and perplexing.

There are always new shoots on the fungus, and new shades of yellow all over it. I cannot keep count of them, though I have tried conscientiously.

It is the strangest yellow, that wallpaper! It makes me think of all the yellow things I ever saw – not beautiful ones like buttercups, but old, foul, bad yellow things.

But there is something else about that paper – the smell! I noticed it the moment we came into the room, but with so much air and sun it was not bad. Now we have had a week of fog and rain, and whether the windows are open or not, the smell is here.

It creeps all over the house.

I find it hovering in the dining-room, skulking in the parlour, hiding in the hall, lying in wait for me on the stairs.

It gets into my hair.

Even when I go to ride, if I turn my head suddenly and surprise it – there is that smell!

Such a peculiar odour, too! I have spent hours in trying to analyse it, to find what it smelled like.

It is not bad – at first, and very gentle, but quite the subtlest, most enduring odour I ever met.

In this damp weather it is awful. I wake up in the night and find it hanging over me.

It used to disturb me at first. I thought seriously of burning the house – to reach the smell.

But now I am used to it. The only thing I can think of that it is like is the *colour* of the paper! A yellow smell.

There is a very funny mark on this wall, low down, near the mop board. A streak that runs round the room. It goes behind every piece of furniture, except the bed, a long, straight, even *smooch*, as if it had been rubbed over and over.

I wonder how it was done, and who did it, and what they did it for. Round and round and round – round and round and round – it makes me dizzy!

I really have discovered something at last.

Through watching so much at night, when it changes so, I have finally found out.

The front pattern *does* move – and no wonder! The woman behind shakes it!

Sometimes I think there are a great many women behind, and sometimes only one, and she crawls around fast, and her crawling shakes it all over.

Then in this very bright spots she keeps still, and in the very shady spots she just takes hold of the bars and shakes them hard.

And she is all the time trying to climb through. But nobody could climb through that pattern – it strangles so; I think that is why it has so many heads.

They get through, and then the pattern strangles them off and turns them upside down, and makes their eyes white!

If those heads were covered or taken off it would not be half so bad.

I think that woman gets out in the daytime!

And I'll tell you why – privately – I've seen her!

I can see her out of every one of my windows!

It is the same woman, I know, for she is always creeping, and most women do not creep by daylight.

I see her on that long road under the trees, creeping along, and when a carriage comes she hides under the blackberry vines.

I don't blame her a bit. It must be very humiliating to be caught creeping by daylight!

I always lock the door when I creep by daylight. I can't do it at night, for I know John would suspect something at once.

And John is so queer now that I don't want to irritate him. I wish he would take another room! Besides, I don't want anybody to get that woman out at night but myself.

I often wonder if I could see her out of all the windows at once.

But, turn as fast as I can, I can only see out of one at one time.

And though I always see her, she *may* be able to creep faster than I can turn!

I have watched her sometimes away off in the open country, creeping as fast as a cloud shadow in a high wind.

If only that top pattern could be gotten off from the under one! I mean to try it, little by little.

I have found out another funny thing, but I shan't tell it this time! It does not do to trust people too much.

There are only two more days to get this paper off, and I believe

John is beginning to notice. I don't like the look in his eyes.

And I heard him ask Jennie a lot of professional questions about me. She had a very good report to give.

She said I slept a good deal in the daytime.

John knows I don't sleep very well at night, for all I'm so quiet!

He asked me all sorts of questions, too, and pretended to be very loving and kind.

As if I couldn't see through him!

Still, I don't wonder he acts so, sleeping under this paper for three months.

It only interests me, but I feel sure John and Jennie are secretly affected by it.

Hurrah! This is the last day, but it is enough. John is to stay in town overnight, and won't be out until this evening.

Jennie wanted to sleep with me – the sly thing! but I told her I should undoubtedly rest better for a night all alone.

That was clever, for really I wasn't alone a bit! As soon as it was moonlight and that poor thing began to crawl and shake the pattern, I got up and ran to help her.

I pulled and she shook, I shook and she pulled, and before morning we had peeled off yards of that paper.

A strip about as high as my head and half around the room.

And then when the sun came and that awful pattern began to laugh at me, I declared I would finish it today!

We go away tomorrow, and they are moving all my furniture down again to leave things as they were before.

Jennie looked at the wall in amazement, but I told her merrily that I did it out of pure spite at the vicious thing.

She laughed and said she wouldn't mind doing it herself, but I must not get tired.

How she betrayed herself that time!

But I am here, and no person touches this paper but me – not *alive!*

She tried to get me out of the room – it was too patent! But I said it was so quiet and empty and clean now that I believed I would lie down again and sleep all I could; and not to wake me even for dinner – I would call when I woke.

So now she is gone, and the servants are gone, and the things are gone, and there is nothing left but that great bedstead nailed down, with the canvas mattress we found on it.

We shall sleep downstairs tonight, and take the boat home tomorrow.

I quite enjoy the room, now it is bare again.

How those children did tear about here!

This bedstead is fairly gnawed!

But I must get to work.

I have locked the door and thrown the key down on to the front path.

I don't want to go out, and I don't want to have anybody come in, till John comes.

I want to astonish him.

I've got a rope up here that even Jennie did not find. If that woman does get out, and tries to get away, I can tie her!

But I forgot I could not reach far without anything to stand on!

This bed will *not* move!

I tried to lift and push it until I was lame, and then I got so angry I bit off a little piece at one corner – but it hurt my teeth.

Then I peeled off all the paper I could reach standing on the floor. It sticks horribly and the pattern just enjoys it! All those strangled heads and bulbous eyes and waddling fungus growths just shriek with derision!

I am getting angry enough to do something desperate. To jump out of the window would be admirable exercise, but the bars are too strong even to try.

Besides I wouldn't do it. Of course not. I know well enough that a step like that is improper and might be misconstrued.

I don't like to *look* out of the windows even – there are so many of those creeping women, and they creep so fast.

I wonder if they all come out of that wallpaper as I did?

But I am securely fastened now by my well-hidden rope – you don't get *me* out in the road there!

I suppose I shall have to get back behind the pattern when it comes night, and that is hard!

It is so pleasant to be out in this great room and creep around as I please!

I don't want to go outside. I won't, even if Jennie asks me to.

For outside you have to creep on the ground, and everything is green instead of yellow.

But here I can creep smoothly on the floor, and my shoulder just fits in that long smooch around the wall, so I cannot lose my way.

Why there's John at the door!

It is no use, young man, you can't open it!

How he does call and pound!

Now he's crying for an axe.

It would be a shame to break down that beautiful door!

'John dear!' said I in the gentlest voice, 'the key is down by the front steps, under a plantain leaf!'

That silenced him for a few moments.

Then he said – very quietly indeed, 'Open the door, my darling!'

'I can't,' said I. 'The key is down by the front door under a plantain leaf!'

And then I said it again, several times, very gently and slowly, and said it so often that he had to go and see, and he got it of course, and came in. He stopped short by the door.

'What is the matter?' he cried. 'For God's sake, what are you doing!'

I kept on creeping just the same, but I looked at him over my shoulder.

'I've got out at last,' said I, 'in spite of you and Jane. And I've pulled off most of the paper, so you can't put me back!'

Now why should that man have fainted? But he did, and right across my path by the wall, so that I had to creep over him every time!

The Death of Halpin Frayser

AMBROSE BIERCE

I

For by death is wrought greater change than hath been shown. Whereas in general the spirit that removed cometh back upon occasion, and is sometimes seen of those in flesh (appearing in the form of the body it bore) yet it hath happened that the veritable body without the spirit hath walked. And it is attested of those encountering who have lived to speak thereon that a lich so raised up hath no natural affection, nor remembrance thereof, but only hate. Also, it is known that some spirits which in life were benign become by death evil altogether.   HALI

ONE DARK NIGHT in midsummer a man waking from a dreamless sleep in a forest lifted his head from the earth, and staring a few moments into the blackness, said: 'Catherine Larue.' He said nothing more; no reason was known to him why he should have said so much.

The man was Halpin Frayser. He lived in St Helena, but where he lives now is uncertain, for he is dead. One who practises sleeping in the woods with nothing under him but the dry leaves and the damp earth, and nothing over him but the branches from which the leaves have fallen and the sky from which the earth has fallen, cannot hope for great longevity, and Frayser had already attained the age of thirty-two. There are persons in this world, millions of persons, and far and away the best persons, who regard that as a very advanced age. They are the children. To those who view the voyage of life from the port of departure, the bark that has accomplished any considerable distance appears already in close approach to the farther shore. However, it is not certain that Halpin Frayser came to his death by exposure.

He had been all day in the hills west of the Napa Valley, looking for doves and such small game as was in season. Late in the afternoon it had come on to be cloudy, and he had lost his bearings; and although he had only to go always downhill – everywhere the way to safety when one is lost – the absence of trails had so impeded him that he was overtaken by night while still in the forest. Unable in the darkness to penetrate the thickets of manzanita and other under-growth, utterly bewildered and overcome with fatigue, he had lain down near the root of a large madroño and fallen into a dreamless sleep. It was hours later, in the very middle of the night, that one of God's mysterious messengers, gliding ahead of the incalculable host of his companions sweeping westward with the dawn line, pro-nounced the awakening word in the ear of the sleeper, who sat upright and spoke, he knew not why, a name, he knew not whose.

Halpin Frayser was not much of a philosopher, nor a scientist. The circumstance that, waking from a deep sleep at night in the midst of a forest, he had spoken aloud a name that he had not in memory and hardly had in mind did not arouse an enlightened curiosity to investigate the phenomenon. He thought it odd, and with a little perfunctory shiver, as if in deference to a seasonal presumption that the night was chill, he lay down again and went to sleep. But his sleep was no longer dreamless.

He thought he was walking along a dusty road that showed white in the gathering darkness of a summer night. Whence and whither it led, and why he travelled it, he did not know, though all seemed simple and natural, as is the way in dreams; for in the Land Beyond the Bed surprises cease from troubling and the judgement is at rest. Soon he came to a parting of the ways; leading from the highway was a road less travelled, having the appearance, indeed, of having been long abandoned, because, he thought, it led to something evil; yet he turned into it without hesitation, impelled by some imperious necessity.

As he pressed forward he became conscious that his way was haunted by invisible existences whom he could not definitely figure to his mind. From among the trees on either side he caught broken and incoherent whispers in a strange tongue which yet he partly understood. They seemed to him fragmentary utterances of a mon-strous conspiracy against his body and soul.

It was now long after nightfall, yet the interminable forest through which he journeyed was lit with a wan glimmer having no point of diffusion, for in its mysterious lumination nothing cast a shadow. A shallow pool in the guttered depression of an old wheel rut, as from a recent rain, met his eye with a crimson gleam. He stooped and plunged his hand into it. It stained his fingers; it was blood! Blood, he then observed, was about him everywhere. The weeds growing rankly by the roadside showed it in blots and splashes on their big, broad leaves. Patches of dry dust between the wheelways were pitted and spattered as with a red rain. Defiling the trunks of the trees were broad maculations of crimson, and blood dripped like dew from their foliage.

All this he observed with a terror which seemed not incompatible with the fulfilment of a natural expectation. It seemed to him that it was all in expiation of some crime which, though conscious of his guilt, he could not rightly remember. To the menaces and mysteries of his surroundings the consciousness was an added horror. Vainly he sought, by tracing life backward in memory, to reproduce the moment of his sin; scenes and incidents came crowding tumultuously into his mind, one picture effacing another, or commingling with it in confusion and obscurity, but nowhere could he catch a glimpse of what he sought. The failure augmented his terror; he felt as one who has murdered in the dark, not knowing whom nor why. So frightful was the situation – the mysterious light burned with so silent and awful a menace; the noxious plants, the trees that by common consent were invested with a melancholy or baleful character, so openly in his sight conspired against his peace; from overhead and all about came so audible and startling whispers and the sighs of creatures so obviously not of earth – that he could endure it no longer, and with a great effort to break some malign spell that bound his faculties to silence and inaction, he shouted with the full strength of his lungs! His voice, broken, it seemed, into an infinite multitude of unfamiliar sounds, went babbling and stammering away into the distant reaches of the forest, died into silence, and all was as before. But he had made a beginning at resistance and was encouraged. He said: 'I will not submit unheard. There may be powers that are not malignant travelling this accursed road. I shall leave them a record and an appeal. I shall relate my wrongs, the persecutions that I endure – I, a helpless mortal, a penitent, an unoffending poet!' Halpin Frayser was a poet only as he was a penitent: in his dream.

Taking from his clothing a small red-leather pocketbook, one-half of which was leaved for memoranda, he discovered that he was without a pencil. He broke a twig from a bush, dipped it into a pool of blood and wrote rapidly. He had hardly touched the paper with the point of his twig when a low, wild peal of laughter broke out at a measureless distance away, and growing ever louder, seemed approaching ever nearer; a soulless, heartless and unjoyous laugh, like that of the loon, solitary by the lakeside at midnight; a laugh which culminated in an unearthly shout close at hand, then died away by slow gradations, as if the accursed being that uttered it had withdrawn over the verge of the world whence it had come. But the man felt that this was not so – that it was near by and had not moved.

A strange sensation began slowly to take possession of his body and his mind. He could not have said which, if any, of his senses was affected; he felt it rather as a consciousness – a mysterious mental assurance of some overpowering presence – some supernatural malevolence different in kind from the invisible existences that swarmed about him, and superior to them in power. He knew that it had uttered that hideous laugh. And now it seemed to be approaching him; from what direction he did not know – dared not conjecture. All his former fears were forgotten or merged in the gigantic terror that now held him in thrall. Apart from that, he had but one thought; to complete his written appeal to the benign powers who, traversing the haunted wood, might some time rescue him if he should be denied the blessing of annihilation. He wrote with terrible rapidity, the twig in his fingers rilling blood without renewal; but in the middle of a sentence his hands denied their service to his will, his arms fell to his sides, the book to the earth; and powerless to move or cry out, he found himself staring into the sharply drawn face and blank, dead eyes of his own mother, standing white and silent in the garments of the grave!

2

In his youth Halpin Frayser had lived with his parents in Nashville, Tennessee. The Fraysers were well-to-do, having a good position in such society as had survived the wreck wrought by civil war. Their children had the social and educational opportunities of their time and place, and had responded to good associations and instruction with agreeable manners and cultivated minds. Halpin, being the youngest and not over-robust, was perhaps a trifle 'spoiled'. He had the double disadvantage of a mother's assiduity and a father's neglect. Frayser *père* was what no Southern man of means is not – a politician. His country, or rather his section and State, made demands upon his time and attention so exacting that to those of his family he was compelled to turn an ear partly deafened by the thunder of the political captains and the shouting, his own included.

Young Halpin was of a dreamy, indolent and rather romantic turn, somewhat more addicted to literature than law, the profession to which he was bred. Among those of his relations who professed the

modern faith of heredity it was well understood that in him the
character of the late Myron Bayne, a maternal great-grandfather, had
revisited the glimpses of the moon[1] – by which orb Bayne had in his
lifetime been sufficiently affected to be a poet of no small Colonial
distinction. If not specially observed, it was observable that while a
Frayser who was not the proud possessor of a sumptuous copy of the
ancestral 'poetical works' (printed at the family expense, and long ago
withdrawn from an inhospitable market) was a rare Frayser indeed,
there was an illogical indisposition to honour the great deceased in
the person of his spiritual successor. Halpin was pretty generally
deprecated as an intellectual black sheep who was likely at any
moment to disgrace the flock by bleating in meter. The Tennessee
Fraysers were a practical folk – not practical in the popular sense of
devotion to sordid pursuits, but having a robust contempt for any
qualities unfitting a man for the wholesome vocation of politics.

   In justice to young Halpin it should be said that while in him were
pretty faithfully reproduced most of the mental and moral characteristics ascribed by history and family tradition to the famous Colonial
bard, his succession to the gift and faculty divine[2] was purely inferen-
tial. Not only had he never been known to court the muse, but in
truth he could not have written correctly a line of verse to save
himself from the Killer of the Wise. Still, there was no knowing
when the dormant faculty might wake and smite the lyre.

   In the meantime the young man was rather a loose fish, anyhow.
Between him and his mother was the most perfect sympathy, for
secretly the lady was herself a devout disciple of the late and great
Myron Bayne, though with the tact so generally and justly admired
in her sex (despite the hardy calumniators who insist that it is
essentially the same thing as cunning) she had always taken care to
conceal her weakness from all eyes but those of him who shared it.
Their common guilt in respect of that was an added tie between
them. If in Halpin's youth his mother had 'spoiled' him, he had
assuredly done his part toward being spoiled. As he grew to such
manhood as is attainable by a Southerner who does not care which
way elections go, the attachment between him and his beautiful
mother – whom from early childhood he had called Katy – became
yearly stronger and more tender. In these two romantic natures was
manifest in a signal way that neglected phenomenon, the dominance
of the sexual element in all the relations of life, strengthening,
softening and beautifying even those of consanguinity. The two were
nearly inseparable and by strangers observing their manner were not
infrequently mistaken for lovers.

Entering his mother's boudoir one day Halpin Frayser kissed her upon the forehead, toyed for a moment with a lock of her dark hair which had escaped from its confining pins, and said, with an obvious effort at calmness: 'Would you greatly mind, Katy, if I were called away to California for a few weeks?'

It was hardly needful for Katy to answer with her lips a question to which her telltale cheeks had made instant reply. Evidently she would greatly mind; and the tears, too, sprang into her large brown eyes as corroborative testimony.

'Ah, my son,' she said, looking up into his face with infinite tenderness, 'I should have known that this was coming. Did I not lie awake half of the night weeping because, during the other half, Grandfather Bayne had come to me in a dream, and standing by his portrait – young, too, and handsome as that – pointed to yours on the same wall? And when I looked it seemed that I could not see the features; you had been painted with a face cloth, such as we put upon the dead. Your father has laughed at me, but you and I, dear, know that such things are not for nothing. And I saw below the edge of the cloth the marks of hands on your throat – forgive me, but we have not been used to keep such things from each other. Perhaps you have another interpretation. Perhaps it does not mean that you will go to California. Or maybe you will take me with you?'

It must be confessed that this ingenious interpretation of the dream in the light of newly discovered evidence did not wholly commend itself to the son's more logical mind; he had, for the moment at least, a conviction that it foreshadowed a more simple and immediate, if less tragic, disaster than a visit to the Pacific Coast. It was Halpin Frayser's impression that he was to be garrotted on his native heath.

'Are there not medicinal springs in California?' Mrs Frayser resumed before he had time to give her the true reading of the dream – 'places where one recovers from rheumatism and neuralgia? Look – my fingers feel so stiff; and I am almost sure they have been giving me great pain while I slept.'

She held out her hands for his inspection. What diagnosis of her case the young man may have thought it best to conceal with a smile the historian is unable to state, but for himself he feels bound to say that fingers looking less stiff, and showing fewer evidences of even insensible pain, have seldom been submitted for medical inspection by even the fairest patient desiring a prescription of unfamiliar scenes.

The outcome of it was that of these two odd persons having equally odd notions of duty, the one went to California, as the interest of his client required, and the other remained at home in compliance with a wish that her husband was scarcely conscious of entertaining.

While in San Francisco Halpin Frayser was walking one dark night along the waterfront of the city, when, with a suddenness that surprised and disconcerted him, he became a sailor. He was in fact 'shanghaied' aboard a gallant, gallant ship,[3] and sailed for a far countree.[4] Nor did his misfortunes end with the voyage; for the ship was cast ashore on an island of the South Pacific, and it was six years afterward when the survivors were taken off by a venturesome trading schooner and brought back to San Francisco.

Though poor in purse, Frayser was no less proud in spirit than he had been in the years that seemed ages and ages ago. He would accept no assistance from strangers, and it was while living with a fellow survivor near the town of St Helena, awaiting news and remittances from home, that he had gone gunning and dreaming.

3

The apparition confronting the dreamer in the haunted wood – the thing so like, yet so unlike his mother – was horrible! It stirred no love nor longing in his heart; it came unattended with pleasant memories of a golden past – inspired no sentiment of any kind; all the finer emotions were swallowed up in fear. He tried to turn and run from before it, but his legs were as lead; he was unable to lift his feet from the ground. His arms hung helpless at his sides; of his eyes only he retained control, and these he dared not remove from the lustreless orbs of the apparition, which he knew was not a soul without a body but that most dreadful of all existences infesting that haunted wood – a body without a soul! In its blank stare was neither love, nor pity, nor intelligence – nothing to which to address an appeal for mercy. 'An appeal will not lie,' he thought, with an absurd reversion to professional slang, making the situation more horrible, as the fire of a cigar might light up a tomb.

For a time, which seemed so long that the world grew grey with age and sin, and the haunted forest, having fulfilled its purpose in this monstrous culmination of its terrors, vanished out of his consciousness with all its sights and sounds, the apparition stood within a pace, regarding him with the mindless malevolence of a wild brute; then thrust its hands forward and sprang upon him with appalling ferocity! The act released his physical energies without unfettering his will; his mind was still spellbound, but his powerful body and agile limbs, endowed with a blind, insensate life of their own, resisted stoutly and well. For an instant he seemed to see this unnatural contest between a dead intelligence and a breathing mechanism only as a spectator – such fancies are in dreams; then he regained his identity almost as if by a leap forward into his body, and the straining automaton had a directing will as alert and fierce as that of its hideous antagonist.

But what mortal can cope with a creature of his dream? The imagination creating the enemy is already vanquished; the combat's result is the combat's cause. Despite his struggles – despite his strength and activity, which seemed wasted in a void, he felt the cold fingers close upon his throat. Borne backward to the earth, he saw above him the dead and drawn face within a hand's breadth of his own, and then all was black. A sound as of the beating of distant drums – a murmur of swarming voices, a sharp, far cry signing all to silence, and Halpin Frayser dreamed that he was dead.

4

A warm, clear night had been followed by a morning of drenching fog. At about the middle of the afternoon of the preceding day a little whiff of light vapour – a mere thickening of the atmosphere, the ghost of a cloud – had been observed clinging to the western side of Mount St Helena, away up along the barren altitudes near the summit. It was so thin, so diaphanous, so like a fancy made visible, that one would have said: 'Look quickly! in a moment it will be gone.'

In a moment it was visibly larger and denser. While with one edge it clung to the mountain, with the other it reached farther and farther out into the air above the lower slopes. At the same time it extended itself to north and south, joining small patches of mist that appeared to come out of the mountainside on exactly the same level, with an intelligent design to be absorbed. And so it grew and grew until the summit was shut out of view from the valley, and over the valley itself was an ever-extending canopy, opaque and grey. At Calistoga, which lies near the head of the valley and the foot of the mountain, there were a starless night and a sunless morning. The fog, sinking into the valley, had reached southward, swallowing up ranch after ranch, until it had blotted out the town of St Helena, nine miles away. The dust in the road was laid; trees were adrip with moisture; birds sat silent in their coverts; the morning light was wan and ghastly, with neither colour nor fire.

Two men left the town of St Helena at the first glimmer of dawn and walked along the road northward up the valley toward Calistoga. They carried guns on their shoulders, yet no one having knowledge of such matters could have mistaken them for hunters of bird or beast. They were a deputy sheriff from Napa and a detective from San Francisco – Holker and Jaralson, respectively. Their business was manhunting.

'How far is it?' enquired Holker, as they strode along, their feet stirring white the dust beneath the damp surface of the road.

'The White Church? Only a half-mile farther,' the other answered. 'By the way,' he added, 'it is neither white nor a church; it is an abandoned schoolhouse, grey with age and neglect. Religious services were once held in it – when it was white, and there is a graveyard that would delight a poet. Can you guess why I sent for you, and told you to come heeled?'

'Oh, I never have bothered you about things of that kind. I've always found you communicative when the time came. But if I may hazard a guess, you want me to help you arrest one of the corpses in the graveyard.'

'You remember Branscom?' said Jaralson, treating his companion's wit with the inattention that it deserved.

'The chap who cut his wife's throat? I ought; I wasted a week's work on him and had my expenses for my trouble. There is a reward of five hundred dollars, but none of us ever got a sight of him. You don't mean to say – '

'Yes, I do. He has been under the noses of you fellows all the time. He comes by night to the old graveyard at the White Church.'

'The devil! That's where they buried his wife.'

'Well, you fellows might have had sense enough to suspect that he would return to her grave some time.'

'The very last place that anyone would have expected him to return to.'

'But you had exhausted all the other places. Learning your failure at them, I "laid for him" there.'

'And you found him?'

'Damn it! he found *me*. The rascal got the drop on me – regularly held me up and made me travel. It's God's mercy that he didn't go through me. Oh, he's a good one, and I fancy the half of that reward is enough for me if you're needy.'

Holker laughed good-humouredly, and explained that his creditors were never more importunate.

'I wanted merely to show you the ground, and arrange a plan with you,' the detective explained. 'I thought it as well for us to be heeled, even in daylight.'

'The man must be insane,' said the deputy sheriff. 'The reward is for his capture and conviction. If he's mad he won't be convicted.'

Mr Holker was so profoundly affected by that possible failure of justice that he involuntarily stopped in the middle of the road, then resumed his walk with abated zeal.

'Well, he looks it,' assented Jaralson. 'I'm bound to admit that a more unshaven, unshorn, unkempt and uneverything wretch I never saw outside the ancient and honourable order of tramps. But I've gone in for him, and can't make up my mind to let go. There's glory in it for us, anyhow. Not another soul knows that he is this side of the Mountains of the Moon.'

'All right,' Holker said; 'we will go and view the ground,' and he added, in the words of a once favourite inscription for tombstones: ' "where you must shortly lie" – I mean, if old Branscom ever gets tired of you and your impertinent intrusion. By the way, I heard the other day that "Branscom" was not his real name.'

'What is?'

'I can't recall it. I had lost all interest in the wretch, and it did not fix itself in my memory – something like Pardee. The woman whose throat he had the bad taste to cut was a widow when he met her. She had come to California to look up some relatives – there are persons who will do that sometimes. But you know all that.'

'Naturally.'

'But not knowing the right name, by what happy inspiration did you find the right grave? The man who told me what the name was said it had been cut on the headboard.'

'I don't know the right grave.' Jaralson was apparently a trifle reluctant to admit his ignorance of so important a point of his plan. 'I have been watching about the place generally. A part of our work this morning will be to identify that grave. Here is the White Church.'

For a long distance the road had been bordered by fields on both sides, but now on the left there was a forest of oaks, madroños and gigantic spruces, whose lower parts only could be seen, dim and ghostly in the fog. The undergrowth was, in places, thick, but nowhere impenetrable. For some moments Holker saw nothing of the building, but as they turned into the woods it revealed itself in faint grey outline through the fog, looking huge and far away. A few steps more, and it was within an arm's length, distinct, dark with moisture, and insignificant in size. It had the usual country-school-house form – belonged to the packing-box order of architecture; had an underpinning of stones, a moss-grown roof and blank window spaces, whence both glass and sash had long departed. It was ruined, but not a ruin – a typical Californian substitute for what are known to guide-bookers abroad as 'monuments of the past'. With scarcely a glance at this uninteresting structure Jaralson moved on into the dripping undergrowth beyond.

'I will show you where he held me up,' he said. 'This is the graveyard.'

Here and there among the bushes were small enclosures containing graves, sometimes no more than one. They were recognised as graves by the discoloured stones or rotting boards at head and foot, leaning at all angles, some prostrate; by the ruined picket fences surrounding them; or, infrequently, by the mound itself showing its gravel through the fallen leaves. In many instances nothing marked the spot where lay the vestiges of some poor mortal – who, leaving 'a large circle of sorrowing friends', had been left by them in turn – except a depression in the earth, more lasting than that in the spirits of the mourners. The paths, if any paths had been, were long obliterated; trees of a considerable size had been permitted to grow up from the graves and thrust aside with root or branch the enclosing fences. Over all was that air of abandonment and decay which seems nowhere so fit and significant as in a village of the forgotten dead.

As the two men, Jaralson leading, pushed their way through the growth of young trees, that enterprising man suddenly stopped and brought up his shotgun to the height of his breast, uttered a low note of warning, and stood motionless, his eyes fixed upon something ahead. As well as he could, obstructed by brush, his companion, though seeing nothing, imitated the posture and so stood, prepared for what might ensue. A moment later Jaralson moved cautiously forward, the other following.

Under the branches of an enormous spruce lay the dead body of a man. Standing silent above it they noted such particulars as first strike the attention – the face, the attitude, the clothing; whatever most promptly and plainly answers the unspoken question of a sympathetic curiosity.

The body lay upon its back, the legs wide apart. One arm was thrust upward, the other outward; but the latter was bent acutely, and the hand was near the throat. Both hands were tightly clenched. The whole attitude was that of desperate but ineffectual resistance to – what?

Nearby lay a shotgun and a game bag through the meshes of which was seen the plumage of shot birds. All about were evidences of a

furious struggle; small sprouts of poison oak were bent and denuded
of leaf and bark; dead and rotting leaves had been pushed into heaps
and ridges on both sides of the legs by the action of other feet than
theirs; alongside the hips were unmistakable impressions of human
knees.

The nature of the struggle was made clear by a glance at the dead
man's throat and face. While breast and hands were white, those
were purple – almost black. The shoulders lay upon a low mound,
and the head was turned back at an angle otherwise impossible, the
expanded eyes staring blankly backward in a direction opposite to
that of the feet. From the froth filling the open mouth the tongue
protruded, black and swollen. The throat showed horrible contu-
sions; not mere fingermarks, but bruises and lacerations wrought by
two strong hands that must have buried themselves in the yielding
flesh, maintaining their terrible grasp until long after death. Breast,
throat, face, were wet; the clothing was saturated; drops of water,
condensed from the fog, studded the hair and moustache.

All this the two men observed without speaking – almost at a
glance. Then Holker said: 'Poor devil! he had a rough deal.'

Jaralson was making a vigilant circumspection of the forest, his
shotgun held in both hands and at full cock, his finger upon the trigger.

'The work of a maniac,' he said, without withdrawing his eyes
from the enclosing wood. 'It was done by Branscom – Pardee.'

Something half hidden by the disturbed leaves on the earth caught
Holker's attention. It was a red-leather pocketbook. He picked it up
and opened it. It contained leaves of white paper for memoranda,
and upon the first leaf was the name 'Halpin Frayser'. Written in red
on several succeeding leaves – scrawled as if in haste and barely
legible – were the following lines, which Holker read aloud, while his
companion continued scanning the dim grey confines of their narrow world and hearing matter of apprehension in the drip of water
from every burdened branch:

> Enthralled by some mysterious spell, I stood
> In the lit gloom of an enchanted wood.
>   The cypress there and myrtle twined their boughs,
> Significant, in baleful brotherhood.
>
> The brooding willow whispered to the yew;
> Beneath, the deadly nightshade and the rue,
>   With immortelles self-woven into strange
> Funereal shapes, and horrid nettles grew.

No song of bird nor any drone of bees,
Nor light leaf lifted by the wholesome breeze:
     The air was stagnant all, and Silence was
A living thing that breathed among the trees.

Conspiring spirits whispered in the gloom,
Half-heard, the stilly secrets of the tomb.
     With blood the trees were all adrip; the leaves
Shone in the witch-light with a ruddy bloom.

I cried aloud! – the spell, unbroken still,
Rested upon my spirit and my will.
     Unsouled, unhearted, hopeless and forlorn,
I strove with monstrous presages of ill!

At last the viewless –

Holker ceased reading; there was no more to read. The manuscript
broke off in the middle of a line.

'That sounds like Bayne,' said Jaralson, who was something of a
scholar in his way. He had abated his vigilance and stood looking
down at the body.

'Who's Bayne?' Holker asked rather incuriously.

'Myron Bayne, a chap who flourished in the early years of the
nation – more than a century ago. Wrote mighty dismal stuff; I have
his collected works. That poem is not among them, but it must have
been omitted by mistake.'

'It is cold,' said Holker; 'let us leave here; we must have up the
coroner from Napa.'

Jaralson said nothing, but made a movement in compliance. Passing the end of the slight elevation of earth upon which the dead
man's head and shoulders lay, his foot struck some hard substance
under the rotting forest leaves, and he took the trouble to kick it into
view. It was a fallen headboard, and painted on it were the hardly
decipherable words, 'Catherine Larue'.

'Larue, Larue!' exclaimed Holker, with sudden animation. 'Why,
that is the real name of Branscom – not Pardee. And – bless my soul!
how it all comes to me – the murdered woman's name had been
Frayser!'

'There is some rascally mystery here,' said Detective Jaralson. 'I
hate anything of that kind.'

There came to them out of the fog – seemingly from a great
distance – the sound of a laugh, a low, deliberate, soulless laugh,
which had no more of joy than that of a hyena night-prowling in the

desert; a laugh that rose by slow gradation, louder and louder, clearer, more distinct and terrible, until it seemed barely outside the narrow circle of their vision; a laugh so unnatural, so unhuman, so devilish, that it filled those hardy manhunters with a sense of dread unspeakable! They did not move their weapons nor think of them; the menace of that horrible sound was not of the kind to be met with arms. As it had grown out of silence, so now it died away; from a culminating shout which had seemed almost in their ears, it drew itself away into the distance, until its failing notes, joyless and mechanical to the last, sank to silence at a measureless remove.

Canon Alberic's Scrapbook

M. R. JAMES

St Bertrand de Comminges is a decayed town on the spurs of the
Pyrenees, not very far from Toulouse and still nearer to Bagnères-
de-Luchon. It was the site of a bishopric until the Revolution, and
has a cathedral which is visited by a certain number of tourists. In the
spring of 1883 an Englishman arrived at this old-world place – I can
hardly dignify it with the name of city, for there are not a thousand
inhabitants. He was a Cambridge man, who had come specially from
Toulouse to see St Bertrand's Church, and had left two friends, who
were less keen archaeologists than himself, in their hotel at Toulouse, under promise to join him on the following morning. Half an
hour at the church would satisfy *them*, and all three could then
pursue their journey in the direction of Auch. But our Englishman
had come early on the day in question, and proposed to himself to fill
a notebook and to use several dozens of plates in the process of
describing and photographing every corner of the wonderful church
that dominates the little hill of Comminges. In order to carry out this
design satisfactorily, it was necessary to monopolise the verger of the
church for the day. The verger or sacristan (I prefer the latter
appellation, inaccurate as it may be) was accordingly sent for by the
somewhat brusque lady who keeps the inn of the Chapeau Rouge;
and when he came, the Englishman found him an unexpectedly
interesting object of study. It was not in the personal appearance of
the little, dry, wizened old man that the interest lay, for he was
precisely like dozens of other church-guardians in France, but in a
curious furtive, or rather hunted and oppressed, air which he had. He
was perpetually half glancing behind him; the muscles of his back
and shoulders seemed to be hunched in a continual nervous contrac-
tion, as if he were expecting every moment to find himself in the
clutch of an enemy. The Englishman hardly knew whether to put
him down as a man haunted by a fixed delusion, or as one oppressed
by a guilty conscience, or as an unbearably henpecked husband. The

probabilities, when reckoned up, certainly pointed to the last idea; but, still, the impression conveyed was that of a more formidable persecutor even than a termagant wife.

However, the Englishman (let us call him Dennistoun) was soon too deep in his notebook and too busy with his camera to give more than an occasional glance to the sacristan. Whenever he did look at him, he found him at no great distance, either huddling himself back against the wall or crouching in one of the gorgeous stalls. Dennistoun became rather fidgety after a time. Mingled suspicions that he was keeping the old man from his *déjeuner*, that he was regarded as likely to make away with St Bertrand's ivory crozier, or with the dusty stuffed crocodile that hangs over the font, began to torment him.

'Won't you go home?' he said at last; 'I'm quite well able to finish my notes alone; you can lock me in if you like. I shall want at least two hours more here, and it must be cold for you, isn't it?'

'Good heavens!' said the little man, whom the suggestion seemed to throw into a state of unaccountable terror, 'such a thing cannot be thought of for a moment. Leave monsieur alone in the church? No, no; two hours, three hours, all will be the same to me. I have breakfasted and I am not at all cold, with many thanks to monsieur.'

'Very well, my little man,' quoth Dennistoun to himself: 'you have been warned, and you must take the consequences.'

Before the expiration of the two hours, the stalls, the enormous dilapidated organ, the choir-screen of Bishop John de Mauléon, the remnants of glass and tapestry and the objects in the treasure-chamber had been well and truly examined, the sacristan still keeping at Dennistoun's heels, and every now and then whipping round as if he had been stung when one or other of the strange noises that trouble a large empty building fell on his ear. Curious noises they were sometimes.

'Once,' Dennistoun said to me, 'I could have sworn I heard a thin metallic voice laughing high up in the tower. I darted an enquiring glance at my sacristan. He was white to the lips. "It is he – that is – it is no one; the door is locked," was all he said, and we looked at each other for a full minute.'

Another little incident puzzled Dennistoun a good deal. He was examining a large dark picture that hangs behind the altar, one of a series illustrating the miracles of St Bertrand. The composition of the picture is well-nigh indecipherable, but there is a Latin legend below, which runs thus:

Qualiter S. Bertrandus liberavit hominem quem diabolus diu volebat strangulare. [How St Bertrand delivered a man whom the Devil long sought to strangle.]

Dennistoun was turning to the sacristan with a smile and a jocular remark of some sort on his lips, but he was confounded to see the old man on his knees, gazing at the picture with the eye of a suppliant in agony, his hands tightly clasped and a rain of tears on his cheeks. Dennistoun naturally pretended to have noticed nothing, but the question would not go away from him, 'Why should a daub of this kind affect anyone so strongly?' He seemed to himself to be getting some sort of clue to the reason of the strange look that had been puzzling him all the day: the man must be a monomaniac; but what was his monomania?

It was nearly five o'clock; the short day was drawing in, and the church began to fill with shadows, while the curious noises – the muffled footfalls and distant talking voices that had been perceptible all day – seemed, no doubt because of the fading light and the consequently quickened sense of hearing, to become more frequent and insistent.

The sacristan began for the first time to show signs of hurry and impatience. He heaved a sigh of relief when camera and notebook were finally packed up and stowed away, and hurriedly beckoned Dennistoun to the western door of the church, under the tower. It was time to ring the Angelus. A few pulls at the reluctant rope, and the great bell Bertrande, high in the tower, began to speak, and swung her voice up among the pines and down to the valleys, loud with mountain-streams, calling the dwellers on these lonely hills to remember and repeat the salutation of the angel to her whom he called Blessed among women. With that a profound quiet seemed to fall for the first time that day upon the little town, and Dennistoun and the sacristan went out of the church.

On the doorstep they fell into conversation.

'Monsieur seemed to interest himself in the old choir-books in the sacristy.'

'Undoubtedly. I was going to ask you if there were a library in the town.'

'No, monsieur; perhaps there used to be one belonging to the Chapter, but it is now such a small place – ' Here came a strange pause of irresolution, as it seemed; then, with a sort of plunge, he went on: 'But if monsieur is *amateur des vieux livres*, I have at home something that might interest him. It is not a hundred yards.'

At once all Dennistoun's cherished dreams of finding priceless manuscripts in untrodden corners of France flashed up, to die down again the next moment. It was probably a stupid missal of Plantin's printing, about 1580. Where was the likelihood that a place so near Toulouse would not have been ransacked long ago by collectors? However, it would be foolish not to go; he would reproach himself for ever after if he refused. So they set off. On the way the curious irresolution and sudden determination of the sacristan recurred to Dennistoun, and he wondered in a shamefaced way whether he was being decoyed into some purlieu to be made away with as a supposed rich Englishman. He contrived, therefore, to begin talking with his guide, and to drag in, in a rather clumsy fashion, the fact that he expected two friends to join him early the next morning. To his surprise, the announcement seemed to relieve the sacristan at once of some of the anxiety that oppressed him.

'That is well,' he said quite brightly – 'that is very well. Monsieur will travel in company with his friends; they will be always near him. It is a good thing to travel thus in company – sometimes.'

The last word appeared to be added as an afterthought, and to bring with it a relapse into gloom for the poor little man.

They were soon at the house, which was one rather larger than its neighbours, stone-built, with a shield carved over the door, the shield of Alberic de Mauléon, a collateral descendant, Dennistoun tells me, of Bishop John de Mauléon. This Alberic was a Canon of Comminges from 1680 to 1701. The upper windows of the mansion were boarded up, and the whole place bore, as does the rest of Comminges, the aspect of decaying age.

Arrived on his doorstep, the sacristan paused a moment.

'Perhaps,' he said, 'perhaps, after all, monsieur has not the time?'

'Not at all – lots of time – nothing to do till tomorrow. Let us see what it is you have got.'

The door was opened at this point, and a face looked out, a face far younger than the sacristan's, but bearing something of the same distressing look: only here it seemed to be the mark not so much of fear for personal safety as of acute anxiety on behalf of another. Plainly, the owner of the face was the sacristan's daughter; and, but for the expression I have described, she was a handsome girl enough. She brightened up considerably on seeing her father accompanied by an able-bodied stranger. A few remarks passed between father and daughter, of which Dennistoun only caught these words, said by the sacristan, 'He was laughing in the church,' words which were answered only by a look of terror from the girl.

But in another minute they were in the sitting-room of the house, a small, high chamber with a stone floor, full of moving shadows cast by a wood-fire that flickered on a great hearth. Something of the character of an oratory was imparted to it by a tall crucifix, which reached almost to the ceiling on one side; the figure was painted of the natural colours, the cross was black. Under this stood a chest of some age and solidity, and when a lamp had been brought, and chairs set, the sacristan went to this chest, and produced therefrom, with growing excitement and nervousness, as Dennistoun thought, a large book, wrapped in a white cloth, on which cloth a cross was rudely embroidered in red thread. Even before the wrapping had been removed, Dennistoun began to be interested by the size and shape of the volume. 'Too large for a missal,' he thought, 'and not the shape of an antiphoner; perhaps it may be something good, after all.' The next moment the book was open, and Dennistoun felt that he had at last lit upon something better than good. Before him lay a large folio, bound, perhaps, late in the seventeenth century, with the arms of Canon Alberic de Mauléon stamped in gold on the sides. There may have been a hundred and fifty leaves of paper in the book, and on almost every one of them was fastened a leaf from an illuminated manuscript. Such a collection Dennistoun had hardly dreamed of in his wildest moments. Here were ten leaves from a copy of Genesis, illustrated with pictures, which could not be later than AD 700. Further on was a complete set of pictures from a Psalter, of English execution, of the very finest kind that the thirteenth century could produce; and, perhaps best of all, there were twenty leaves of uncial writing in Latin, which, as a few words seen here and there told him at once, must belong to some very early unknown patristic treatise. Could it possibly be a fragment of the copy of Papias, 'On the Words of Our Lord', which was known to have existed as late as the twelfth century at Nîmes?* In any case, his mind was made up; that book must return to Cambridge with him, even if he had to draw the whole of his balance from the bank and stay at St Bertrand till the money came. He glanced up at the sacristan to see if his face yielded any hint that the book was for sale. The sacristan was pale, and his lips were working.

'If monsieur will turn on to the end,' he said.

So monsieur turned on, meeting new treasures at every rise of a

---

* We now know that these leaves did contain a considerable fragment of that work, if not of that actual copy of it.

leaf; and at the end of the book he came upon two sheets of paper, of much more recent date than anything he had yet seen, which puzzled him considerably. They must be contemporary, he decided, with the unprincipled Canon Alberic, who had doubtless plundered the Chapter library of St Bertrand to form this priceless scrapbook. On the first of the paper sheets was a plan, carefully drawn and instantly recognisable by a person who knew the ground, of the south aisle and cloisters of St Bertrand's. There were curious signs looking like planetary symbols and a few Hebrew words in the corners; and in the north-west angle of the cloister was a cross drawn in gold paint. Below the plan were some lines of writing in Latin, which ran thus:

Responsa 12^{mi} Dec. 1694. Interrogatum est: Inveniamne? Responsum est: Invenies. Fiamne dives? Fies. Vivamne invidendus? Vives. Moriarne in lecto meo? Ita. [Answers of the 12th of December, 1694. It was asked: Shall I find it? Answer: Thou shalt. Shall I become rich? Thou wilt. Shall I live an object of envy? Thou wilt. Shall I die in my bed? Thou wilt.]

'A good specimen of the treasure-hunter's record – quite reminds one of Mr Minor-Canon Quatremain in *Old St Paul's*,'[1] was Dennistoun's comment, and he turned the leaf.

What he then saw impressed him, as he has often told me, more than he could have conceived any drawing or picture capable of impressing him. And, though the drawing he saw is no longer in existence, there is a photograph of it (which I possess) which fully bears out that statement. The picture in question was a sepia drawing from the end of the seventeenth century representing, one would say at first sight, a biblical scene; for the architecture (the picture represented an interior) and the figures had that semi-classical flavour about them which the artists of two hundred years ago thought appropriate to illustrations of the Bible. On the right was a king on his throne, the throne elevated on twelve steps, a canopy overhead, lions on either side – evidently King Solomon. He was bending forward with outstretched sceptre, in attitude of command; his face expressed horror and disgust, yet there was in it also the mark of imperious will and confident power. The left half of the picture was the strangest, however. The interest plainly centred there. On the pavement before the throne were grouped four soldiers, surrounding a crouching figure which must be described in a moment. A fifth soldier lay dead on the pavement, his neck distorted, and his eyeballs starting from his head. The four surrounding guards were looking at the king. In their faces the sentiment of horror was intensified; they seemed, in fact, only restrained from flight by their implicit trust in their master. All this terror was plainly excited by the being that crouched in their midst. I entirely despair of conveying by any words the impression which this figure makes upon anyone who looks at it. I recollect once showing the photograph of the drawing to a lecturer on morphology – a person of, I was going to say, abnormally sane and unimaginative habits of mind. He absolutely refused to be alone for the rest of that evening, and he told me afterwards that for many nights he had not dared to put out his light before going to sleep. However, the main traits of the figure I can at least indicate. At first you saw only a mass of coarse, matted black hair; presently it was seen that this covered a body of fearful thinness, almost a skeleton, but with the muscles standing out like wires. The hands were of a dusky pallor, covered, like the body, with long, coarse hairs, and hideously taloned. The eyes, touched in with a burning yellow, had intensely black pupils, and were fixed upon the throned king with a look of beast-like hate. Imagine one of the awful bird-catching spiders of South America translated into human form, and endowed with intelligence just less than human, and you will have some faint conception of the terror inspired by this appalling effigy. One remark is universally made by those to whom I have shown the picture: 'It was drawn from the life.'

As soon as the first shock of his irresistible fright had subsided, Dennistoun stole a look at his hosts. The sacristan's hands were pressed upon his eyes; his daughter, looking up at the cross on the wall, was telling her beads feverishly.

At last the question was asked, 'Is this book for sale?'

There was the same hesitation, the same plunge of determination that he had noticed before, and then came the welcome answer, 'If monsieur pleases.'

'How much do you ask for it?'

'I will take two hundred and fifty francs.'

This was confounding. Even a collector's conscience is sometimes stirred, and Dennistoun's conscience was tenderer than a collector's.

'My good man!' he said again and again, 'your book is worth far more than two hundred and fifty francs, I assure you – far more.'

But the answer did not vary: 'I will take two hundred and fifty francs, not more.'

There was really no possibility of refusing such a chance. The money was paid, the receipt signed, a glass of wine drunk over the transaction, and then the sacristan seemed to become a new man. He stood upright, he ceased to throw those suspicious glances

behind him, he actually laughed or tried to laugh. Dennistoun rose
to go.

'I shall have the honour of accompanying monsieur to his hotel?'
said the sacristan.

'Oh no, thanks! it isn't a hundred yards. I know the way perfectly,
and there is a moon.'

The offer was pressed three or four times, and refused as often.

'Then, monsieur will summon me if – if he finds occasion; he will
keep the middle of the road, the sides are so rough.'

'Certainly, certainly,' said Dennistoun, who was impatient to
examine his prize by himself; and he stepped out into the passage
with his book under his arm.

Here he was met by the daughter; she, it appeared, was anxious
to do a little business on her own account; perhaps, like Gehazi, to
'take somewhat' from the foreigner whom her father had spared.

'A silver crucifix and chain for the neck; monsieur would perhaps
be good enough to accept it?'

Well, really, Dennistoun hadn't much use for these things. What
did mademoiselle want for it?

'Nothing – nothing in the world. Monsieur is more than welcome
to it.'

The tone in which this and much more was said was unmistakably
genuine, so that Dennistoun was reduced to profuse thanks, and
submitted to have the chain put round his neck. It really seemed as
if he had rendered the father and daughter some service which they
hardly knew how to repay. As he set off with his book, they stood at
the door looking after him, and they were still looking when he
waved them a last good-night from the steps of the Chapeau
Rouge.

Dinner was over, and Dennistoun was in his bedroom, shut up
alone with his acquisition. The landlady had manifested a particular
interest in him since he had told her that he had paid a visit to the
sacristan and bought an old book from him. He thought, too, that he
had heard a hurried dialogue between her and the said sacristan in
the passage outside the *salle à manger*; some words to the effect that
'Pierre and Bertrand would be sleeping in the house' had closed the
conversation.

All this time a growing feeling of discomfort had been creeping
over him – nervous reaction, perhaps, after the delight of his
discovery. Whatever it was, it resulted in a conviction that there was
someone behind him, and that he was far more comfortable with his
back to the wall. All this, of course, weighed light in the balance as

against the obvious value of the collection he had acquired. And now, as I said, he was alone in his bedroom, taking stock of Canon Alberic's treasures, in which every moment revealed something more charming.

'Bless Canon Alberic!' said Dennistoun, who had an inveterate habit of talking to himself. 'I wonder where he is now? Dear me! I wish that landlady would learn to laugh in a more cheering manner; it makes one feel as if there was someone dead in the house. Half a pipe more, did you say? I think perhaps you are right. I wonder what that crucifix is that the young woman insisted on giving me? Last century, I suppose. Yes, probably. It is rather a nuisance of a thing to have round one's neck – just too heavy. Most likely her father has been wearing it for years. I think I might give it a clean up before I put it away.'

He had taken the crucifix off, and laid it on the table, when his attention was caught by an object lying on the red cloth just by his left elbow. Two or three ideas of what it might be flitted through his brain with their own incalculable quickness.

'A penwiper? No, no such thing in the house. A rat? No, too black. A large spider? I trust to goodness not – no. Good God! a hand like the hand in that picture!'

In another infinitesimal flash he had taken it in. Pale, dusky skin, covering nothing but bones and tendons of appalling strength; coarse black hairs, longer than ever grew on a human hand; nails rising from the ends of the fingers and curving sharply down and forward, grey, horny and wrinkled.

He flew out of his chair with deadly, inconceivable terror clutching at his heart. The shape, whose left hand rested on the table, was rising to a standing posture behind his seat, its right hand crooked above his scalp. There was black and tattered drapery about it; the coarse hair covered it as in the drawing. The lower jaw was thin – what can I call it? – shallow, like a beast's; teeth showed behind the black lips; there was no nose; the eyes, of a fiery yellow, against which the pupils showed black and intense, and the exulting hate and thirst to destroy life which shone there, were the most horrifying features in the whole vision. There was intelligence of a kind in them – intelligence beyond that of a beast, below that of a man.

The feelings which this horror stirred in Dennistoun were the intensest physical fear and the most profound mental loathing. What did he do? What could he do? He has never been quite certain what words he said, but he knows that he spoke, that he grasped blindly at the silver crucifix, that he was conscious of a movement towards him on the part of the demon and that he screamed with the voice of an animal in hideous pain.

Pierre and Bertrand, the two sturdy little serving-men, who rushed in, saw nothing, but felt themselves thrust aside by something that passed out between them, and found Dennistoun in a swoon. They sat up with him that night, and his two friends were at St Bertrand by nine o'clock next morning. He himself, though still shaken and nervous, was almost himself by that time, and his story found credence with them, though not until they had seen the drawing and talked with the sacristan.

Almost at dawn the little man had come to the inn on some pretence, and had listened with the deepest interest to the story retailed by the landlady. He showed no surprise.

'It is he – it is he! I have seen him myself,' was his only comment; and to all questionings but one reply was vouchsafed: 'Deux fois je l'ai vu; mille fois je l'ai senti.' He would tell them nothing of the provenance of the book, nor any details of his experiences. 'I shall soon sleep, and my rest will be sweet. Why should you trouble me?' he said.*

We shall never know what he or Canon Alberic de Mauléon suffered. At the back of that fateful drawing were some lines of writing which may be supposed to throw light on the situation:

> *Contradictio Salomonis cum demonio nocturno.*
> *Albericus de Mauleone delineavit.*
> *V. Deus in adiutorium. Ps. Qui habitat.*
> *Sancte Bertrande, demoniorum effugator, intercede*
> *pro memiserrimo.*
> *Primum vidi nocte 12^{mi} Dec. 1694: videbo mox ultimum.*
> *Peccavi et passus sum, plura adhuc passurus. Dec. 29, 1701.*†

I have never quite understood what was Dennistoun's view of the

---

* He died that summer; his daughter married and settled at St Papoul. She never understood the circumstances of her father's 'obsession'.

† i.e., The Dispute of Solomon with a demon of the night. Drawn by Alberic de Mauléon. *Versicle*. O Lord, make haste to help me. *Psalm*. Whoso dwelleth (xci). St Bertrand, who puttest devils to flight, pray for me most unhappy. I saw it first on the night of Dec. 12, 1694: soon I shall see it for the last time. I have sinned and suffered, and have more to suffer yet. Dec. 29, 1701.

The 'Gallia Christiana' gives the date of the canon's death as December 31, 1701, 'in bed, of a sudden seizure'. Details of this kind are not common in the great work of the Sammarthani.

events I have narrated. He quoted to me once a text from Ecclesiasticus: 'Some spirits there be that are created for vengeance, and in their fury lay on sore strokes.' On another occasion he said: 'Isaiah was a very sensible man; doesn't he say something about night monsters living in the ruins of Babylon? These things are rather beyond us at present.'

Another confidence of his impressed me rather, and I sympathised with it. We had been, last year, to Comminges, to see Canon Alberic's tomb. It is a great marble erection, with an effigy of the canon in a large wig and soutane, and an elaborate eulogy of his learning below. I saw Dennistoun talking for some time with the vicar of St Bertrand's, and as we drove away he said to me: 'I hope it isn't wrong: you know I am a Presbyterian – but I – I believe there will be "saying of mass and singing of dirges" for Alberic de Mauléon's rest.' Then he added, with a touch of the northern British in his tone, 'I had no notion they came so dear.'

The book is in the Wentworth Collection at Cambridge. The drawing was photographed and then burnt by Dennistoun on the day when he left Comminges on the occasion of his first visit.

No. 252 Rue M. le Prince[1]

RALPH ADAMS CRAM

WHEN IN MAY 1886 I found myself at last in Paris, I naturally determined to throw myself on the charity of an old chum of mine, Eugène Marie d'Ardéche, who had forsaken Boston a year or more ago on receiving word of the death of an aunt who had left him such property as she possessed. I fancy this windfall surprised him not a little, for the relations between the aunt and nephew had never been cordial, judging from Eugène's remarks touching the lady, who was, it seems, a more or less wicked and witchlike old person, with a penchant for black magic, at least such was the common report.

Why she should leave all her property to d'Ardéche, no one could tell, unless it was that she felt his rather hobbledehoy tendencies toward Buddhism and occultism might someday lead him to her own unhallowed height of questionable illumination. To be sure, d'Ardéche reviled her as a bad old woman, being himself in that state of enthusiastic exaltation which sometimes accompanies a boyish fancy for occultism; but in spite of his distant and repellent attitude, Mlle Blaye de Tartas made him her sole heir, to the violent wrath of a questionable old party known to infamy as the Sar Torrevieja, the 'King of the Sorcerers'. This malevolent old portent, whose grey and crafty face was often seen in the Rue M. le Prince during the life of Mlle de Tartas, had, it seems, fully expected to enjoy her small wealth after her death; and when it appeared that she had left him only the contents of the gloomy old house in the Quartier Latin, giving the house itself and all else of which she died possessed to her nephew in America, the Sar proceeded to remove everything from the place, and then to curse it elaborately and comprehensively, together with all those who should ever dwell therein.

Whereupon he disappeared.

This final episode was the last word I had received from Eugène, but I knew the number of the house, 252 Rue M. le Prince. So, after a day or two given to a first cursory survey of Paris, I started across the Seine to find Eugene and compel him to do the honours of the city.

Everyone who knows the Latin Quarter knows the Rue M. le Prince, running up the hill towards the Garden of the Luxembourg. It is full of queer houses and odd corners – or was in '86 – and certainly No. 252 was, when I found it, quite as queer as any. It was nothing but a doorway, a black arch of old stone between and under two new houses painted yellow. The effect of this bit of seventeenth-century masonry, with its dirty old doors and rusty broken lantern sticking gaunt and grim out over the narrow sidewalk, was, in its frame of fresh plaster, sinister in the extreme.

I wondered if I had made a mistake in the number; it was quite evident that no one lived behind those cobwebs. I went into the doorway of one of the new *hôtels* and interviewed the concierge.

No, M. d'Ardéche did not live there, though to be sure he owned the mansion; he himself resided in Meudon, in the country house of the late Mlle de Tartas. Would monsieur like the number and the street?

Monsieur would like them extremely, so I took the card that the concierge wrote for me, and forthwith started for the river, in order that I might take a steamboat for Meudon. By one of those coincidences which happen so often, being quite inexplicable, I had not gone twenty paces down the street before I ran directly into the arms of Eugène d'Ardéche. In three minutes we were sitting in the queer little garden of the Chien Bleu, drinking vermouth and absinthe, and talking it all over.

'You do not live in your aunt's house?' I said at last, interrogatively.

'No, but if this sort of thing keeps on I shall have to. I like Meudon much better, and the house is perfect, all furnished, and nothing in it newer than the last century. You must come out with me tonight and see it. I have got a jolly room fixed up for my Buddha. But there is something wrong with this house opposite. I can't keep a tenant in it – not four days. I have had three, all within six months, but the stories have gone around and a man would as soon think of hiring the Cour des Comptes to live in as No. 252. It is notorious. The fact is, it is haunted the worst way.'

I laughed and ordered more vermouth.

'That is all right. It is haunted all the same, or enough to keep it empty, and the funny part is that no one knows how it is haunted. Nothing is ever seen, nothing heard. As far as I can find out, people just have the horrors there, and have them so bad they have to go to the hospital afterwards. I have one ex-tenant in the Bicêtre[2] now. So the house stands empty, and as it covers considerable ground and is taxed for a lot, I don't know what to do about it. I think I'll either give it to that child of sin, Torrevieja, or else go and live in it myself. I shouldn't mind the ghosts, I am sure.'

'Did you ever stay there?'

'No, but I have always intended to, and in fact I came up here today to see a couple of rake-hell fellows I know, Fargeau and Duchesne, doctors in the Clinical Hospital beyond here, up by the Parc Mont Souris. They promised that they would spend the night with me some time in my aunt's house – which is called around here, you must know, *la Bouche d'Enfer* – and I thought perhaps they would make it this week, if they can get off duty. Come up with me while I see them, and then we can go across the river to Véfour's and have some luncheon, and you can get your things at the Chatham, and we will go out to Meudon, where of course you will spend the night with me.'

The plan suited me perfectly, so we went up to the hospital and found Fargeau, who declared that he and Duchesne were ready for anything, the nearer the real *bouche d'Enfer* the better; that the following Thursday they would both be off duty for the night, and that on that day they would join in an attempt to outwit the devil and clear up the mystery of No. 252.

'Does M. l'Américan go with us?' asked Fargeau.

'Why, of course,' I replied, 'I intend to go, and you must not refuse me, d'Ardéche; I decline to be put off. Here is a chance for you to do the honours of your city in a manner which is faultless. Show me a real live ghost, and I will forgive Paris for having lost the Jardin Mabille.'[3]

So it was settled. Later we went down to Meudon and ate dinner in the terrace room of the villa, which was all that d'Ardéche had said, and more, so utterly was its atmosphere that of the seventeenth century. At dinner Eugène told me more about his late aunt, and the queer goings on in the old house. Mlle Blaye lived, it seems, all alone, except for one female servant of her own age; a severe, taciturn creature, with massive Breton features and a Breton tongue, whenever she vouchsafed to use it. No one was ever seen to enter the door of No. 252 except Jeanne the servant and the Sar Torrevieja, the latter coming constantly from none knew whither, and always entering, *never leaving*. Indeed, the neighbours, who for eleven years had watched the old sorcerer sidle crabwise up to the bell almost every day, declared vociferously that *never* had he been seen to leave the house. Once, when they decided to keep absolute guard, the watcher, none other than Maître Garceau of the Chien Bleu, after keeping his eyes fixed on the door from ten o'clock one morning when the Sar arrived until four in the afternoon, during which time the door was unopened (he knew this, for had he not gummed a ten-centime stamp over the joint and was not the stamp unbroken?), nearly fell down when the sinister figure of Torrevieja slid wickedly by him with a dry, 'Pardon, monsieur!' and disappeared again through the black doorway.

This was curious, for No. 252 was entirely surrounded by houses, its only windows opening on a courtyard into which no eye could look from the *hôtels* of the Rue M. le Prince and the Rue de l'Ecole, and the mystery was one of the choice possessions of the Latin Quarter.

Once a year the austerity of the place was broken, and the denizens of the whole quarter stood open-mouthed watching many carriages drive up to No. 252, many of them private, not a few with crests on the door panels, from all of them descending veiled female figures and men with coat collars turned up. Then followed curious sounds of music from within, and those whose houses joined the blank walls of No. 252 became for the moment popular, for by placing the ear against the wall strange music could distinctly be heard, and the sound of monotonous chanting voices now and then. By dawn the last guest would have departed, and for another year the *hôtel* of Mlle de Tartas was ominously silent.

Eugène declared that he believed it was a celebration of 'Walpurgisnacht', and certainly appearances favoured such a fancy.

'A queer thing about the whole affair is,' he said, 'the fact that everyone in the street swears that about a month ago, while I was out in Concarneau for a visit, the music and voices were heard again, just as when my revered aunt was in the flesh. The house was perfectly empty, as I tell you, so it is quite possible that the good people were enjoying an hallucination.'

I must acknowledge that these stories did not reassure me; in fact, as Thursday came near, I began to regret a little my determination to spend the night in the house. I was too vain to back down, however, and the perfect coolness of the two doctors, who ran down Tuesday to Meudon to make a few arrangements, caused me to swear that I would die of fright before I would flinch. I suppose I believed more or less in ghosts, I am sure now that I am older I believe in them, there are in fact few things I cannot believe. Two or three inexplicable things had happened to me, and, although this was before my adventure with Rendel in Paestum, I had a strong predisposition to believe some things that I could not explain, wherein I was out of sympathy with the age.

Well, to come to the memorable night of the twelfth of June, we had made our preparations, and after depositing a big bag inside the doors of No. 252, went across to the Chien Bleu, where Fargeau and Duchesne turned up promptly, and we sat down to the best dinner Père Garceau could create. I remember I hardly felt that the conversation was in good taste. It began with various stories of Indian fakirs and Oriental jugglery, matters in which Eugène was curiously well read, swerved to the horrors of the great Sepoy mutiny, and thus to reminiscences of the dissecting-room. By this time we had drunk more or less, and Duchesne launched into a photographic and Zolaesque account of the only time (as he said) when he was possessed of the panic of fear: namely, one night many years ago, when he was locked by accident into the dissecting-room of the Loucine, together with several cadavers of a rather unpleasant nature. I ventured to protest mildly against the choice of subjects, the result being a perfect carnival of horrors, so that when we finally drank our last *crème de cacao* and started for *la Bouche d'Enfer*, my nerves were in a somewhat rocky condition.

It was just ten o'clock when we came into the street. A hot dead wind drifted in great puffs through the city, and ragged masses of vapour swept the purple sky; an unsavoury night altogether, one of those nights of hopeless lassitude when one feels, if one is at home, like doing nothing but drink mint juleps and smoke cigarettes.

Eugène opened the creaking door, and tried to light one of the lanterns; but the gusty wind blew out every match, and we finally had to close the outer doors before we could get a light. At last we had all the lanterns going, and I began to look around curiously. We were in a long vaulted passage, partly carriageway, partly footpath, perfectly bare but for the street refuse which had drifted in with eddying winds. Beyond lay the courtyard, a curious place rendered more curious still by the fitful moonlight and the flashing of four dark lanterns. The place had evidently been once a most noble palace. Opposite rose the oldest portion, a three-story wall of the time of Francis I, with a great wistaria vine covering half. The wings on either side were more modern, seventeenth century, and ugly, while towards the street was nothing but a flat unbroken wall.

The great bare court, littered with bits of paper blown in by the wind, fragments of packing cases, and straw, mysterious with flashing lights and flaunting shadows, while low masses of torn vapour drifted overhead, hiding, then revealing the stars, and all in absolute silence, not even the sounds of the streets entering this prison-like place, was weird and uncanny in the extreme. I must confess that already I began to feel a slight disposition towards the horrors, but with that curious inconsequence which so often happens in the case of those who are deliberately growing scared, I could think of nothing more reassuring than those delicious verses of Lewis Carroll's:

> Just the place for a Snark! I have said it twice,
>   That alone should encourage the crew.
> Just the place for a Snark! I have said it thrice
>   *What I tell you three times is true* – [4]

which kept repeating themselves over and over in my brain with feverish insistence.

Even the medical students had stopped their chaffing, and were studying the surroundings gravely.

'There is one thing certain,' said Fargeau, '*anything* might have happened here without the slightest chance of discovery. Did ever you see such a perfect place for lawlessness?'

'And *anything* might happen here now, with the same certainty of impunity,' continued Duchesne, lighting his pipe, the snap of the match making us all start. 'D'Ardéche, your lamented relative was certainly well fixed; she had full scope here for her traditional experiments in demonology.'

'Curse me if I don't believe that those same traditions were more or less founded on fact,' said Eugène. 'I never saw this court under these conditions before, but I could believe anything now. What's that!'

'Nothing but a door slamming,' said Duchesne loudly.

'Well, I wish doors wouldn't slam in houses that have been empty eleven months.'

'It is irritating,' and Duchesne slipped his arm through mine; 'but we must take things as they come. Remember we have to deal not only with the spectral lumber left here by your scarlet aunt, but as well with the supererogatory curse of that hellcat Torrevieja. Come on! Let's get inside before the hour arrives for the sheeted dead to squeak and gibber[5] in these lonely halls. Light your pipes, your tobacco is a sure protection against "your whoreson dead bodies";[6] light up and move on.'

We opened the hall door and entered a vaulted stone vestibule, full of dust and cobwebby.

'There is nothing on this floor,' said Eugène, 'except servants' rooms and offices, and I don't believe there is anything wrong with them. I never heard that there was, anyway. Let's go upstairs.'

So far as we could see, the house was apparently perfectly uninteresting inside, all eighteenth-century work, the façade of the main building being, with the vestibule, the only portion of the Francis I work.

'The place was burned during the Terror,' said Eugène, 'for my great-uncle, from whom Mlle de Tartas inherited it, was a good and true Royalist; he went to Spain after the Revolution, and did not come back until the accession of Charles X, when he restored the house, and then died, enormously old. This explains why it is all so new.'

The old Spanish sorcerer to whom Mlle de Tartas had left her personal property had done his work thoroughly. The house was absolutely empty, even the wardrobes and bookcases built in had been carried away; we went through room after room, finding all absolutely dismantled, only the windows and doors with their casings, the parquet floors and the florid Renaissance mantels remaining.

'I feel better,' remarked Fargeau. 'The house may be haunted, but it don't look it, certainly; it is the most respectable place imaginable.'

'Just you wait,' replied Eugène. 'These are only the state apartments, which my aunt seldom used, except, perhaps, on her annual "Walpurgisnacht". Come upstairs and I will show you a better *mise en scène*.'

On this floor, the rooms fronting the court, the sleeping-rooms, were quite small – 'They are the bad rooms all the same,' said Eugène – four of them, all just as ordinary in appearance as those below. A corridor ran behind them connecting with the wing corridor, and from this opened a door, unlike any of the other doors in that it was covered with green baize, somewhat moth-eaten. Eugène selected a key from the bunch he carried, unlocked the door, and with some difficulty forced it to swing inward; it was as heavy as the door of a safe.

'We are now,' he said, 'on the very threshold of hell itself; these rooms in here were my scarlet aunt's unholy of unholies. I never let them with the rest of the house, but keep them as a curiosity. I only wish Torrevieja had kept out; as it was, he looted them, as he did the rest of the house, and nothing is left but the walls and ceilings and floors. They are something, however, and may suggest what the former condition must have been. Tremble and enter.'

The first apartment was a kind of anteroom, a cube of perhaps twenty feet each way, without windows, and with no doors except that by which we entered and another to the right. Walls, floor and ceiling were covered with a black lacquer, brilliantly polished, that flashed the light of our lanterns in a thousand intricate reflections. It was like the inside of an enormous Japanese box, and about as empty. From this we passed to another room, and here we nearly dropped our lanterns. The room was circular, thirty feet or so in diameter, covered by a hemispherical dome; walls and ceiling were dark blue, spotted with gold stars; and reaching from floor to floor across the dome stretched a colossal figure in red lacquer of a nude woman kneeling, her legs reaching out along the floor on either side, her head touching the lintel of the door through which we had entered, her arms forming its sides, with the forearms extended and stretching along the walls until they met the long feet. The most astounding, misshapen, absolutely terrifying thing, I think, I ever saw. From the navel hung a great white object, like the traditional roc's egg of *The Arabian Nights*. The floor was of red lacquer, and in it was inlaid a pentagram the size of the room, made of wide strips of brass. In the centre of this pentagram was a circular disk of black stone, slightly saucer-shaped, with a small outlet in the middle.

The effect of the room was simply crushing, with this gigantic red figure crouched over it all, the staring eyes fixed on one, no matter what his position. None of us spoke, so oppressive was the whole thing.

The third room was like the first in dimensions, but instead of being black it was entirely sheathed with plates of brass – walls, ceiling and floor – tarnished now, and turning green, but still brilliant under the lantern light. In the middle stood an oblong altar of porphyry, its longer dimensions on the axis of the suite of rooms, and at one end, opposite the range of doors, a pedestal of black basalt.

This was all. Three rooms, stranger than these, even in their emptiness, it would be hard to imagine. In Egypt, in India, they would not be entirely out of place, but here in Paris, in a common-place *hôtel*, in the Rue M. le Prince, they were incredible.

We retraced our steps, Eugène closed the iron door with its baize covering, and we went into one of the front chambers and sat down, looking at each other.

'Nice party, your aunt,' said Fargeau. 'Nice old party, with amiable tastes; I am glad we are not to spend the night in *those* rooms.'

'What do you suppose she did there?' inquired Duchesne. 'I know more or less about black art, but that series of rooms is too much for me.'

'My impression is,' said d'Ardéche, 'that the brazen room was a kind of sanctuary containing some image or other on the basalt base, while the stone in front was really an altar – what the nature of the sacrifice might be I don't even guess. The round room may have been used for invocations and incantations. The pentagram looks like it. Anyway, it is all just about as queer and *fin de siècle* as I can well imagine. Look here, it is nearly twelve. Let's dispose of ourselves, if we are going to hunt this thing down.'

The four chambers on this floor of the old house were those said to be haunted, the wings being quite innocent, and, so far as we knew, the floors below. It was arranged that we should each occupy a room, leaving the doors open with the lights burning, and at the slightest cry or knock we were all to rush at once to the room from which the warning sound might come. There was no communication between the rooms to be sure, but, as the doors all opened into the corridor, every sound was plainly audible.

The last room fell to me, and I looked it over carefully.

It seemed innocent enough, a commonplace, square, rather lofty Parisian sleeping-room, finished in wood painted white, with a small marble mantel, a dusty floor of inlaid maple and cherry, walls hung with an ordinary French paper, apparently quite new, and two deeply embrasured windows looking out on the court.

I opened the swinging sash with some trouble, and sat down in the window seat with my lantern beside me trained on the only door, which gave on the corridor.

The wind had gone down and it was very still without – still and hot. The masses of luminous vapour were gathering thickly over-head, no longer urged by the gusty wind. The great masses of rank wistaria leaves, with here and there a second blossoming of purple flowers, hung dead over the window in the sluggish air. Across the roofs I could hear the sound of a belated *fiacre* in the streets below. I filled my pipe again and waited.

For a time the voices of the men in the other rooms were a companionship, and at first I shouted to them now and then, but my voice echoed rather unpleasantly through the long corridors, and had a suggestive way of reverberating around the left wing beside me, and coming out at a broken window at its extremity like the voice of another man. I soon gave up my attempts at conversation, and devoted myself to the task of keeping awake. It was not easy; why did I eat that lettuce salad at Père Garceau's? I should have known better. It was making me irresistibly sleepy, and wakefulness was absolutely necessary. It was certainly gratifying to know that I could

sleep, that my courage was by me to that extent, but in the interests
of science I must keep awake. But almost never, it seemed, had sleep
looked so desirable. Half a hundred times, nearly, I would doze for
an instant, only to awake with a start and find my pipe gone out. Nor
did the exertion of relighting it pull me together. I struck my match
mechanically, and with the first puff dropped off again. It was most
vexing. I got up and walked around the room. It was most annoying.
My cramped position had almost put both my legs to sleep. I could
hardly stand. I felt numb, as though with cold. There was no longer
any sound from the other rooms, nor from without. I sank down in
my window seat. How dark it was growing! I turned up the lantern.
That pipe again, how obstinately it kept going out! and my last
match was gone. The lantern, too, was that going out? I lifted my
hand to turn it up again. It felt like lead, and fell beside me.

Then I awoke – absolutely. I remembered the story of 'The
Haunters and the Haunted'.[6] *This* was the Horror. I tried to rise, to
cry out. My body was like lead, my tongue was paralysed. I could
hardly move my eyes. And the light was going out. There was no
question about that. Darker and darker yet, little by little the pattern
of the paper was swallowed up in the advancing night. A prickling
numbness gathered in every nerve, my right arm slipped without
feeling from my lap to my side, and I could not raise it – it swung
helpless. A thin, keen humming began in my head, like the cicadas on
a hillside in September. The darkness was coming fast.

Yes, this was it. Something was subjecting me, body and mind, to a
slow paralysis. Physically I was already dead. If I could only hold my
mind, my consciousness, I might still be safe, but could I? Could I
resist the mad horror of this silence, the deepening dark, the creeping numbness? I knew that, like the man in the ghost story, my only
safety lay here.

It had come at last. My body was dead, I could no longer move my
eyes. They were fixed in that last look on the place where the door
had been, now only a deepening of the dark.

Utter night: the last flicker of the lantern was gone. I sat and
waited; my mind was still keen, but how long would it last? There
was a limit even to the endurance of the utter panic of fear.

Then the end began. In the velvet blackness came two white eyes,
milky, opalescent, small, far away – awful eyes, like a dead dream.
More beautiful than I can describe, the flakes of white flame moving
from the perimeter inward, disappearing in the centre, like a never-
ending flow of opal water into a circular tunnel. I could not have
moved my eyes had I possessed the power: they devoured the fearful,

beautiful things that grew slowly, slowly larger, fixed on me, advancing, growing more beautiful, the white flakes of light sweeping more swiftly into the blazing vortices, the awful fascination deepening in its insane intensity as the white, vibrating eyes grew nearer, larger.

Like a hideous and implacable engine of death the eyes of the unknown Horror swelled and expanded until they were close before me, enormous, terrible, and I felt a slow, cold, wet breath propelled with mechanical regularity against my face, enveloping me in its fetid mist, in its charnel-house deadliness.

With ordinary fear goes always a physical terror, but with me in the presence of this unspeakable Thing was only the utter and awful terror of the mind, the mad fear of a prolonged and ghostly nightmare. Again and again I tried to shriek, to make some noise, but physically I was utterly dead. I could only feel myself go mad with the terror of hideous death. The eyes were close on me – their movement so swift that they seemed to be but palpitating flames, the dead breath was around me like the depths of the deepest sea.

Suddenly a wet, icy mouth, like that of a dead cuttlefish, shapeless, jellylike, fell over mine. The Horror began slowly to draw my life from me, but, as enormous and shuddering folds of palpitating jelly swept sinuously around me, my will came back, my body awoke with the reaction of final fear, and I closed with the nameless death that enfolded me.

What was it that I was fighting? My arms sank through the unresisting mass that was turning me to ice. Moment by moment new folds of cold jelly swept round me, crushing me with the force of Titans. I fought to wrest my mouth from this awful Thing that sealed it, but, if ever I succeeded and caught a single breath, the wet, sucking mass closed over my face again before I could cry out. I think I fought for hours, desperately, insanely, in a silence that was more hideous than any sound – fought until I felt final death at hand, until the memory of all my life rushed over me like a flood, until I no longer had strength to wrench my face from that hellish succubus, until with a last mechanical struggle I fell and yielded to death.

Then I heard a voice say, 'If he is dead, I can never forgive myself; I was to blame.'

Another replied, 'He is not dead, I know we can save him if only we reach the hospital in time. Drive like hell, *cocher!* Twenty francs for you, if you get there in three minutes.'

Then there was night again, and nothingness, until I suddenly awoke and stared around. I lay in a hospital ward, very white and sunny, some yellow *fleurs-de-lis* stood beside the head of the pallet, and a tall sister of mercy sat by my side.

To tell the story in a few words, I was in the Hôtel Dieu, where the men had taken me that fearful night of the twelfth of June. I asked for Fargeau or Duchesne, and by and by the latter came, and sitting beside the bed told me all that I did not know.

It seems that they had sat, each in his room, hour after hour, hearing nothing, very much bored and disappointed. Soon after two o'clock Fargeau, who was in the next room, called to me to ask if I was awake. I gave no reply, and, after shouting once or twice, he took his lantern and came to investigate. The door was locked on the inside! He instantly called d'Ardéche and Duchesne, and together they hurled themselves against the door. It resisted. Within they could hear irregular footsteps dashing here and there, with heavy breathing. Although frozen with terror, they fought to destroy the door and finally succeeded by using a great slab of marble that formed the shelf of the mantel in Fargeau's room. As the door crashed in, they were suddenly hurled back against the walls of the corridor, as though by an explosion, the lanterns were extinguished, and they found themselves in utter silence and darkness.

As soon as they recovered from the shock, they leaped into the room and fell over my body in the middle of the floor. They lighted one of the lanterns, and saw the strangest sight that can be imagined. The floor and walls to the height of about six feet were running with something that seemed like stagnant water, thick, glutinous, sickening. As for me, I was drenched with the same cursed liquid. The odour of musk was nauseating. They dragged me away, stripped off my clothing, wrapped me in their coats, and hurried to the hospital, thinking me perhaps dead. Soon after sunrise d'Ardéche left the hospital, being assured that I was in a fair way to recovery, with time, and with Fargeau went up to examine by daylight the traces of the adventure that was so nearly fatal. They were too late. Fire engines were coming down the street as they passed the Acadèmie. A neighbour rushed up to d'Ardéche: 'Oh, monsieur! what misfortune, yet what fortune! It is true *la Bouche d'Enfer* – I beg pardon, the residence of the lamented Mlle de Tartas – was burned, but not wholly, only the ancient building. The wings were saved, and for that great credit is due the brave firemen. Monsieur will remember them, no doubt.'

It was quite true. Whether a forgotten lantern, overturned in the excitement, had done the work, or whether the origin of the fire was more supernatural, it was certain that the 'Mouth of Hell' was no more. A last engine was pumping slowly as d'Ardéche came up; half a dozen limp hoses and one distended hose stretched through the *porte-cochère*, and within, only the façade of Francis I remained, draped still with the black stems of the wistaria. Beyond lay a great vacancy, where thin smoke was rising slowly. Every floor was gone, and the strange halls of Mlle Blaye de Tartas were only a memory.

With d'Ardéche I visited the place last year, but in the stead of the ancient walls was then only a new and ordinary building, fresh and respectable; yet the wonderful stories of the old *Bouche d'Enfer* still lingered in the quarter and will hold there, I do not doubt, until the Day of Judgement.

The Lame Priest

S. CARLETON

IF THE AIR had not been December's, I should have said there was balm in it. Balm there was, to me, in the sight of the road before me. The first snow of winter had been falling for an hour or more; the barren hill was white with it. What wind there was was behind me, and I stopped to look my fill.

The long slope stretched up till it met the sky, the softly rounded white of it melting into the grey clouds – the dove-brown clouds – that touched the summit, brooding, infinitely gentle. From my feet led the track, sheer white, where old infrequent wheels had marked two channels for the snow to lie; in the middle a clear filmy brown – not the shadow of a colour, but the light of one; and the grey and white and brown of it all was veiled and strange with the blue-grey mist of falling snow. So quiet, so kind, it fell, I could not move for looking at it, though I was not halfway home.

My eyes are not very good. I could not tell what made that brown light in the middle of the track till I was on it, and saw it was only grass standing above the snow; tall, thin, feathery autumn grass, dry and withered. It was so beautiful I was sorry to walk on it.

I stood looking down at it, and then, because I had to get on, lifted my eyes to the skyline. There was something black there, very big against the low sky; very swift, too, on its feet, for I had scarcely wondered what it was before it had come so close that I saw it was a man, a priest in his black soutane. I never saw any man who moved so fast without running. He was close to me, at my side, passing me even as I thought it.

'You are hurried, father,' said I, meaning to be civil. I see few persons in my house, twelve miles from the settlement, and I had my curiosity to know where this strange priest was going. For he was a stranger.

'To the churchyard, my brother – to the churchyard,' he answered, in a chanting voice, yet not the chanting you hear in churches. He was past me as he spoke – five yards past me down the hill.

The churchyard! Yes, there was a burying. Young John Noel was dead these three days. I heard that in the village.

'This priest will be late,' I thought, wondering why young John must have two priests to bury him. Father Moore was enough for everyone else. And then I wondered why he had called me 'brother'.

I turned to watch him down the hill, and saw what I had not seen before. The man was lame. His left foot hirpled, either in trick or infirmity. In the shallow snow his track lay black and uneven where the sound foot had taken the weight. I do not know why, but that black track had a desolate look on the white ground, and the black priest hurrying down the hill looked desolate, too. There was something infinitely lonely, infinitely pathetic, in that scurrying figure, indistinct through the falling snow.

I had grown chilled standing, and it made me shiver; or else it was the memory of the gaunt face, the eyes that did not look at me, the incredible, swift lameness of the strange priest. However it was, virtue had gone from me. I went on to the top of the hill without much spirit, and into the woods. And in the woods the kindliness had gone from the snowfall. The familiar rocks and stumps were unfamiliar, threatening. Half a dozen times I wondered what a certain thing could be that crouched before me in the dusk, only to find it a rotten log, a boulder in the bare bushes. Whether I hurried faster than I knew, for that unfriendliness around me, I did not trouble to think, but I was in a wringing sweat when I came out at my own clearing. As I crossed it to my door something startled me; what, I do not know. It was only a faint sound, far off, unknown, unrecognisable, but unpleasing. I forgot the door was latched (I leave my house by the window when I go out for the day), and pushed it sharply. It gave to my hand. There was no stranger inside, at least. An old Indian sat by the smouldering fire, with my dog at his feet.

'Andrew!' said I. 'Is anything wrong?' I had it always in my mind, when he came unexpectedly, that his wife might be dead. She had been smoking her pipe and dying these ten years back.

'I don't know.' The old man smiled as he carefully shut and barred the door I had left ajar. 'He want tobacco, so I come. You good man to me. You not home; I wait and make supper; my meat.' He nodded proudly at the dull embers, and I saw he had an open pot on them, with a hacked-off joint of moose meat. 'I make him stew.'

He had done the same thing before, a sort of tacit payment for the tobacco he wanted. I was glad to see him, for I was so hot and tired from my walk home that I knew I must be getting old very fast. It is not good to sit alone in a shack of a winter's night and know you are getting old very fast.

When there was no more moose meat we drew to the fire. Outside the wind had risen, full of a queer wailing that sounded something like the cry of a loon. I saw Andrew was not ready to start for home, though he had his hat on his head, and I realised I had not got out the tobacco. But when I put it on the table he let it lie.

'You keep me here tonight?' he asked, without a smile, almost anxiously. 'Bad night, tonight. Too long way home.'

I was pleased enough, but I asked if the old woman would be lonely.

'He get tobacco tomorrow.' (Andrew had but the masculine third person singular; and why have more, when that serves?) 'Girl with him when I come. Tomorrow' – He listened for an instant to the wind, stared into the fire, and threw so mighty a bark-covered log on it that the flames flew up the chimney.

'Red deer come back to this country!' exclaimed he irrelevantly. 'Come down from Maine. Wolves come back, too, over the north ice. I s'pose smell 'em? I don' know.'

I nodded. I knew both things, having nothing but such things to know in the corner of God's world I call my own.

Andrew filled his pipe. If I had not been used to him, I could never have seen his eyes were not on it, but on me.

'Tomorrow,' he harked back abruptly, 'we go 'way. Break up here; go down Lake Mooin.'

'Why?' I was astounded. He had not shifted camp for years.

'I say red deer back. Not good here any more.'

'But' – I wondered for half a minute if he could be afraid of the few stray wolves which had certainly come, from heaven knew how far, the winter before. But I knew that was nonsense. It must be something about the deer. How was I to know what his mind got out of them?

'No good,' he repeated; he lifted his long brown hand solemnly – 'no good here. You come too.'

I laughed. 'I'm too old! Andrew, who was the strange priest I met today crossing the upland farm?'

'Father Moore – no? Father Underhill?'

'No. Thin, tired-looking, lame.'

'Lame! Drag leg? Hurry?' I had never seen him so excited, never seen him stop in full career as now. 'I don' know.' It was a different man speaking. 'Strange priest, not belong here. You come Lake Mooin with me.'

'Tell me about the priest first,' though I knew it was useless as I ordered it.

He spat into the fire. 'Lame dog, lame woman, lame priest – all no good!' said he. 'What time late you sit up here?'

Not late that night, assuredly. I was more tired than I wanted to own. But long after I had gone to my bunk in the corner I saw Andrew's wrinkled face alert and listening in the firelight. He played with something in his hand, and I knew there was that in his mind which he would not say. The wind had died away; there was no more loon-calling, or whatever it was. I fell to sleep to the sound of the fire, the soft pat of snow against the window. But the straight old figure in my chair sat rigid, rigid.

I opened my eyes to broad, dull daylight. Andrew and the tobacco were gone. But on the table was something I did not see till I was setting my breakfast there: three bits of twig, two uprights and a crosspiece; a lake-shore pebble; a bit of charred wood. I supposed it was something about coming back from Lake Mooin to sit by my fire again, and I swept the picture-writing away as I put down my teapot. Afterwards I was glad.

I began to wonder if it would ever stop snowing. Andrew's track from my door was filled up already. I sat down to my fly-tying and my books, with a pipe in my mouth and an old tune at my heart, when I heard a hare shriek out. I will have no traps on my grant – a beggarly hundred acres, not cleared, and never will be; I have no farmer blood – and for a moment I distrusted Andrew. I put on my boots and went out.

The dog plumped into the woods ahead of me, and came back. The hare shrieked again, and was cut off in mid cry.

'Indian is Indian!' said I savagely. 'Andrew!' But no one answered.

The dog fell behind me, treading in my steps.

In the thick spruces there was nothing; nothing in the opener hardwood, till I came out on a clear place under a big tree, with the snow falling over into my boot legs. There, stooping in the snow with his back to me, was a man – the priest of yesterday. Priest or no priest, I would not have it; and I said so.

He smiled tightly, his soutane gathered up around him.

'I do not snare. Look!' He moved aside, and I saw the bloody snow, the dead hare. 'Something must have killed it and been frightened away. It is very odd.' He looked round him, as I did, for the fox or wild-cat tracks that were not there. Except for my bootprints from my side, and his uneven track from his, there was not a mark on the snow. It might have been a wild cat who jumped to some tree, but even so it was queer.

'Very odd,' he said again. 'Will you have the hare?'

I shook my head. I had no fancy for it.

'It is good meat.'

I had turned to see where my dog had gone, but I looked back at the sound of his voice, and was ashamed. Pinched, tired, bedraggled, he held up the hare; and his eyes were sharp with hunger.

I looked for no more phantom tracks; I forgot he had sinned about the hare. I was ashamed that I, well fed, had shamed him, empty, by wondering foolishly about wild cats. Yet even so I had less fancy for that hare than ever.

'Let it lie,' said I. 'I have better meat, and I suppose the beasts are hungry as well as we. If you are not hurried, come in and have a bite with me. I see few strangers out here. You would do me a kindness.'

A very strange look came on his face. 'A kindness!' he exclaimed. 'I – do a kindness!'

He seemed so taken aback that I wondered if he were not a little mad. I do not like madmen, but I could not turn round on him.

'You are off the track to anywhere,' I explained. 'There are no settlements for a hundred miles back of me. If you come in, I will give you your bearings.'

'Off the track!' he repeated, almost joyfully. 'Yes, yes. But I am very strong. I suppose' – his voice dragged into a whisper – 'I shall not be able to help getting back to a settlement again. But' – He looked at me for the first time, with considering eyes like a dog's, only more afraid, less gentle. 'You are a good man, brother,' he said. 'I will come.'

He cast a shuddering glance at the hare, and threw it behind him. As I turned to go he drifted lamely after me, just as a homeless dog does, half hope, half terrified suspicion. But I fancied he laid a greedy eye at the bloody hare after he had turned away from it.

Somehow, he was not a comfortable companion, and I was sorry I had no lunatic asylum. I whistled for my dog, but he had run home. He liked neither snow nor strangers. I saw his great square head in my bed as I let the priest in, and I knew he was annoyed. Dogs are funny things.

Mad or sane, that priest ate ravenously. When he had finished his eyes were steadier, though he started frightfully when I dropped some firewood – started toward the door.

'Were you in time for the funeral yesterday, father?' I asked, to put him at his ease. But at first he did not answer.

'I turned back,' he said at last, in the chanting voice of yesterday. 'You live alone, brother? Alone, like me, in the wilderness?'

I said yes. I supposed he was one of the Indian priests who live alone indeed. He was no town priest, for his nails were worn to the quick.

'You should bar your door at night,' he continued slowly, as if it were a distasteful duty. 'These woods are not – not as they were.'

Here was another warning, the second in twenty-four hours. I forgot about his being crazy.

'I always bar it.' I answered shortly enough. I was tired of these child's terrors, all the more that I myself had felt evil in the familiar woods only yesterday.

'Do more!' cried the priest. He stood up, a taller man than I had thought him; a gaunt, hunted-looking man in his shabby black. 'Do more! After nightfall keep your door shut, even to knocking; do not open it for any calling. The place is a bad place, and treachery' – He stopped, looked at the table, pointed at something. 'Would you mind,' said he, 'turning down that loaf? It is not – not true!'

I saw the loaf bottom up on the platter, and remembered. It is an old custom of silent warning that the stranger in the house is a traitor. But I had no one to warn. I laughed, and turned the loaf.

'Of course there is no traitor.'

If ever I saw gratitude, it was in his eyes, yet he spoke peevishly: 'Not now; but there might be. And so I say to you, after nightfall do not open your door – till the Indians come back.'

Then he was an Indian priest. I wondered why Andrew had lied about him.

'What is this thing' – I was impatient – 'that you and they are afraid of? Look out there' – I opened the door (for the poor priest, to be truthful, was not savoury) and pointed to the quiet clearing, the soft falling snow, the fringe of spruces that were the vanguard of the woods – 'look there, and tell me what there is in my own woods that has not been there these twelve years past! Yet first an Indian comes with hints and warnings, and then you.'

'What warnings?' he cried. 'The Indian's, I mean! What warnings?'

'I am sure I do not know.' I was thoroughly out of temper; I was not always a quiet old man in a lonely shack. 'Something about the red deer coming back, and the place being bad.'

'That is nonsense about the red deer,' returned the priest, not in the least as if he meant it.

'Nonsense or not, it seems to have sent the Indians away.' I could not help sounding dry. I hate these silly mysteries.

He turned his back to me, and began to prowl about the room. I had opened my mouth to speak, when he forestalled me.

'You have been kind to an outcast priest.' He spoke plainly. 'I tell

you in return to go away; I tell you earnestly. Or else I ask you to
promise me that for no reason will you leave your house after dark,
or your door on the latch, till the Indians come ba – ' He stopped in
the middle of a word, the middle of a step, his lame leg held up
drolly. 'What is that?'

It was more like the howl of a wild beast than a question, and I
spun round pretty sharply. The man was crazier than I liked.

'That rubbish of twigs and stones? The Indian left them. They
mean something about his coming back, I suppose.'

I could not see what he was making such a fuss about. He stood in
that silly, arrested attitude, and his lips had drawn back from his
teeth in a kind of snarl. I stooped for the things, and it was exactly as
if he snapped at me.

'Let them be. I – I have no fancy for them. They are a heathen
charm.' He backed away from them, drew close to the open door,
and stood with a working face – the saddest sight of fierce and weary
ruin, of effort to speak kindly, that ever I saw.

'They're just a massage,' I began.

'That you do not understand.' He held up his hand for silence,
more priest and less madman than I had yet seen him. 'I will tell you
what they mean. The twigs, two uprights and a crosspiece, mean to
keep your door shut; the stone is – the stone does not matter – call it
a stranger; the charcoal' – for all the effort he was making his hand
fell, and I thought he trembled – 'the charcoal' –

I stooped mechanically to put the things as he described them, as
Andrew had left them; but his cry checked me.

'Let the cruel things be! The charcoal means the unlucky, the
burned-out souls whose bodies live accursed. No, I will not touch
them, either. But do you lay them as you found them, night after
night, at your door, and – and' – he was fairly grinding his teeth with
the effort; even an outcast priest may feel shame at believing in
heathenry – 'and the unlucky, the unhappy, must pass by.'

I do not know why such pity came on me, except that it is not right
to see into the soul of any man, and I knew the priest must be
banned, and thought Andrew had meant to warn me against him. I
took the things – twigs, stone and charcoal – and threw them into the
fire.

'I'd sooner they came in,' I said.

But the strange priest gave me a look of terror, of agony. I thought
he wrung his hands, but I could not tell. As if I had struck him he was
over my threshold and scurrying away with his swift lameness into
the woods and the thin-falling snow. He went the way we had come

in the morning, the way of the dead hare. I could not help wondering
if he would take it with him if it were still there. I was sorry I had not
asked him where he was going; sorrier I had not filled his pockets
with food. I turned to put away my map of the district, and it was
gone. He must have moved more silently than a wolf to have stolen
it, but stolen it was. I could not grudge it, if I would rather have given
it. I went to the bunk to pull out my sulky dog, and stood amazed.
Those books lie which say dogs do not sweat.

'The priest certainly had a bad smell,' I exclaimed, 'but nothing to
cause all this fuss! Come out!'

But he only crawled abjectly to the fire, and presently lifted his
great head and howled.

'Snow or no snow, priest or no priest,' said I, 'we will go out to get
rid of these vapours;' for I had not felt much happier with my guest
than had the dog.

When we came back we had forgotten him; or why should I lie? –
the dog had. I could not forget his lameness, his poor, fierce, hungry
face. I made a prayer in my bed that night. (I know it is not a devout
practice, but if the mind kneels I hold the body does not matter and
my mind has been kneeling for twenty years.)

'For all that are in agony and have none to pray for them, I beseech
thee, O God!' And I meant the priest, as well as some others. But,
however it was, I heard – I mean I saw – no more of him. I had never
heard of him so much as his name.

Christmas passed. In February I went down to the village, and
there I heard what put the faint memory of the lame man out of my
head. The wolves who had followed the red deer were killing, not
deer in the woods, but children in the settlements. The village talked
of packs of wolves, and heaven knew how many children. I thought,
if it came to bare truth, there might have been three children eaten,
instead of the thirty rumour made them, and that for the fabled pack
there probably stood two or three brutes, with a taste for human
flesh, and a distaste for the hard running of pulling down a deer. And
before I left the village I met a man who told the plain tale.

There had been ten children killed or carried off, but there had
been no pack of wolves concerned, nor even three nor two. One lame
wolf's track led from each robbed house, only to disappear on some
highroad. More than that, the few wolves in the woods seemed to
fear and shun the lonely murderer; were against him as much as the
man who meant to hunt him down.

It was a queer story; I hardly thought it held water, though the man
who told it was no romance-maker. I left him, and went home over

the hard shining of the crusted snow, wondering why the good God, if he had not meant his children to kill, should have made the winter so long and hard.

Yellow shafts of low sunlight pierced the woods as I threaded them, and if they had not made it plain that there was nothing abroad I should have thought I heard something padding in the underbrush. But I saw nothing till I came out on my own clearing; and there I jerked up with surprise.

The lame priest stood with his back to my window – stood on a patch of tramped and bloody snow.

'Will you never learn sense?' he whined at me. 'This is no winter to go out and leave your window unfastened. If I had not happened by, your dog would be dead.'

I stared at him. I always left the window ajar, for the dog to go out and in.

'I came by,' drawled the priest, as if he were passing every day, 'and found your dog out here with three wolves on him. I – I beat them off.' He might speak calmly, but he wiped the sweat from his face. 'I put him in by the window. He is only torn.'

'But you' – My wits came back to me. I thanked him as a man does who has only a dumb beast to cherish. 'Why did you not go in, too? You must be frozen.'

He shook his head. 'The dog is afraid of me; you saw that,' he answered simply. 'He was better alone. Besides, I had my hands full at the time.'

'Are you hurt?' I would have felt his ragged clothes, but he flinched away from me.

'They were afraid, too!' He gave a short laugh. 'And now I must go. Only be careful. For all you knew, there might have been wolves beside you as you came. And you had no gun.'

I knew now why he looked neither cold nor like a man who has been waiting. He had made the window safe for the dog inside, and run through the woods to guard me. I was full of wonder at the strangeness of him, and the absurd gratitude; I forgot – or rather, I did not speak of – the stolen map. I begged him to come in for the night. But he cut me off in the middle.

'I am going a long way. No, I will not take a gun. I have no fear.'

'These wolves are too much!' I cried angrily. 'They told me in the village that a lame one had been harrying the settlements. I mean a wolf' – Not for worlds would I have said anything about lameness if I had remembered his.

'Do they say that?' he asked, his gaunt and furrowed face without expression. 'Oh, you need not mind me. It is no secret that I – I too am lame. Are they sure?'

'Sure enough to mean to kill him.' Somehow, my tongue faltered over it.

'So they ought.' He spoke in his throat. 'But – I doubt if they can!' He straightened himself, looked at the sun with a queer face. 'I must be going. You need not thank me – except, if there comes one at nightfall, do not, for my memory, let him in. Good-night, brother.'

And, 'Good-night, brother,' said I.

He turned, and drifted lamely out of the clearing. He was out of my sight as quickly as if he had gone into the ground. It was true about the wolves; there were their three tracks, and the priest's tracks running to the place where they had my dog down. If, remembering the hare, I had had other thoughts, I was ashamed of them. I was sorry I had not asked in the village about this strange man who beat off wolves with a stick; but I had, unfortunately, not known it in the village.

I was to know. Oh, I was to know!

It might have been a month after – anyhow, it was near sunset of a bitter day – when I saw the lame priest again.

Lame indeed. Bent double as if with agony, limping horribly, the sweat on his white face, he stumbled to my door. His hand was at his side; there was a dry blood stain round his mouth; yet even while he had to lean against the doorpost he would not let me within arm's reach of him, but edged away.

'Come in, man.' I was appalled. 'Come in. You – are you hurt?' I thought I saw blood on his soutane, that was in flinders.

He shook his head. Like a man whose minutes are numbered, he looked at the sun; and, like a man whose minutes are numbered, could not hurry his speech.

'Not I,' he said at last. 'But there is a poor beast out there,' nodding vaguely, 'a – a dog, that has been wounded. I – I want some rags to tie up the wound, a blanket to put over him. I cannot leave him in his – his last hour.'

'You can't go. I'll put him out of his misery: that will be better than blankets.'

'It might,' muttered he, 'it might, if you could! But I must go.'

I said I would go, too. But at that he seemed to lose all control of himself, and snarled out at me.

'Stay at home. I will not have you. Hurry. Get me the things.'

His eyes – and, on my soul, I thought death was glazing them – were on the sinking sun when I came out again, and for the first time

he did not edge away from me. I should have known without telling
that he had been caring for some animal by the smell of his clothes.

'My brother that I have treated brotherly, as you me,' he said,
'whether I come back this night or not, keep your door shut. Do not
come out – *if I had strength to kneel, I would kneel to you* – for any
calling. And I – I that ask you have loved you well; I have tried to
serve you, except' (he had no pause, no awkwardness) 'in the matter
of that map; but you had burnt the heathen charm, and I had to find
a way to keep far off from you. I am – I am a driven man!'

'There will be no calling.' I was puzzled and despairing. 'There has
been none of that loon-crying, or whatever it was, since the night I
first met you. If you would treat me as a brother, come back to my
house and sleep. I will not hurt your wounded dog,' though even
then I knew it was no dog.

'I treat you as I know best,' he answered passionately. 'But if in the
morning I do not come' – He seized the blanket, the rags; bounded
from me in the last rays of sunlight, dragging his burden in the snow.
As he vanished with his swift, incredible lameness, his voice came
back high and shrill: 'If I do not come in the morning, come out and
give – give my dog burial. For the love of' – he was screaming – 'for
the love I bore you – Christian burial!'

If I had not stayed to shut the door, I should not have lost him.
Until dark I called, I beat every inch of cover. All the time I had a
feeling that he was near and evading me, and at last I stopped looking
for him. For all I knew he might have a camp somewhere; and camp
or none, he had said pretty plainly he did not want me. I went home,
angry and baffled.

It was a freezing night. The very moon looked fierce with cold.
The shack snapped with frost as I sat down to the supper I could not
eat for the thought of the poor soul outside; and as I sat I heard a
sound, a soft, imploring call – the same, only nearer and more
insistent, as the cry on the wind the night after I first saw the priest. I
was at the door, when something stopped me. I do not exaggerate
when I say the mad priest's voice was in my ears: 'If there comes one
to your door after nightfall, do not let him in. Do not open for any
crying. *If I had strength to kneel, I would kneel to you.*'

I do not think any pen on earth could put down the entreaty of that
miserable voice, but even remembering it I would have disregarded
it if, before I could so much as draw breath, that soft calling had not
broken into a great ravening howl, bestial, full of malice. For a
moment I thought the priest had come back raving mad; I thought
silly thoughts of my cellar and my medicine chest; but as I turned for

my knitted sash to tie him with, the horrid howl came again, and I knew it was no man, but a beast. Or I think that is a lie. I knew nothing, except that outside was something more horrible than I had ever dreamed of, and that I could not open my door.

I did go to the window; I put a light there for the priest to see, if he came; but I did no more. That very day I had said, 'There will be no more calling,' and here, in my sober senses, stood and sweated because my words were turned into a lie.

There seemed to be two voices, yet I knew it was but one. First would come the soft wailing, with the strange drawing in it. There was more terror for me in that than in the furious snarl to which it always changed; for while it was imploring it was all I could do not to let in the one who cried out there. Just as I could withstand no longer, the ravening malice of the second cry would stop me short. It was as if one called and one forbade me. But I knew there were no two things outside.

I may as well set down my shame and be done. I was afraid. I stood holding my frantic dog, and dared not look at the unshuttered window, black and shining like new ice in the lamplight, last I should see I knew not what inhuman face looking at me through the frail pane. If I had had the heathen charm, I should have fallen to the cowardice of using it.

It may have been ten minutes that I stood with frozen blood. All I am sure of is that I came to my senses with a great start, remembering the defenceless priest outside. I shut up my dog, took my gun, opened my door in a fury, and – did not shoot.

Not ten yards from me a wolf crouched in the snow, a dark and lonely thing. My gun was in my shoulder, but as he came at me the sound that broke from his throat loosened my arm. It was human. There is no other word for it. As I stood, sick and stupid, the poor brute stopped his rush with a great slither in the snow that was black with his blood in the moonlight, and ran – ran terribly, lamely, from my sight – but not before I had seen a wide white bandage bound round his grey-black back and breast.

'The priest's dog!' I said. I thought a hundred things, and dared not meddle with what I did not understand.

I searched as best I might for what I knew I should not find – searched till the dawn broke in a lurid sky; and under that crimson light I found the man I had called brother on the crimson snow. And as I hope to die in a house and in my bed, my rags I gave for the dying beast were round his breast, my blanket huddled at his hand. But his face, as I looked on him, I should not have known, for it was young. I put down my loaded gun, that I was glad was loaded still, and I carried the dead home. I saw no wounded wolf nor the trace of one, except the long track from my door to the priest's body, and *that* was marked by neither teeth nor claws, but, under my rags, with bullets.

Well, he had his Christian burial! – though Father Moore, good, smooth man, would not hear my tale.

The dead priest had been outcast by his own will, not the Church's; had roamed the country for a thousand miles, a thing afraid and a thing of fear. And now someone had killed him, perhaps by mistake.

'Who knows?' finished Father Moore softly. 'Who knows? But I will have no hue and cry made about it. He was once, at least, a servant of God, and these' – he glanced at the queer-looking bullets that had fallen from the dead man's side as I made him ready for burial – 'I will encourage no senseless superstition in my people by trying to trace these. Especially – ' But he did not finish.

So we dug the priest's grave, taking turn by turn, for we are not young; and his brother in God buried him. What either of us thought about the whole matter he did not say.

But the very day after, while the frozen mound of consecrated earth was raw in the sunshine, Andrew walked in at my door.

'We come back,' he announced. 'All good here now! Lame wolf dead. Shoot him after dark, silver bullet. *Weguladimooch. Bochtusum.*'[1]

He said never a word about the new grave. And neither did I.

Luella Miller

MARY WILKINS FREEMAN

CLOSE TO THE VILLAGE STREET stood the one-storey house in which Luella Miller, who had an evil name in the village, had dwelt. She had been dead for years, yet there were those in the village who, in spite of the clearer light which comes on a vantage-point from a long-past danger, half believed in the tale which they had heard from their childhood. In their hearts, although they scarcely would have owned it, it was a survival of the wild horror and frenzied fear of their ancestors who had dwelt in the same age with Luella Miller. Young people even would stare with a shudder at the old house as they passed, and children never played around it as was their wont around an untenanted building. Not a window in the old Miller house was broken: the panes reflected the morning sunlight in patches of emerald and blue, and the latch of the sagging front door was never lifted although no bolt secured it. Since Luella Miller had been carried out of it, the house had had no tenant except one friendless old soul who had no choice between that and the far-off shelter of the open sky. This old woman, who had survived her kindred and friends, lived in the house one week, then one morning no smoke came out of the chimney, and a body of neighbours, a score strong, entered and found her dead in her bed. There were dark whispers as to the cause of her death, and there were those who testified to an expression of fear so exalted that it showed forth the state of the departing soul upon the dead face. The old woman had been hale and hearty when she entered the house, and in seven days she was dead; it seemed that she had fallen a victim to some uncanny power. The minister talked in the pulpit with covert severity against the sin of superstition; still the belief prevailed. Not a soul in the village but would have chosen the almshouse rather than that dwelling. No vagrant, if he heard the tale, would seek shelter beneath that old roof, unhallowed by nearly half a century of superstitious fear.

There was only one person in the village who had actually known

Luella Miller. That person was a woman well over eighty, but a marvel of vitality and unextinct youth. Straight as an arrow, with the spring of one recently let loose from the bow of life, she moved about the streets, and she always went to church, rain or shine. She had never married, and had lived alone for years in a house across the road from Luella Miller's.

This woman had none of the garrulousness of age, but never in all her life had she ever held her tongue for any will save her own, and she never spared the truth when she essayed to present it. She it was who bore testimony to the life, evil, though possibly wittingly or designedly so, of Luella Miller, and to her personal appearance. When this old woman spoke – and she had the gift of description, although her thoughts were clothed in the rude vernacular of her native village – one could seem to see Luella Miller as she had really looked. According to this woman, Lydia Anderson by name, Luella Miller had been a beauty of a type rather unusual in New England. She had been a slight, pliant sort of creature, as ready with a strong yielding to fate and as unbreakable as a willow. She had glimmering lengths of straight, fair hair, which she wore softly looped round a long, lovely face. She had blue eyes full of soft pleading, little slender, clinging hands, and a wonderful grace of motion and attitude.

'Luella Miller used to sit in a way nobody else could if they sat up and studied a week of Sundays,' said Lydia Anderson, 'and it was a sight to see her walk. If one of them willows over there on the edge of the brook could start up and get its roots free of the ground, and move off, it would go just the way Luella Miller used to. She had a green shot silk she used to wear, too, and a hat with green ribbon streamers, and a lace veil blowing across her face and out sideways, and a green ribbon flyin' from her waist. That was what she came out bride in when she married Erastus Miller. Her name before she was married was Hill. There was always a sight of 'l's' in her name, married or single. Erastus Miller was good lookin', too, better lookin' than Luella. Sometimes I used to think that Luella wa'n't so handsome after all. Erastus just about worshipped her. I used to know him pretty well. He lived next door to me, and we went to school together. Folks used to say he was waitin' on me, but he wa'n't. I never thought he was except once or twice when he said things that some girls might have suspected meant somethin'. That was before Luella came here to teach the district school. It was funny how she came to get it, for folks said she hadn't any education, and that one of the big girls, Lottie Henderson, used to do all the

teachin' for her, while she sat back and did embroidery work on a
cambric pocket-handkerchief. Lottie Henderson was a real smart
girl, a splendid scholar, and she just set her eyes by Luella, as all the
girls did. Lottie would have made a real smart woman, but she died
when Luella had been here about a year – just faded away and died:
nobody knew what ailed her. She dragged herself to that schoolhouse and helped Luella teach till the very last minute. The
committee all knew how Luella didn't do much of the work herself,
but they winked at it. It wa'n't long after Lottie died that Erastus
married her. I always thought he hurried it up because she wa'n't fit
to teach. One of the big boys used to help her after Lottie died, but
he hadn't much government, and the school didn't do very well, and
Luella might have had to give it up, for the committee couldn't have
shut their eyes to things much longer. The boy that helped her was a
real honest, innocent sort of fellow, and he was a good scholar, too.
Folks said he over-studied, and that was the reason he was took crazy
the year after Luella married, but I don't know. And I don't know
what made Erastus Miller go into consumption of the blood the year
after he was married: consumption wa'n't in his family. He just grew
weaker and weaker, and went almost bent double when he tried to
wait on Luella, and he spoke feeble, like an old man. He worked
terrible hard till the last trying to save up a little to leave Luella. I've
seen him out in the worst storms on a wood sled – he used to cut and
sell wood – and he was hunched up on top lookin' more dead than
alive. Once I couldn't stand it: I went over and helped him pitch
some wood on the cart – I was always strong in my arms. I wouldn't
stop for all he told me to, and I guess he was glad enough for the
help. That was only a week before he died. He fell on the kitchen
floor while he was gettin' breakfast. He always got the breakfast and
let Luella lay abed. He did all the sweepin' and the washin' and the
ironin' and most of the cookin'. He couldn't bear to have Luella lift
her finger, and she let him do for her. She lived like a queen for all
the work she did. She didn't even do her sewin'. She said it made her
shoulder ache to sew, and poor Erastus's sister Lily used to do all her
sewin'. She wa'n't able to, either; she was never strong in her back,
but she did it beautifully. She had to, to suit Luella, she was so
dreadful particular. I never saw anythin' like the fagottin' and
hemstitchin' that Lily Miller did for Luella. She made all Luella's
weddin' outfit, and that green silk dress, after Maria Babbit cut it.
Maria she cut it for nothin', and she did a lot more cuttin' and fittin'
for nothin' for Luella, too. Lily Miller went to live with Luella after
Erastus died. She gave up her home, although she was real attached

to it and wa'n't a mite afraid to stay alone. She rented it and she went to live with Luella right away after the funeral.'

Then this old woman, Lydia Anderson, who remembered Luella Miller, would go on to relate the story of Lily Miller. It seemed that on the removal of Lily Miller to the house of her dead brother to live with his widow, the village people first began to talk. This Lily Miller had been hardly past her first youth, and a most robust and blooming woman, rosy-cheeked, with curls of strong, black hair overshadowing round, candid temples and bright dark eyes. It was not six months after she had taken up her residence with her sister-in-law that her rosy colour faded and her pretty curves became wan hollows. White shadows began to show in the black rings of her hair, and the light died out of her eyes, her features sharpened and there were pathetic lines at her mouth, which yet wore always an expression of utter sweetness and even happiness. She was devoted to her sister; there was no doubt that she loved her with her whole heart, and was perfectly content in her service. It was her sole anxiety lest she should die and leave her alone.

'The way Lily Miller used to talk about Luella was enough to make you mad and enough to make you cry,' said Lydia Anderson. 'I've been in there sometimes toward the last, when she was too feeble to cook, and carried her some blancmange or custard – somethin' I thought she might relish, and she'd thank me and, when I asked her how she was, say she felt better than she did yesterday, and ask me if I didn't think she looked better, dreadful pitiful, and say poor Luella had an awful time takin' care of her and doin' the work – she wa'n't strong enough to do anythin' – when all the time Luella wa'n't liftin' her finger and poor Lily didn't get any care except what the neighbours gave her, and Luella ate up everythin' that was carried in for Lily. I had it real straight that she did. Luella used to just sit and cry and do nothin'. She did act real fond of Lily, and she pined away considerable, too. There was those that thought she'd go into a decline herself. But after Lily died, her Aunt Abby Mixter came, and then Luella picked up and grew as fat and rosy as ever. But poor Aunt Abby begun to droop just the way Lily had, and I guess somebody wrote to her married daughter, Mrs Sam Abbot, who lived in Barre, for she wrote her mother that she must leave right away and come and make her a visit, but Aunt Abby wouldn't go. I can see her now. She was a real good-lookin' woman, tall and large, with a big, square face and a high forehead that looked of itself kind of benevolent and good. She just tended out on Luella as if she had been a baby, and when her married daughter sent for her she wouldn't stir one inch. She'd always thought a lot of her daughter, too, but she said Luella needed her and her married daughter didn't. Her daughter kept writin' and writin', but it didn't do any good. Finally she came, and when she saw how bad her mother looked, she broke down and cried and all but went on her knees to have her come away. She spoke her mind out to Luella, too. She told her that she'd killed her husband and everybody that had anythin' to do with her, and she'd thank her to leave her mother alone. Luella went into hysterics, and Aunt Abby was so frightened that she called me after her daughter went. Mrs Sam Abbot she went away fairly cryin' out loud in the buggy, the neighbours heard her, and well she might, for she never saw her mother again alive. I went in that night when Aunt Abby called for me, standin' in the door with her little green-checked shawl over her head. I can see her now. "Do come over here, Miss Anderson," she sang out, kind of gasping for breath. I didn't stop for anythin'. I put over as fast as I could, and when I got there, there was Luella laughin' and cryin' all together, and Aunt Abby trying to hush her, and all the time she herself was white as a sheet and shakin' so she could hardly stand. "For the land sakes, Mrs Mixter," says I, "you look worse than she does. You ain't fit to be up out of your bed."

' "Oh, there ain't anythin' the matter with me," says she. Then she went on talkin' to Luella. "There, there, don't, don't, poor little lamb," says she. "Aunt Abby is here. She ain't goin' away and leavin' you. Don't, poor little lamb."

' "Do leave her with me, Mrs Mixter, and you get back to bed," says I, for Aunt Abby had been layin' down considerable lately, though somehow she contrived to do the work.

' "I'm well enough," says she. "Don't you think she had better have the doctor, Miss Anderson?"

' "The doctor," says I, "I think *you* had better have the doctor. I think you need him much worse than some folks I could mention." And I looked right straight at Luella Miller, laughin' and cryin' and goin' on as if she was the centre of all creation. All the time she was actin' so – seemin' as if she was too sick to sense anythin' – she was keepin' a sharp lookout as to how we took it out of the corner of one eye. I see her. You could never cheat me about Luella Miller. Finally I got real mad and I run home and I got a bottle of valerian I had, and I poured some boilin' hot water on a handful of catnip, and I mixed up that catnip tea with most half a wineglass of valerian, and I went with it over to Luella's. I marched right up to Luella, a-holdin' out of that cup, all smokin'. "Now," says I, "Luella Miller, *you swaller this!*"

' "What is – what is it, oh, what is it?" she sort of screeches out. Then she goes off a-laughin' enough to kill.

' "Poor lamb, poor little lamb," says Aunt Abby, standin' over her, all kind of tottery, and tryin' to bathe her head with camphor.

' "*You swaller this right down*," says I. And I didn't waste any ceremony. I just took hold of Luella Miller's chin and I tipped her head back, and I caught her mouth open with laughin', and I clapped that cup to her lips, and I fairly hollered at her: "Swaller, swaller, swaller!" and she gulped it right down. She had to, and I guess it did her good. Anyhow, she stopped cryin' and laughin' and let me put her to bed, and she went to sleep like a baby inside of half an hour. That was more than poor Aunt Abby did. She lay awake all that night and I stayed with her, though she tried not to have me; said she wa'n't sick enough for watchers. But I stayed, and I made some good corn-meal gruel and I fed her a teaspoon every little while all night long. It seemed to me as if she was jest dyin' from bein' all wore out. In the mornin' as soon as it was light I ran over to the Bisbees and sent Johnny Bisbee for the doctor. I told him to tell the doctor to hurry, and he come pretty quick. Poor Aunt Abby didn't seem to know much of anythin' when he got there. You couldn't hardly tell she breathed, she was so used up. When the doctor had gone, Luella came into the room lookin' like a baby in her ruffled nightgown. I can see her now. Her eyes were as blue and her face all pink and white like a blossom, and she looked at Aunt Abby in the bed sort of innocent and surprised. "Why," says she, "Aunt Abby ain't got up yet?"

' "No, she ain't," says I, pretty short.

' "I thought I didn't smell the coffee," says Luella.

' "Coffee," says I. "I guess if you have coffee this mornin' you'll make it yourself."

' "I never made the coffee in all my life," says she, dreadful astonished. "Erastus always made the coffee as long as he lived, and then Lily she made it, and then Aunt Abby made it. I don't believe I *can* make the coffee, Miss Anderson."

' "You can make it or go without, jest as you please," says I.

' "Ain't Aunt Abby goin' to get up?" says she.

' "I guess she won't get up," says I, "sick as she is." I was gettin' madder and madder. There was somethin' about that little pink-and-white thing standin' there and talkin' about coffee, when she had killed so many better folks than she was, and had jest killed another, that made me feel 'most as if I wished somebody would up and kill her before she had a chance to do any more harm.

' "Is Aunt Abby sick?' says Luella, as if she was sort of aggrieved and injured.

' "Yes,' says I, "she's sick, and she's goin' to die, and then you'll be left alone, and you'll have to do for yourself and wait on yourself, or do without things." I don't know but I was sort of hard, but it was the truth, and if I was any harder than Luella Miller had been I'll give up. I ain't never been sorry that I said it. Well, Luella, she up and had hysterics again at that, and I jest let her have 'em. All I did was to bundle her into the room on the other side of the entry where Aunt Abby couldn't hear her, if she wa'n't past it – I don't know but she was – and set her down hard in a chair and told her not to come back into the other room, and she minded. She had her hysterics in there till she got tired. When she found out that nobody was comin' to coddle her and do for her she stopped. At least I suppose she did. I had all I could do with poor Aunt Abby tryin' to keep the breath of life in her. The doctor had told me that she was dreadful low, and give me some very strong medicine to give to her in drops real often, and told me real particular about the nourishment. Well, I did as he told me real faithful till she wa'n't able to swaller any longer. Then I had her daughter sent for. I had begun to realise that she wouldn't last any time at all. I hadn't realised it before, though I spoke to Luella the way I did. The doctor he came, and Mrs Sam Abbot, but when she got there it was too late; her mother was dead. Aunt Abby's daughter just give one look at her mother layin' there, then she turned sort of sharp and sudden and looked at me.

' "Where is she?" says she, and I knew she meant Luella.

' "She's out in the kitchen," says I. "She's too nervous to see folks die. She's afraid it will make her sick."

'The doctor he speaks up then. He was a young man. Old Dr Park had died the year before, and this was a young fellow just out of college. "Mrs Miller is not strong," says he, kind of severe, "and she is quite right in not agitating herself."

' "You are another, young man; she's got her pretty claw on you," thinks I, but I didn't say anythin' to him. I just said over to Mrs Sam Abbot that Luella was in the kitchen, and Mrs Sam Abbot she went out there, and I went, too, and I never heard anythin' like the way she talked to Luella Miller. I felt pretty hard to Luella myself, but this was more than I ever would have dared to say. Luella she was too scared to go into hysterics. She jest flopped. She seemed to jest shrink away to nothin' in that kitchen chair, with Mrs Sam Abbot standin' over her and talkin' and tellin' her the truth. I guess the truth was most too much for her and no mistake, because Luella presently actually did faint away, and there wa'n't any sham about it, the way I always suspected there was about them hysterics. She fainted dead away and we had to lay her flat on the floor, and the doctor he came runnin' out and he said somethin' about a weak heart dreadful fierce to Mrs Sam Abbot, but she wa'n't a mite scared. She faced him jest as white as even Luella was layin' there lookin' like death and the doctor feelin' of her pulse.

'"Weak heart," says she, "weak heart; weak fiddlesticks! There ain't nothin' weak about that woman. She's got strength enough to hang on to other folks till she kills 'em. Weak? It was my poor mother that was weak: this woman killed her as sure as if she had taken a knife to her."

'But the doctor he didn't pay much attention. He was bendin' over Luella layin' there with her yellow hair all streamin' and her pretty pink-and-white face all pale, and her blue eyes like stars gone out, and he was holdin' on to her hand and smoothin' her forehead, and tellin' me to get the brandy in Aunt Abby's room, and I was sure as I wanted to be that Luella had got somebody else to hang on to, now Aunt Abby was gone, and I thought of poor Erastus Miller, and I sort of pitied the poor young doctor, led away by a pretty face, and I made up my mind I'd see what I could do.

'I waited till Aunt Abby had been dead and buried about a month, and the doctor was goin' to see Luella steady and folks were beginnin' to talk; then one evenin', when I knew the doctor had been called out of town and wouldn't be around, I went over to Luella's. I found her all dressed up in a blue muslin with white polka dots on it, and her hair curled jest as pretty, and there wa'n't a young girl in the place could compare with her. There was somethin' about Luella Miller seemed to draw the heart right out of you, but she didn't draw it out of *me*. She was settin' rocking in the chair by her sittin'-room window, and Maria Brown had gone home. Maria Brown had been in to help her, or rather to do the work, for Luella wa'n't helped when she didn't do anythin'. Maria Brown was real capable and she didn't have any ties; she wa'n't married, and lived alone, so she'd offered. I couldn't see why she should do the work any more than Luella; she wa'n't any too strong; but she seemed to think she could and Luella seemed to think so, too, so she went over and did all the work – washed, and ironed and baked, while Luella sat and rocked. Maria didn't live long afterward. She began to fade away just the same fashion the others had. Well, she was warned, but she acted real mad when folks said anythin': said Luella was a poor, abused woman, too delicate to help herself, and they'd ought to be ashamed, and if she died helpin' them that couldn't help themselves she would – and she did.

' "I s'pose Maria has gone home," says I to Luella, when I had gone in and sat down opposite her.

' "Yes, Maria went half an hour ago, after she had got supper and washed the dishes," says Luella, in her pretty way.

' "I suppose she has got a lot of work to do in her own house tonight, says I, kind of bitter, but that was all thrown away on Luella Miller. It seemed to her right that other folks that wa'n't any better able than she was herself should wait on her, and she couldn't get it through her head that anybody should think it *wa'n't* right."

' "Yes," says Luella, real sweet and pretty, "yes, she said she had to do her washin' tonight. She has let it go for a fortnight along of comin' over here."

' "Why don't she stay home and do her washin' instead of comin' over here and doin' *your* work, when you are just as well able, and enough sight more so, than she is to do it?" says I.

'Then Luella she looked at me like a baby who has a rattle shook at it. She sort of laughed as innocent as you please. "Oh, I can't do the work myself, Miss Anderson," says she. "I never did. Maria *has* to do it."

'Then I spoke out: "Has to do it!" says I. "Has to do it! She don't have to do it, either. Maria Brown has her own home and enough to live on. She ain't beholden to you to come over here and slave for you and kill herself."

'Luella she jest set and stared at me for all the world like a doll-baby that was so abused that it was comin' to life.

' "Yes," says I, "she's killin' herself. She's goin' to die just the way Erastus did, and Lily, and your Aunt Abby. You're killin' her jest as you did them. I don't know what there is about you, but you seem to bring a curse," says I. "You kill everybody that is fool enough to care anythin' about you and do for you."

'She stared at me and she was pretty pale.

' "And Maria ain't the only one you're goin' to kill," says I. "You're goin' to kill Dr Malcom before you're done with him."

'Then a red colour came flamin' all over her face. "I ain't goin' to kill him, either," says she, and she began to cry.

' "Yes, you *be*!" says I. Then I spoke as I had never spoke before. You see, I felt it on account of Erastus. I told her that she hadn't any business to think of another man after she'd been married to one that had died for her; that she was a dreadful woman; and she was, that's true enough, but sometimes I have wondered lately if she knew it – if she wa'n't like a baby with scissors in its hand cuttin' everybody without knowin' what it was doin'.

'Luella she kept gettin' paler and paler, and she never took her eyes off my face. There was somethin' awful about the way she looked at me and never spoke one word. After awhile I quit talkin' and I went home. I watched that night, but her lamp went out before nine o'clock, and when Dr Malcom came drivin' past and sort of slowed up, he see there wa'n't any light and he drove along. I saw her sort of shy out of meetin' the next Sunday, too, so he shouldn't go home with her, and I began to think mebbe she did have some conscience after all. It was only a week after that that Maria Brown died – sort of sudden at the last, though everybody had seen it was comin'. Well, then there was a good deal of feelin' and pretty dark whispers. Folks said the days of witchcraft had come again, and they were pretty shy of Luella. She acted sort of offish to the doctor and he didn't go there, and there wa'n't anybody to do anythin' for her. I don't know how she *did* get along. I wouldn't go in there and offer to help her – not because I was afraid of dyin' like the rest, but I thought she was just as well able to do her own work as I was to do it for her, and I thought it was about time that she did it and stopped killin' other folks. But it wa'n't very long before folks began to say that Luella herself was goin' into a decline jest the way her husband, and Lily, and Aunt Abby and the others had, and I saw myself that she looked pretty bad. I used to see her goin' past from the store with a bundle as if she could hardly crawl, but I remembered how Erastus used to wait and 'tend when he couldn't hardly put one foot before the other, and I didn't go out to help her.

'But at last one afternoon I saw the doctor come drivin' up like mad with his medicine chest, and Mrs Babbit came in after supper and said that Luella was real sick.

' "I'd offer to go in and nurse her," says she, "but I've got my children to consider, and mebbe it ain't true what they say, but it's queer how many folks that have done for her have died."

'I didn't say anythin', but I considered how she had been Erastus's wife and how he had set his eyes by her, and I made up my mind to go in the next mornin', unless she was better, and see what I could do; but the next mornin' I see her at the window, and pretty soon she came steppin' out as spry as you please, and a little while afterward Mrs Babbit came in and told me that the doctor had got a girl from out of town, a Sarah Jones, to come there, and she said she was pretty sure that the doctor was goin' to marry Luella.

'I saw him kiss her in the door that night myself, and I knew it was true. The woman came that afternoon, and the way she flew around was a caution. I don't believe Luella had swept since Maria died. She swept and dusted, and washed and ironed; wet clothes and dusters and carpets were flyin' over there all day, and every time Luella set her foot out when the doctor wa'n't there there was that Sarah Jones helpin' of her up and down the steps, as if she hadn't learned to walk.

'Well, everybody knew that Luella and the doctor were goin' to be married, but it wa'n't long before they began to talk about his lookin' so poorly, jest as they had about the others; and they talked about Sarah Jones, too.

'Well, the doctor did die, and he wanted to be married first, so as to leave what little he had to Luella, but he died before the minister could get there, and Sarah Jones died a week afterward.

'Well, that wound up everything for Luella Miller. Not another soul in the whole town would lift a finger for her. There got to be a sort of panic. Then she began to droop in good earnest. She used to have to go to the store herself, for Mrs Babbit was afraid to let Tommy go for her, and I've seen her goin' past and stoppin' every two or three steps to rest. Well, I stood it as long as I could, but one day I see her comin' with her arms full and stoppin' to lean against the Babbit fence, and I run out and took her bundles and carried them to her house. Then I went home and never spoke one word to her though she called after me dreadful kind of pitiful. Well, that night I was taken sick with a chill, and I was sick as I wanted to be for two weeks. Mrs Babbit had seen me run out to help Luella and she came in and told me I was goin' to die on account of it. I didn't know whether I was or not, but I considered I had done right by Erastus's wife.

'That last two weeks Luella she had a dreadful hard time, I guess. She was pretty sick, and as near as I could make out nobody dared go near her. I don't know as she was really needin' anythin' very much, for there was enough to eat in her house and it was warm weather, and she made out to cook a little flour gruel every day, I know, but I guess she had a hard time, she that had been so petted and done for all her life.

'When I got so I could go out, I went over there one morning. Mrs Babbit had just come in to say she hadn't seen any smoke and she didn't know but it was somebody's duty to go in, but she couldn't help thinkin' of her children, and I got right up, though I hadn't been out of the house for two weeks, and I went in there, and Luella she was layin' on the bed, and she was dyin'.

'She lasted all that day and into the night. But I sat there after the new doctor had gone away. Nobody else dared to go there. It was about midnight that I left her for a minute to run home and get some medicine I had been takin', for I begun to feel rather bad.

'It was a full moon that night, and just as I started out of my door to cross the street back to Luella's, I stopped short, for I saw something.'

Lydia Anderson at this juncture always said with a certain defiance that she did not expect to be believed, and then proceeded in a hushed voice: 'I saw what I saw, and I know I saw it, and I will swear on my deathbed that I saw it. I saw Luella Miller and Erastus Miller, and Lily, and Aunt Abby, and Maria, and the doctor, and Sarah, all goin' out of her door, and all but Luella shone white in the moonlight, and they were all helpin' her along till she seemed to fairly fly in the midst of them. Then it all disappeared. I stood a minute with my heart poundin', then I went over there. I thought of goin' for Mrs Babbit, but I thought she'd be afraid. So I went alone, though I knew what had happened. Luella was layin' real peaceful, dead on her bed.'

This was the story that the old woman, Lydia Anderson, told, but the sequel was told by the people who survived her, and this is the tale which has become folklore in the village.

Lydia Anderson died when she was eighty-seven. She had continued wonderfully hale and hearty for one of her age until about two weeks before her death.

One bright moonlight evening she was sitting beside a window in her parlour when she made a sudden exclamation, and was out of the house and across the street before the neighbour who was taking care of her could stop her. She followed as fast as possible and found Lydia Anderson stretched on the ground before the door of Luella Miller's deserted house and she was quite dead.

The next night there was a red gleam of fire athwart the moonlight and the old house of Luella Miller was burned to the ground. Nothing is now left of it except a few old cellar stones and a lilac bush, and in summer a helpless trail of morning glories among the weeds, which might be considered emblematic of Luella herself.

The Bird in the Garden

RICHARD MIDDLETON

THE ROOM in which the Burchell family lived in Love Street, SE, was underground and depended for light and air on a grating let into the pavement above.

Uncle John, who was a queer one, had filled the area with green plants and creepers in boxes and tins hanging from the grating, so that the room itself obtained very little light indeed, but there was always a nice bright green place for the people sitting in it to look at. Toby, who had peeped into the areas of other little boys, knew that his was of quite exceptional beauty, and it was with a certain awe that he helped Uncle John to tend the plants in the morning, watering them and taking the pieces of paper and straws that had fallen through the grating from their hair. 'It is a great mistake to have straws in one's hair,' Uncle John would say gravely; and Toby knew that it was true.

It was in the morning after they had just been watered that the plants looked and smelt best, and when the sun shone through the grating and the diamonds were shining and falling through the forest, Toby would tell the baby about the great bird who would one day come flying through the trees – a bird of all colours, ugly and beautiful, with a harsh sweet voice. 'And that will be the end of everything,' said Toby, though of course he was only repeating a story his Uncle John had told him.

There were other people in the big, dark room besides Toby and Uncle John and the baby; dark people who flitted to and fro about secret matters, people called father and mother and Mr Hearn, who were apt to kick if they found you in their way, and who never laughed except at nights, and then they laughed too loudly.

'They will frighten the bird,' thought Toby; but they were kind to Uncle John because he had a pension. Toby slept in a corner on the ground beside the baby, and when father and Mr Hearn fought at nights he would wake up and watch and shiver; but when this happened it seemed to him that the baby was laughing at him, and he would pinch her to make her stop. One night, when the men were fighting very fiercely and mother had fallen asleep on the table, Uncle John rose from his bed and began singing in a great voice. It was a song Toby knew very well about Trafalgar's Bay, but it frightened the two men a great deal because they thought Uncle John would be too mad to fetch the pension any more. Next day he was quite well, however, and he and Toby found a large green caterpillar in the garden among the plants.

'This is a fact of great importance,' said Uncle John, stroking it with a little stick. 'It is a sign!'

Toby used to lie awake at nights after that and listen for the bird, but he only heard the clatter of feet on the pavement and the screaming of engines far away.

Later there came a new young woman to live in the cellar – not a dark person, but a person you could see and speak to. She patted Toby on the head; but when she saw the baby she caught it to her breast and cried over it, calling it pretty names.

At first father and Mr Hearn were both very kind to her, and mother used to sit all day in the corner with burning eyes, but after a time the three used to laugh together at nights as before, and the woman would sit with her wet face and wait for the coming of the bird, with Toby and the baby and Uncle John, who was a queer one.

'All we have to do,' Uncle John would say, 'is to keep the garden clean and tidy, and to water the plants every morning so that they may be very green.' And Toby would go and whisper this to the baby, and she would stare at the ceiling with large, stupid eyes.

There came a time when Toby was very sick, and he lay all day in his corner wondering about wonder. Sometimes the room in which he lay became so small that he was choked for lack of air, sometimes it was so large that he screamed out because he felt lonely. He could not see the dark people then at all, but only Uncle John and the woman, who told him in whispers that her name was 'Mummie'. She called him Sonny, which is a very pretty name, and when Toby heard it he felt a tickling in his sides which he knew to be gladness. Mummie's face was wet and warm and soft, and she was very fond of kissing. Every morning Uncle John would lift Toby up and show him the garden, and Toby would slip out of his arms and walk among the trees and plants. And the place would grow bigger and bigger until it was all the world, and Toby would lose himself amongst the tangle of trees and flowers and creepers. He would see butterflies there and tame animals, and the sky was full of birds of all colours, ugly and beautiful; but he knew that none of these was the bird, because their voices were only sweet. Sometimes he showed these wonders to a little boy called Toby, who held his hand and called him Uncle John, sometimes he showed them to his mummie and he himself was Toby; but always when he came back he found himself lying in Uncle John's arms, and, weary from his walk, would fall into a pleasant dreamless sleep.

It seemed to Toby at this time that a veil hung about him which, dim and unreal in itself, served to make all things dim and unreal. He did not know whether he was asleep or awake, so strange was life, so vivid were his dreams. Mummie, Uncle John, the baby, Toby himself came with a flicker of the veil and disappeared vaguely without cause. It would happen that Toby would be speaking to Uncle John, and suddenly he would find himself looking into the large eyes of the baby, turned stupidly towards the ceiling, and again the baby would be Toby himself, a hot, dry little body without legs or arms, that swayed suspended as if by magic a foot above the bed.

Then there was the vision of two small feet that moved a long way off, and Toby would watch them curiously, as kittens do their tails, without knowing the cause of their motion.

It was all very wonderful and very strange, and day by day the veil grew thicker; there was no need to wake when the sleeptime was so pleasant; there were no dark people to kick you in that dreamy place.

And yet Toby woke – woke to a life and in a place which he had never known before.

He found himself on a heap of rags in a large cellar which depended for its light on a grating let into the pavement of the street above. On the stone floor of the area and swinging from the grating were a few sickly, grimy plants in pots. There must have been a fine sunset up above, for a faint red glow came through the bars and touched the leaves of the plants.

There was a lighted candle standing in a bottle on the table, and the cellar seemed full of people. At the table itself two men and a woman were drinking, though they were already drunk, and beyond in a corner Toby could see the head and shoulders of a tall old man. Beside him there crouched a woman with a faded, pretty face, and between Toby and the rest of the room there stood a box in which lay a baby with large, wakeful eyes.

Toby's body tingled with excitement, for this was a new thing; he had never seen it before, he had never seen anything before.

The voice of the woman at the table rose and fell steadily without a pause; she was abusing the other woman, and the two drunken men were laughing at her and shouting her on; Toby thought the other woman lacked spirit because she stayed crouching on the floor and said nothing.

At last the woman stopped her abuse, and one of the men turned and shouted an order to the woman on the floor. She stood up and came towards him, hesitating; this annoyed the man and he swore at her brutally; when she came near enough he knocked her down with his fist, and all the three burst out laughing.

Toby was so excited that he knelt up in his corner and clapped his hands, but the others did not notice because the old man was up and swaying wildly over the woman. He seemed to be threatening the man who had struck her, and that one was evidently afraid of him, for he rose unsteadily and lifted the chair on which he had been sitting above his head to use as a weapon.

The old man raised his fist and the chair fell heavily on to his wrinkled forehead and he dropped to the ground.

The woman at the table cried out, 'The pension!' in her shrill voice, and then they were all quiet, looking.

Then it seemed to Toby that through the forest there came flying, with a harsh sweet voice and a tumult of wings, a bird of all colours, ugly and beautiful, and he knew, though later there might be people to tell him otherwise, that that was the end of everything.

The Room in the Tower

E. F. BENSON

IT IS PROBABLE that everybody who is at all a constant dreamer has had at least one experience of an event or a sequence of circumstances which have come to his mind in sleep being subsequently realised in the material world. But, in my opinion, so far from this being a strange thing, it would be far odder if this fulfilment did not occasionally happen, since our dreams are, as a rule, concerned with people whom we know and places with which we are familiar, such as might very naturally occur in the awake and daylit world. True, these dreams are often broken into by some absurd and fantastic incident, which puts them out of court in regard to their subsequent fulfilment, but on the mere calculation of chances, it does not appear in the least unlikely that a dream imagined by anyone who dreams constantly should occasionally come true. Not long ago, for instance, I experienced such a fulfilment of a dream which seems to me in no way remarkable and to have no kind of psychical significance. The manner of it was as follows.

A certain friend of mine, living abroad, is amiable enough to write to me about once in a fortnight. Thus, when fourteen days or thereabouts have elapsed since I last heard from him, my mind, probably, either consciously or subconsciously, is expectant of a letter from him. One night last week I dreamed that as I was going upstairs to dress for dinner I heard, as I often heard, the sound of the postman's knock on my front door, and diverted my direction downstairs instead. There, among other correspondence, was a letter from him. Thereafter the fantastic entered, for on opening it I found inside the ace of diamonds and scribbled across it in his well-known handwriting, 'I am sending you this for safe custody, as you know it is running an unreasonable risk to keep aces in Italy.' The next evening I was just preparing to go upstairs to dress when I heard the postman's knock, and did precisely as I had done in my dream. There, among other letters, was one from my friend. Only it did not contain the ace of diamonds. Had it done so, I should have attached more weight to the matter, which, as it stands, seems to me a perfectly ordinary coincidence. No doubt I consciously or subconsciously expected a letter from him, and this suggested to me my dream. Similarly, the fact that my friend had not written to me for a fortnight suggested to him that he should do so. But occasionally it is not so easy to find such an explanation, and for the following story I can find no explanation at all. It came out of the dark, and into the dark it has gone again.

All my life I have been a habitual dreamer: the nights are few, that is to say, when I do not find on awaking in the morning that some mental experience has been mine, and sometimes, all night long, apparently, a series of the most dazzling adventures befalls me. Almost without exception these adventures are pleasant, though often merely trivial. It is of an exception that I am going to speak.

It was when I was about sixteen that a certain dream first came to me, and this is how it befell. It opened with my being set down at the door of a big red-brick house, where, I understood, I was going to stay. The servant who opened the door told me that tea was being served in the garden, and led me through a low dark-panelled hall, with a large open fireplace, on to a cheerful green lawn set round with flower beds. There were grouped about the tea-table a small party of people, but they were all strangers to me except one, who was a schoolfellow called Jack Stone, clearly the son of the house, and he introduced me to his mother and father and a couple of sisters. I was, I remember, somewhat astonished to find myself here, for the boy in question was scarcely known to me, and I rather disliked what I knew of him; moreover, he had left school nearly a year before. The afternoon was very hot, and an intolerable oppression reigned. On the far side of the lawn ran a red-brick wall, with an iron gate in its centre, outside which stood a walnut tree. We sat in the shadow of the house opposite a row of long windows, inside which I could see a table, with cloth laid, glimmering with glass and silver. This garden front of the house was very long, and at one end of it stood a tower of three stories, which looked to me much older than the rest of the building.

Before long, Mrs Stone, who, like the rest of the party, had sat in absolute silence, said to me, 'Jack will show you your room: I have given you the room in the tower.'

Quite inexplicably my heart sank at her words. I felt as if I had known that I should have the room in the tower, and that it contained something dreadful and significant. Jack instantly got up, and I understood that I had to follow him. In silence we passed through the hall, and mounted a great oak staircase with many corners, and arrived at a small landing with two doors set in it. He pushed one of these open for me to enter, and without coming in himself, closed it after me. Then I knew that my conjecture had been right: there was something awful in the room, and with the terror of nightmare growing swiftly and enveloping me, I awoke in a spasm of terror.

Now that dream or variations on it occurred to me intermittently for fifteen years. Most often it came in exactly this form, the arrival, the tea laid out on the lawn, the deadly silence succeeded by that one deadly sentence, the mounting with Jack Stone up to the room in the tower where horror dwelt, and it always came to a close in the nightmare of terror at that which was in the room, though I never saw what it was. At other times I experienced variations on this same theme. Occasionally, for instance, we would be sitting at dinner in the dining-room, into the windows of which I had looked on the first night when the dream of this house visited me, but wherever we were, there was the same silence, the same sense of dreadful oppression and foreboding. And the silence I knew would always be broken by Mrs Stone saying to me, 'Jack will show you your room: I have given you the room in the tower.' Upon which (this was invariable) I had to follow him up the oak staircase with many corners, and enter the place that I dreaded more and more each time that I visited it in sleep. Or, again, I would find myself playing cards, still in silence, in a drawing-room lit with immense chandeliers that gave a blinding illumination. What the game was I have no idea; what I remembered, with a sense of miserable anticipation, was that soon Mrs Stone would get up and say to me, 'Jack will show you your room: I have given you the room in the tower.' This drawing-room where we played cards was next to the dining-room, and, as I have said, was always brilliantly illuminated, whereas the rest of the house was full of dusk and shadows. And yet, how often, in spite of those bouquets of lights, have I not pored over the cards that were dealt me, scarcely able for some reason to see them. Their designs, too, were strange: there were no red suits, but all were black, and among them there were certain cards which were black all over. I hated and dreaded those.

As this dream continued to recur, I got to know the greater part of the house. There was a smoking-room beyond the drawing-room, at the end of a passage with a green-baize door. It was always very dark there, and as often as I went there I passed somebody whom I could not see in the doorway coming out. Curious developments, too, took place in the characters that peopled the dream as might happen to living persons. Mrs Stone, for instance, who, when I first saw her, had been black-haired, became grey, and instead of rising briskly, as she had done at first when she said, 'Jack will show you your room: I have given you the room in the tower,' got up very feebly, as if the strength was leaving her limbs. Jack also grew up, and became a rather ill-looking young man, with a brown moustache, while one of the sisters ceased to appear, and I understood she was married.

Then it so happened that I was not visited by this dream for six months or more, and I began to hope, in such inexplicable dread did I hold it, that it had passed away for good. But one night after this interval I again found myself being shown out on to the lawn for tea, and Mrs Stone was not there, while the others were all dressed in black. At once I guessed the reason, and my heart leaped at the thought that perhaps this time I should not have to sleep in the room in the tower, and though we usually all sat in silence, on this occasion the sense of relief made me talk and laugh as I had never yet done. But even then matters were not altogether comfortable, for no one else spoke, but they all looked secretly at each other. And soon the foolish stream of my talk ran dry, and gradually an apprehension worse than anything I had previously known gained on me as the light slowly faded.

Suddenly a voice which I knew well broke the stillness, the voice of Mrs Stone, saying, 'Jack will show you your room: I have given you the room in the tower.' It seemed to come from near the gate in the red-brick wall that bounded the lawn, and looking up, I saw that the grass outside was sown thick with gravestones. A curious greyish light shone from them, and I could read the lettering on the grave nearest me, and it was, 'In evil memory of Julia Stone.' And as usual Jack got up, and again I followed him through the hall and up the staircase with many corners. On this occasion it was darker than usual, and when I passed into the room in the tower I could only just see the furniture, the position of which was already familiar to me. Also there was a dreadful odour of decay in the room, and I woke screaming.

The dream, with such variations and developments as I have mentioned, went on at intervals for fifteen years. Sometimes I would dream it two or three nights in succession; once, as I have said, there was an intermission of six months, but taking a reasonable average, I should say that I dreamed it quite as often as once in a month. It had, as is plain, something of nightmare about it, since it always ended in the same appalling terror, which so far from getting less, seemed to me to gather fresh fear every time that I experienced it. There was, too, a strange and dreadful consistency about it. The characters in it, as I have mentioned, got regularly older, death and marriage visited this silent family, and I never in the dream, after Mrs Stone had died, set eyes on her again. But it was always her voice that told me that the room in the tower was prepared for me, and whether we had tea out on the lawn, or the scene was laid in one of the rooms overlooking it, I could always see her gravestone standing just outside the iron gate. It was the same, too, with the married daughter, usually she was not present, but once or twice she returned, in company with a man, whom I took to be her husband. He, too, like the rest of them, was always silent. But, owing to the constant repetition of the dream, I had ceased to attach, in my waking hours, any significance to it. I never met Jack Stone again during all those years, nor did I ever see a house that resembled this dark house of my dream. And then something happened.

I had been in London in this year, up till the end of the July, and during the first week in August went down to stay with a friend in a house he had taken for the summer months in the Ashdown Forest district of Sussex. I left London early, for John Clinton was to meet me at Forest Row Station and we were going to spend the day golfing and go to his house in the evening. He had his motor with him and we set off, about five of the afternoon, after a thoroughly delightful day, for the drive, the distance being some ten miles. As it was still so early we did not have tea at the clubhouse, but waited till we should get home. As we drove, the weather, which up till then had been, though hot, deliciously fresh, seemed to me to alter in quality, and become very stagnant and oppressive, and I felt that indefinable sense of ominous apprehension that I am accustomed to before thunder. John, however, did not share my views, attributing my loss of lightness to the fact that I had lost both my matches. Events proved, however, that I was right, though I do not think that the thunderstorm that broke that night was the sole cause of my depression.

Our way lay through deep high-banked lanes, and before we had gone very far I fell asleep, and was only awakened by the stopping of the motor. And with a sudden thrill, partly of fear but chiefly of curiosity, I found myself standing in the doorway of my house of dream. We went, I half wondering whether or not I was dreaming still, through a low oak-panelled hall and out on to the lawn, where tea was laid in the shadow of the house. It was set in flower-beds, a

red-brick wall, with a gate in it, bounded one side, and out beyond
that was a space of rough grass with a walnut tree. The façade of the
house was very long, and at one end stood a three-storeyed tower,
markedly older than the rest.

Here for the moment all resemblance to the repeated dream
ceased. There was no silent and somehow terrible family, but a large
assembly of exceedingly cheerful persons, all of whom were known
to me. And in spite of the horror with which the dream itself had
always filled me, I felt nothing of it now that the scene of it was thus
reproduced before me. But I felt intensest curiosity as to what was
going to happen.

Tea pursued its cheerful course, and before long Mrs Clinton got
up. And at that moment I think I knew what she was going to say. She
spoke to me, and what she said was: 'Jack will show you your room: I
have given you the room in the tower.'

At that, for half a second, the horror of the dream took hold of me
again. But it quickly passed, and again I felt nothing more than the
most intense curiosity. It was not very long before it was amply
satisfied.

John turned to me.

'Right up at the top of the house,' he said, 'but I think you'll be
comfortable. We're absolutely full up. Would you like to go and see
it now? By Jove, I believe that you are right and we are going to have
a thunderstorm. How dark it has become.'

I got up and followed him. We passed through the hall, and up the
perfectly familiar staircase. Then he opened the door, and I went in.
And at that moment sheer unreasoning terror again possessed me. I
did not know what I feared: I simply feared. Then like a sudden
recollection, when one remembers a name which has long escaped
the memory, I knew what I feared. I feared Mrs Stone, whose grave
with the sinister inscription, 'In evil memory', I had so often seen in
my dream, just beyond the lawn which lay below my window. And
then once more the fear passed so completely that I wondered what
there was to fear, and I found myself, sober and quiet and sane, in the
room in the tower, the name of which I had so often heard in my
dream, and the scene of which was so familiar.

I looked around it with a certain sense of proprietorship, and
found that nothing had been changed from the dreaming nights in
which I knew it so well. Just to the left of the door was the bed,
lengthways along the wall, with the head of it in the angle. In a line
with it was the fireplace and a small bookcase; opposite the door the
outer wall was pierced by two lattice-paned windows, between which

stood the dressing-table, while ranged along the fourth wall was the washing-stand and a big cupboard. My luggage had already been unpacked, for the furniture of dressing and undressing lay orderly on the washstand and toilet-table, while my dinner clothes were spread out on the coverlet of the bed. And then, with a sudden start of unexplained dismay, I saw that there were two rather conspicuous objects which I had not seen before in my dreams: one a life-sized oil painting of Mrs Stone, the other a black-and-white sketch of Jack Stone, representing him as he had appeared to me only a week before in the last of the series of these repeated dreams, a rather secret and evil-looking man of about thirty. His picture hung between the windows, looking straight across the room to the other portrait, which hung at the side of the bed. At that I looked next, and as I looked I felt once more the horror of nightmare seize me.

It represented Mrs Stone as I had seen her last in my dreams: old and withered and white-haired. But in spite of the evident feebleness of body, a dreadful exuberance and vitality shone through the envelope of flesh, an exuberance wholly malign, a vitality that foamed and frothed with unimaginable evil. Evil beamed from the narrow, leering eyes; it laughed in the demon-like mouth. The whole face was instinct with some secret and appalling mirth; the hands, clasped together on the knee, seemed shaking with suppressed and nameless glee. Then I saw also that it was signed in the left-hand bottom corner, and wondering who the artist could be, I looked more closely, and read the inscription, 'Julia Stone by Julia Stone'.

There came a tap at the door, and John Clinton entered.

'Got everything you want?' he asked.

'Rather more than I want,' said I, pointing to the picture.

He laughed.

'Hard-featured old lady,' he said. 'By herself, too, I remember. Anyhow she can't have flattered herself much.'

'But don't you see?' said I. 'It's scarcely a human face at all. It's the face of some witch, of some devil.'

He looked at it more closely.

'Yes; it isn't very pleasant,' he said. 'Scarcely a bedside manner, eh? Yes; I can imagine getting the nightmare if I went to sleep with that close by my bed. I'll have it taken down if you like.'

'I really wish you would,' I said. He rang the bell, and with the help of a servant we detached the picture and carried it out on to the landing and put it with its face to the wall.

'By Jove, the old lady is a weight,' said John, mopping his forehead. 'I wonder if she had something on her mind.'

The extraordinary weight of the picture had struck me too. I was about to reply, when I caught sight of my own hand. There was blood on it, in considerable quantities, covering the whole palm.

'I've cut myself somehow,' said I.

John gave a little startled exclamation. 'Why, I have too,' he said.

Simultaneously the footman took out his handkerchief and wiped his hand with it. I saw that there was blood also on his handkerchief.

John and I went back into the tower room and washed the blood off; but neither on his hand nor on mine was there the slightest trace of a scratch or cut. It seemed to me that, having ascertained this, we both, by a sort of tacit consent, did not allude to it again. Something in my case had dimly occurred to me that I did not wish to think about. It was but a conjecture, but I fancied that I knew the same thing had occurred to him.

The heat and oppression of the air, for the storm we had expected was still undischarged, increased very much after dinner, and for some time most of the party, among whom were John Clinton and myself, sat outside on the path bounding the lawn where we had had tea. The night was absolutely dark, and no twinkle of star or moon ray could penetrate the pall of cloud that overset the sky. By degrees our assembly thinned, the women went up to bed, men dispersed to the smoking- or billiard-room, and by eleven o'clock my host and I were the only two left. All the evening I thought that he had something on his mind, and as soon as we were alone he spoke.

'The man who helped us with the picture had blood on his hand, too, did you notice?' he said.

'I asked him just now if he had cut himself, and he said he supposed he had, but that he could find no mark of it. Now where did that blood come from?'

By dint of telling myself that I was not going to think about it, I had succeeded in not doing so, and I did not want, especially just at bedtime, to be reminded of it.

'I don't know,' said I, 'and I don't really care so long as the picture of Mrs Stone is not by my bed.'

He got up.

'But it's odd,' he said. 'Ha! Now you'll see another odd thing.'

A dog of his, an Irish terrier by breed, had come out of the house as we talked. The door behind us into the hall was open, and a bright oblong of light shone across the lawn to the iron gate which led on to the rough grass outside, where the walnut tree stood. I saw that the dog had all his hackles up, bristling with rage and fright, his lips were curled back from his teeth, as if he was ready to spring at something, and he was growling to himself. He took not the slightest notice of his master or me, but stiffly and tensely walked across the grass to the iron gate. There he stood for a moment, looking through the bars and still growling. Then of a sudden his courage seemed to desert him: he gave one long howl, and scuttled back to the house with a curious crouching sort of movement.

'He does that half a dozen times a day,' said John. 'He sees something which he both hates and fears.'

I walked to the gate and looked over it. Something was moving on the grass outside, and soon a sound which I could not instantly identify came to my ears. Then I remembered what it was: it was the purring of a cat. I lit a match, and saw the purrer, a big blue Persian, walking round and round in a little circle just outside the gate, stepping high and ecstatically, with tail carried aloft like a banner. Its eyes were bright and shining, and every now and then it put its head down and sniffed at the grass.

I laughed.

'The end of that mystery, I am afraid,' I said. 'Here's a large cat having Walpurgis Night all alone.'

'Yes, that's Darius,' said John. 'He spends half the day and all night there. But that's not the end of the dog mystery – for Toby and he are the best of friends – but the beginning of the cat mystery. What's the cat doing there? And why is Darius pleased, while Toby is terror-stricken?'

At that moment I remembered the rather horrible detail of my dreams – when I saw through the gate, just where the cat was now, the white tombstone with the sinister inscription. But before I could answer the rain began, as suddenly and heavily as if a tap had been turned on, and simultaneously the big cat squeezed through the bars of the gate and came leaping across the lawn to the house for shelter. Then it sat in the doorway, looking out eagerly into the dark. It spat and struck at John with its paw as he pushed it in in order to close the door.

Somehow, with the portrait of Julia Stone in the passage outside, the room in the tower had absolutely no alarm for me, and as I went to bed, feeling very sleepy and heavy, I had nothing more than interest for the curious incident about our bleeding hands, and the conduct of the cat and dog. The last thing I looked at before I put out my light was the square empty space by my bed where the portrait had been. Here the paper was of its original full tint of dark red: over the rest of the walls it had faded. Then I blew out my candle and instantly fell asleep.

My awaking was equally instantaneous, and I sat bolt upright in bed under the impression that some bright light had been flashed in my face, though it was now absolutely pitch dark. I knew exactly where I was, in the room which I had dreaded in dreams, but no horror that I ever felt when asleep approached the fear that now invaded and froze my brain. Immediately after, a peal of thunder crackled just above the house, but the probability that it was only a flash of lightning which had awoken me gave no reassurance to my galloping heart. Something I knew was in the room with me, and instinctively I put out my right hand, which was nearest the wall, to keep it away. And my hand touched the edge of a picture-frame hanging close to me.

I sprang out of bed, upsetting the small table that stood by it, and I heard my watch, candle and matches clatter on to the floor. But for the moment there was no need of light, for a blinding flash leaped out of the clouds and showed me that by my bed again hung the picture of Mrs Stone. And instantly the room went into blackness again. But in that flash I saw another thing also, namely a figure that leaned over the end of my bed, watching me. It was dressed in some close-clinging white garment, spotted and stained with mold, and the face was that of the portrait.

Overhead the thunder cracked and roared, and when it ceased and the deathly stillness succeeded, I heard the rustle of movement coming nearer me, and, more horrible yet, perceived an odour of corruption and decay. And then a hand was laid on the side of my neck, and close beside my ear I heard quick-taken, eager breathing. Yet I knew that this thing, though it could be perceived by touch, by smell, by eye and by ear, was still not of this earth, but something that had passed out of the body and had power to make itself manifest. Then a voice, already familiar to me, spoke.

'I knew you would come to the room in the tower,' it said. 'I have been long waiting for you. At last you have come. Tonight I shall feast; before long we will feast together.'

And the quick breathing came closer to me; I could feel it on my neck.

At that the terror, which I think had paralysed me for the moment, gave way to the wild instinct of self-preservation. I hit wildly with both arms, kicking out at the same moment, and heard a little animal-squeal, and something soft dropped with a thud beside me. I took a couple of steps forward, nearly tripping up over whatever it was that lay there, and by the merest good-luck found the handle of the door. In another second I was out on the landing and had banged the door behind me. Almost at the same moment I heard a door open somewhere below, and John Clinton, candle in hand, came running upstairs.

'What is it?' he said. 'I sleep just below you, and heard a noise as if – Good heavens, there's blood on your shoulder.'

I stood there, so he told me afterwards, swaying from side to side, white as a sheet, with the mark on my shoulder as if a hand covered with blood had been laid there.

'It's in there,' I said, pointing. 'She, you know. The portrait is in there, too, hanging up in the place we took it from.'

At that he laughed.

'My dear fellow, this is mere nightmare,' he said.

He pushed by me, and opened the door, I standing there simply inert with terror, unable to stop him, unable to move.

'Phew! What an awful smell,' he said.

Then there was silence; he had passed out of my sight behind the open door. Next moment he came out again, as white as myself, and instantly shut it.

'Yes, the portrait's there,' he said, 'and on the floor is a thing – a thing spotted with earth, like what they bury people in. Come away, quick, come away.'

How I got downstairs I hardly know. An awful shuddering and nausea of the spirit rather than of the flesh had seized me, and more than once he had to place my feet upon the steps, while every now and then he cast glances of terror and apprehension up the stairs. But in time we came to his dressing-room on the floor below, and there I told him what I have here described.

The sequel can be made short; indeed, some of my readers have perhaps already guessed what it was, if they remember that inexplicable affair of the churchyard at West Fawley, some eight years ago, where an attempt was made three times to bury the body of a certain woman who had committed suicide. On each occasion the coffin was found in the course of a few days again protruding from the ground. After the third attempt, in order that the thing should not be talked about, the body was buried elsewhere, in unconsecrated ground. Where it was buried was just outside the iron gate of the garden belonging to the house where this woman had lived. She had committed suicide in a room at the top of the tower in that house. Her name was Julia Stone.

Subsequently the body was again secretly dug up, and the coffin was found to be full of blood.

NOTES ON AUTHORS AND STORIES

Sir Bertrand: A Fragment

Anna Letitia Aikin (1743–1825), also known by her married name of Anna Letitia Barbauld, was the daughter of a schoolmaster from the nonconformist tradition. She in her turn married a dissenting clergyman of French descent and for several years together they ran a boys' school in Sussex. During a productive literary career, she wrote poetry and political pamphlets and was a prolific literary editor. 'Sir Bertrand' appeared in 1773, in a volume entitled *Miscellaneous Pieces in Prose* by Anna and her brother, John Aikin.

Captive of the Banditti

This story appeared in the form reproduced here the 1801 'blue book', *New Collection of Gothic Stories*. The author of the first part, Nathan Drake (1766–1836), was born in York, son of a minor painter of the same name, studied medicine at the University of Edinburgh and for most of his life practised medicine in Suffolk. He was also, however, a Shakespearian scholar and collector and a literary critic. The unusual origin and composition of the story are discussed in the Introduction, pp. x–xii.

Extracts from Gosschen's Diary: No. 1

This story appeared anonymously in *Blackwood's Edinburgh Magazine* in August 1818. In their anthology *Tales of Terror from Blackwood's Magazine* (Oxford University Press, 1995), Robert Morrison and Chris Baldick identify the author as John Wilson (1785–1854), a Scot who had careers in literature and law as well as being Professor of Moral Philosophy at Edinburgh University from 1820 to 1851. He was a regular contributor to *Blackwood's* under the pseudonym, 'Christopher North'.

The Parricide's Tale

This story (title supplied by the present editor) is told within Chapter IX of the 1820 novel *Melmoth the Wanderer* by Irish writer and clergyman Charles Robert Maturin (1782–1824). In the complex narrative structure of the novel, a Spaniard, Monçada, is recounting to John Melmoth his experiences as a young man when he was forced into monastic life by his parents. At this point he is endeavouring to escape from the monastery with the assistance of a sinister monk who is known to have murdered his own father. The two are obliged to hide in an underground chamber during the day before effecting their escape by night, and it is during this interval that the parricide monk tells Monçada this story.

1 (p. 21) *Phalaris*   The most celebrated cruelty of the Sicilian tyrant Phalaris was that he roasted his victims alive in a hollow bronze bull, so that their howling resembled the bellowing of the animal.

2 (p. 25) *amateurs*   used in its older sense meaning something closer to 'connoisseurs'

3 (p. 25) *auto-da-fé*   a burning at the stake

4 (p. 29) *Madame Sevigné*   a seventeenth-century writer whose letters to her daughter were much read and admired in the following century

5 (p. 31) *Zeno . . . Burgersdicius*   respectively an early Stoic philosopher and a professor of logic at Leyden in the early seventeenth century

6 (p. 31) *ascititious*   'assumed' in the sense of 'adopted' or 'put-on'

The Spectre Bride

This story appeared anonymously in *Arliss's Pocket Magazine* in 1822. It has sometimes been attributed to William Harrison Ainsworth, who later wrote a large number of historical novels, such as *Rookwood* (1834), *Old St Paul's* (1841), *Windsor Castle* (1843) and *The Lancashire Witches* (1849), highly esteemed at the time but now largely unread. Dr Dick Collins, who knows more about early Ainsworth than anyone, informs me privately that issues of authorship of pieces in the *Pocket Magazine* are so confused that this attribution cannot securely be confirmed or denied. If the story is his he must have been only seventeen at the time of its publication. Some obvious minor errors in *Arliss's* text have been silently corrected here, but there remains an apparent omission on p. 37 (see Note below).

1 (p. 37) *'Tomorrow?' faltered out . . . cancelled'*   Here the second half of the speech would appear to belong to the dead father, not to Clotilda, suggesting that the compositor eye-skipped, probably because 'tomorrow' was repeated again in the first part of the father's reply.

The Tapestried Chamber

Sir Walter Scott (1771–1832) was nearing the end of his phenomenally productive career when this story was written. He was internationally known as a poet before his first novel, *Waverley*, was published in 1814. Between then and his death he wrote a further twenty-four novels plus shorter fiction, and he was also a prolific editor, reviewer and essayist. 'The Tapestried Chamber' was one of a number of short stories that Scott intended for a second series of *Chronicles of the Canongate*, the first series of which had appeared in 1827. At his publisher's suggestion, these stories were not incorporated in the *Chronicles*, and Scott later published them in an annual called *The Keepsake*, in the issue for 1829, actually published with an eye on the Christmas market late in 1828. When it was reprinted in the *Magnum Opus* edition of his works, Scott prefaced the tale with a note claiming that it had been told to him several years earlier by Anna Seward, a writer (1747–1809) with whom Scott had kept up an extended literary correspondence and whose poems he had published in 1810 after her death. An earlier version of the story, which appears to be by Scott himself but was signed with the initials 'A. B.', had been published in *Blackwood's Magazine* in September 1818. (See Coleman Oscar Parsons, 'Scott's Prior Version of "The Tapestried Chamber"', *Notes and Queries*, 207 [1962], pp. 417–20.)

Scott's opening sentence places the events of the story in around 1783, following the end of the 'American War of Independence', as it is known to British history, or the 'American Revolution', as it is known in America. The British surrender at Yorktown had occurred in October 1781.'The wars of York and Lancaster' (the Wars of the Roses), mentioned on the first page, took place from the 1450s to the 1480s.

1 (p. 41) *Eton* Eton College in Berkshire, then as now the foremost public school for sons of the English establishment and those who aspire to enter it, where 'fagging' is a system whereby junior pupils are assigned to positions subservient to their seniors

2 (p. 41) *Christ Church* the college of that name at the University of Oxford

Berenice

This story first appeared in March 1835 in the *Southern Literary Messenger*, of which Poe was then the assistant literary editor, and was later collected in his *Tales of the Grotesque and Arabesque* (1840). Poe was born in Boston in 1809, attended school in England from 1815–20 and then the University of Virginia, which he left with many debts and no degree in 1826. His whole career, including an abortive spell at West Point in

1830–1, was dogged by poverty, scandal and ill-health, aggravated by drink and drugs. He wrote, none the less, numerous stories, essays, poems, journalistic pieces and one novel, and gained in his own lifetime a degree of literary celebrity as well as personal notoriety. He died after going on a bender in Baltimore in 1849.

The Latin epigraph, repeated later in the story, comes from a poem by the second-century Middle-Eastern poet Ebn Zaiat, and translates as, 'My companions told me I might find some little alleviation of my misery in visiting the grave of my beloved.'

1 (p. 55) *Coelius Secundus Curio . . . impossibile est*   The narrator's rather arcane reading may call for some explanation. Coelius Secundus Curio was a sixteenth-century theologian, the title of whose book, as given (slightly incorrectly) here, means *Concerning the Extent of the Blessed Kingdom of God*. 'St Austin', more usually called Augustine, lived from 354 to 430, and *City of God* is his best-known work. The influential early Christian theologian Tertullian lived from the mid-first to the mid-second century and *De Carne Christi* (*Concerning the Flesh of Christ*) was one of his longer works. The famous paradox that is quoted here means, 'The son of God died; it is believable because it is absurd; and buried he rose again; it is certain because it is impossible.'

2 (p. 57) *Mad'selle Sallé*   a celebrated French *danseuse* in the eighteenth century. The phrase in French applied to her means 'that all her steps were feelings'; adapted to Berenice by her cousin, it is transmuted into 'that all her teeth were ideas'.

A Madman's Manuscript

This story is one of several short, generally dark, narratives embedded in Dickens's early novel *Pickwick Papers*, where they are told to the main characters or, as here, read by them. It occurs in Chapter xi, in the fourth number of the serial publication of the book, which appeared in June 1836. The *Pickwick Papers* text has been cropped here so as to show Mr Pickwick's reading of the story and to include the comments on the story written in the manuscript 'in another hand'. These are usually omitted when the tale is reprinted in isolation.

Dickens went on to write many free-standing ghost stories, which can be found in *Best Ghost Stories* (of Charles Dickens), published by Wordsworth in 1997.

Strange Event in the Life of Schalken the Painter

Irish-born Joseph Sheridan Le Fanu (1814–73) was the author of many stories and novels of the bizarre and the supernatural. His most admired novels are *Wylder's Hand* and *Uncle Silas* (both 1864), and he has a secure place in the history of vampire literature due to his striking novella of lesbian vampirism *Carmilla* (1871–2). His early story, 'A Chapter in the History of a Tyrone Family'(1839), which he later reworked into the full-length *Wyvern Mystery* (1869), has been suggested as a source for Charlotte Brontë's 'madwoman in the attic' plot in *Jane Eyre*, but possibly his most celebrated short story is 'Green Tea', which can be found in the anthology *Classic Horror Stories*, edited by Christine Baker, published by Wordsworth in 1998.

'Strange Event in the Life of Schalken the Painter' first appeared in the *Dublin University Magazine* in 1839. Two slightly different versions of the story exist, the original one which was part of Le Fanu's ongoing set of *Purcell Papers*, a frame device in which several of his early stories originally belonged, and one that Le Fanu revised for inclusion in his collection *Ghost Stories and Tales of Mystery* in 1851. The version reproduced here is the former. Gerard Douw (or 'Dou') and Godfrey (Gottfried) Schalken were real historical figures.

Ethan Brand

Nathaniel Hawthorne (1804–64), author of *The Scarlet Letter* (1850) and *The House of the Seven Gables* (1851) among other novels, was one of the pre-eminent American writers of the first half of the nineteenth century.

'Ethan Brand' appeared first in *'The Snow-Image' and other Twice-Told Tales* (1850). The subtitle suggests that Hawthorne had planned a longer narrative of which this was to be the climactic episode. However, only in the phrase, 'as we have seen' (p. 90), in the allusion to the 'earlier' introduction of the village doctor (p. 96) and in the reference to 'the Esther of our tale . . . ' (p. 98) is the shadow of that 'abortive romance' visible. The reference early in the story to 'the shepherds of the Delectable Mountains' is to an episode in *The Pilgrim's Progress* (1678) by John Bunyan, in which the said shepherds show Christian, the pilgrim of the title, a 'dark and smoky' doorway that is 'a by-way to Hell, a way that hypocrites go in at'.

The Old Nurse's Story

Elizabeth Gaskell (1810–65) is best known as the author of a number of trenchant novels of Victorian society in which the position of women and the difficulties of their lives are especially subtly represented. These include *Mary Barton* (1848), *Ruth* (1853) and *North and South* (1855). She wrote an early and influential biography of Charlotte Brontë and was also a prolific writer of shorter fictions, many of them dealing in the macabre and supernatural.

'The Old Nurse's Story' first appeared in the Christmas number of Dickens's journal *Household Words* in 1852. The present text comes from the Cranford Edition of Mrs Gaskell's works. Careful readers will spot that the name of the under-servant at the Manor House changes from Agnes to Bessy and then back again.

1 (p. 110) *Flesh is grass*   from I Peter 1:24: 'For all flesh is as grass, and all the glory of man as the flower of grass.'

2 (p. 111) *gowk*   literally cuckoo – a northern-English and Scottish colloquial word for a fool

3 (p. 114) *maud*   a kind of plaid that used to be worn in winter by shepherds in that region

The Body-Snatcher

Most famous today, perhaps, as the author of *The Strange Case of Dr Jekyll and Mr Hyde*, Robert Louis Stevenson (1850–94) had an extraordinarily large and varied literary output, given his lifelong ill health and resultant early death. He wrote several novels set in his native Scotland, such as *Kidnapped* (1886), its sequel *Catriona* (1893), *The Master of Ballantrae* (1889) and the unfinished *Weir of Hermiston*, as well as the classic pirate adventure *Treasure Island* (1883) and others. He was also a travel-writer, poet, essayist and editor.

'The Body-Snatcher' was begun by Stevenson in 1881 but he laid it aside, as he explained in a letter to Sidney Colvin, 'in a justifiable disgust, the tale being horrid'. He completed it for publication in the *Pall Mall Magazine*'s Christmas number in 1884. The story is carefully grafted on to the real events that surrounded the regime of Dr Robert Knox, the 'K—' of the story, who became the head of Edinburgh University Anatomical School in 1826. His keenness on practical dissection created a market for corpses which was supplied by the notorious William Burke and William Hare. Burke, who is mentioned by name on p. 128, was tried and executed for murder in 1829.

The Yellow Wallpaper

This is the most famous story by Charlotte Perkins Gilman (1860–1935), sometimes also known by her first married name of Charlotte Perkins Stetson. She was born in Hartford, Connecticut, the daughter of Frederick Beecher Perkins, a librarian, through whom she was related to Harriet Beecher Stowe, author of *Uncle Tom's Cabin*. It was while married to Charles Walter Stetson that she experienced a period of intense post-natal depression, or 'hysteria' as it was sometimes then called, during which her husband, on the advice of Dr Weir Mitchell, put her through a 'treatment' that involved isolating her and depriving her of almost all kinds of mental stimulation, an experience that is clearly the point of departure for this story, whose narrator is threatened with Weir Mitchell by name on p. 146. Perkins and Stetson were divorced in 1894 and she married George Houghton Gilman in 1900. After her divorce she was an active writer on women's issues, the author of a volume of poetry, *In This Our World*, and of three novels, *What Diantha Did*, *The Crux* and *Herland*. Terminally ill with cancer, she took her own life in August 1935.

In 1913 Gilman published a short essay, 'Why I Wrote *The Yellow Wallpaper*', in which she told of the origins of the story in her own period of mental illness and indicated also the line between truth and what she called her 'embellishments' in the tale, remarking, 'I never had hallucinations or objections to my mural decorations.'

The Death of Halpin Frayser

Ambrose Bierce was born in 1842 in Ohio and disappeared, never to be seen again, in Mexico during the revolution in 1914. It was an appropriate exit for an author who had often delighted in tales of unexplained disappearances. He had led a varied, rootless, often unhappy life, cutting himself off from his family, fighting on the Union side in the Civil War, and subsequently working as a journalist based in San Francisco, where he became editor of the *News Letter*. From 1872 to 1876 he lived in England with his new wife, the first four years of an unhappy marriage that ended in divorce in 1891. Back in the United States, a lot of his journalistic work consisted of waspish satirical commentary, but he wrote also a great deal of short fiction, most of it dealing with the bizarre and supernatural. His best-known stories are probably 'An Occurrence at Owl-Creek Bridge' and 'The Damned Thing'. The latter can be found in the Wordsworth anthology *Classic Horror Stories*.

This story comes from the collection *Can Such Things Be?*, published in 1893. The epigraph from 'Hali' is a piece of cod-mysticism by Bierce himself, a trick he learned from Poe – 'Hali' never existed.

1 (p. 160) *revisited the glimpses of the moon* This phrase comes from *Hamlet*, 1, 4, 53.

2 (p. 160) *the gift and faculty divine* adapted from a passage in William Wordsworth's *The Excursion*, 1, 77–9:

Oh! many are the Poets that are sown
By Nature; men endowed with highest gifts,
The vision and the faculty divine;
Yet wanting the accomplishment of verse.

3 (p. 162) *gallant, gallant ship* comes from a poem, 'Gloucester Moors'
(l. 36), by the American poet William Vaughn Moody (1869–1910)

4 (p. 162) *a far countree* from S. T. Coleridge's 'The Rime of the
Ancient Mariner' (l. 518)

Canon Alberic's Scrapbook

Montague Rhodes James (1862–1936) had a distinguished career as a
Cambridge scholar. He was the Director of the Fitzwilliam Museum,
Provost of King's College and Vice-Chancellor of the University before
returning to Eton College, where he had been a pupil, as Provost in
1918. He has acquired the reputation of being the foremost British
writer of ghost stories, although not all of the manifestations in his tales
are ghosts, as this example illustrates. It appeared first in the *National
Review* in March 1895 and was collected by James in his *Ghost Stories of an
Antiquary* published in 1904. James's *Collected Ghost Stories* were published by Wordsworth Editions in 1992.

1 (p. 175) The reference to 'Mr Minor-Canon Quatremain in *Old St
Paul's*' is an allusion to the 1841 novel by Harrison Ainsworth (on
whom, see Note on 'The Spectre Bride' above) which is set in the year
of the Great Plague (1665) and climaxes with the destruction of the
old cathedral in the Great Fire of London in 1666. In Chapter 8,
Thomas Quatremain, 'a grave, sallow-complexioned man, with a
morose and repulsive physiognomy', participates in a macabre dig in
the crypt of the cathedral for a treasure chest which he supposes to be
buried there.

No. 252 Rue M. Le Prince

American writer Ralph Adams Cram (1863–1942) was primarily an
architectural historian, the author of books on European, Japanese and
modern American architectural traditions, including studies of the
Gothic style. He had also an interest in the occult and spiritualism, and
in 1919 wrote a preface to a book devoted to claiming that the Great
War had been predicted in the 'automatic writings' of mediums. His
book of macabre stories, *Black Spirits and White*, from which this story is
taken, was published in America in 1895 and in London a year later, and
has never been reprinted.

1 (p. 181) *Rue M. Le Prince*   The Rue des Fosses Monsieur le Prince in Paris is exactly where Cram describes it – on the left bank, intersecting with the Boulevard St Michel, close to the Luxembourg Gardens.

2 (p. 182) *Bicêtre*   a hospital, as Eugène's comment implies, specialising at that period in the study and treatment of insanity

3 (p. 183) *Jardin Mabille*   This had been a fashionable pleasure-garden earlier in the century and is the setting for a scene in Émile Zola's novel *Nana*. A visit to the Jardin Mabille also takes place in Chapter 14 of Mark Twain's *The Innocents Abroad* (1869).

4 (p. 186) *Just the place . . . times is true*   lines from the second stanza of the first Fit of Lewis Carroll's nonsense epic 'The Hunting of the Snark' (1876)

5 (p. 186) *for the sheeted dead to squeak and gibber*   from Shakespeare's *Hamlet*, where Horatio recalls the portents of Julius Caesar's murder: 'The graves stood tenantless, and the sheeted dead / Did squeak and gibber in the Roman streets . . . ' (1, 1, 115–16)

6 (p. 186) *whoreson dead bodies*   the words of the gravedigger in *Hamlet*, 5, 1, 167–8: ' . . . your water is a sore decayer of your whoreson dead body.'

7 (p. 190) *'The Haunters and the Haunted'*   Properly titled 'The Haunted and the Haunters', the story is by Edward Bulwer Lytton (1803–73) and can be found in the anthology *Classic Horror Stories* published by Wordsworth in 1998.

The Lame Priest

This story, signed simply 'S. Carleton', appeared in the magazine *The Atlantic Monthly* in December 1901, sandwiched between essays on poetry of the American Civil War and 'Maeterlinck and Music'. In a corner of the *Literary Gothic* website (see the Select Bibliography that follows the Introduction) it is said that this is one Susan Carleton Jones and her dates are there given as 1864 (?) to 1926. I have been unable to confirm this identification or to find out anything else by, or about, the author.

1 (p. 206) *Weguladimooch. Bochtusum*   These two words in the Native American language are translated in a note to the original as 'evil spirit' and 'wolf', with the added comment: '*Weguladimooch* is a word no Indian cares to say.'

Luella Miller

Mary Wilkins Freeman (1852–1930) was born and spent most of her life in Massachusetts. Until she was thirty she lived with her family, but her father, mother and sister all died in the same year, 1883, and for the next twenty years of her life she lived with her childhood friend, Mary Wells. When she married Dr Charles Freeman in 1902 she was fifty years old and was a prolific writer of fiction and poetry. During her troubled twenty-year marriage she lived in New Jersey before separating from her husband and returning to Massachusetts.

Once almost forgotten, her work began to receive more critical attention towards the end of the twentieth century, in part because of her writing's subtle address to the problems and self-experience of women in turn-of-the-century American society. She wrote a number of ghost stories which have begun to appear in anthologies – such as 'The Wind in the Rose-bush', 'The Lost Child' and 'The Shadows on the Wall'. 'Luella Miller' first appeared in *Everybody's Magazine* in December 1902 and was collected the following year in *'The Wind in the Rose-bush' and Other Tales of the Supernatural*, from which the text used here comes.

The Bird in the Garden

Richard Middleton (b. 1882) was a promising British poet and story-writer at the time of his early death in 1911, but at that stage had published only one-off pieces in various literary magazines. Post-humously his poetry was collected into two volumes of *Poems and Songs* published in 1912, and some of his stories were collected under the title *'The Ghost Ship' and Other Stories*, also published in 1912, with an enthusiastic Preface by Arthur Machen. One of these stories, 'On the Brighton Road', has sometimes been reprinted in anthologies of ghost stories. It is from *'The Ghost Ship' and Other Stories* that 'The Bird in the Garden' comes. I have not been able to trace the earlier magazine publication of the story and so have dated it to (pre)1912.

The Room in the Tower

Edward Frederic Benson (1867–1940) was a prolific writer, the son of E.W. Benson, who was Archbishop of Canterbury from 1883 to 1896, and the brother of A. C. Benson, Master of Magdalene College, Cam-bridge, and himself a notable author. He attracted a new, enthusiastic audience when his 'Mapp and Lucia' novels, written in the 1930s, with their comic representations of English middle-class *mores* of that period, were adapted for television in the 1980s. 'The Room in the Tower' was the title-story of a volume of supernatural stories published in 1912.